THE GUNCLE ABROAD

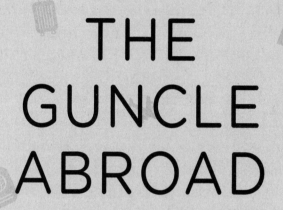

THE
GUNCLE
ABROAD

— a novel —

STEVEN ROWLEY

G. P. PUTNAM'S SONS
NEW YORK

PUTNAM
— EST. 1838 —

G. P. PUTNAM'S SONS
Publishers Since 1838
An imprint of Penguin Random House LLC
penguinrandomhouse.com

Library of Congress Cataloging-in-Publication Data

Names: Rowley, Steven, 1971– author. | Rowley, Steven, 1971– Guncle.
Title: The guncle abroad: a novel / Steven Rowley.
Description: New York: G.P. Putnam's Sons, 2024.
Identifiers: LCCN 2023053085 (print) | LCCN 2023053086 (ebook) |
ISBN 9780593540459 (hardcover) | ISBN 9780593540466 (e-book)
Subjects: LCGFT: Domestic fiction. | Gay fiction. | Novels.
Classification: LCC PS3618.O888 G863 2024 (print) |
LCC PS3618.O888 (ebook) | DDC 813/.6—dc23/eng/20231121
LC record available at https://lccn.loc.gov/2023053085
LC ebook record available at https://lccn.loc.gov/2023053086

International edition ISBN: 9780593718254

Printed in the United States of America
1st Printing

For my readers

"The trouble with children is that they're not returnable."

—QUENTIN CRISP

"When they're handin' out the heartaches you know you got to have you some."

—JUICE NEWTON, "QUEEN OF HEARTS"

THE GUNCLE ABROAD

NOW

Patrick O'Hara removed the cloche from his room service breakfast with a flourish it did not deserve; he grimaced at what lay beneath. *You have to hand it to the Italians,* he thought as he sat on his terrazza overlooking Lake Como. They hit lunch and dinner so hard there was never anything left for breakfast, unless you count the driest pastry you'd ever seen as a meal (and Patrick did not—this particular brick looked like it should be on display in Pompeii). He sighed. Neither the pastry nor the acrid coffee that came with it would alleviate the pounding in his head or the uneasiness of his stomach, as he ached for a good, greasy American breakfast to help him sop up the disaster that was the previous night.

"Why is your coffee so small?" Grant bellowed from inside his uncle's hotel room. The boy was eleven now, and had mostly outgrown his lisp, even if Patrick's trained ear still caught echoes of it—*tho thmall*—every now and again.

"Why is your voice *so loud*?" Grant and his sister, Maisie, had the magic ability to amplify his every hangover. Patrick took a sip of his caffè normale and winced. The boy's question was a decent one (as far as his inane questions went), but it had an easy answer: the espresso was so bitter he wouldn't survive a full cup. He was so hungover, even his hair seemed to hurt.

"What's wrong with you?" Grant asked.

"I prefer a French breakfast, if you know what I mean." They didn't, so Patrick scrapped the rest of the joke—*a roll in bed with some honey*—as it would most likely go over their heads and he didn't have the energy to explain double entendre.

Grant lifted the room phone from its cradle. "I'll see if they offer one." The kid had become far too adept at ordering room service over the course of their travels.

"See if they offer euthanasia."

Below, two passengers made their way down the hotel's docks and stepped onto the back of a wooden speedboat. Patrick squinted as diamonds of sunlight rippled off the lake; slowly his brother, Greg, came into focus, as well as Livia, his brother's soon-to-be wife. Or *maybe* soon-to-be wife. Too many things remained unresolved in the wake of a disastrous rehearsal dinner. He watched as they settled onto the boat's rear vinyl seat, Livia fanning her patterned Marimekko dress as she crossed her legs just so, Greg extending his arm around her, whispering in her ear until she giggled. They seemed genuinely happy. Patrick had to hand it to her. The night before he was certain Livia was a cooked goose, but she was an absolute bird of paradise in the fresh light of day. Patrick narrowed his eyes further until he could see his brother pouring two flutes of prosecco from a bottle that sat in an ice bucket between them—he extended his arm, as if reaching for a glass, his best hope a little hair of the dog that bit him. But as the boat's motor gurgled and churned, the only bubbles before him were in the water as the boat pushed back from the dock.

"Look at them," Maisie scoffed without glancing up from the phone she'd been given when she turned fourteen.

"Oh, you *are* talking to me." Maisie had been giving her uncle the silent treatment all morning, mortified still by the absolute spectacles they had made of themselves at dinner. Of course, the kids had an excuse: it was difficult watching their father remarry. Patrick, as the adult, did not.

"How can you eat at a time like this?" Maisie's question dripped with teenage judgment.

Patrick took a bite of the pastry and it disintegrated down the front of his hotel robe. "Not well, clearly." He let the dry crumbs roll off his tongue. Then he said in his most confident tone, "We can fix this."

"Why would we want to?" Maisie asked, and Patrick motioned toward Grant, who approached them with his game console. Her brother was the reason why.

Grant sidled up next to his uncle. "They didn't have what you asked for, but I got us a pitcher of grape juice."

"Wonderful. I'm sure the conversation it inspires will be just as intoxicating." Patrick stood up to wipe himself clean over the edge of the terrace before taking a swig of Acqua Panna, turning what little of the pastry was left in his mouth into some sort of wallpaper glue.

"Don't you have any feelings?" Maisie had finally looked up from her phone.

Patrick laughed, recalling Goldie Hawn's answer to that question from *The First Wives Club*. "Yes, I have feelings. I'm an actor. I have all of them." His niece didn't think that was funny.

They were at the Grand Hotel Tremezzo, an iconic art nouveau masterpiece on the western shore of Lake Como, for four nights of a planned six. The wedding was to be that evening, followed by a day of rest, and then Patrick would take the kids home to the States while their father and Livia honeymooned in Greece. Or at least that had been the plan. Patrick had a hard time grasping that any of this was real. The wedding. The setting. His whole family in Italy. Now it was all one big mess.

Maisie tucked her phone into the shallow front pocket of her cut-off shorts; it did not fit all the way inside.

"Did you finally reach the end of TikTok?" Patrick mocked, but in all honesty he should thank the Chinese for keeping her calm.

Maisie leaned awkwardly in the doorway with one arm at her side, her left hand clasping the wrist on her right, looking not out at the floating pool in the lake, which was an incredible sight for its unnecessary opulence (a swimming pool *in* a lake?), but instead like she'd rather disappear from this place. "I just don't see it. Dad and *Livia*?"

Everyone needed a nemesis; Patrick had instructed Maisie well. And if Walt Disney himself had taught children anything, it's that stepmothers are wicked, even if Patrick no longer found Livia to be all that bad. But it was long past time for his niece to ease up.

"The connection between two people is not always something others are meant to see." Patrick thought of himself and his ex-boyfriend Emory, and how many on the outside could think them mismatched. "Like fireworks in the daytime." Since ending their nearly five-year relationship, Patrick had never felt so alone. It used to be his default setting, but now solitude was an ill-fitting garment that once-trusted cleaners had shrunk.

Grant's game console made a sound like something swirling a drain and he groaned. "Why can't Dad marry Palmina?"

Speaking of nemeses, a cold chill ran down Patrick's spine. "Palmina's a lesbian, you know that."

Grant didn't seem to view that as disqualifying. "Yeah, but gay marriage is legal now."

"Yes, for gay people to marry *other* gay peop— Why would you want your dad to marry Palmina?"

Grant shrugged, but they all knew the answer: Palmina was the very definition of *sprezzatura*. In every way, she exuded an effortless cool. "Maybe *you* should marry her."

"Gay men can't marry lesbians," Patrick said, appalled.

"Oh no. Here come the Guncle Rules." Maisie stuck out her tongue in protest. Guncle Rules were Patrick's little bons mots and instructions for living that he previously doled out like candy—*brunch is awesome, when a gay man hands you his phone look only at what he is showing you, bottomless mimosas are not the same as pantless mimosas.* Those sorts of things.

Grant pressed, undeterred. "Why not? She's gay, you're gay. You just said!"

"BECAUSE THAT'S NOT HOW IT WORKS!" Patrick swallowed the rest of his coffee like a bitter pill and motioned for Grant to sit. "That's not a Guncle Rule, that's just common sense." As their gay uncle, Patrick had once been the apple of their eye. Now he had been swept aside in favor of Livia's younger lesbian sister, Palmina, who just seventy-two hours earlier had crashed down on his world—an asteroid wiping him out like the dinosaur he was. Over was the era of the guncle; behold the dawn of the launt!

Grant circled three times like a dog and plopped down next to his uncle with such force it caused Patrick to rise an inch off the cushion. "I want you to understand something. Your mother would welcome this day. She wanted your dad to be happy. It's been five years and that's a respectable amount of time and we should celebrate your father and Livia."

Maisie disagreed. "Mom never could have imagined this day."

Patrick glanced up at the sun's yolk; colors seemed more saturated in Italy. "Well, no. Not *this* day, exactly." Even he could not have foreseen his lawyer brother representing the American business interests of an Italian noble family, then falling for his client's daughter, a marchesa of all things, and Patrick's imagination was quite robust. But Sara, his best friend from college, had planned for a lot of contingencies that others had not, including his summer with the kids in Palm Springs immediately after her death, when Patrick had been thrust into the role of caregiver, cementing their special bond; he was loathe not to afford her due credit. "But I know she would have been happy about it. Remember I knew her before any of you."

Maisie held firm. "I don't like the way I feel inside."

Patrick tried to make light. "Too much pasta and formaggio. That has nothing to do with your father."

Maisie's face soured. "It's not that."

Patrick had been warned by Maisie in stark terms not to inquire about her period again. But it was all still new and some things couldn't be helped. "Do you need another . . . 'women's aspirin'?" He grimaced as he pulled the bottle from his robe pocket and tossed it for her to catch; it landed like a baby's rattle on the floor.

Maisie stomped her feet and Patrick jumped, knocking over his tiny coffee cup. "I swear to god, if you say women's aspirin one more—!"

"Okay! I'm sorry. I just want you to know I'm an ally. I've read almost everything by Judy Blume."

"Who's Judy Blume?" Grant asked.

Patrick's head pounded anew as he reclined back onto his chaise. *Are you there, god? It's me, Patrick.* But he was also clearly relieved. If it wasn't Maisie's period, it was grief, something he was more adept at handling, as he'd helped the kids navigate so much of it when he had custody of them in Palm Springs. "That pit you feel in your gut, that's just love persevering." He looked solemnly at the kids to make sure each understood. "Remember our summer together? In many ways that was just the beginning."

"And this is, what? *The end?*" Maisie sneered. That was the thing about grief, none of us wanted to travel with it, exactly, but the suggestion that we would or should be over it was somehow an even more unwelcome passenger.

"Of course not. Maybe the beginning of a new phase."

"When *does* it end?" Grant asked, nestling against Patrick's side. Patrick tousled his hair and imagined that his nephew was still six. This is the kind of question that would have thrown him for a loop when the kids first walked into his life, but now he was able to answer honestly.

"It doesn't end. Not really." Patrick spoke from experience. His first love, Joe, died in a car crash fifteen years prior. In the wake of Patrick's recent breakup with Emory, Joe had been on his mind again. "But here's the good news. You get so much stronger." He tackled Grant and the boy burst out in fits of unguarded giggles. It made Patrick happy, as if it were proof that Grant survived the last five years with his childhood intact. "Now drop and give me ten."

Grant flexed his biceps, his arms two noodles like always. He then fell to the floor and completed seven push-ups, then three more from his knees. "TEN!"

"Come on. You can't be this unhappy. I mean, look where you are! George Clooney has a house just down the shore, and he could live *anywhere*." Patrick gestured at the crystalline waters and then across the lake toward Bellagio. "And yeah, I know—who's George Clooney." He'd walked himself into a trap. "He's like the reigning Spencer Tracy." Patrick stood to his full height, tightening the hotel's robe over his sleep pants, and then held a finger aloft before Grant could inquire about Spencer Tracy. "Look. You remember the Bellagio hotel when I took you to Vegas? The one with a lake built in front?"

"It had dancing fountains." Grant's eyes grew wide with the memory. "That was a *great* lake!"

"That's *this* lake! Or it's supposed to be."

"This lake has dancing fountains, too?" Grant ran to the edge of the terrace, as if he might have to fight for the perfect spot to catch the next water show.

"No. Just *that* lake has fountains."

"You said that lake was this lake."

"A re-creation of it."

Grant peered down over the edge, having lost total interest. "Oh. Then that lake was better."

"No, this lake is better because it's the real deal. The other one is for tourists who wear matching tracksuits and need to breathe oxygen from a tank." Patrick scuttered into the shade.

"We're tourists," Maisie pointed out.

"We're not *tourists*." Patrick said it with the disdain the word deserved.

"What are we, then?" she challenged.

Patrick leaned in the doorway of his suite. "Well, wedding guests, for one. Beyond that, itinerants, birds of passage . . ." Patrick disappeared inside to look for a cold compress and instead stumbled upon the room service menu Grant left on his bed. "The French would call us bon vivants!" He wondered aloud if a Bloody Mary, light on the tomato juice, might do the trick.

"Why do you need a drink at ten o'clock in the morning?" Maisie asked, following him inside.

Patrick gave her a loving jab at the nape of her neck. "Because I suffer from a rare condition where my body doesn't produce its own alcohol."

There was a knock at the door. Grant's pitcher of grape juice. "Un momento," he said as he fished for euros to tip. The door opened and his sister, Clara, waltzed in.

"Patrick. It's not even noon. What a surprise to find you upright." Clara's look had softened since her divorce (with Patrick's help she'd found a hair color and style that worked), and Italy had done even more to suit her. His sister's demeanor, however, was sharp as ever, as she was wearing a surprising amount of makeup.

"What's with the war paint?"

"Oh! Livia brought in a makeup artist for the wedding party." Clara touched her face gently like a silent-era star. She was clearly ready for her close-up.

"Does that mean . . . ?" Patrick asked. Maisie braced herself for an answer.

"I talked to Greg, but your guess is as good as mine." Clara gently tucked Maisie's hair behind one of her ears. "But it never hurts to be ready. Perhaps they have a bronzer they could use on you, Patrick. You look tired."

Patrick glared at Clara. "That's because you and Harvey Wall-banger kept me up half the night."

Even under Clara's makeup, Patrick could see his sister's face redden; it was unlike her to have one-night stands.

"You heard us?" she asked, horrified.

"We share a wall. Not that it matters. *Belgium* heard you."

Grant tugged on his aunt's sleeve. "Aunt Clara, can we go to the buffet?"

Patrick saw an opening and he nudged his family toward the door. "Yes. Take these ankle biters down to breakfast and secure us a table. The pastry they brought to my room leaves something to be desired."

"Only if we can find seats in the shade. I don't want my face to melt."

"Like in *Raiders of the Lost Ark!*" Grant pumped his fist. Face melting was right in his wheelhouse.

"All of you, out. I promise I'm right behind you." He closed the door on his family, revealing he was anything but.

Silence at last.

Alone, Patrick ran a washcloth under cold water and pressed it against his forehead, then stepped out onto the terrazza and inhaled deeply. He gripped the balustrade, his fingers curling tightly over the edge, and looked intently over the lake. He watched as a young couple ran across the narrow street toward the lounge chairs near the beachfront. Beach club employees were just starting to raise the umbrellas for shade from the intense July sun, their orange-and-cream-colored stripes and scalloped edges looking like delicious ice cream treats from above. "*Would* you be happy about this?" he whispered to Sara, less certain now that she would be than he was before. *Yes*, he thought, *of course she would.* What was good for her family was always best for her. But he wished he could know for sure that she agreed Greg and Livia were a match. It was the sad truth about losing someone—your certainty about who they were faded with memory.

Patrick stepped back into his room and frowned at the side of the bed where the kids always sat with their shoes. Their European adventure was drawing to a close. Soon he would be returning to the States to start over, at the age of forty-nine, alone.

A knock on the door startled him. Grant's grape juice at last. Again he tightened his robe, and as he reached for the door he instinctively stepped aside to allow his server to enter. Except it wasn't a porter standing in front of him with a pitcher of juice, but rather someone else—someone who took his breath away.

"*It's you.*"

FOUR WEEKS
EARLIER

ONE

Patrick mustered the last of his patience to smile warmly at the Claridge's doorman before slumping against the revolving door into the hotel to jump-start its spin. *Nothing.* Even employing his full weight he didn't have the strength to nudge the London hotel's door from a dead stop, and he looked pathetically at the doorman for an assist. Over his weeks-long stay he had come to find the doorman's commitment to the top hat to be, well, a tad over the top—a bit of a bad habitdashery—but as the man tipped his brim with a wink and sprang to help, Patrick was charmed in spite of himself. At last he was inside the hotel.

"Evening, Pip." Patrick waved as he emerged from the door at last. The night clerk looked up from his paperwork with wide eyes; instead of the string bean his name might suggest, Pip was squat and muscular and filled out his classic uniform quite nicely. Claridge's was a London institution situated between Hyde and Green Parks, triangulating it perfectly with Buckingham and Kensington Palaces, and everyone who worked there was seemingly named after a Dickens character, even Pip, who had moved to England just three years prior from Jaipur. During Patrick's first week in residence at the hotel, he amused himself by assigning names to the people he did not know.

Mr. Bumbleporridge. Jiminy Pocket. Madame Squeers. But no such made-up name was required for his favorite employee. "Have anything for me?"

"Evening, sir. Nothing for *you*, I'm afraid, but I do have an envelope for Jack Curtis."

Patrick chuckled as he accepted his mail. Jack Curtis was the name he used when he didn't want to attract attention (a combination of Jack Lemmon and Tony Curtis from the movie *Some Like It Hot*). He used the envelope to salute Pip.

"I see you're leaving us on Friday," Pip said.

"The party had to end sometime." Shooting a film wasn't exactly a party, and certainly not this one, which had been plagued by both poor weather and endless rewrites, but Patrick was committed to use the last of his energy to charm.

"Shame." Pip held Patrick's gaze and a spark of electricity crackled between them. "You look pretty knackered. I could have something else for you. Turndown service, perhaps?"

Patrick had invited Pip up to his room once, weeks earlier, and so he knew this turndown would be full-service. Was he up for this tonight? He studied how sharp the desk clerk looked in his waistcoat and thought maybe it was worth getting a second wind. "Sure. Give me a few minutes?"

Pip playfully slapped the front bell. "I'll find someone to cover the desk."

As he waited for the elevator, Patrick weighed the envelope in his tired hands and snarled at the overwrought calligraphy. Ivory. An invitation, he surmised, which was the last thing he wanted—when this movie wrapped he was booking a trip for himself somewhere far away from everyone else (or at least all the people he knew). He reached for his phone, but there was no service in the elevator. His hands were dry, and the skin on his knuckles creped. The hours on this film had been insane and he'd been neglecting his self-care, and for early summer, London was surprisingly cold. That's what his upcoming vacation was meant to address. It was time to put himself first, in a warm climate—Sitges perhaps or Tenerife, or even the South of France—someplace with a climate that might remind him of his old home in Palm Springs. When he spied the envelope again he was almost surprised to find he was still holding it. He slid one finger under the seal; it caught a hangnail, and he sucked on his finger until he was sure it wasn't bleeding. Indeed it was an invitation. A *wedding* invitation.

As the elevator reached his floor, he glanced at the time; it was still early evening in Connecticut. He opened the door to his room, which was both cozy and too formal in that British drawing room kind of way. The furniture looked inviting but was stuffed with sawdust or some other filling that made it not at all comfortable (and most certainly a fire hazard). The chairs were narrow and encouraged good posture and there was some sort of tufted left-arm chaise, which he had weeks ago drafted into service to hold his dirty clothes. (The underbutler, he called it.) His brother, Greg, answered his call on the third ring.

"So you're actually doing it."

"Doing what?"

"Marrying the Baroness."

"You got our summons!" Greg joked, but Patrick did feel like he was being called for jury service. He could hear his brother fumbling with something on the other end of the line. "I worried my assistant got the international postage all wrong. Livia should never have put me in charge of the mailing." More fumbling. "Also, she's not a baroness, she's a marchesa."

"Yeah, like that's a real thing." Patrick picked up the RSVP card and looked at the back side, thinking it might reveal this all to be a practical joke. Instead it was blank.

"It's very much a real thing." Indeed Livia hailed from an Italian noble family whose company was a client at Greg's firm. Attorneys weren't really supposed to date clients, but he worked mostly with her father and apparently there was no way for the partners to enforce these things.

Patrick thumbed through the rest of the envelope, the tissue and some information about hotels, before losing interest and ditching the entire thing on the room's quaint writing desk. He turned his attention once again to his hands. "Listen, you're a doctor—"

"I'm a lawyer."

"Same difference. Why do my hands look so much older than the rest of me?"

"You only say that because you can't see your face."

Patrick took the punch, but didn't strike back. There was no denying it, especially with family: he was looking down both barrels at fifty and didn't quite know how to feel about that. He wished he had more role models for gay aging; sadly, many men—*too* many men—in the generation above him were lost.

More clanging. "Are you fixing the kids dinner or building them a car?"

"I'm making pasta. A little regional cuisine to get them excited for Italy."

"Why, what's in Italy?"

Greg groaned. "Did you read the invitation, or are you waiting for the movie?"

Patrick picked up the invitation again and this time glanced at the actual words. The Grand Hotel Tremezzo. Lake Como, Italy. And then he noticed the date. "Aw, man. I was going to take a vacation."

"People vacation in Italy."

Not with their entire family. "It's in four weeks! That's not much notice."

"We sent a save the date!" More clanging. "Maybe we sent it to your apartment in New York."

"I'm not in my apartment, as you know."

"Patrick, it took us a lifetime to find one another. We don't believe in waiting longer."

Patrick rolled his eyes, but the thing about Greg, if his first wife was any indication, was that he had *great* taste in women. Sara had, after all, been Patrick's best friend from college. "Livia's rich, in any case. Good for you for locking it down." Although to Patrick's great surprise, Greg seemed about as interested in her fortune as he did in her title, which is to say not much at all. He genuinely seemed into the woman, or at least he projected as much. "First marriage for love, second for money."

"And the third?"

"Is there going to be a third?"

"No. But you sounded like you were on a roll." More clanging from Greg's end. Honestly, it was like he was fixing a carburetor. "I'm worried about the kids, Patrick."

"Why. What did you do to them?"

"I didn't do anything. They're just . . . They're having a difficult time."

"With the pasta? Cook it longer."

"With *this*."

Patrick took a deep breath. In many ways he knew this day would come. He had hoped perhaps that Grant and Maisie would be a little older. If they were closer to leaving the nest and spreading their wings to begin exciting lives of their own, they might welcome their father having someone new enter his life. But they were still young, eleven and fourteen—a long way from independence. Their mother's loss was still a wound that had yet to fully scab.

Patrick wasn't ready to tackle his brother's dilemma. "Remember when we were kids and we thought al dente was a way to say pregnant in mixed company? She's, *you know*, al dente."

Greg laughed. "By the way, Livia thinks I'm still in my late thirties, so can it with the shared memories when she's around."

Patrick pushed his laundry aside and plopped onto the underbutler. *So that's what these couches are for.* "Aren't you forty-five?"

"Forty-six."

"Why would she think you're in your thirties? Can't she see *your* face?"

Deserving that, Greg dismissed the insult. "She was really into the young-widower thing when we met. She made assumptions, I didn't correct her. It fueled some fantasy in her and the sex was great, like *really* great. This one time—"

"What are we, girlfriends?"

Silence on the other end of the line. Patrick pulled his phone away from his ear to make sure they hadn't accidentally been disconnected. Greg continued. "She knows the truth deep down. It's just our little game. Anyway, don't draw attention to it."

Livia herself was in her late forties and she probably liked the idea of being the older (and more well-to-do) woman; Europeans didn't have such hang-ups about age and wealth, which was a point in their favor. So on one hand, Patrick didn't see the harm. On the other, falsehoods were no way to start a marriage. He was hardly a traditionalist, but he believed that much to be true.

Patrick ran the bath, hoping he would have time to get in a soak before entertaining. "You're getting married, Gregory."

"Do you think it's too soon?"

A knock at the door. So much for the bath.

"Who's that? Are you expecting company?"

"It's just Pip."

"PIMP?" Greg asked, horrified.

"No, Pip. *Pip*. PIP. What's wrong with you? He's here for turndown service. ONE SECOND!"

"Now, that's a euphemism. And are you running a bath?"

Patrick sat on the edge of the tub. "Should I take a dip with Pip?"

"Why? So he can hop on Pop?"

Patrick groaned. "I'm hanging up now."

"Patrick," Greg began, before hissing like he'd been burned, and Patrick could hear him dumping water out of a pot. "I really do need your help with the kids."

Patrick promised to call back soon. A guncle's work was never done.

◇◇◇◇◇◇◇◇

Pip brought with him a bottle of scotch, and he poured two glasses, which they drank on the balcony. Patrick's view was the rooftops of affluent Mayfair, which was charming, even at night—exactly what you'd want from London, as if Mary Poppins and her merry band of chimney sweeps might shoot out of smokestacks with a gentle cough of ash and start stepping in time.

"Mayfair lays claim to the most expensive spot on London's Monopoly board," Pip offered as conversation.

"Does it?" Not that Patrick booked his travel by way of Parker Brothers, but he was nonetheless tickled by this piece of trivia. He sniffed his scotch; its fragrance was both salty and sweet.

"It's a single malt. Fifteen-year. Aged primarily in bourbon barrels, then the last three in oloroso casks. Not our most expensive bottle, but certainly far from the worst."

"Did you charge it to my room?"

"Nah. This is on Claridge's. A going-away gift of sorts. You'll be missed around here."

Patrick's face grew hot. "I don't know about that."

"Hold this." Pip handed Patrick his glass and disappeared inside the room. A moment later Patrick heard him turn off the faucet; Pip reappeared a moment later. "That's better. Don't want the tub over-flowing."

"Sorry. I was a bit distracted, I guess."

"No apologies necessary," Pip said, reclaiming his glass. "So long as I'm the distraction."

Patrick offered his own glass to cheers, as he didn't want to seem rude. But the truth was he was occupied with thoughts of the kids. They were unhappy, Greg had reported. Maisie was acting out at school and Grant had developed a tic, constantly picking at moles on his body; Patrick heard in horror that Grant had nearly ripped one clean off, requiring a trip to urgent care. They needed their uncle, his brother had told him. Patrick had made the kids a promise a long time ago: if they needed him he would be there. But he wasn't so sure he was anyone's magic solution; he, too, was unhappy these days, at least since his breakup with Emory. And he'd promised himself this up-coming trip, time alone to re-center himself and make new plans as he moved forward once again on his own. That was important, too, wasn't it? A bit of selfless selfishness, like the securing of your own oxygen mask before helping others with theirs?

"Earth to Patrick," Pip said, and Patrick realized he had drifted.

"Sorry." He snapped back to attention just as Pip relieved him of his scotch. Pip set both glasses down on a little side table before nuz-zling into his host. With the difference in their heights, his head rested perfectly on Patrick's chest.

Housekeeping had placed a fresh arrangement of magnolias by the door and they smelled like sugar and champagne. They reminded him of flowers Emory had once given him and he imagined it was Emory there now, pressed against him, with his goofy grin and infec-tious laugh. Patrick had done the right thing, hadn't he? Emory was young, still in his twenties when they met. He was five years older now (they had a blast in Mexico celebrating his thirtieth), but then again, so was Patrick, who had a big birthday himself coming up— one he felt less celebratory about. "How old are you, Pip?"

"Twenty-eight. Why?"

Jesus. Patrick was going in the wrong direction. "No reason. Just thought we should know each other a little better."

This delighted Pip. "My favorite old movie is *In the Mood for Love.* My favorite new movie is *RRR.* My favorite food is my mother's daal."

"*In the Mood for Love* is an old movie?" Patrick winced. If he recalled, it came out this century.

"I think so. Why? How old are you?"

Patrick wondered if Pip could hear his heart momentarily stop. "We'll have to look it up on IMDb. Pip . . ." he began. "I'm pretty beat. I wonder if maybe we shouldn't call it a night." May to December was all fine and good, but no one talked about what was supposed to happen in the long, cold month called January.

"How about I at least get you into your bath. It's already drawn." Patrick glanced toward the bathroom. He could see a bit of steam billowing from the door. "Come on. I'll wash your hair. You can be Meryl Streep in that *really* old movie *Out of Africa.*"

Patrick hesitated, unsure. "And that would make you Robert Redford?"

Pip dipped his head, looking up at Patrick with soulful brown eyes, and ultimately Patrick relented, even though it was a movie released ten years before Pip was born. Yes, he was too young, younger even than Emory. But if he knew the reference, he was old enough. At least for one night.

TWO

Patrick struggled to find his trailer in the sea of production vehicles, which today were parked just outside Hampstead Heath on the Cricklewood side. (Again with *these names*.) When he finally located the vehicle with his placard, he trudged up the two steps, hoping to have time for a catnap before he was called to set. Half-asleep, he screamed when he saw a figure inside, and was just about to call for security, when he noticed this person was perhaps more scared of him than he was of her.

"Cassie?" he asked as he watched the startled figure grab tissues to mop up her sloshed coffee from the floor.

"You made me spill."

Patrick stepped inside and closed the door quickly behind him, so as not to attract the attention of the first and second ADs who were always milling about with headsets. Cassie Everest was his agent now for five lucrative years. She landed Patrick as her first client when she was working as his former agent Neal's assistant and Patrick was desperately in need of a change. "What are you doing here?"

"You're wrapping your first leading role in a feature. I thought I would stop by to celebrate my favorite client."

"Your only client."

Cassie stood up with the clump of wet tissue and turned around in a tight circle, looking for where to dispose of it. Patrick pointed to the rubbish just next to the makeup table. "That used to be a fun joke, I'll grant you, but it's just not true anymore. I have lots of clients, thank you. And a bigger office, too."

She certainly looked the part, having pulled off a major glow-up these past few years; her clothes were impeccably tailored and her haircut looked like it cost more than a week's salary as an assistant. Yes, Patrick had taken her shopping once when they were first working together, around the time Barneys in Beverly Hills morphed into Saks. But this may be a case where the student had now eclipsed the teacher. Patrick pointed to her shoes. "Are those the . . ."

"Gianvito Rossi PVC mules?" she replied, doing her best Anne Hathaway from *The Devil Wears Prada*.

Patrick stared, bemused. "But it's daytime."

She casually tossed the hair out of her face. "I flew all night."

Patrick chuckled in disbelief that she took the red-eye just to see him; he absentmindedly thumbed through a stack of scripts on the table. "What are these?"

"Scripts."

"I can see that they're scripts."

"Then why ask?"

Patrick picked up the stack to move them and winced, as they were surprisingly heavy. "You can email these, you know."

"You don't read them when I email them."

"I don't read them when you print them out, either. And emailing is better for the environment."

Cassie scoffed. "Didn't you fly in a private plane?"

"That was one time!" Patrick blurted before he could see she was intentionally trying to ruffle his feathers. "Four times. Okay, seven max." He picked up the script on top of the stack and opened it. "Are these better than the last stack you sent?" Patrick was still sore, as one of his recent films managed only nineteen percent on Rotten Tomatoes. In that instance he was grateful to have had only a small part.

"The last stack was good! Three of those scripts made the Black List."

Patrick kicked off his shoes and reached for his costume, which had been dry-cleaned and was hanging on the back of the door. "The body-switching movie about identical twins? Come on."

"What was wrong with that one?"

"They were *identical twins*! No one gives a shit if they switch bodies! A hundred pages of them *whining*. What difference does it make?! Just get on with your lives!"

Cassie laughed. "It was avant-garde. And I'll have you know the filmmaker attached to that won a Student Oscar."

"When he wins a grown-up Oscar I'll read it again."

"You're no fun."

"Nineteen percent!" he shouted, reminding her of the Rotten Tomatoes fiasco. It had become somewhat of a rallying cry for him to only commit to projects he believed in.

Cassie awkwardly offered him the second coffee from her tray, but Patrick waved her away. That should be hers, to make up for the one that spilled. Someone walked by outside playing an accordion.

"Is that an—"

"It's been going on for days."

"It's cheerful," Cassie offered, trying to remain upbeat, before remembering, as his agent, it might be her job to intercede. "Do you want me to . . ."

"No, it's fine. It'll be the soundtrack to my demise." After an awkward moment, he softened. "You really flew all this way to see me?"

"And for the miles," she said, grinning. "I can finally take that trip to Belize."

◇◇◇◇◇◇◇

They were escorted to their table at Isabel's by a woman in a tulip dress; Patrick couldn't decide if she looked more like an air hostess from the 1960s or an emissary from the near future. The restaurant was one of the most beautiful in London, centered around a four-sided bar that was made for people watching. Hoping for a more discreet evening, Patrick had reserved a private table to the side, where he and Cassie could quietly gossip about the film he was wrapping and what might come next.

Patrick pulled back a chair for his agent. "I was surprised you were staying at Claridge's," she began as she took her seat. A napkin was placed across her lap. "I pictured you somewhere more modern."

Patrick eyed their hostess as he pushed back his own chair, a little puzzled as he mulled a quippy response. He liked Claridge's. Was he growing less cutting-edge with age?

"So how are you?" Cassie asked, moving on. "I saw Emory at a premiere. He asked about you."

Patrick's knee hit a table leg and their silverware jumped. "What did you tell him?"

"I said you were a broken man living off crumbs of the former limelight."

"Limelight doesn't crumb."

"A panache of Marlon Brando, Greta Garbo, and the Unabomber is how I think I put it." Cassie rested her chin on her hands with a smirk.

"I think you mean pastiche," Patrick said as he straightened his silverware.

She thought for a moment. "I do. I do mean pastiche."

"Panache almost works."

"I'm sure I said pastiche."

"Maybe you said pistachio." A nut almost worked, too. "I like the

Unabomber, though. Well, I don't *like* the Unabomber. But you know what I mean."

"Thank you. I thought that was a nice touch. Although I've never once seen you wear a hoodie." Cassie picked up the knife from her setting and used it to see if she had lipstick on her teeth before coming clean. "I said you were filming a movie in London."

Patrick agreed this was good. "The truth is always the best policy."

"May I offer a little personal criticism?"

"Personal?" This marked a shift in their relationship. Patrick wasn't so sure he wanted to hear it. "I can take any amount of criticism as long as it's unqualified praise. Noël Coward."

"Never mind, then." Cassie placed her knife back where she found it. She was treading in dangerous waters. "So how are you, *really*?"

"Really?" Patrick was eyeing a sea bream tartare with pink grapefruit and white turnip that was placed on their neighbor's table when he finally answered. "Tired."

"You seemed so energized on set!"

"That's called acting and I'm good at it."

"No. It's more than that. I mean, look at you, you're practically glowing."

Patrick reached for his fork and pointed toward the ceiling. "We're all of us glowing. We're sitting under three hundred brass lamps."

Cassie glanced upward and, sure enough, recessed into the ceiling were hundreds of domes in a flattering alloy, each one looking like it had been delicately scooped out with a melon baller.

"Well, I'm glad you summoned the strength to join me."

"I've got to eat." Patrick could tell she was disappointed he wasn't as excited as she was, so he added, "You have a marvelous glow about you, too."

Cassie shifted in her seat, uncomfortable as always in the spotlight, let alone under the glare of three hundred of them. She blushed as she perused the main courses.

"In truth, it's been a great experience. I was hoping to get another season or two out of the sitcom, but I think this movie is going to be really good." The sitcom was *Guncle Knows Best*; Patrick had recently completed a four-season run of the show modeled on his relationship with Maisie and Grant.

Cassie was happy that her client was pleased. "Four years is good for networks nowadays. Besides, the problem with kids is they grow up too fast. Do you think they'd still need your character when they're looking at colleges?" Cassie's smile faded when she realized she'd skirted too close to Patrick's real life. She then raised her menu to hide her faux pas. "I'm debating between the ratatouille and the cod."

"English food," Patrick said in a tone that was hard to read without elaboration.

"Did you have time to glance through those scripts?" Cassie asked, determined not to let her carelessness derail their evening.

"I told you no sequels."

"There was just *one* sequel," she protested. "It wouldn't kill you, you know, to do something that others already enjoy."

"I don't agree with what others enjoy and I don't want to be responsible for giving them more of it."

"What's wrong with sequels? *Avatar 2*, *Toy Story 3*, *Top Gun: Maverick*—all received Best Picture nominations."

"Did any of them win?"

"No, but . . ."

"You can't lead with exceptions to the rule. Sequels are either too bloated, too stuffed with B-team actors or characters or Ewoks—things that weren't good enough for the original. A cash grab to profit off something that was probably a fluke in the first place."

Cassie glanced at the surrounding patrons, perhaps wishing she could dine with one of them.

"The only time it maybe works—and I mean the *only* time—is when there wasn't an ending that was entirely happy, when not everything was tied up in a neat little bow. Otherwise you have to undo someone's happy ending to create more drama for your characters, and no one likes a happy ending undone. And what stories these days don't have happy endings? They all do, because the planet is on fire and our rights are being stripped and we're slipping into fascism and people need *some* distraction from their miserable lives—"

"Okay," Cassie said very slowly, backing away from a poked bear.

"I'm sorry, I'm not *actually* Noël Coward. I could have said that with more panache." Patrick placed a finger alongside one nostril and then pointed at her. That, in the business, is what they referred to as a callback.

"Okay, no sequels. So what do you want to play next?"

Patrick didn't have an answer, but he was rescued by a server with the night's specials. He ordered a vodka martini dry, very dry, and Cassie a Kir Royale. Part of the problem was that he didn't know who he wanted to *be* next. He did his best to explain. Not only was there not much of a career model for a gay man of fifty to follow, there wasn't much of a life model. Cassie listened intently, and he saw his pain reflected back at him in her rigorously focused gaze. She was positively Bill Clinton–esque in that way.

"What about Nathan Lane?" she asked sympathetically.

"Is that how you see me?" Patrick retorted, although Nathan Lane had given a career-redefining performance in the revival of *Angels in America* that had taken Patrick's breath away, and had won a Tony for his efforts. A Tony would look nice next to his Golden Globe, Patrick thought; the G in EGOT was for Grammy and not Globe, but it would still put him one step closer to a dream.

"Why not? Or Ian McKellen."

Patrick gay-gasped. Cassie jumped.

"What?"

"I open my heart to you about gay men and aging, and you come at me with Gandalf?"

"Well, I—" Cassie stammered, but it was too late.

"Why not Dumbledore? He was gay. Why not stop dyeing my hair and rent out the Shubert or the Lunt-Fontanne for a whole evening of homosexual wizards!"

"You dye your hair?" Cassie whispered.

Patrick pounded his fists on the table. "FUCKING GANDALF?" Several patrons in the restaurant turned, and there was a tense moment where people just stared in their direction. And then Patrick started to laugh. That was the absurdity of his situation, wasn't it? There was no good answer. Patrick waved at the other diners and they lost interest and returned to their meals, salads with peas and sprigs of mint. "I use a mousse," Patrick confessed, "to strip out some of the gray."

"It looks very natural."

He smoothed out the napkin in his lap with both hands. "I guess maybe I need a break while I figure a few things out."

Cassie's lips disappeared as she forced a weak grin. "I get nervous about you and breaks." His last break after Joe's death a decade and a half ago had nearly derailed his career. It wasn't until his summer in Palm Springs with the kids that he'd found his way back to the light. "Besides. I thought you were turning forty-nine. Fifty is still a year off."

Patrick narrowed his eyes, deciding whether or not to come clean. "Neal advised shaving a year off my age before sending me on my first audition. Back then you could be twenty-five and play a student at West Beverly High, but twenty-six was starting to push it. It was the best thing he ever did for me. Then my new age kind of stuck."

Cassie seemed surprised by this. It sounded like something that happened in old Hollywood, not new. "And now is the time to clear the air?"

"What can I say?" Patrick offered. "I'm a work in progress."

Their server appeared with a sampling of gordal olives with Manchego cheese along with their drinks.

"By the way, you're not available to babysit, are you? It pays fourteen dollars an hour."

Cassie did her best to mask whiplash from the change in subject. "Babysit? When?"

"Say, now through . . ." He began to count the weeks in his head, but didn't know how long Greg and Livia planned to honeymoon. "August?"

Cassie laughed nervously. They raised their glasses and offered cheers.

"Greg's getting remarried in a few weeks. Did I mention that? I said I would take the kids for a while. They're having a rough time with it."

"Well, of course." Cassie's expression turned pained. "I remember when my father remarried, and *my* mother was still very much alive. It's never easy. Does she have kids?"

Patrick shook his head, but then second-guessed himself. He really knew very little about Livia.

"I don't know if that makes it easier or harder, and it will be another issue entirely if she and Greg have their own."

"Oh, I think that ship has sailed." Fudging the truth about his age was one thing, but there were biological realities for women that made it harder for them to do the same. Not that more children would be impossible per se, and rich people had more options than most. But Patrick was tired, and he didn't do anything really. Even on days when he wasn't on set he needed a nap. He couldn't imagine anyone close to his age with an infant.

"So what are you going to do for them?"

"For Greg and Livia? I dunno. They're probably registered somewhere. Although what they might need is impossible to imagine, maybe one of those toasters with four slots."

Cassie looked at him, disappointed. "For the kids."

Patrick took a long, slow sip of his martini. The vodka his server recommended (apparently distilled in France specifically for the restaurant) had a nutty, rich taste. He set the glass down on the table, the olive floating on the surface like a tiny bird in a bath.

Cassie proceeded with caution. "You did kind of make them an oath."

Patrick carefully spun his cocktail on the marble tabletop, which had a handsome inlay. He stopped a passing server. "We're going to need some wine. Could I see a list?" The server disappeared to fetch one. "I kind of did, didn't I." He lifted the martini glass holding only the stem and admired the small ice chips that rose to the surface. "Any suggestions?"

Cassie repositioned her napkin just so on her lap to draw attention away from her smile. "I thought I was limited to giving career advice."

"Oh, Cassie." Patrick threw one arm over the back of his chair. "I think we're well beyond that."

Over dessert, Cassie promised to find him work that would *feel* like a break without actually being one and he wished her good luck with that; they parted on a cheerful note. When he was safely back in his room Patrick turned on the TV and flipped through channels until he found an old *Ab Fab* rerun. Eddie was jogging around the kitchen island in an obnoxiously loud tracksuit making a spectacle of herself as usual, declaring to anyone who would listen, "Inside of me there is a thin person just screaming to get out." The brilliant June Whitfield, as Eddie's mother, deadpans, "Just the one, dear?" Patrick laughed as he always did when he heard that line. It was such an inspired take-down. And it's how he often felt. Inside of him was a good person just screaming to get out. He had his moments, sure. But it was easier than not to revert to old ways. But he still wanted to do better, be better. He slumped his head back against the upholstered, scalloped headboard. A midlife identity crisis? Really? It was all so cliché that it was categorically boring.

He picked up his phone and searched for the travel agent he still used in LA; he was relieved when someone answered his call, as he was pretty sure he was the only one keeping them in business. One day soon travel agents would be like phone booths—decommissioned. The last one removed by some public works department and hauled off to live in a museum.

His next call was to Greg.

"Oh. Cheerio," Greg said, surprised to hear from his brother so soon. "It's late where you are. Have you given any more thought to the kids?"

Patrick unlaced his shoes and shimmied his bare feet under the duvet. He had done nothing *but* think of the kids. "You know, I went to a museum here in London on one of my days off."

"Do you want like a medal?"

Patrick cleared his throat. "The museum only had mirrors."

"Okay, but what about Maisie and Grant?"

"Old mirrors, antique mirrors, futuristic mirrors. Quite fascinating, really."

"Am I in a different conversation?" Greg asked, confused.

"Almost always," Patrick replied. *"Anyhow.* I thought, 'This is a hustle.'"

Greg gave up. "The mirrors? How so?"

"Charging people to look at themselves. I mean, don't get me wrong, I admired it. But it truly was quite the swindle."

"Ah," Greg said, finally understanding. "This is a roundabout way of saying you've done some introspection."

Patrick was certain he had a point in telling the mirror story, but in the moment he couldn't remember it. And if he was doing some introspection, he wasn't going to talk about it with Greg—at least not yet. "I booked tickets for the kids. Plane tickets. JFK to Heathrow."

There was a long silence on the other end of the line.

"Hello?"

"Patrick, I—" Greg didn't quite know what to say.

"They'll come spend a couple weeks with me in Europe while you and the Baroness take care of last-minute details—"

"She's not a baroness."

"And we'll meet you in Italy for the wedding. It'll take their minds off things, and who knows. Maybe it will be good for all three of us." Patrick hoped that would once again prove to be true. "Just don't expect another wedding gift. Oven mitts or a casserole dish."

"Livia's family comes from seven hundred years of generational wealth, so I think we'll be fine."

"Yes, but Suze Orman says it's not until eight hundred years that you feel truly secure."

"Who's Suze Orman?"

"A lesbian financial gu— What difference does it make? Do you need her curriculum vitae?"

Greg laughed.

"What?"

"They're related to three popes. I think this situation is different."

"*Three* popes."

"One by marriage."

Patrick, too, had to laugh. They were not raised Catholic, but his parents took all three of their children to some kind of Lutheran church in Connecticut until his sister, Clara, started high school and had her own life on weekends, and Patrick, several years younger, declared his disinterest. Their mother was all too happy to throw in the towel. Only Greg, the youngest, seemed to enjoy it at all—something about the ritual of the service—until he learned that Lutherans did not worship at the altar of *Lex* Luthor. And now here he was all grown up, about to be a third cousin twice removed or some nonsense to three popes.

The last thing he instructed Greg was to tell the kids to pack light. He'd also purchased three flexible Eurail passes. Thirty-three countries at their fingertips. No fixed route. The world was about to be their oyster.

"It'll be hard to convince Maisie to leave her books," Greg warned.

"Is Livia planning on being buried with her generational wealth? Get your bumptious offspring Kindles, for heaven's sake."

"She likes physical books, what can I say. And she's started her period. Can you handle that?"

Patrick hesitated, but supposed he'd handled worse.

"It came later than most of her friends and she's very sensitive, so you have to tread carefully."

"I'm sensitive, too, you know."

"She just had it, so maybe you won't—"

"Okay."

"It's a twenty-eight-day cycle."

"The length of this conversation has now exceeded my interest in it."

"I just figured you haven't had that kind of experience with women."

"I'm saying goodbye now."

"PATRICK, WAIT."

Patrick pulled the phone from his ear and stared at it.

"Are you still there?"

"Yes," he said, listening again.

There was only a slight hesitation on Greg's end before he said, "I love you."

THREE

"GUP!" the kids screamed as they emerged from the passenger bridge and spotted their uncle at the gate. Celebrities had access to a whole host of perks while flying, but apparently so did adults meeting children flying alone. Maisie and Grant ran straight into his arms as a gate agent followed closely to check the paperwork they wore around their necks. They both had backpacks, Maisie's bulging with books.

"Mr. O'Hara?" the gate agent asked, making sure all was in order. Patrick presented his passport as ID and she cross-checked everything one final time with her records. "Thank you for flying British Airways, children. I was going to offer you a pin, but I suppose you're rather big for one."

"I'll take a pin," Grant said excitedly.

"A brooch to go with your clownish necklaces." Patrick held aloft the lanyards clipped to their documents.

"You know what the best insult is?" Grant asked.

Patrick braced himself. "Is it about to be directed at me?"

Grant ignored his uncle. "It's 'Who is this clown?' Because you're calling someone a clown, but not even like one of the better-known clowns." He grinned from ear to ear, exposing most of his adult teeth.

"Ignore him," Patrick instructed the agent. "He's what happens when the ventriloquist dies and the dummy keeps talking." He pinched Grant playfully in the ticklish spot on the back of his arm and the boy squealed with laughter.

The gate agent was charmed as she fished in her pocket for pins. "I'll give you two. In case your sister decides she'd like one later." She winked at Grant and mussed his hair. "And so you don't think I'm a clown. Welcome to London."

Patrick sized up his niblings as she retreated to bring the completed paperwork to the airline's attendant. She was right about one thing: the kids were rather big. Bigger even than when he last saw them in March.

"Maisie, I can't believe you're starting high school."

"If I survive the summer."

"And Grant?"

"Middle school. I already met my teachers. Mr. Arroyo said I can get extra credit if I write a report about my trip. Is this England?" The kid produced a little notebook and pen from his pocket.

"It is," Patrick said as he relieved Grant of the British Airways pins and fastened one to the kid's backpack. He offered the second to Maisie and she refused. "London is in England."

"I thought it was in Great Britain," Maisie said.

"It's in that, too."

Grant frowned. "What's the United Kingdom, then?"

"It's all of these things."

Grant flipped his notebook closed. "This report is going to be harder than I thought, GUP."

Patrick gripped his temples. "You've grown in every imaginable way, but you're still going to fuck with me by calling me GUP?" GUP was short for Gay Uncle Patrick, a nickname the kids' mother had fed them before she died. They tortured him with it the summer they'd spent in Palm Springs and it clung to their relationship like a sock fresh out of the dryer. He lowered Grant's arm, which the boy had raised to point out his cursing. "It's okay if you swear around kids here. Europeans believe in treating children like adults, just like I do. You could probably get a pint, if you were so inclined."

"Of beer?!"

Patrick nodded.

Grant's eyes grew wide. "Fuckin' A!"

Patrick buried his face in his hands. "I said to swear *around* kids." He took them each by the hand. "Kids can only swear in Australia because it was once a penal colony."

"Penal," Grant giggled, but Patrick could only bite his lip in response.

Maisie, however, was ready to dive into business. "This is a real mess, GUP."

"Heathrow? Get outta here. It's a world-class airport."

"Dad and Livia." Maisie looked more like Sara every day; Patrick was alarmed to see she had the hint of a figure and in her shorts seemed sixty percent leg. Everything was changing too fast. He squeezed her hand twice, a little code they'd worked out that meant "I love you" without having to say it in public, and started them moving.

"Whenever I get gloomy about the state of the world, I think about the arrivals gate at Heathrow Airport." He gestured around them as they took their first steps toward baggage claim.

"Huh?" Grant asked, stumped. "Why?"

"It's from *Love Actually*. Have you seen it?" Both kids gave him blank stares. He thought about showing them the movie on this trip—they'd always loved a little Christmas in July—but none of them were in a romantic comedy mood given the glum states of their little worlds. "It sounded better when Hugh Grant said it. Most things do. You know what? Never mind. Everything about that movie is psychotic. Except for Emma Thompson, who can do no wrong. Guncle Rule one hundred twenty-nine."

Maisie rumbled a small protest. "We're well into the three hundreds."

Patrick had long ago stopped counting his rules and he waved at them to keep stride.

Over eleven billion dollars had been spent upgrading London Heathrow and great care had been put into the designs, vaulting the ceilings where passengers were likely to congregate and spend valuable waiting time, and lowering them at places like security and customs so that people did not feel overwhelmed. Even acoustic performance was a design consideration, allowing people to easily communicate in a crowd. Even if the three of them had yet to fall back into their old patter and ways.

"Ooh, a Sunglass Hut!" Grant pointed excitedly when they had been quiet too long. Somehow this echoed through the entire terminal.

"Stop it," Patrick hissed as they stepped onto a people mover. Travelers were afforded the highest-end shopping and finest restaurants; on his way to the gate to meet the kids, Patrick had passed Harrods and Burberry and Cartier. They would not so much as slow their pace for a Sunglass Hut, he would not allow it. Especially since they had a long way to go before daylight. A transit train to passport control. Then baggage claim. Then customs. Then, and only if they were lucky, the last light of day.

They ascended the platform just as the transit arrived. Patrick relieved Grant of his backpack to lighten his load. "Did you just come from the gym?" he asked, noticing the boy's T-shirt and basketball shorts.

"That's the style," Maisie said, bored. "All boys wear that. It's like a uniform."

"Not to school." Patrick recoiled. He remembered wearing corduroy pants and oxford shirts when he was Grant's age. Young Patrick had been equally outfitted to sell insurance or go to the sixth grade.

"Especially to school," Grant said.

"What do you wear to gym class? A tuxedo?"

"Noooo!" Grant exclaimed, punctuated with a *dumbass* that, for his sake, was fortunately silent. "Sometimes we change into different gym clothes, but then we change back."

The transport doors opened and they stepped on board. There was no point in arguing, but Patrick made a note that perhaps a lecture on the decline of personal presentation was warranted later. "Grab on to the rail," he instructed as the transport doors closed. Maisie was more acceptably dressed in shorts and a cropped sweater over some sort of light top. It was a far cry from the boyish looks she preferred as a young girl.

"Can we go to Hogwarts?" Grant asked once they were underway.

"On this train? No."

"On this *trip*."

"No. We're not going to Hogwarts."

"Why not?" Grant was a dog with a bone.

"It doesn't exist, for one. Also, Jo Rowling's a TERF."

"What's a TERF?"

"It's an acronym." A man near them looked up from his phone. Patrick stared at him until he blinked and returned to his scrolling.

"For what?" Maisie asked.

"I don't know, but it's not good."

"Not good, how?"

Patrick was at a loss to explain. "It's a person without any magic or kindness."

"Oh, like a muggle," Grant said.

"Yes, but worse."

"I'm confused."

"So is she." Patrick had forgotten what it was like to be barraged with such questions. When he spent time with the kids these days, visiting them at home, they were more often than not distracted by friends or screens. So if they were already peppering him to this degree, undivided in their attention, it was bound to be a long several weeks. The train went dark as it entered a tunnel, and thankfully Grant's questions did, too.

When they stepped off the transport they were shepherded to immigration and passport control. The ceiling had hundreds of circular lights, much like the restaurant he'd been to with Cassie, but they were fluorescent and not brass and therefore did nothing for his complexion.

"You look worn out," Grant said, as if to confirm this, and Maisie continued her moody silence.

"Thank you, one never tires of hearing that." Patrick stopped them to read the signage. "I've been shooting nights on this film, but we're almost wrapped."

Maisie's dam finally burst. Exasperated, she blurted, "We're wasting our time! What are we going to do about *Dad*?"

Patrick held his hand out for each kid's passport. "We're not wasting our time, we're going through customs. But tell me, how do you mean?"

"The wedding. It's a sham."

"You know what's a sham? Cirque du Soleil. Charging that much money to watch people bend in that way."

"GUP!" To get his attention, Maisie snatched their passports back.

"Gah! Papercuts." Patrick waved his hand like it stung, then relented. "Why is the wedding a sham? They don't love each other?"

Maisie awkwardly crossed her arms under her crop top. "Ew, gross."

"They're just in it for the gifts?"

"Livia's rich," Grant boasted.

"Is Livia a decorative pillowcase?" Patrick asked.

Maisie threw up her arms at her uncle's nonsense.

"Then how is it a sham?!"

Foot traffic was flowing around them like salmon moving upstream, and so he pulled them over against a nearby wall. A digital poster boasted that London Heathrow serviced two hundred fourteen destinations across eighty-four countries via eighty-nine different airlines. "Is it something specific about Livia? Is she already married to someone else?" Patrick's eyes grew wide.

"Why do you look so excited?" Grant asked.

"Because gay people live for drama. What is it? You have to tell me. Does she snore? Does she mispronounce words, like 'shed-ule' for 'schedule'? Does she pick her nose?" Speaking of picking, Grant was picking at a mole on his neck and Patrick had to swat his hand away.

"No," Maisie reluctantly admitted.

"Is she mean to you?"

"No."

"To the dog?"

"No!" Grant cried.

"Does she wear vulgar Italian fashion to pick you up from school? Burn salad? Drive on the wrong side of the road?"

"None of those things."

"Smell funny?"

"Not more funny than other rich women," Maisie observed.

"Then I'm losing interest."

Maisie stomped her feet in despair. "You just don't get it!" Patrick imagined he'd be hearing that phrase a lot over the next few years.

"No, I get it. I really do." Patrick watched as the digital poster changed to a fresh image boasting about the new solar panels powering the Queen's Terminal. "But I think we all want your dad to be happy, don't we? Even if it requires some sacrifice on our parts." Patrick and his brother had grown close in the years since Greg's successful completion of rehab after he was widowed. The summer five years ago when Patrick had taken in the kids was a gift in so many ways, and Greg's gratitude had far-reaching tentacles that had massaged the previous tension in their relationship. And likewise, Patrick actually enjoyed spending time with Greg as someone who appreciated and missed Sara as much (if not more) than he did. Grieving together allowed them to entertain memories, to laugh—to find genuine happiness—faster than they otherwise might have on their own. Perhaps it was even Patrick's fault, Greg's openness to getting caught up in this new relationship, for the seemingly whirlwind nature of the whole affair. Should he tell Maisie as much? Or perhaps it was better to do what he did best. To divert. To distract. To offer a fresh perspective. To be a confidant. To listen. And to show them a better way. "Not to be all Pollyanna about it, but sometimes people can pleasantly surprise you."

"Who's Pollyanna?" Grant asked.

Patrick bent down on one knee to look them in the eye, steadying himself as Grant's backpack clumsily slipped off his shoulder. "She's no one. What I'm trying to say is that you were skeptical of me at first, but we get on pretty good now. You were skeptical of Emory, but then you ended up liking him once we got together. So you never really know until you give people a chance."

Grant picked at the pilot wings freshly pinned to his bag. "We did not like it when you two broke up."

Patrick felt his stomach knot. "Is that what you're worried about? Getting attached to Livia, and then having it not work out?"

"Please," Maisie groaned.

Patrick ignored her protest. "Because, I don't know. Your father seems pretty committed."

Maisie tilted her head down and looked up as if over an invisible pair of glasses, giving her best teenage *You're kidding, right?* expression. "Our father should *be* committed."

"That's funny," Patrick said admiringly, but he didn't laugh. Out of the corner of his eye he saw two security guards in menacing uniforms eyeing them. He needed to wrap this up before they were urged to move along. "You two have had to deal with so much. More than any kids your age should have to. And now your dad's getting remarried. And it's not what you want. I get that. And sometimes that's the raw deal of being a kid. Adults make decisions that affect you and you really don't have a say."

Maisie's arms reappeared from the sleeves of her sweater. She stood up to her full height and lifted her chin, looking valiant. "You're not making this better."

Patrick held up his finger. He wasn't done yet. "But there are great things about being a kid, too."

"Like what?" Grant interrupted, his interest piqued. He reached for the mole on his neck a second time, so Patrick took the boy's hand in his own.

"There are still so many beautiful things to see and experience for the first time. And rich uncles with exquisite taste in art and antiquities to show them to you. That's what this trip is all about. I thought we could see a whole bunch of new things together. And then we'll decide what to do about the Baroness. Deal?"

"The Baroness?" Maisie exchanged looks with Grant.

Patrick hummed a few bars of "The Lonely Goatherd" and both kids laughed. Thank god they loved *The Sound of Music* as much as he did.

Maisie's expression soured again as she studied her uncle's face. "Why do you have sideburns?"

"For work. Any more questions?" He stood up and slung Grant's backpack over his shoulder again. The kids, for once, were silent. "Good. Because before we can do anything, we have to get through customs."

FOUR

Patrick's movie was titled *Tongue-in-Cheek*, in reference to the style of British humor, but in itself was tongue-in-cheek, as it also suggested a very specific sexual act at the center of the film's plot. It all took place in the mid-1970s, a gloomy period in Britain after Harold Wilson's swinging sixties and before the rise of Margaret Thatcher. It was a decade of strikes—postal workers, miners, and dustmen— where the Queen's Silver Jubilee was followed by the Winter of Discontent. Jude Law was cast as fictional prime minister Lyle Bancroft, whose taste for the aforementioned sexual act comes to light in his divorce proceedings just as he's taken residency at Number 10 Downing. He becomes embroiled in scandal and the—ahem—*butt* of the nation's jokes and, being a deeply serious man, lacks the talent and grit to effectively strike back and neutralize a rather precarious political predicament. Patrick played Peter Wiggins, a disgraced American sitcom star ("Imagine that," he'd said to Cassie when she'd sent him the script, first via email and then printed) running from his own scandal (being outed as bisexual), whom Bancroft's advisers hire to teach their man to be funny. An unlikely friendship develops between the British politician and the American comedian as they bond over being other people's punch lines, and Patrick's character gets to the heart of why Lyle's sense of humor had been so stymied.

"It's all very *King's Speech*," Cassie had explained when she was trying to sell him on the project. "Except, you know. *Funny*."

"You're being unusually *ass*-ertive." It would be the first of many puns between them.

"I think you should do it. *The King's Speech* did wonders for Colin Firth's career."

"I recall," Patrick said. Firth played King George VI and the film centered on his friendship with an unorthodox speech therapist played by Geoffrey Rush. "It won him his *firth* Oscar," Patrick quipped in honor of Grant and his old lisp.

Jude had been a most generous scene partner, and while he'd aged into more interesting roles, he retained a magnetism that had yet to dim. It was easy to imagine not only his party electing him prime minister, but an ex-wife allowing him to do the dirty deed at the heart of the film. Jude seemed unbothered by growing older, almost relieved, and Patrick admired him for it. Patrick himself had never been burdened with quite such good looks. He was handsome, no doubt, especially in his youth. But his looks were not driving his fame. In real life, Jude was slyly funny, and he and Patrick had developed their own camaraderie, which served them both on set and off. And now Patrick was almost sad the movie was wrapping.

On the last day of shooting, Patrick arranged for Maisie and Grant to play small parts as extras; they were to be members of a cheering crowd who warmly greet the prime minister as he triumphantly leaves the House of Commons and all seems forgiven. Patrick thought they'd get a kick out of being in the film; if nothing else they had bragging rights for when they returned home (it was the ultimate "What I did on my summer vacation" answer). For Patrick's part it was free babysitting, as he wasn't sure what else he would do with them while he was at work.

When Patrick emerged from hair and makeup, the kids were already waiting for him; Maisie was dressed in a jumpsuit made of drab olive corduroy and her hair pulled back in a braid, while Grant was clad in gray dress shorts and long socks as part of a primary school uniform.

"Don't you both look groovy." Patrick himself was sporting a maroon leisure suit with its shirt-like jacket and long bell-bottom pants.

An actress named Thomasin walked by on her way to the set and pointed at Grant. "He looks just like you," she said, and kept walking.

"Thanks, that's a great compliment!" Patrick called after her. He then turned to Grant and said, "For you."

"Oooh," Maisie said when she finally took in his whole getup. "Your sideburns are for the *film*."

"Yes, I told you that."

"Yeah, but we don't listen to you."

Patrick longed for the days when they hung on his every word.

"What did you think, I was just reliving some latent Jason Priestley thing?" Blank stares. "Never mind, come here. We have to take a picture for your dad."

Patrick lowered himself on one knee and Grant rested against his uncle's thigh as he motioned for Maisie to lean in. A breeze caught the kid's hair just as he looked away from the camera at something off in the distance; the resulting photo was just so cool and badass. They looked like a band of thieves on a wanted poster, Patrick the mastermind, Maisie and Grant street-smart orphans who could swindle you for all you were worth. It was the kind of movie Hollywood used to make with Ryan O'Neal. "Are you two excited?"

The kids' response lacked a certain vivacity.

"Oh, come on. You're in a *movie*. You're going to see how the magic is made. You can't be that blasé. We could probably even get you Taft-Hartley waivers. You ever thought about joining SAG?"

"SAG?" Maisie said. Once again it was clear from their expressions they thought he was speaking in tongues.

"SAG. The Screen Actors Guild. That's how I get my health insurance."

Maisie was unimpressed. "We get our insurance from Dad. Besides, we don't even have any lines."

"Ooh, I want to have a line!" Grant exclaimed.

"You're not getting lines."

Grant put his hands on his hips in frustration. "You have lines!"

"What do you think this is, some sort of Montessori-type thing?" Patrick balked. "Not everyone's part is the same. Now, come on. You're extras in a Hollywood film. I don't know what more you could want out of the summer."

Maisie challenged him with a glare. "We'd like to stop our dad from making a huge mistake."

Patrick looked at them both, remembering when they were six and nine. It was easier then; they didn't understand everything that came out of his mouth, but they were always open and enchanted. Now they had agency to push back against his wilder antics and they were more immune to his charms. On top of that they devised their own agendas and had no problem advocating for them; everything was all so straightforward in their minds. "One thing at a time, okay?" There would be plenty of long days ahead to work out the Greg situation as they traveled by rail around Europe.

Patrick sent the kids to set with a second AD, adding, "It wouldn't be the worst thing in the world if you packed them up with wardrobe and sent them back to the States." The director laughed; everyone always assumed he was kidding.

They shot the scene several times, Patrick trying his level best not to break character while cameras were rolling to scan for Maisie and Grant in the crowd. He kept his focus on Jude (or rather, Prime Minister Lyle Bancroft), and it honestly felt thrilling to be greeted with cheers each time they emerged from the building, even if everyone was being paid to cheer and the hoots and hollers were for their characters and not them. He couldn't believe he'd taken such a long leave from acting, hiding away in the desert, as he did for the better part of ten years. Now that he was back in front of the cameras, he realized how much an integral part of him acting was. Yes, Palm Springs had almost constant sunshine, but it was nothing compared to the hot lights of a movie set. The excitement, the bustle, the camera on a crane that panned over them before swooping high above to take in a crowd that would be digitally replicated and expanded later. It was just so exciting. Even his leisure suit was growing on him; he wondered if there was any way he could keep it when filming was done. Maybe he'd even wear it to Greg's wedding, just to see the look on his brother's face. Perhaps that alone would be enough to stop the ceremony in its tracks. Although it was just as likely that in Italy no one would blink an eye at his seventies fashion; in Europe it was hard to tell.

Between takes, however, Patrick kept a firm eye on the kids. They'd been placed in the crowd alongside two actors dressed, he supposed, as their mom and dad. These more experienced extras were offering the kids both encouragement and ideas, and he watched as they rehearsed little bits they could do for the camera together. Patrick's heart grew heavy as he studied Maisie and Grant with a proxy mother and father. The kids were part of a complete family again, fictional as it was, looking happy and cheering, and he was struck in that moment by how much these children had lost. Of course he knew what they had missed out on these past five years—he missed their mother terribly, too. But to see it so plainly, through this window into an alternate universe, he felt it all anew.

◇◇◇◇◇◇◇

"Would you let your kids go into acting?" Sara had asked him once when they were still in their freshman year at school. Patrick was newly out and had yet to even go on a formal date. Kids were light-years away.

"Kids?" Patrick replied. They had just returned from rehearsals for the fall play and were buzzing with how much more professional their college theater department was than their respective high school drama clubs. "What world are you living in?"

Sara scrutinized him with a look that made Patrick panic; she always saw a future for him that he could not.

"Where is this coming from all of a sudden?" Usually late at night they would gripe about things that had transpired that day—their castmates' reluctance to get off book, for instance, or the director's ridiculous insistence they rehearse in spandex pants—rather than ponder a time to come.

Sara lay on her dorm room floor and looked up at the tapestry she'd pinned to the ceiling, a stand-in for the night sky. She stared so intently Patrick wondered if she was waiting to see a shooting star. "My parents are threatening to cut off tuition unless I study something more practical."

"More practical to who?" Patrick asked, but the answer was crystal clear. "They can't do that!" One thing about coming out, it made Patrick enraged with all of the world's injustices. But he knew they very well could, as his own parents had threatened the same before school even began. "The only sane course of action is announcing a keen interest in something even less employable than drama. Tell them you're taking up the French horn."

"That's the sane course of action?" Sara pressed.

"I'm not saying actually do it," Patrick replied. Try as he might, he could not picture her in a band uniform.

"I just think if I had kids, I would want them to be happy. At all costs. I'd want them to find their happiness."

The simplicity of it was profound. "Happiness," Patrick repeated, like it was a novel concept. He wasn't even certain he'd ever thought to visualize that for himself and here she was wishing it on others who did not yet exist, perhaps at the cost of her own. He reached for a book on her shelf, a collection of one-acts for two people, published by Samuel French. "Want to read a play?" It was something they did for amusement in the wee hours.

"No. You have to get out of here. The Faucet is coming over."

Patrick groaned. "I'm being sexiled for the Faucet?" The Faucet was a sophomore Sara had hooked up with twice who leaked an alarming amount whenever the least bit excited; his penis was quite like a spigot. "You can't have kids with the Faucet."

"What's wrong with the Faucet?"

"The way his anatomy works? He's more likely to impregnate his pants."

Sara laughed. "There's a special place in hell for people like you."

Patrick stood up and spun on one heel. "Yes, obviously I'll be in VIP."

Sara pulled the pillows off her bed and threw them at Patrick one by one until he opened the door to leave. "Good night, Patrick."

He leaned in the doorway, and looked adoringly at his friend. They'd known each other only a matter of weeks and he already wanted to repay her for everything she'd done for him, nudging him closer to happiness than he'd ever been. "Someday I'll introduce you to someone else. Someone better. And your kids will be all the happier for it. Whether they're actors or not."

Patrick became aware of a tugging on his sleeve and it snapped him out of his trance. It was one of the actors pulling him back inside as the director called for another take. Patrick found his starting mark and stood, listening as the crowd of extras was once more quieted and stilled. Maisie and Grant could have this again. A complete family. If only they would open themselves up to Livia. Sure, he liked to have his fun, calling her the Baroness and whatnot, needling his brother about her wealth and family lineage. But he had to sell the kids on all the good that could come from their father remarrying. Not for his sake, not for Greg's. But for *theirs*. Having, if not a mother again, a mother figure who could make them happy. He felt certain of it, even if they were not. They were young still, they needed that.

He had a mission now for their summer trip as they wound their way slowly to Italy for the wedding. He hoped that he was up for it, and he almost convinced himself he was just as the director called, "ACTION!"

FIVE

The train for Paris left London's St. Pancras International, a brick paragon of Victorian engineering with a majestic clock tower that stood at the southern end of the London borough of Camden. It was a beautiful morning in late June with a magnificent blue sky marred only by the trail of a single passing plane. The city of London was pulling out all the stops for its goodbye; it made Patrick even more sorry to leave. Maisie kept pace with her uncle, who moved at a purposeful clip, but placed a small distance between them, as if annoyed by his very presence. Grant trailed behind, pulling an overstuffed suitcase, which he struggled to get up on the curb.

"Can I have my own bed in Paris? I don't want to sleep with the underbutler," he complained.

"*On* the underbutler," Patrick corrected, referring to his Claridge's room's fainting couch. Not that that sounded any better.

As Grant gave his suitcase one last tug, he spotted neighboring King's Cross station, which had been erected across Pancras Road.

"Look! King's Cross station!"

"What?" Patrick pressed. It sounded like the boy said *crustacean*, as if His Majesty had a pet crab.

"That's where you get the train to Hogwarts!"

Patrick pulled Grant forward to St. Pancras. "What did I say about Hogwarts?"

It had already been a morning; Patrick not only had to pack his own bags after an extended stay, but bags for two kids who'd somehow made more of a mess in four days than he did in six weeks. He would have been impressed if he hadn't also been horrified. He quickly organized their belongings in two piles, keep and toss—toss was by far the bigger of the two.

"We need those things!" Maisie had protested.

"No you don't."

"Yes we do!" Grant concurred.

Patrick held strong. "We're going to Paris, which is, with all apologies to Milan, the fashion capital of the world. We'll get new things. We can't go with suitcases that are already stuffed to the gills. That's offensive to . . ." Patrick hesitated, not quite sure what it was offensive to. He grasped for straws. "*Shopping.*"

Maisie made the biggest fuss about her books and Patrick allowed her to keep three and then paid the hotel to ship the rest on ahead to Lake Como. "It's quite possible you read too much," Patrick told her. Maisie scowled and said the problem with adults is that they read too little.

Just as Grant finally had his suitcase up onto the curb, a red double-decker plowed by. Patrick made a sweeping gesture.

"You see that? It's like right out of a postcard."

"Grant getting pancaked?" Maisie asked with growing frustration.

"No, the double-decker— Look around, would you?"

"You look around!" Maisie yelled. "Grant was almost hit by a bus!"

Patrick seemed unfazed. "That's only because they drive on the left. Don't worry, the French are civilized and drive on the right."

Maisie was at her wit's end. "Maybe it would have been easier if you had just *sent* us a postcard. Instead of dragging us all the way here."

Patrick stopped in his tracks, stood his suitcase up on four wheels, and lowered the handle. "You kids don't know how lucky you are."

Maisie pushed her hair out of her face and gave him a defiant look, like she spent her days on her hands and knees scrubbing Miss Hannigan's floors. Patrick realized perhaps *lucky* was ripe for misinterpretation, but they *were*, in certain regards.

"I know, it's a hard-knock life. I hear you, Pepper—"

"—my name is Maisie."

"But you hear me. You kids are about to see and experience so much. Certainly more than I ever had the opportunity to do and see at your age. Which was probably more the economic realities of my upbringing in the nineteen—" Patrick covered his mouth as he garbled a decade. "—than it was being raised by boors."

"What are boors?" Grant asked.

"Boars are tusked pigs," Maisie explained.

"That's B-O-A-R," Patrick corrected, quickly becoming B-O-R-E-D.

"Then what did you say?"

"IT DOESN'T MATTER." When purchasing their rail tickets and charting their trip, Patrick had read that St. Pancras was a Roman boy who converted to Christianity, then was beheaded for his unwavering faith in the persecution of Christians by the emperor Diocletian in the year 303. It seemed an extreme punishment for a boy of only fourteen, but Patrick had newfound sympathy for the emperor; teens could test one's resolve. "Now can we please focus on catching our train?" Patrick extended the handle of his suitcase once again and spun dramatically toward the station entrance, praying his niece and nephew would follow.

The St. Pancras main hall was an impressive construction of steel and glass, with shops, pubs, and some departures on the lower level, topped with an impressive champagne bar and further tracks above. Almost as if to prove Patrick's point, Maisie and Grant stopped in their own tracks at the center of the hall to marvel at the size of the station and the bustle of people around them. They'd rode into New York plenty of times to visit their uncle, but this far surpassed in grandeur the size of either Penn or Grand Central Station, and the quavering sounds of travel sent their imaginations buzzing.

"*See?*" Patrick asked if the spectacle of this single train station justified his plans to drag them all over Europe. "Now hurry along so that we can split a gimlet. The pub is meant to be a world-class establishment." He looped behind and nudged them forward like an Australian cattle dog.

"We're going to share a gimlet?" Maisie asked skeptically.

"More or less," Patrick replied. "I'll have the gin, and you two can squabble over the Rose's lime."

They walked the Eurostar premier-class car's rich burgundy carpet like they'd arrived at a movie premiere dragging luggage. The car was quiet and calming, upholstered in a two-tone taupe, and had sliding glass partitions every few aisles; it felt like a lovely place to spend a few hours. Patrick thought it a shame the US never invested in trains like these, he would have considered taking the kids to see national parks. They found a free cluster of four seats, and Patrick sat on one side of a small table, while Maisie and Grant slid into seats on the other. Across the aisle, an older couple in dusty overcoats sat in a two-seater and griped at each other in French, looking like extras from a film by Godard or Truffaut. Soon they were underway.

"Why are you both on that side of the table?" Patrick pressed after the train had been moving for half an hour. "You look like you're interviewing me for a job."

Maisie exchanged a look with her brother like they'd been busted. Then she studied her uncle and said, "You looked better with sideburns."

Patrick slammed his head against the back of the seat and exhaled. He'd shaved them as soon as filming had wrapped.

Grant folded his hands on the table like a cog on the wrong side of forty who'd never risen above middle management. "Look. We hate to ask you this."

Patrick glanced over his shoulder to see if he could spot the café car. "It's not too late to stop yourselves."

The kids were undeterred and Maisie picked right up where her brother left off. "We need you to talk to Dad."

"Talk some sense into him," Grant explained.

Patrick turned back to his niece and nephew and frowned. There were times when they looked incredibly big and there were times, like now, when they looked very small. He sighed, wondering how on earth he'd ever explain. "Your father's in love. It's been my experience there's no talking sense into people in love."

"Why not?"

"Because they're properly unhinged! Temporarily, at least, but unhinged nonetheless."

"He wasn't with Mom!" Maisie protested.

Patrick scoffed. "Oh, really. Were you there?"

"Yes."

"Not at the beginning!" Greg had absolutely lost his mind when Patrick had introduced him to Sara, and it was indeed upsetting for Patrick to witness. Overnight he had gone from being Greg's brother and Sara's best friend to being an unwelcome third wheel in their presence. To make matters worse, Greg called him at all hours wanting to talk about Sara as if she were a long-held prized possession of Patrick's, one he was intent on stealing, and asking him to betray the confidentiality of close friendship. That whole time was a mess; for a while he lost them both. "When you grow up you'll see."

Maisie disagreed. "We don't have that kind of time."

"Let's talk about something else," Patrick said, scrambling for a topic. "You guys were on a real film set. What did you think of movie-making?" He'd wondered with the kids seeing his career back in full swing if one of them might express an interest in acting or working on set. So far he had no takers.

Grant squirmed as he tried his best to get comfortable. "It's a lot of waiting around."

"Yeah, but pretty good crafty."

"What's crafty?"

"Craft services. Food. Snacks."

"Lunch was okay," Maisie offered.

"No, lunch is catering. Crafty is the table where—"

Suddenly everything went pitch-black and lights came on in their car. The gentle rocking of the train continued unabated.

"What's happening?" Grant pressed himself against the window to peer at the darkness, only to see his own concerned face reflected back. "Was there an eclipse?" he asked, but the only shadow was that of his former lisp.

"That's not how eclipses work. We entered the Chunnel."

"The *what*?" Grant's eyes filled with horror.

"The Channel Tunnel," Patrick overpronounced. "It goes under the English Channel, connecting the island of Great Britain with France."

Maisie began to panic. "We're underwater?"

Patrick nodded. *Hello darkness, my old friend.*

"Like, the *ocean*?" Grant covered his mouth in horror.

"Under the Channel, which I suppose is part of the ocean, sure." Patrick directed his gaze over his shoulder again.

"How deep?"

"Twenty thousand leagues under the sea." Patrick had no idea, but the least he could do was amuse himself.

Grant swallowed hard. "How deep is that?"

"I don't know. I couldn't fathom it." Patrick bit the inside of his cheek to keep from laughing at his own little joke. He again looked toward the back of the car.

Maisie crossed her arms. "Why do you keep looking over your shoulder?"

"I wonder if the café car has champagne."

"Dad is sober."

"So am I, which is why I was wondering about champagne."

"No, *sober* sober. He doesn't like for you to drink so much when you're taking care of us."

Patrick turned his attention back. "We'll tell him you drove me to it."

"I don't like this," Grant said, cautiously taking in their surroundings. His uncle knew him well enough to know he was imagining sharks and whales and giant squid swimming all around them.

Patrick leaned toward the older couple seated across the aisle. The man was trying to peel the skin off a peach with a plastic knife and not getting very far; the woman looked at her husband with disdain. "Excusez-moi," Patrick interrupted. "Quelle est la profondeur du tunnel?"

The man looked at the woman as if she might know. "Soixante-quinze mètres, plus ou moins?" The woman agreed.

"Merci. Mon neveu voulait savoir." Patrick turned to Grant. "Seventy-five meters. Give or take." Grant leaned forward and opened his mouth to speak, but Patrick didn't give him the chance to ask his question. "Like two hundred and fifty feet, since you Americans insist on clinging to the imperial system." Grant whipped out his notebook to write that down.

"*You're* American," Maisie replied. Patrick turned to the couple across from them and shook his head. She stared at her uncle with bemused skepticism. "What just happened?"

"How do you mean?"

"You were speaking in tongues."

"I wasn't speaking in tongues, I was speaking in French. You should know some French, it's one of the Romance languages." And then, to get a rise out of them, he added, "Tongues are exclusively for French kissing." Sure enough, both of them squirmed with disgust, with Grant going so far as grabbing his throat with both hands and pretending to vomit.

Patrick wondered if that wasn't in part how Livia had Greg under her spell, given that Italian was a Romance language, too.

"How do you know French?"

"How does anyone know anything? I learned in school. In New England they used to make you take French to speak with the Québécois."

"The who?"

"My god. Don't they teach anything anymore? Canadians. Or at least the ones from Quebec. But you should probably take Spanish."

Maisie glanced heavenward, as if her mother might give her strength.

"One or both of you should think about continuing your education in Europe. It's very chic to be schooled abroad. Oxford. The Sorbonne. RADA."

"What's RADA?"

"The Royal Academy of Dramatic Art. Although, that one's very hard to get into."

Maisie pulled out her phone and twisted her mouth to one side. "I need the Wi-Fi."

As if it were old hat, Patrick pulled a brochure from a pocket next to the seat, slapped it on the table, and pointed to the network name and password. "Wi-Fi," he said, but used the French pronunciation *wee-fee.*

Seeing that Grant was obviously still stressed about their surroundings, Patrick thought a change of subject was in order. "You remember the first time you spent the summer with me. Right after your mom died. We flew to California together."

Maisie and Grant nodded.

"You freaked out on me then, too. Remember, Grant? On the plane. You screamed when you lost a tooth."

"Oh, yeah," he recalled. "I was only six."

"That's right."

"You were only forty-four."

Patrick closed his eyes for a second. *That was uncalled for.* He turned once again to the couple across from them in case they were eavesdropping. "J'avais quarante-trois ans." They dipped their heads politely and the man's peach slipped out of his bony hands and onto his lap. "My point is," Patrick continued as he looked at the kids, "I got you through it. And I'll get you through this tunnel. And when we come out the other side we'll be in France."

"And you'll also help with this thing with Dad?"

Patrick closed his eyes to center himself. He would get them through that, too. "Look, I'll make you a deal. Europe is the perfect place to learn about love. Are you familiar with the five love languages?"

"Yeah, one of them is French."

"No."

Maisie looked at her uncle as if he'd just been hit in the head with a mallet. "You just said!"

"I said it was a *Romance* language. That's very different. The five love languages are words of affirmation, gifts, acts of service, quality time, and physical touch."

Grant retched again at the mention of physical touch.

"Those aren't languages."

"Sure they are. Unspoken ones. Except, I suppose, the affirmation one. They are different ways people can express love, and different ways people can ask to receive it."

"What's yours?" Grant asked, finally sitting still in his seat.

"I don't know if we subscribe to those five exactly. You and I travel to the beat of a different drum." He then added, "Linda Ronstadt," to attribute the lyric.

"Mine's gifts," Grant said. It was the only one that made logical sense.

"You don't even know what you're talking about," Maisie said; she could have been directing her observation to either of them. But Grant took the bait.

"Yes, I do. I like gifts!" He lunged for his sister and they descended into a shoving match.

Patrick reached across the table to separate them. "My point is, we're about to do and see and eat and experience so many incredible things. Things that I consider *my* love languages. Guncle Love Languages. Okay? Similar to Guncle Rules. They will make you understand love, and maybe even appreciate it, too, and if at the end of all that, if we arrive in Italy and you still object to your father marrying Livia, I'll talk to him. Okay? I don't know if it will do any good, but I'll talk to him and I'll plead your case and we'll see what comes of it. Do we have a deal?"

Maisie and Grant looked at each other. They'd done enough wheeling and dealing with their uncle over the years to know when the offer was best and final. "Okay, deal," Grant said, spitting into his hand and offering it for Patrick to shake.

"That's disgusting."

Grant squealed with delight.

"Maisie?"

Maisie clutched her phone and slumped down in her chair so far that Patrick was concerned she was going to slide under the table and onto the floor.

"What are you doing?"

"Downloading SayHi."

"Hi," Patrick obeyed, though somewhat befuddled.

"No, SayHi is a language-translation app for my phone."

"Why do you need a language-translation app when you have me?" Patrick asked, and the look Maisie gave him was withering. He snatched her phone in retaliation and slipped it into his shirt pocket. "No more screens until Paris."

Maisie didn't protest; instead she opened her backpack and pulled out a book. "Of course it's a deal. All we have to do is hold our ground and you will talk to Dad." She held her book in front of her face: *Murder on the Orient Express. Perfect.* Patrick laughed.

"You're reading Agatha Christie?"

"You made me ship all my Stephen King!"

"That I did." Patrick drummed his fingers on the window. "Okay, then. We have a deal. But you'll see." That was the thing about love; even its harshest critics were not immune, love finding its way into even the darkest spaces.

"Now, Guncle Love Language number one." Patrick decided in the moment to name all of his love languages after songs, starting with one from Tori Amos. "Silent All These Years."

They rode without another word as they waited for the light at the end of this Chunnel.

SIX

They arrived in Paris by midafternoon and headed straight to the Hôtel Plaza Athénée, a luxury establishment on Avenue Montaigne in the 8th arrondissement near the Champs-Élysées, Patrick thinking about love languages the whole way. They were not just a form of expression, but rather ways to reveal yourself that others found meaningful. The key was not so much for the kids to understand their own languages (that would be the job of their future partners one day), but for Patrick to open their eyes to ways in which Greg and Livia might be a good match, and ways in which Livia might be expressing love for the two of them that they were currently missing. Guncle Love Languages. Were they as practical as his Guncle Rules? Maybe not in the short run. But his mission was clear nonetheless. He would teach these kids about love, how to love others, and how to be loved in return. Was he the best conduit for this lesson in the wake of his own breakup? He hoped the kids wouldn't ask. But the best teachers were also students, as learning was never done.

As they stepped out of their taxi, both Maisie and Grant looked up with wonder at the red awnings that hung outside the hotel's every room and at the window boxes, which were positively spilling with geraniums. Maisie closed her eyes and inhaled deeply. Patrick smiled knowingly. Paris was to be taken in with all five senses. Even the air felt different here; it sparkled with romance and possibility. His plan was already working.

"Why are we staying here?" Maisie asked. She didn't sound judgmental as much as she did curious.

"Because it's the Hôtel Plaza Athénée, that's why. It's classically French. You'd prefer a Courtyard by Marriott?"

"It looks familiar." Grant scratched his head as he waited for recognition to set in.

"Of course it's familiar, just like the Empire State Building is familiar, or Julia Roberts is familiar—it's world-famous." Their driver handed Patrick their luggage from the taxi's trunk as Patrick handed him a generous tip in return. "We probably shouldn't stay here, in all honesty, as it was bought by the sultan of Brunei. It's illegal to be gay in Brunei. Damn the Bruneians for ruining all the best hotels. Well, not *ruining* them, ruining them, look at this place, it's gorgeous. Just *morally* ruining them. They could probably take away my gay card simply for staying here."

"You have a card?" Grant asked. "Like Costco?"

"Costco? Bite your tongue."

"They could take it away? Who's *they*?" Maisie wondered, looking around as if they might be jumped by the team from *Queer Eye*.

"I mean, they wouldn't dare. The first time I came to Paris I had a brief affair with a Parisian street mime—that ought to earn me residual gay goodwill. By the way, stay away from the mimes, they're all hands." Grant opened his notebook, but Patrick snatched his pen before he could write. "That's not going in your report. You let me worry about keeping my gay card, okay? But you probably shouldn't call me GUP while we're here. They might hang me up by my thumbs."

"The *G* in GUP could mean anything," Maisie dissented. "You could be our Great-Uncle Patrick."

"Good lord, I'm not old enough to be your Great-Uncle Patrick." He took three steps toward the door, wondering why he was burdened with all the luggage. "Unless you mean great as in magnificent, formidable, preeminent. Then we can have that discussion." Patrick's face soured as he imagined them calling him MUP or FUP. "But even then, we should probably come up with something else." Patrick handed each kid a suitcase and saluted the doorman, who welcomed them inside.

"Gargantuan?" Grant asked as they entered the lobby.

"No."

"Grumpy? Grimy?" They were both having too much fun with this game. "I know. Ghastly."

"Grotesque," Grant giggled, and Maisie doubled over laughing. Patrick turned to chide them, but didn't; he was a sucker for seeing them laugh. Both kids stumbled around like little drunks trying to find their footing, their faces turning a beet red. No doubt many guests visiting Paris had staggered through their hotel lobbies a similar shade after imbibing too much wine.

The lobby of the Hôtel Plaza Athénée was bathed in ivory, and majestic pillars stood like circular guards protecting an extravagant crystal chandelier. Strapped to each pillar was an ornate vase holding opulent arrangements with irises and crocuses and tall leafy greens.

"I know!" Grant exclaimed.

"What do you know?" Patrick asked, bracing himself, thinking the kid had found the ultimate insult beginning with g.

"Why I recognize this place."

Patrick exhaled, relieved. Maybe his nephew had some taste after all.

Grant turned in a complete circle to consider the rest of the lobby. "Yup. Just as I suspected. It was in the movie *Smurfs 2*."

Patrick turned to bang his head against one of the pillars.

Grant looked up at his uncle. "Have you not seen it?"

"Do I look like I've seen *Smurfs 2*?"

Grant studied his uncle's face. "Well, that's understandable. If you haven't seen the first one, it probably wouldn't make sense."

Patrick knocked his head against the pillar a second time. An agitated red spot marked the center of his forehead. "*Smurfs 2*?! This is where Big found Carrie at the end of *Sex and the City*. Where he finally told her she was the one."

Dubious, Maisie put her hands on her hips. "There was a person named Big?"

"Yes! Well, Mr. Big. Big was his last name. He rescued Carrie after she was kidnapped by Mikhail Baryshnikov."

"Was he a pirate?" Grant asked.

Patrick took in their blank faces. How would he get them to understand love if he couldn't get them to appreciate Carrie and Big? "No, a Russian sculptor. Never mind. Just wait here, the both of you. Grotesque Uncle Patrick needs to check us in. And then we have a busy afternoon planned."

Patrick nudged their luggage off to the side and proceeded to the hotel's elaborately carved front desk. "*Smurfs 2*," he muttered, reaching for his ID.

Paris was known for many things, world-class museums, towering monuments and cathedrals from every era that were renowned the world over. The highest-class gastronomy in dimly lit restaurants and robust coffee on the sun-dappled terraces of the city's many cafés. History and architecture, not to mention fashion: Chanel, Saint Laurent, Vuitton, Dior, Hermès. The city was famous for its pastry and macarons in sumptuous colors and the mellifluous sound of street buskers with big instruments and even bigger dreams. Catacombs,

parks, bridges, romance, greenery, strolls along the River Seine—
Paris had it all, including the richest hot chocolate a kid could ever
dream of drinking. Which was where Patrick decided they should
start.

Perhaps the city's finest chocolat chaud was at the renowned Angelina's. Patrick marched the kids into the tearoom at 226 rue de
Rivoli, and after a short wait they were seated at a table for three. It
was summer, yes, but inside, the room had a warm glow that was
a welcome embrace and despite the muggy afternoon it was easy to
imagine they had just stepped in from the cold. Steam rose from
ornate tea sets, and towers of pastry welcomed guests with hearty
appetites. It was a bit touristy for Patrick's taste, the place was over-
flowing with Americans—if he didn't have an agenda he would have
chosen anyplace else—but the kids seemed unbothered and in fact
were subdued by their surroundings.

"I can't read the menu," Grant confessed after a moment of study,
and he sent it sailing across the table at Patrick.

"That's because it's in French."

"Why is it in French?"

"Because we're in France. Are you going to be like this the whole
trip?"

Grant considered his answer carefully while Maisie acquainted
herself with her newly downloaded SayHi app, looking for an option
to scan the specials.

"Forget the menu. I'm ordering for all three of us."

Maisie glared at him skeptically. "*You're* ordering?"

"That's what I said."

"Ordering what? There are a lot of things we don't like," she reminded him, but she was too distracted by her app to list them.

"I saw a McDonald's, we passed it on the way," Grant offered helpfully, never one to miss the Golden Arches, but Patrick shushed him.

"You want pomme frites?"

"No," Grant replied firmly. "But I could go for some fries."

"I told you, I'm here to teach you about love. No one is going to fall in love at McDonald's. Not in Paris, certainly."

Their server was dressed in a tie and white apron meticulously tied at his waist. His clothes were tailored and he stood with great pride, as if he were serving nobility. He twitched a thin mustache that made him look like John Waters had been animated to be in the film *Ratatouille*. "Bonjour messieurs et mademoiselle." Grant was too panic-stricken to respond, but Patrick didn't hesitate. Maisie held up her phone to capture the exchange.

"Bonjour. Nous voudrions vos chocolats chauds célèbres pour trois."

"Trés bien, monsieur. Tout de suite." The server disappeared to place their order.

"Famous hot chocolate?" Maisie asked, tapping her phone on the table three times as if her app had grossly misfired. People could be famous, she knew that. Places, too. But hot cocoa?

"Guncle Love Language number one. 'The Finer Things.' I believe it was the great philosopher Steve Winwood who said that finer things keep shining through. But don't be a snob about it, not everyone can come to Paris. I'm saying if you have good dishes, use the good dishes for a meal with someone you care about. If you have nice shoes, but you're afraid to get them dirty, wear the good shoes and complete your outfit. Finer things. Don't save them for a day that may never come, enjoy them with someone you love now. And if you're going to have simple things like a hot beverage, you might as well have the world's best."

"I thought number one was silence," Maisie challenged.

"Oh, blessed silence, that's right. Let's observe that as we wait on Love Language deux."

"Duh," Grant repeated, but, except for another inquiry as to why they spoke French in France, said nothing more and instead took in his surroundings.

Angelina's was founded by Anton Rumpelmayer as a gourmet temple to the French way of life. Among other things (like its Mont-Blanc pastry, which appealed to the keenest of palates), Angelina's was known for its hot chocolate, which was created using three carefully collected cocoas from Niger, Ghana, and Côte d'Ivoire; its recipe had been kept a closely guarded secret for more than a century.

"How did you know about this place?" Maisie asked, eventually breaking their silence.

"I'm a citizen of the world."

"No you're not. Your passport is the same as ours."

Patrick ignored her. There was no passport stamp for emotional destinations.

Their hot chocolate arrived in two ceramic pitchers, which made it seem all very French, and was presented to them alongside three delicate cups with matching saucers. Their server graciously poured, expertly not spilling a drop. The chocolate was unlike its American cousin. It was not runny, or tepid, or bland, needing marshmallows or Cool Whip or other such nonsense to make it palatable. No, this drink was rich, molten, and looked like an actual flood of melted chocolate might, mixed with a just a hint of milk. It wasn't difficult to imagine a gluttonous German kid drowning in a stream of it in Willy Wonka's whimsical factory. Their dessert came with a small bowl of whipped, unsweetened cream.

"This is hot chocolate?" Grant asked doubtfully, concerned it might be some kind of gravy or fine consommé made with something from the long list of things they abhorred.

"Yes. I'm sorry it wasn't delivered by a cloying Swiss miss in a dirndl."

Maisie held her phone up to Patrick's face. "A what?" she asked in an effort to get him to repeat it.

"What are you doing?" Patrick pushed the phone away from his face.

"SayHi," she explained.

Patrick waved his finger. "I'm not falling for that again."

Grant inhaled deeply and married an expression of relief with actual delight as Patrick spooned a dollop of cream into his own mug and gave it a gentle stir. "Maisie?" he offered, and she consented to have cream added to hers as well. Grant, however, saw no need to mar a perfectly delectable treat and he hoisted his cup with both hands. "Careful, your mug might be hot."

But to Grant, scalding his tongue was only a mild deterrent. He took a small sip to test the beverage's temperature, blew on his mug twice, then knocked back the whole thing.

"Hey hey hey," Patrick cautioned as he tasted his with a spoon. "This hot chocolate is for sipping, not gulping like a pelican."

"I wish I was a pelican," came Grant's reply. "Then I could store more of this in my throat pouch."

Patrick shuddered. "Don't say 'throat pouch' in a chocolaterie."

Maisie's phone dinged. "Chocolate shop," she explained, her translation app already working overtime. Patrick glared at his niece's phone; he did not consent to having their conversations eavesdropped on by an app, but also wondered if this could save him crucial time constantly having to explain himself. When Maisie finally deigned to sip from her cup she confessed, "This is quite . . . something," with an air of delighted surprise.

"Would you look at that. I left you flummoxed on my first try."

Maisie glanced at her phone, but there was no ding.

"Give it a rest, would you? Flummoxed is an everyday English word." Maisie raised an eyebrow; their definitions of "everyday" were quite different. Her expression, coupled with the way she held her cup, properly, gently supporting it with her second hand, made her look uncharacteristically like a Jane Austen heroine.

"Well, I like it," Grant said, placing his now empty cup on its saucer with a clang and wiping his mouth with the back of his hand.

"You like it, where did it go?"

Grant pointed straight down his gullet, so Patrick poured him what was left from the second pot, while urging the boy to show some restraint—and use a napkin.

"I'm not really a chocolate person," Maisie began. "But even I have to admit this is pretty good." She was like her father that way, she had a strange palate and preferred savory to sweet.

"*Pretty good.* Coco Chanel had one every day from this very spot, if you can believe tha—"

Grant didn't hesitate. "I can." It was clear he didn't know who Coco Chanel was, but that was of secondary importance.

The clink of a spoon, a teacup, a saucer. The room was alive with chatter and the ringing of china in a way that filled Patrick with momentary warmth.

Maisie set her cup down. "Oh, GUP. You are so wise to teach us about love."

Grant peered into a now empty pitcher, then tried to fit his entire fist inside. "I'd like another lesson just like this one." He licked the chocolate off his hand, hoping Patrick would order them a second round.

"I see what you're doing. You're trying to disarm me with flattery, to get me to give up on this quest. But let me tell you something. I eat flattery for breakfast. Flattery fuels me, okay? So you'll have to try another tactic."

"Fine," Grant said, tending to his paw like a dog.

"Food is love, don't you see? Never more so than when you treat yourself to the very best of something. Doesn't this make you open your eyes to the world around you? You don't have to become gourmands, but aren't you the least bit . . . epicurious?"

Maisie reached for her phone, but Patrick snatched it from her before she could grab it; SayHi was no match for his wordplay.

"Come on. Livia has great taste. Does she treat you to food?"

"She doesn't like it when we order pizza," Grant griped.

"She says it's not *real* pizza," Maisie added.

"She *is* Italian. I think she would know." Patrick wasn't sure how he would win this argument on Livia's behalf with two kids who preferred Domino's. "We'll get you some pizza in Italy and we can see if she knows what she's talking about."

"She never knows what she's talking about," Maisie explained. Patrick knitted his brows. It was going to take much more than a language app to bridge the gap between those two.

"Oh, come on. She's from Italy. She knows pizza and risotto and wine. You're lucky she's not from one of the European countries that boils potatoes and cabbage. Do you know what kohlrabi is? I don't think anyone does."

"It's not just food. She thinks you're a clown."

Patrick tried not to give them the satisfaction of a reaction. "She said that? Clown?"

Maisie made an indecipherable face.

Grant pointed to his uncle and said, "Who's this clown?" sounding like a little Robert De Niro. He then doubled over laughing, recalling his favorite insult.

"Your sister is just trying to start something. It could have been a difference in language. She said clown when she meant comedian." It was true Livia traded in a currency that was very different from his. She was not seduced by his type of stardom when she herself was nobility, and her wealth seemed to dwarf his. But that didn't mean she didn't respect him. Did it? He nudged his niece as he tried to shake the thought from his mind. "Come on, drink up. It's good for you."

Maisie wasn't convinced. "*This* is good for us?"

"Yes, it is."

Even Grant voiced his skepticism. "*Chocolate* is good for you?"

Patrick nodded. "The New England School of Medicine did a study," he lied. Chocolate like this was good for the soul, and the finer things good for the heart.

SEVEN

The Sacré-Coeur Basilica was located at the summit of the butte Montmartre, the city's highest natural point, and boasted the best views of Paris; it was the second most popular tourist attraction in France after the Eiffel Tower. As darkness fell, Patrick marched the kids up the two hundred and thirty-seven steps built to reach the entrance to the massive stone cathedral.

"Pick up your feet!" he cheerily instructed like a spirited tour guide waving a little flag to lead his group, but then after ten more steps griped, "Jiminy Christmas, you need to be a mountain goat to access this place."

"I brought the wrong shoes," Grant moaned.

"What's the matter with your shoes?" Patrick pressed, glancing down at his nephew's feet. Of the three of them, Grant was most consistently dressed for activity.

Despite being appropriately outfitted, both children were losing steam and making a meal of trudging up each step. "They're too shoes-y."

Patrick made a mental note to get his nephew shoes that were *less* shoes-y and therefore more to the kid's liking, or were at the very least more comfortable for traipsing across France. His wallet was open for any purchase that reduced whining.

"What's the deal with this place?" Maisie asked.

"You mean why are we climbing all the way up here?"

She nodded.

"For the best view in all of Paris!"

They were already tired, as Patrick had footslogged them through le Louvre that afternoon, which SayHi had translated merely as *the* Louvre, much to Maisie's consternation. Grant made the most of their visit by counting breasts he saw in the art, torn whether to count them individually or as pairs. Patrick chose not to get involved as they breezed by some old favorites of his—the Venus de Milo, Jean-Honoré Fragonard's painting *The Bolt*, Eugène Delacroix's *Liberty Leading the People*—on their way to the Salle des États, which housed works of the Venetian masters, artists like Titian, Tintoretto, and Veronese. Although visitors mostly had eyes for one: Leonardo da Vinci.

"What's everyone looking at?" Grant had asked, surprised by the crowd's sudden swelling.

Patrick pointed straight ahead and replied, "That's the *Mona Lisa.*"

"*That's* the *Mona Lisa?*" Maisie blurted, sounding both impressed and disappointed. And indeed, housed behind bulletproof glass and surrounded by so many people, she looked surprisingly dim.

Grant tilted his head and put his hand on his chin. "The world's most famous painting?"

"That's right."

Maisie put her hands on her hips. "She's supposed to be some mysterious beauty, right?"

"I don't get it," Grant dismissed, his enthusiasm clearly dampened.

"It's just her face." Draped in fabric as she was, she didn't even add to his running tally.

Patrick glanced down at his nephew. "Are you kidding? A person's face says a lot about their looks."

"Why is *she* so special?" Grant asked as they got in the queue to move closer. "Like, what's the appeal?"

Patrick leaned in for a closer look. "No one really knows."

"Oh, so she's like you, then. Famous, but no one knows why."

Museums were one thing, but even the Louvre couldn't contain Paris itself; Patrick knew from experience that the way you fall in love with a place was to see it for the first time. *Really* see it. Both its beauty and its flaws. All of it. And there was no better vantage point to see Paris than Sacré-Coeur, except perhaps atop the Eiffel Tower. Even if being trapped in a wrought-iron tower with the worst tourists in France didn't sound like an absolute nightmare to Patrick, he knew part of the sheer joy of Paris was seeing the tower as part of the city's skyline, which you couldn't very well do if you were deep inside of it.

A small cable car filled with people glided past as they continued their ascent. The car looked like a tiny spaceship and the people inside waved at them; a bit of the future skyrocketing past the hardships of the present. Grant's imagination was immediately captured. "What's that?"

"The funicular."

Maisie stopped in her tracks. "Do you ever get tired of just making up words?"

Patrick ascended the step behind her and gave his niece a friendly nudge. "Never."

With another fifty or so steps they reached the butte's summit and they faced the Basilica with their arms on their hips to catch their collective breath. Patrick was surprised anew each time he found himself winded. Growing older, as they say, was not for the faint of heart. Fortunately the kids were distracted by the monument before them, spectacularly lit up at night, and not the least bit concerned with their uncle or his diminishing stamina. Which is exactly as it should be. Patrick looked at the immense structure in front of them and it gleamed white against the darkening sky. He'd read that it was built with the stone of Château-Landon, the same rock used to construct the Arc de Triomphe. When hit with rainwater, the stone's natural coating secreted a white substance that hardened in the sun. In essence, the Basilica had a chemical peel every time it rained, keeping it eternally young. If it was possible to be jealous of a stone, Patrick in this moment was. Then, after he'd wiped his brow, he slowly spun Maisie and Grant around so that they faced all of Paris at dusk; it was, after all, his reason for bringing them here. Maisie gasped at the shimmering sea of lights that stretched out endlessly before them.

"Guncle Love Language number three: 'Don't need no credit card to ride this train.'" Patrick led them to a spot on the crowded steps to sit.

"This isn't a train, it's a staircase," Maisie complained.

"Everything is so literal with you. I just mean that there's nothing money can buy that beats life's free joys with the people you care about. So, let's sit here for a bit and take it all in."

"The museum wasn't free," Maisie said, determined to fight him on everything.

"It was for you, as you're under eighteen. And it would have been for me if I lived in the European Union, which perhaps I should."

"Is this free for you?" Grant asked, and Patrick motioned for him to sit to quiet him. He then felt his own racing heart; all it had cost him was ten years off his life. He then sat between them on the steps.

Patrick was reminded of his early days in Hollywood, going up to the top of Mulholland Drive to get lost in the city's lights. So many dreams he had, so many plans he'd made. He would take his late partner, Joe, and Sara, too, when she was in town, and they would park his car on a precarious dirt outcropping and look across a sea of diamonds, trying not to think about how steep the drop was below, or how many dreams the city had broken. It was a view he hoped to have for himself one day, and he did for a short time; when his sitcom *The People Upstairs* had been renewed for a second season and he understood the show would be a success, he bought a little house in Laurel Canyon for him and Joe.

"Do you ever get tired of this view?" Sara asked the first time she flew out to visit. They stood on the shallow deck that ran the length of the house and gave them the best canyon views.

Patrick bit the inside of his cheek to keep himself from bursting into a smile. He was proud of the life he'd built for himself. "Sometimes at night we sit out here and listen to the music that other people play as it echoes through the canyon. You just feel like a member of the Byrds or the Doors."

"Mama Cass," Sara said, playing along.

"Or any of Crosby or Stills or Nash or Young." Patrick was not a religious person, but from a vantage point such as this he felt very small, and for the first time understood the idea that there was something much bigger than him. He then turned and faced the house, admiring his real favorite view—Joe in the kitchen. He was putting the finishing touches on a charcuterie board.

"Are you still mad?" Sara asked Patrick. Their friendship of late had been fraught. It was Greg who suggested she visit to see if it wouldn't help their relationship mend.

Patrick hadn't decided. He took her left hand to look one more time at the ring.

"Your brother's on partnership track, thank you very much." She held the stone up to the porch light, then screamed when a large insect buzzed by.

"No, I'm not mad," Patrick came clean. He had just needed some distance to see things clearly.

"It's the real deal, Patrick, I promise." There was no denying that she was happy. "For ever and ever and ever. Until death do us part."

"Okay," Patrick said, urging her to calm down. "You're on the verge of overselling it."

"Can you blame me for being excited? We're going to be *sisters*, Patrick."

"You and Greg?" he asked, not following.

Sara shoved him against the railing, and just as he started to lose his balance, she grabbed him by the collar and kissed his cheek. "No, silly. You and me."

It was the first moment it dawned on him that they would be family. And would have new entanglements that came with it.

◇◇◇◇◇◇◇

"What do you think?" Patrick asked, encouraging the kids to share their reactions. The Eiffel Tower flashed a beam that cut through the night, circling like a warning from a lighthouse. Both kids were transfixed.

"It's better than television," Grant conceded, which was, from him, high praise.

"That's because television is best for appearing on, not for looking at."

But Grant seemed less interested in what lay in front of him than in what towered behind them. He looked over his shoulder and pointed up at the Basilica. "Is that a church?"

"It is," Patrick said. Notre Dame was Paris's most notable cathedral, but it was recovering still from a devastating fire, and the resulting construction and scaffolding made it, from certain vantage points, less awe-inspiring than it once was.

"It's very white. Even in the dark." Grant made circles with his fists and raised them to his eyes like binoculars. "Just like your teeth."

"That's because for thirty minutes a day, nuns come out and cover the whole building in Crest Whitestrips."

"They do not. The whole thing? That would be too expensive."

"Congregants give vouchers and coupons."

The kid bent his head back so that he was looking at the church upside down. "Can we go inside?"

"We can try. It might be closed to the public for the night." At least that much was true.

"What's in there?"

Patrick wasn't really certain. "Usual church things, I imagine. Stained glass windows. Pews. Candles. A crypt. An organ. A belfry."

"For bats?" Grant's eyes grew wide.

Patrick blinked. He'd been expecting pushback on "crypt." "For bells. I read that this one houses the biggest bell in all of France." Patrick didn't know if that factoid was all that impressive or not; perhaps France was overall a small-belled country. "But, yes, I imagine also a shit ton of bats."

"Livia goes to church," Maisie said, breaking an uncharacteristic silence. "She wanted us to go with her, and Dad said if we went once we didn't have to go again."

"So what did you do?"

Maisie looked at him as if to say, *We had no other choice.* "We went once. It was the only way to shut her up." It was the same humoring tactic they were taking with him.

Patrick was not one to go to bat for organized religion, but he also wanted to clear the kids' own belfries of negative thoughts. "Lots of people go to church."

"Not in Connecticut," Maisie reminded him. "At least not a lot that we know."

An egg-bald man glossy with sweat stopped right next to them, bent over, and placed his hands on his knees. He was breathing heavily as he charted a path through the crowd.

"Did you think about what you're going to say to Dad?" Maisie asked.

"About what?"

"About Livia! Because I have some ideas."

"Monsieur," Patrick called out, ignoring his niece. He gestured to their spot on the steps and he and the kids vacated their seats so the man could sit down.

"Look," Maisie continued, once they found an open spot to stand away from the crowd. "We can help you with this or not help you."

"I choose not help me."

"GUP!"

"You're not going to do to me what you did to Livia, humor me and then get your way. I'm on to you! And I'm trying to teach you something important."

Maisie gave him her best teenage *We'll see* look, but Grant acquiesced; he pointed at the cathedral as they wandered in that general direction. "What else?"

"About Sacré-Coeur?" Patrick didn't know how to top a crypt and a belfry of bats. He pulled out his phone and did a quick Google search. "There has been a continuous prayer happening inside the

chapel since the year 1885." He could see Grant working out the par-
ticulars of how such a thing might work, and knew his nephew well
enough to know his vision included one-hundred-and-fifty-year-old
monks, little more than skin and bones drowning in now-oversized
vestments. "People take turns," Patrick explained before that image
could take hold. "In shifts, day and night."

"Oh," Grant said, disappointed.

"Can we take a turn?" Maisie asked.

"I thought you didn't like church."

"I don't like Livia, that's different. Besides, she's not here."

"Do you pray?" It was well established the kids weren't regular
churchgoers, but that didn't mean they entirely dismissed religion.

Maisie chewed on her lip, like she was deciding whether or not to
be honest. "Sometimes I talk to Mom."

"I do, too," Grant quickly confirmed, chewing on his lip, too.

"Stop copying me!" Maisie shoved her brother into her uncle, then
scuffed her feet on the pavement. "I'm not really sure that's praying."

Patrick helped a dazed Grant find his footing, before extending an
arm around her shoulder. "I'm not really sure that it isn't." He wasn't
the expert on such things, but Patrick thought the kids talking to their
late mother, who was once very real, was far more practical and ther-
apeutic than talking to a god that he felt adamantly was not. "But I
don't think we should risk breaking a chain that has been happening
for a century and a half just to satisfy our impudent interest as day-
trippers." He had to imagine the system was fail-safe: perhaps that the
church enlisted multiple people to pray at once just in case a nonbe-
liever infiltrated the ranks or a well-intentioned worshipper's mind
drifted toward inappropriate thoughts. It only made sense, he thought,
like backing up a computer.

"Do *you* talk to Mom?"

Patrick bowed his head, before bending down to retie his shoelace and buy himself time to think. He used to talk to Sara, especially that first summer after she died, in part to ask for strength with the kids. But it had been a long time since it had even occurred to him to do so. But maybe that was a mistake. He could have found comfort in talking to her after his breakup with Emory, or now in helping her kids anew.

"GUP?" Maisie prompted, when he had been quiet too long.

"I replay conversations we had. Especially the funny ones. But that's not quite the same thing. She called you two carnies once, and that made me laugh."

"What's a carny?" Grant asked.

"Oh, it doesn't matter. I do think about your mom a lot, though. Especially at times like this."

Maisie looked up at him earnestly. "How does that make you feel?"

How did it make him feel? More alone? Less alone? In the moment he wasn't quite sure. "Feelings for adults are like treasures. And by that I mean we should bury them." He put his arms around both kids so that it was clear he was kidding. *Sort of.* "Don't you think if your mom was watching over us, her view would look something like this?"

Maisie was still for a long time before wriggling her way out from underneath Patrick's arm. "She's getting fuzzier and fuzzier. Mom. The further and further we get from her she seems less sharp." Maisie's eyes grew wet.

Patrick remembered telling them once that one day they would miss the acute pain of grief, the grief that meant their mother was still close. He had a hard time acknowledging that time was here, or understanding how five years had already passed. He watched as the city's lights danced a bit of magic, hoping Paris itself might offer him the answer. "See how the lights twinkle?" Patrick pointed at the horizon. He held on tight to Grant, who he imagined felt even further from Sara; Maisie, after all, had nine years with her mother, while her brother only had six. "They're not actually flickering, not really. The lights themselves are static. It's all the things we cannot see between us and them that make them shimmer. Atmospheric densities, dust, moisture, humidity, that sort of thing. I'm not really the expert. But all the invisible things. Like your mom, she's one of them now, too. When she starts to feel far away, I like to imagine she's not as far away as we might think. She's right here between us and the lights."

For a moment they both seemed satisfied with his explanation. But then Maisie's mouth wilted back into a frown. "That's why we don't like Livia. If she comes in here trying to replace Mom, she's going to erase the rest of her, too."

Patrick wondered if part of him didn't feel the same way. That Livia had swept into their lives on a chaotic wind bent on clearing their cobwebs to make way for something new, not understanding that they found comfort in some of their gloom. At the very least she aimed to distract them from a past they were not ready to move on from. Patrick linked his arm with Maisie's. "She can't do that."

Maisie turned to Patrick, newly seeing her uncle as an ally in this fight. "Because you won't allow it?"

"No, I mean she *can't* do that. It's not moral outrage, she simply doesn't have that power. You have a mother, and that's the simple truth of it. No one can take her away."

"KA-POW!" Grant said, raising a fist, one of those inexplicable things boys did.

It was natural that Livia would want to make space for herself in this family, but that didn't have to mean it was nefarious or that it had the consequences they feared. "You know, most things we think of as good we find out eventually are bad. Ice cream. Cigarettes. Plastic straws, as it turns out, can go right up a turtle's nose. But every once in a while, something that seems bad turns out to be good."

"Like Livia?" Maisie stuck her index finger in her mouth, pretending to make herself vomit.

Patrick laughed. "Jeez, tough crowd." He turned to Grant. "What about you, Grantelope? Think you could keep an open mind?"

Grant stomped his foot. "I asked you not to call me that, remember?"

Patrick honestly didn't remember; kids grew fast and their preferences for things changed on a dime. "No, I don't, I'm sorry."

"I asked you like six times! I'm too old to be a Grantelope." He anxiously started picking at the mole on his neck.

"Well, I'm sorry! I was diagnosed with auditory recency bias."

Grant scrunched his face. "What's that?"

"It means I only ever remember the last thing you say."

"That's not real."

"*That's not real*," Patrick mimicked, proving he had at least heard that. "Yes it is, it's very much real."

"Don't listen to him," Maisie instructed.

"What happened to you two?" Patrick protested. "You used to think I was fun."

Maisie gave him a pitying look. "We grew up."

"Then grow back down! I'm not ready for you to be so adult."

"Can we get more hot chocolate?" Grant asked perfectly on cue, and then immediately piggybacked his question with another. "Can we ride the funic— Whatever that thing is called?"

"The funicular? Sure, we can ride the funicular."

"What about the hot chocolate?" Grant pressured.

Patrick pointed to his ear. "What about the hot chocolate?"

"Can we have some!" Grant implored, exasperated. It was getting late and he was exhausted from a full day in the wrong shoes and was quickly losing his patience.

"Oh, right. See? Auditory recency bias." Patrick wiggled his ear like

Carol Burnett, wondering if he could use this new condition to weasel out of the usual onslaught of questions. If so, he should have thought of it years ago. "Yes, we can get hot chocolate." There was even a slight chill in the evening air that made a hot drink sound appealing. *The finer things*. He smiled to himself. For the first time he thought his plan might be working.

"Oh no," Grant said, panic in his voice. He quickly compressed his neck with one hand.

"What?"

Grant held his other hand out, showing Patrick and Maisie what looked like a chocolate chip. "This mole came clean off."

EIGHT

Julie Andrews was still in her twenties when she was cast in *The Sound of Music*, not much older than Patrick and Sara were when they auditioned for a summer stock production of the Rodgers and Hammerstein musical in Louisville. Sara was a born Maria, warm, free-spirited, with an easy conspiratorial wink and a soprano range well-suited for the part. Patrick fashioned himself as Captain von Trapp, and no doubt at that age he would have looked dashing in a military uniform, even if his face was still a tad boyish. They must have watched the movie a half-dozen times in Patrick's dorm room and marveled at how much they both ached for Christopher Plummer. Each evening at dusk leading up to their audition, Patrick twirled Sara around a gazebo that anchored a nearby park as they made no shortage of plans for the summer. Alas, neither booked the part they were after; Patrick was offered the role of Max Detweiler, the children's rakish uncle (which, looking back on it, was a pretty unsubtle precursor for his life as both an uncle and second banana), and Sara was cast as a nun. Patrick quickly made peace with the decision. He quite liked Max—the ultimate bachelor, cheeky and always well-kept—and also felt a kinship with him and his outlook on living. "I like rich people," Max would confess. "I like the way they live, I like the way I live when I'm with them." Patrick didn't really know any rich people then, but he suspected he would quite like their lifestyle, too. Sara, however, was not at all happy with her role as a background player. If she couldn't be the rebellious Sister that broke out of the abbey to bed a navy captain, she didn't much see the point. She convinced Patrick they should drop out before rehearsals even began. Louisville was no Salzburg and Kentucky no Austria; she felt there were better ways to spend a perfectly good summer. Patrick agreed—he always agreed—and they spent the summer at the beach instead, like Sandy and Danny from *Grease*.

Patrick wasn't quite sure when Austria came to mind as the next destination to take the kids, but knew he had all this talk of Greg marrying the Baroness to thank. He had shown them the 1965 Robert Wise film on several occasions after their mother had passed, explaining it was a favorite of hers, and while they enjoyed it more than he perhaps expected them to, he wasn't sure they enjoyed it at the time quite as much as he *needed* them to on their mother's behalf. But taking them to Salzburg on the official *Sound of Music* tour—something he and Sara promised they would one day do, but of course never did? This would be another lesson in love—doing something simply because you knew it would make someone you care about happy.

Patrick booked the overnight train to Salzburg, which was perhaps slightly less poetic than a midnight train to Georgia (singing nuns were fine and all, but they were no match for the Pips). It was an eight-hour journey, much of which he hoped to sleep through. Not that he needed a break from the kids per se (although he had come to appreciate a quiet hour or two to himself each night after they fell asleep), but rather the opportunity to reflect on their journey so far and plan a recalibration if needed. Night travel didn't allow for much of a view; in fact in his exhaustion he forgot if this was the train that went through Zurich or Stuttgart and the absolute darkness transported him back to Grant's freak-out in the Chunnel. With Italy drawing closer with each stop and Sara very much on his mind, Patrick was nearing his own breakdown.

With Maisie curled up on the seats across from him and Grant passed out by his side, two stitches and a fresh bandage on his neck where his mole used to be, Patrick wondered what *would* Sara think of him once again having custody of her kids? Was this what she imagined when she orchestrated their first summer together all those years ago? Certainly, she would approve of their next destination, but would she really be comfortable knowing her children were having a grand adventure with no one more responsible in charge? Patrick had regularly checked in with Greg via a series of texts and the kids had Face-Timed with him to both boast and gripe about the itinerary. But Greg was also busy readying himself for his own European travels, so Patrick didn't bore him with every detail of their trip. If anyone, it was really Sara he wanted to update, and the question he was left with was this: Can grief and gratitude coexist? Could he miss the kids' mother and also be grateful for his time with Maisie and Grant? Or did the gratitude just make him miss Sara more and wish she was the one on this train with him instead of her sleeping kids? And in helping them these past few years with their grief, had he once again neglected his own?

Patrick glanced out the window into the darkness, and for a brief second he thought he saw Sara's reflection sitting with Maisie; it was nothing but a cruel optical illusion, the woman across the aisle from them reading her book, her red hair spilling over her face. He closed his eyes to shake the sight of it, and eventually fell asleep.

They checked into their hotel bright and early to catch some much-needed rest; Patrick was both disappointed and relieved to find the windows in their room were covered with linen shades and not old drapes in desperate need of replacing.

"I guess I won't be making you any playclothes," he bemoaned. Maisie replied with a sour face. *Stop being such a dork.*

"I love making jokes about *The Sound of Music*," Patrick confessed.

"Why?" Grant asked.

"I can't help it. It's my idle vice. Get it? 'Edelweiss'? Idle vi—"

Both of them stared at him blankly.

"You kids are no fun." Not that Patrick knew how to sew, but he'd witnessed enough designers on *Project Runway* fake their way through a challenge with little more than spit, pins, and a glue gun to be tempted. If nothing else, it would have made for a great photo, the three of them in lederhosen that looked tragically homemade. *Content!* Something Cassie was always encouraging him to make more of for his social media. He slowly lowered the shades until the room fell dark. "Come on. Let's get some sleep."

Patrick had reserved three tickets for the two o'clock tour, and when they arrived at their point of departure he was appalled to find their bus shrink-wrapped in a life-sized image of Julie Andrews leading the von Trapp children through the Alps. Yes, he was teaching the kids an act of love and to proudly embrace their passions, but as usual he had hoped to do it in style; the coach didn't even have tinted windows. On top of everything, they were surrounded by dyed-in-the-wool fans from all over the world dressed like their favorite characters, Indian schoolchildren in the aforementioned playclothes, three goatherds who talked loudly about how they had traveled from Brazil, and two Japanese women dressed as nuns guiltily holding carburetors from Nazi vehicles they had just stripped.

"Why is everyone dressed like that?" Maisie asked.

He wished he had a snarky comment at the ready. Indeed he

agreed many of them looked absurd; instead, only the truth sprang to mind. "They're having fun." And he hoped, despite their ordinary street clothes and general horror at the spectacle, they would eventually, too. "Your mother would get such a kick out of this," he decided. "In fact, if she were here, she would have demanded we call her fräulein." And with that he urged the kids to board the bus before some passerby could see him.

"What Guncle Love Language is this?" Grant asked as they pressed their way toward the back of the bus. Patrick was disappointed by the lack of tiered seating; what he wouldn't give for the extra legroom of first class.

"Don't say anything about goatherds," Maisie warned.

"I'm not going to say anything about *goatherds*," Patrick assured her, disquieted by the very thought. Although, he was making all of this up on the fly, and *goatherd* was the kind of irresistible word he could make a meal of. Plus, he and Sara had many a drunken night in college yodeling along to the movie's most divisive song. He even felt wistful thinking of a particular lyric: *Soon the duet will become a trio, lay ee odl lay ee odl-oo.* His duet was down one member, and yet here they were now three. "Guncle Love Language number four: 'Simply remember your favorite things.'"

"Presents!" Grant exclaimed as he pumped his fist.

"Presents isn't a Guncle Love Language. We have got to move on from that."

"Yuh-huh," Grant protested. "'Brown paper packages tied up with strings.' Sounds like presents to me."

Patrick pinched the bridge of his nose. "Think of your *loved one's* favorite things. And do those."

"Isn't that just acts of service?" Maisie asked. "One of the ones you said was bullshit?"

"Bullshit!" Grant echoed, pointing a finger in the air.

"Stop it. There's no swearing on the *Sound of Music* tour." Patrick grimaced apologetically at two older women dressed to sing in the Salzburg Festival who were grumbling in Polish. "Now quit your pussyfooting and take a seat." He ushered both kids into a row, while he settled himself across the aisle. "But yes, you do have a point. I guess they weren't *all* . . ." He made a gesture alluding back to do-re-mi-fa-so-la-bull-shit.

Their tour began at the Nonnberg Abbey, which is where the real Maria Auguste Kutschera lived as a novice before she was sent to be a governess for the family von Trapp. The nunnery was founded sometime around 715 CE and had operated continuously since, making it the oldest nunnery in the German-speaking region. The grounds were flanked by fortress walls wherever they were not protected by steep slopes. There are no interior shots of the abbey in the film, only of its grounds and cemetery, where the tour group now gathered to take photos.

"Where are we again?" Grant asked as he spun around to take in their surroundings.

"In the eastern foothills of the Festungsberg," Patrick replied, glad at least he was paying attention to their tour guide.

Grant scoffed. "Like that's a real place." He stared up at the fortress walls.

"This is the nunnery."

"Again," Grant said, and then made a gesture like it was all going over his head.

"It's where Maria spent her time before she left to be with the von Trapps."

"Oh," Maisie said. "So the boring parts of the film."

"Why is that the boring part? Is the Mother Abbess boring? Is

Peggy Wood boring? She received an Academy Award nomination, for heaven's sake." (Patrick liked to think it was specifically for her inspired delivery of the line "What is it you *can't* face?" which, with her given accent, sounded perhaps more vulgar than intended.)

"Because!" Grant proclaimed. "It's the part without any kids." When put that way, Patrick had to concede he had a point.

"But also the climax! They hid from Nazis right here in this very cemetery."

Grant looked at the tombstones with some skepticism. On the whole, it did not look like a big-enough place to hide. "So, we're doing this for Mom?" he asked as they walked through the neatly trimmed hedges of the rose garden.

"That's right. She always wanted to take this tour, and now we're here taking it for her because we love her. And in that sense she's here with us."

Grant found that explanation acceptable. "Are we bringing her to Dad's wedding, too?" he asked, quite certain she would be less welcome there.

"We bring her everywhere," Maisie said—helpfully, Patrick thought. "But don't worry. There isn't going to be a wedding." So much for her being of assistance.

◇◇◇◇◇◇◇

The bus traveled on to the stately Leopoldskron Palace, the rococo building that stood in for the von Trapp family home and which currently operated as a hotel. The famed gazebo where Rolf and Liesl sang "Sixteen Going on Seventeen" used to stand on the palace's grounds, but was moved to the park at Schloss Hellbrunn to accommodate more tourists (and would be a later stop on the tour). The palace's interior Venetian Salon, with its intricate gold wall panels and smoky mirrors, was replicated for the film and served as a backdrop for several important scenes, including the big party that concluded the first half of the film (back when cinemas screened films with an intermission), and the puppet theater complete with marionettes.

"This is where the children were introduced to the Baroness," Patrick explained as they walked along the lake to get a better view.

"It's also where they drove her away." Maisie had her arms firmly crossed.

"You've got to give people a chance. Sometimes they surprise you."

"Not often," Maisie replied with a weary tone like she had everyone's number.

"*I* surprised you, didn't I?"

Maisie looked at her uncle earnestly. "I think you surprised yourself."

◇◇◇◇◇◇◇◇

The tour also included stops at the Mondsee Abbey and several other locations, before their bus rolled to its final destination, the Mirabell Gardens, where Maria taught the children to sing by introducing them to the basic notes—the architecture behind music—before they were replaced by words. Actually she taught them on a nearby mountaintop, but continued the lesson through Salzburg, first on bicycle, then by horse and buggy, and finally ending at the gardens, where they marched around the famed Pegasus Fountain before ascending the Angel Staircase. The resulting earworm—"Do-Re-Mi"—was a showstopping moment in the film and Patrick had images of himself leading Maisie and Grant in song throughout the city as an equally showstopping end to their day. But instead of feeling moved to sing, twenty minutes into their stroll around the gardens, the children seemed ready to lie down and nap.

"You know, sooner or later I'm going to show you something that you do find impressive," he said.

Maisie looked at an imaginary watch. They had a deal that expired in Italy. *Tick tock.*

Patrick felt a presence hovering peripherally and he cautiously turned to see a college-aged kid clad in a Wonder Bread T-shirt with sunglasses too big for his face. A few steps behind him was a young woman about the same age in a similarly ill-fitting purple shirt with a Smucker's logo and hair that was begging to be washed.

"Sorry to bother you," the kid began with a hitch in his voice. "We wanted to talk to you when you got off the coach, but you looked unapproachable."

"And yet here you are," Patrick groused.

Undaunted, Smucker's stepped forward. "Are you Patrick O'Hara?" she asked.

Oh god, Patrick thought. He should have known this is where he'd be recognized. "No, I'm sorry I'm not."

"Yes he is," Maisie said, enjoying Patrick's discomfort as he tried to focus on something intangible in the near distance.

"Wow," Wonder Bread exclaimed. "We never thought we'd see someone famous on this tour."

"Stars, they're just like us," Patrick muttered. And then, no longer able to contain himself, he asked, "What are you wearing?"

"Oh! We're jam and bread," the woman said proudly.

"You know, from the song."

"I'm familiar," Patrick confessed. And then he added, "Clever" with a tone somewhere between snark and genuine admiration. "Were you on our bus this whole time?"

"We were on the morning tour, but when it ended we just couldn't bring ourselves to, you know, leave." The young man said it while spinning a full three hundred and sixty degrees with the kind of genuine wonder that was on brand with his shirt—the very wonder Patrick had hoped to see on the faces of Maisie and Grant.

"He's Kevin and I'm Mel," the man's friend interrupted. "We're in the theater program at Tisch. Our friend Brian was supposed to come with us, but then he was cast in three different plays at the Oregon Shakespeare Festival and had to back out." Mel unzipped her backpack and pulled out a third T-shirt with a Lipton tea logo printed across the chest. *Tea, a drink with jam and bread.*

Patrick had never thought highly of Tisch, finding their graduates a tad pretentious, but held his tongue, since he didn't know where this was going. "Are you in a throuple?"

Mel laughed. "With Kevin and Brian? Oh, god no. Why do you ask?"

Patrick pushed his sunglasses up his nose. "No reason. It's just I knew a throuple once."

"No, I'm straight, and they're my gay BFFs." It dawned on Patrick that Kevin and Mel looked like a young Patrick and Sara.

"I know you're with your kids," Mel continued apologetically.

"We're not his kids," Grant said, and Patrick's head turned. It used to be him who made such denials.

"They're my wards," Patrick corrected, lest these Tisch students fear he had kidnapped them.

"Oh," Kevin brightened. "Like Auntie Mame!"

Patrick softened. Exactly like that. Kevin and Mel were growing on him.

"We were wondering if you would take a photo."

"Of you?" Patrick joked. Because of course they wanted a photo with him. He reached out his hand and snatched the Lipton tee. "What size is Kevin?"

"I'm Kevin," Kevin corrected. "You mean Brian."

Same difference. "What size is *Brian*?" Patrick playfully glanced at the label while sensing their growing excitement. Large, a perfect fit. Without being asked he slipped the T-shirt over his own and ushered them to stand by his side. "Maisie?" He gestured for Kevin to hand his phone over to his niece.

Maisie stepped up onto a concrete bench to take the photo.

"Higher," Patrick and Kevin said together. Patrick did a double take.

"I'm standing on a bench!"

"So?"

"So I've been taking photos of you since I was nine. I know to hold the camera higher."

It was true, she had made real progress since they first met. But Patrick was now five years older, and he didn't see the harm in elevating the camera even more. He turned to Kevin and Mel. "Excuse us, we're just having a family spat."

"Maybe we should get you a drone . . ." Maisie suggested.

"Ignore her. She's like a whiskey sour without the whiskey, if you know what I mean."

". . . Or contact the ISS. They can take your picture from space."

Grant produced his little notebook and tugged on Mel's purple tee. "Do you know the chief export of Australia? I'm writing a report for my teacher."

Mel narrowed her eyes, confused. "Do you mean Austria?"

Grant turned to his uncle. "Where are we again?"

"Just tell him kangaroos and let's do this." Patrick stood between Kevin and Mel and extended his arms around them. He pulled them in tight and give his best smirk; Patrick was loathe to be anyone's understudy, but knowing Kevin—BRIAN!—knowing *Brian* would lose his mind when he received the photo in Oregon, ready to go on in *The Taming of the Shrew*, made this worth making an exception.

Maisie snapped the picture and handed the college kids back

their phone. They looked at the photo and Mel in particular seemed quite pleased. "We'll tag you," she said.

"Great. You can post it on the dark web."

"He means Facebook," Maisie clarified.

"Now I need you to do something for me in return," Patrick said to Kevin and Mel as Kevin tucked away his phone.

"Anything," the two replied together, then glanced at each other, unsure of what they were getting themselves into.

"I need you to be Liesl and Friedrich to Maisie's Marta and Grant's what's-his-name so that we can march around the Pegasus Fountain together." Maisie started to turn away—she could see where this was going—but Patrick grabbed her by the scruff like a kitten.

"Kurt!" Mel laughed.

"Yes, Kurt. That's the one I left out. God bless Kurt," Patrick said, imitating Maria from the movie when she finally remembered the younger von Trapp boy's name in her prayers. Maisie continued to squirm. "Where do you think you're going?"

"Connecticut," she replied.

But Patrick held firmly on to her shoulders and quickly started marching the four of them around the Pegasus Fountain with others from their tour falling in line until they were all do-re-mi-fa-so-and-so-ing deep into song. Crowds gathered like they couldn't believe their eyes, but honestly, Patrick wondered, what else did they expect to see at Mirabell Gardens? Even the two Polish women exhibited a crack in their unpleasant demeanors for the first time all day and joined in the singing with surprising gusto. The horde began snapping photos and Patrick grimaced, thinking this might end up on TMZ, even though they were well outside the thirty-mile studio zone the website was named for. But he didn't ultimately care. This was, after all, an act of service.

Just as Maria lifted the children's spirits through song, the absolute ridiculousness of their marching charmed Maisie and Grant until they, too, were singing through preposterous grins. Patrick hopped off the fountain's edge and ran them through the Dwarf Garden, arms in the air, to the Angel Staircase, where they and others approximated the song's climactic choreography, jumping up one step, then bouncing back two. There must have been thirty von Trapp children now following Patrick's lead; they were like little gremlins who'd been pushed into the fountain and multiplied—Patrick could hardly keep count. When he finally reached the top step he plucked Mel from the crowd of "children" and enlisted her in hitting the song's signature high note. *Ti (La, So, Fa, Mi, Re) Ti DOOOOO!* Mel jumped the octave like Julie Andrews without so much as blinking and held the note for so long Patrick was forced to reevaluate his opinion of Tisch. The crowd that had gathered burst into enthusiastic applause and whistled their appreciation. Patrick beamed and took a bow, singling out Jam and Bread for their contributions before looking up to the heavens above. *Acts of service*, he thought as he peeled off his Lipton tee. Not such bullshit after all.

Sara, that was for you.

NINE

People often said Paris was the City of Love, and while it was a fine city for lovers Patrick firmly believed such a title belonged to Venice. He was feeling good about their trip, confident his lessons were taking root and that both Maisie and Grant had a growing appreciation for love. But if he had yet to truly astound his niblings, Venice was certainly the city to capture their sense of wonder. It was a city for romantic love, platonic love, famous love, anonymous love, sacred love, secular love, familial love—Venice ticked all the boxes. It was even a city for *lust*—it had been home to Casanova, for heaven's sake—but they needn't dwell on that. What more could anyone want? And since they were slightly ahead of schedule and Venice was not far from Lake Como, their ultimate destination, it made perfect sense as the final stop on Patrick's instructional tour. If he couldn't get the kids to understand love after visiting Venice, he had failed in spectacular fashion.

The train ride from Salzburg was roughly six hours and this time they made the journey by day; arriving in Venice was a breathtaking experience and Patrick didn't want to sneak the kids in under the cover of night. The train took them due south through Austria's lush and green farmland before crossing the mountainous border into Italy near Slovenia. They had a private car this time, seats still facing one another, but with a large picture window of their own to look out. All the rooms were on one side of the train with a sliding door to a narrow corridor on the other. The doors were glass and the corridors also had large picture windows, so they had decent views of the landscape on all sides. Maisie had her nose in a new book and Grant kept his eyes peeled on the corridor.

"Who are you expecting?" Patrick asked, following the boy's gaze.

"The trolley cart," he replied.

Another wizarding reference. "Again? Aren't you getting too old for Harry Potter?"

Grant looked at his uncle like he'd lost his mind. "I'm eleven. That's exactly when you get your letter from Hogwarts."

Patrick winced. He often forgot how young Grant still was. Like the boy wizard, he had lost a great deal and been forced to grow up too fast, although as a custodial relative Patrick hoped he was quite the opposite of the Dursleys. Annoyed with their obsession with books, Patrick snatched Maisie's from her hands.

"Ow. You gave me like a thousand papercuts."

"Would you please look out the window?" They were passing the quaintest little villages tucked in swooping valleys between mountains.

"Neat," she said flatly. "Can I have my book back now?"

Patrick glanced at the cover. Another Agatha Christie, this time *Appointment with Death.* "Subtle," he said, handing it back to her. She was going to be a real joy at her father's wedding.

"What country is this?" Grant asked, squishing his face against the window.

"Italy. If you're counting, that makes five." Patrick ran a quick tabulation in his head to be sure. Maybe six, if their train had dipped through Germany on their way to Salzburg.

"Yeth!" Grant said, falling back into his lisp. He pumped his fist for exclamation.

"Big fans of Italy, are we?" Patrick asked.

"We're going to see Dad in Italy."

"And Livia," Maisie said, trying to temper her brother's excitement. She raised her book in front of her face. "Don't forget about her."

"Who could forget about her?" Grant asked, but his enthusiasm remained undimmed. "Don't worry. Uncle Patrick is going to stop the wedding."

"Over my dad body!" Patrick joked.

"You said you would!"

"I say a lot of things. I said I would write a stern letter to the Recording Academy for never giving ABBA a Grammy. Doesn't mean I did."

"You promised!"

"I never said I would dramatically throw myself on the altar to stop a wedding, don't put words in my mouth. I said I would talk to your father and voice your concerns. Privately. *If* you still didn't understand after our trip why he was getting married."

Maisie swung sideways and tucked her feet up onto the seat. "Well, we don't. We don't know why anyone would want to get married."

"I do!" Grant offered, and Patrick laughed, as it sounded like the kid was taking his own marital vow. "Cake."

"Ah, yes. Many a marriage entered into for cake."

"Cake is not a reason," Maisie said, her aversion to sweets rearing its head yet again. "So I remain unconvinced."

Patrick massaged his temples to stave off a headache. So much for his confidence.

Their train pulled into Venice in the late afternoon, just as the sun's low rays caressed the colorful buildings that lined the canals. Patrick dragged the kids straight into the heart of the city; there was not a moment to wait. The canal water's tint always made him stop to take it all in, the green surprisingly vibrant. He raced them through St. Mark's Square on the way to the Grand Canal.

"Pigeons!" Grant cried as he pointed into the square, which was flooded with hundreds, perhaps thousands of birds.

"If the goal was to see pigeons, I would have brought you to any Chipotle parking lot back home. But we're not here to see pigeons, so keep up!" Grant protested until Patrick promised them they'd be back to admire the panoply. For now he had one destination in mind, and time was of the essence.

The mouth of the Grand Canal spilled open in front of them and it was one of Patrick's favorite views of Venice. In this city built on the sea, the most consequential street was not a street at all, but rather a two-mile waterway that snaked through the city and formed the letter S. The Grand Canal was bustling with private boats and activity, and the buildings that lined the canal once belonged to Venice's most successful mercantile families. They rose proudly from the water in warm shades of oranges and pinks and reds that reflected beautifully across the cooler colors of the canal. Even standing in the middle of it, it was hard to accept that Venice was real; it was like the three of them had stumbled into a Renaissance painting and now themselves were hanging in the Louvre.

Oh my god, Maisie mouthed, too stunned to summon her voice and put it to her statement of wonder. *Finally*, Patrick thought. He'd shown them something that had left them speechless and they stood quietly savoring Guncle Love Language number one. There was nothing quite like the sound of silence.

"Is this where Livia's from?" Grant asked, breaking the spell after he watched at least a dozen speedboats go by.

"She's from Italy, yes, but a different city. I think her family's from Rome."

"Does Rome have boats instead of cars, too?"

"No, Rome has regular streets with cars, although a lot of people ride Vespas."

"Oh," Grant said with disappointment, as if he had come close to finding something admirable about his stepmother-to-be before all hopes were dashed.

They started to walk along the waterway's cobblestone banks, dodging tourists and merchants alike.

"Livia has a sister, you know," Maisie announced.

"I didn't know," Patrick admitted.

"She's a lesbian," Grant said, "like you."

"Whoa whoa whoa." Patrick pulled them against a wall as a gaggle of tourists with an obnoxious number of shopping bags turned sideways in order to squeeze by. "I am many things, but I am *not* a lesbian."

"He meant she's gay like you. She's going to be our launt."

Patrick inhaled sharply, clutching imaginary pearls. "There's no such thing as a launt."

"There's no such thing as a *guncle*!" Maisie clarified. "I mean, not really. It's just a silly word."

"It's a lot more real than *launt*!" Patrick didn't know quite *why* his feathers were ruffled, like he was one of the many pigeons in St. Mark's Square waiting indignantly to be fed, but they were. *Launt.* The very idea, ridiculous!

"I thought you hated the word 'guncle.'"

"Onomatopoeically! But the reason for its existence is sound. I mean, look where I've brought you. Look at all the things we've done! Is a launt going to take you around the world? No! Will a launt treat you to world-class cuisine? Of course not. You'll be lucky if a launt shoves you in their Subaru to take you to a farmers' market for artisanal dog treats."

"A launt will get us a dog?" Grant asked excitedly.

"I GOT YOU A DOG!"

"Oh, yeah. I meant *another* dog."

"Why do you need another dog?" They were on the move again, walking past a bank of gondolas, where an older couple carefully stepped into a boat with the help of their gondolier. "Look at them," Patrick said, discreetly pointing toward the couple.

"I like their stripes," Grant admitted of the superbly costumed oarsmen.

"No, not the gondolier. The couple. See how they look at each other?" The man could hardly take his eyes off his wife, even though Patrick imagined they had been together for decades; indeed, her face glowed in the last of the day's sun. Maybe they came every summer, maybe they had saved their whole lives for a trip like this. Maybe they lived here. But there was no mistaking how they felt about each other. "That's Venice. That's love." Patrick took a deep breath. "You really can't understand why two people would want to get married?"

Maisie turned to challenge Patrick. "Why do you feel the need to be our favorite?"

"Did you not hear anything I just said?" Patrick took one last look at the elderly couple; they held hands as the gondolier pushed them away from the dock with his oar. Patrick then turned back to his niece. "I don't. I don't need to be your favorite." That, of course, was a lie.

"Then why do you care if we have a launt?"

"Because we're not doing launt. Launt is not a thing. Now stop trying to goad me."

Grant scratched his chin. "What's goad mean?"

"Provoke me into action. Your sister is impressed with Venice, and she's seeing and understanding love and she's afraid she's losing out on our deal. And if she knows I won't try to stop the wedding on your behalf—"

Grant interjected. "You already said you weren't."

Patrick ignored him. "—she's trying to get me to make a disaster of it by creating a nonexistent rivalry with . . ." Patrick could hardly get himself to say the world. "This *launt.*"

"Whatever," Maisie dismissed, caving a little too easily for Patrick's tastes. What did she know that he didn't? Who was this sister of Livia's and why did Maisie wear such an inscrutable expression? It was as if she were saying, *You'll see.*

Grant pointed at the gondolas and broke his chain of thought. "Can we ride in one of those?"

"Tomorrow. Tomorrow we can ride in a gondola and explore all the canals, and there's even a bookstore I want to show you." Patrick gave Maisie a friendly tap on her back. "But tonight we're eating pizza to our heart's content. Who's hungry?"

Grant thrust his hips to one side and pointed a finger in the air like a tiny disco king—all he was missing was a crushed-velvet suit. "Finally!"

"Let me guess," Maisie began. "It's the world's *best* pizza?" She said it with just the right amount of sarcasm to make it truly funny. Patrick put his arm around her and they continued along the canal. *Let's see a launt teach her delivery like that.*

◇◇◇◇◇◇◇

Pizzerias in Venice were a dime a dozen, it would be impossible to throw a stone without hitting one. But good pizza, well that was harder to find. The city offered world-class cuisine, but there were also plenty of places that were just as forgettable. Patrick, however, had done his research and reserved them three spots at the counter at Antico Forno, a small pizzeria not far from the Rialto Bridge. Despite Maisie's ribbing, he had no idea if this was the best pizza in Venice, let alone the world—there were as many pizzas as there were regions and people's favorites were so subjective. But he had a good feeling about the night ahead and would do his best to serve as proxy for Livia's views on Italian cuisine.

"Buonasera!" the proprietor at Antico Forno exclaimed as they took their seats at the counter.

"Buonasera," Patrick greeted him back. Maisie pulled out her phone to have SayHi at the ready before their conversation could go any further.

The scents inside the cozy restaurant were intoxicating and the whole space had the air of a small movie set, something directed by one of the Coppolas. Marble pillars out front, tiled flooring aged just so, and red-and-white-checkered curtains framed the pies in the window.

"Okay, you got me," Maisie marveled, reluctantly as she may have sounded. "This really isn't like anyplace I've seen."

"Except Pizza Hut," Grant replied, and Patrick threw his hands over the boys mouth, hoping the man behind the counter's English was limited, even though everyone in Venice seemed to speak it fluently.

"It does not look like—" Patrick couldn't even bring himself to repeat such a claim.

Maisie reached across Patrick to shove her brother. "I was talking about the city, doofus." Grant shoved her back, but didn't otherwise take the bait.

"You know what would be cool?" Grant asked. "If instead of canals they had waterslides."

Patrick handed them each a menu. "Then you'd be wet everywhere you went."

Maisie picked her T-shirt away from her body. "We're wet anyway. The whole city is . . . *damp*."

"Of course it's *damp*, it's a city of water."

Grant studied his menu. "They misspelled 'pizza,'" he observed, pointing at the menu, which said *pizze.*

"P-i-z-z-e is plural in Italian."

"I thought margherita was a drink," Maisie said, taking her own issue with the offerings.

"It's a drink *and* a pizza. Also different spellings." Patrick explained how the margherita pizza with tomato sauce, mozzarella, and basil was red, white, and green—just like the Italian flag.

"How do you know all this stuff? Like how do you know all these places?" Maisie asked. It was just dawning on her, the idea of being a citizen of the world.

"I mean, I don't. Not really. London I'd been to a few times, but I didn't really know the city until this year when I was living there to film the movie. Austria I'd never been to, we discovered that one together. I'd been to Paris with Emory once when he filmed a French commercial for Peugeot, and years ago I came to Venice with Joe. Granted, that was a long time ago, but a city like Venice you don't forget. You'll see when you come back on your own when you're older."

"What *happened* with you and Emory?" Grant asked, almost exasperated, as if he'd been over it and over it in his head.

"Shall I order for us?" Patrick asked, knowing the best way to answer a question you wanted to avoid was with another question. He flagged down their waiter, who adopted a boisterous persona for those he deemed tourists; Patrick imagined locals grew tired of playing the part. He requested margherita and quattro formaggi pizzas for the three of them to share and was surprised to see both Maisie and Grant staring at him so intently once their order was in. "What, did you want antipasto, too?"

"We want you to answer Grant's question."

"About Emory? It's complicated," he sighed, adding, "in an uninteresting way," hoping he could get them to drop it.

"You're the one who wanted to teach us about love. Doesn't that include what happens when love ends?" The world was a globe, as round as it was wide, but somehow there in a tiny restaurant across a vast ocean, Patrick finally found himself cornered.

"It didn't *end*."

"Then you still love him," Maisie pressed.

"Of course. Very much."

"Then what happened?"

"I told you."

"You didn't, though." Grant pulled his shirt up over his mouth, looking like a little bandit. Indeed he had Patrick at gunpoint.

Many of the kids' friends had parents who were divorced. Those kids knew that sometimes love faded, they witnessed fighting and anger and separation before being swapped back and forth every other weekend. Maisie and Grant's own circumstances were very different. They lost their mother, and their grief came from love that endured. If Patrick was going to teach them about love—really teach them—he owed it to them to be honest. Love also had its shortcomings. So he said simply, "Sometimes love isn't enough."

"Why?"

Patrick closed his eyes and inhaled the scents of dough and tomato and basil emulsion. He listened to the din of the crowd, excited chatter in English and Italian and who knows how many other languages. Passersby bustling past the door on their way to their own dinner plans.

"*Why?* Because I'm going to be fifty, that's why. It's time for me to get serious." Patrick remembered during their first summer together when the kids heard his age and proclaimed that forty-three was almost fifty. He was horrified then, but it was the unvarnished truth now—he was undeniably middle-aged.

"What does that have to do with it?"

Patrick chuckled. "I know this will come as a shock, but Emory is quite a bit younger." He whispered "younger" like it was a dirty word. "Yes, we do all kinds of things and travel to all kinds of places, but at my age I can't just have fun all the time. I have to be serious. I have to grow up."

"Age shouldn't make a difference," Maisie stated plainly. "Not if you really love each other. Besides, Emory is five years older than he was when you first met. He's growing up, too."

"Yes," Patrick said. In theory he agreed. And certainly that was Emory's point of view. "But the problem is, so am I."

There was an unspoken agreement, Patrick thought, in dating someone younger that they would participate in the illusion that you were their age, too, or at the very least that you somehow met at a neutral age in the middle. And Emory had kept up his end of the bargain, at least for a while. He never commented on the graying around Patrick's temples or the salt that grew in his beard. When they played tennis, Emory would get winded, too—or at least pretend he did—allowing for Patrick not to feel his full age. But every once in a while the truth of their ages would show. Emory would rebound more quickly on the court. Patrick would pass a mirror and feel not so much betrayed by his reflection as confused. A reference would go over Emory's head or one would go over Patrick's. Emory would mention watching *Friends* as a kid, and mean not as a young adult but as an actual child. And every so often he would look at Patrick with a curious head tilt and his eyes would grow the faintest bit wet. Of course, Patrick was not privy to Emory's thoughts and if he really wanted to know, all he had to do was just ask, but he was always worried that Emory was performing complicated math—how old Patrick would be when Emory was Patrick's age now, that sort of thing, and he was afraid each time that the answer made Emory die a little inside.

"That's not a real problem," Grant finally said.

"Then what is a real problem?"

Grant thought for a moment before saying, "Quicksand."

"Mmmm," Patrick hummed, stifling a laugh. The kid did have a point. Only, for adults most quicksand was emotional.

A puzzled look fell over Grant's face. "Why are we laughing?"

"We're not laughing, I'm laughing."

"Why is that funny?" Maisie asked. "Emory is an old soul." She said it with confidence, as if that were her own observation, when clearly it was not.

"Who told you that?"

"Emory."

"When? When did Emory tell you that?"

"Before we left on this trip," Maisie replied. "He said I was one, too."

Maisie and Grant still talked to his ex? The thought had never occurred to him and now that it was staring him in the face he wasn't so sure that he liked it. "You shouldn't be talking to Emory." His appetite suddenly dimmed.

"He's our friend!" Grant protested.

"Don't be silly. He's too old to be your friend."

Grant threw his hands in the air. "He's too old to be our friend, he's too young to be yours. I guess Emory is fucked!"

"I guess that's right. Wait, WHAT?"

Two pizzas appeared on the counter in front of them. The focaccia crust had deliciously bubbled and charred, with crushed tomatoes peering through chunks of buffalo mozzarella, and Patrick decided he would force himself to have at least one slice. He reached for the stack of plates as Grant and Maisie eyed their meal. "Don't use language like that in public, it's not polite."

"You do!" Grant charged.

"I do a lot of things," Patrick admitted with the slightest twinge of regret. "Now, mangia."

◇◇◇◇◇◇◇◇

Venice was an entirely different city by night. The crowds cleared out, the streets emptied, and the canals all fell quiet. Restaurants closed around ten, and save for the opera at the Teatro La Fenice, there wasn't much in the way of nightlife; people who were looking for a more traditional scene with bars and nightclubs shuffled over to Mestre on the mainland. What remained was a city that was eerily peaceful and even more mazelike without the sun to light the way; the night glow came from below, off the waters of the canals, reflecting light from the endless docks and bridges. Patrick walked the kids over a series of footbridges back toward St. Mark's Square, checking the navigation on his phone every few hundred feet. They ate gelato, the perfect nightcap: Grant had two scoops of cioccolato al latte, while Maisie—who, despite her foray into Parisian hot chocolate, was never a fan of the flavor—opted for stracciatella; Patrick had pistacchio.

"What do you think? Venice always seems both romantic and sinister at night." It was perhaps all the Venetian masks that hung in store windows suggesting people still engaged in licentious behavior after dark.

"Gelato is supposed to be sinister?" Maisie asked, not falling for it. She took a look around. "I guess it takes a dump like this to underscore how boring sin can be."

Patrick grabbed her in a headlock. "Is that supposed to be sass?"

Maisie laughed. "Yes! I'm kidding."

The student becomes the teacher. Patrick took a spoonful of her gelato as punishment.

"Are we going back to see the pigeons?" Grant asked.

"It's past pigeon bedtime. Just as it's past yours."

"There are so many bridges!" Grant exclaimed. "I think they dug too many canals."

"They didn't dig the canals. Venice is a city of islands. Three big ones and more than a hundred little ones."

"That's a lot," he remarked, his mouth full of chocolate. "So what love language is this?"

"Ah." Patrick thought, scrambling for just what he wanted to say. "Are you ready for this? You're about to get Rickrolled."

"What's Rickrolled?" Grant asked, bracing himself for something awful.

"It's a meme where Rick Astley's 'Never Gonna Give You Up' appears in unexpected places. But I'm extending it to include his other hit, because once again, Americans like all the wrong songs." Maisie looked at him like she wanted to mush her gelato onto his nose. "Guncle Love Language number five: 'Together forever with you.' That's it. That's mostly what marriage is. Spending time together. And wanting to move heaven and earth to make that happen. With the right person, time flies. Forever goes by in a blink. But the good news is, you're the pilot. And when you have a good copilot, it makes the journey all the more bearable."

Maisie remained conspicuously silent as they walked, the only sound the patter of their feet on cobblestones and the echo of other conversations several bridges away.

"Something on your mind?" Patrick asked.

For a time, Maisie didn't answer. Then, out of nowhere, she asked, "All these love languages, but what's so great about love in the first place?"

"How do you mean?"

"You're teaching us everything about it, except *why*."

"Why do we love?"

"Why *should* we love?"

"I think that's an excellent question."

"Like, aren't there people who just don't bother?"

Patrick could tell, like now for instance, when one or both of the kids was genuinely interested, and he prided himself on feeding their starved little minds with an adult perspective. "There are people who are aromantic, people who don't feel romantic love. And that's fine. That's a valid way to be for some. But are there people who don't love anything or anybody? Their families, their pets, books, travel . . . *Taylor Swift?*" They stopped at the center of a bridge and looked down at the water that gently lapped the sides of the canal, rippling reflections of light dancing below them. "That doesn't sound like any way to live."

"It sounds like a way not to get hurt," Maisie opined.

Patrick agreed. It was that. "Listen to me. Even after everything you've been through—and you kids have been through a lot—would you prefer to not have loved your mother? Just so that it would have hurt less when you lost her? Of course not. In fact, I dare say if she somehow came walking over this bridge right now you would love her even more."

"I wish she would." Maisie leaned forward, rested her chin on the bridge's railing, and exhaled, making her own bridge of sighs.

If wishing made it so.

Patrick extended his arm across her shoulders as Grant stepped up on the railing's lower rung and asked, "Can pigeons swim?"

Patrick missed the days where he commanded their attention for greater stretches of time. "Can pigeons *what?*"

"Swim. How deep is this canal?"

"Are you even listening to me?"

Grant looked over the rail, seemingly weighing the benefits and drawbacks of dropping his spoon into the water to see how deep it would sink. Patrick glared at him: *Don't you dare.* "It looks bottomless."

"It won't be bottomless after I throw you in it." Patrick grabbed Grant under the armpits and raised him a few inches off the railing; Grant kicked and squirmed and laughed.

"Look, if you want to live your life without the bother of romantic love, I will support you. Whatever floats your gondola. I'm coming around to that way of thinking myself." Patrick realized as soon as he said it that that last part at least was a lie. "*But*. You can't go through life not loving anything at all. Because then you're a sociopath. Or the people behind the Razzies. You understand?"

The kids acknowledged that they did, then returned their focus to their gelato under the moonlight, leaving Patrick alone with his thoughts. All these rules he was making up. This entire leg of the journey, now that it was coming to a close. Was he selling the kids on the merits of love—or was he secretly selling himself?

They spent two more days in Venice, until Patrick was convinced the kids loved the city as much as he did, Rick Astley stuck in his head the whole time.

TEN

Patrick gripped the wheel of their tiny bubble rental car with both hands, not once moving them from ten and two the length of Lake Como's shoreline drive. There was barely room in the boot for even half of their luggage; Grant was smushed with the rest of their bags in the rear. Patrick himself was comically slumped over the wheel, his six-foot frame much too big for the driver's seat. The cars were small, street signs were all in Italian, and there was only a single lane in each direction, which many raced down like it was the Autobahn—but at least the Italians drove on the side of the street he was used to. Every so often Patrick and the kids would pull into a small town and the traffic would slow to a crawl, and then, as if all European motorists had death wishes, it would resume lightning speeds again. Twice he almost clipped old Italian men out for walks with their brindled fleabags.

It had been a long time since Patrick had driven with the kids and he did a double take seeing Maisie in the passenger seat. "Are you sure you're old enough to be sitting up front with me?" Maisie leaned her forehead against the side window.

"Do I have a choice?" Indeed they were packed in like sardines.

"I'm fourteen, you know. You can drive in South Dakota when you're fourteen."

Are we in *South Dakota?* Patrick thought. "Who told you that?"

"My friend Winsome."

"Winsome?"

"Yes."

"As in you win some, you lose some?"

"It means lighthearted."

Patrick questioned not only where Winsome got her name, but where she got her information, but kept his focus where it belonged. "That's because there's nothing to hit in South Dakota other than Mount Rushmore. Here, on the other hand . . ." And as if to illustrate his point, a Maserati coupe sped by going the opposite way.

"Where can you drive when you're eleven?" Grant asked, muffled by some of their luggage.

"*North* Dakota," Patrick quipped.

Maisie pointed to Patrick's grip. "Also, it's now recommended you keep your hands at nine and three, not ten and two."

"You don't know everything," he replied, but as soon as his niece turned away Patrick's hands involuntarily slid into the newly endorsed position.

"I liked it better when you didn't drive." Maisie was referring to the decade after Joe died in a car accident when Patrick refused to get behind the wheel, which seemed to him like a low blow.

All three of them were more than a little on edge, their time as a tight trio was coming to a close. Greg and Livia were waiting for them dead ahead, and soon even Patrick's older sister, Clara, would arrive. There was this lesbian, too, to contend with—this future *launt*—not to mention the rest of Livia's family of fat cats. It wasn't too late, Patrick thought, to turn the car south to Rome. The kids were excited to see their dad, but he suspected he could interest them in the Colosseum if he went into great detail of how bloody gladiatorial events used to be. The harsh realities of a wedding were settling, in particular the speak now of it all, and the forever holding your peace. For differing reasons, it felt like they were all three about to be tossed to the lions.

"I'm going to hug Dad first," Grant said.

"Ladies first," Maisie said. Patrick glanced at her as long as he dared; five years ago she would have been loath to identify as such.

"I don't see any *ladies*," Grant teased. Maisie pushed her seat back to squish him, but they were already so tightly wedged in it hardly moved half an inch.

Patrick intervened. "What about me? Your dad is *my* brother. Maybe he'll be happiest to see me."

"No one is happy to see their *brother*," Maisie said in retaliation.

Grant pulled her hair while saying, "You can hug Palmina."

"Paulina?" Patrick asked, wondering if the boy meant Porizkova. There was no telling what prominent Europeans Livia knew. "Who is this Paulina?"

"*Palmina.* She's the lesbian," Grant informed him.

"Her name is Palmina?" Patrick's mouth turned instantly dry. "I really got the fuzzy side of that lollipop."

The hotel materialized out of nowhere and Patrick had just enough time to glance in the rearview mirror to make sure they wouldn't be rear-ended before slamming on his brakes. He waited for three oncoming cars to pass and then made one of the tightest left turns of his life onto the property's shallow keyhole-shaped driveway; he hadn't expected the building to sit so close to the road.

"Buongiorno!" the valet said as Patrick exited the car.

"Buongiorno," Patrick replied with a groan as he got out. He'd never been so in need of a good massage. Surely the hotel had a spa.

"Salut," Maisie sullenly added as she emerged from the passenger side. No translation app was needed; she'd mastered the art of abruptness.

"Welcome to the Grand Hotel Tremezzo."

Maisie reluctantly let her brother exit, but not before he gave several swift kicks to the door. Patrick walked around the car to usher them away from the busy road, afraid they might bicker themselves into a tragedy. He'd been a perfectly responsible guardian for the past several weeks, he wasn't about to get a failing grade in the final moments of the exam. He placed himself between the kids and took each of their hands, something he was shocked they allowed him to do. Then, collectively, they looked up at the hotel in awe. The building looked both imposing and twee, like something out of a Wes Anderson film. While Italy's tipping culture was unclear, Patrick handed the valet twenty euros and together he and the kids started their ascent to the lobby.

According to the plaque at the base of the stairs, the Grand Hotel Tremezzo was a palace built in 1910 as a playground for the social elite. The hotel's art nouveau facade was painted a golden yellow, and stood so close to the shores of Lake Como it almost appeared to be rising out of its depths. Ivy-covered stairs snaked to their left and their right, leading up to a ground floor with Creamsicle-colored awnings. Above, each lakefront room had its own balcony, and several were occupied by guests, who once upon a time could have been properly employed models for 1950s travel posters. In short, the whole thing looked like a page ripped from *Travel + Leisure*—the perfect venue for a wedding, *if* that union was an occasion for merriment.

Greg and Livia descended the grand lobby stairs like they owned them, their feet practically floating above the gold and cabernet runner. The reception and concierge desks were tucked off to the side, adding to the illusion that they were entering a private home. The kids dropped their backpacks, ran up the first few steps, and threw their arms around their dad.

At the foot of the stairs was a round banquet in tufted red velvet with an arrangement of the most opulent roses Patrick had ever seen towering above the backrest. He slumped onto the settee as a rose petal fell into his lap. Like *Beauty and the Beast*, he turned to say to the kids, before remembering he no longer held their attention. And then he brushed the petal onto the floor, as he didn't like the symbolism of the rose representing the Beast's dying hope for finding true love. As he studied this family tableau, Patrick felt pangs of loneliness, as if he were destined to remain a beast forever.

"Let me see you," Greg said as he peeled the kids off his legs before crouching with tears in his eyes. Patrick had to imagine this was the longest he'd been apart from his children since Patrick had watched them that first summer after Sara died. But while Greg only had eyes for his children, Patrick's eyes were squarely on Livia, who stood off to one side and two steps above, holding her hands in front of her with her corresponding fingertips touching in a way Patrick had once told Grant looked like a spider doing push-ups on a mirror. She was very attractive, Patrick gave her that, and had a soft demeanor that looked almost maternal. Until she grinned with the smile of a shark, then she really did resemble a brunette Eleanor Parker, Greg the poor fool in over his head without an attractive young woman from the convent to save him.

"Children," Livia said, part greeting, part statement of fact. She tucked her hair behind her ear on one side. Patrick covered his face with one hand to shield himself from the awkwardness; he didn't want to watch, but could also not look away. She stepped between them and they each half hugged their stepmother-to-be, turning their faces safely to the side, as if they might catch something by breathing in her perfume. "Ciao. Benvenuti in Italia. Welcome to Italy."

Greg whisked Grant into his arms in a manner that would have most certainly wrenched Patrick's back, and the boy, despite being too old for such foolishness, squealed. Greg then spotted Patrick, and as soon as his brother locked onto him, against his will, Patrick's own eyes welled with tears. After the years he spent in hibernation blocking out all emotion, and after everything that had happened with Sara and the kids since, it often felt like emotion was making up for lost time. He used to joke that he only cried if a piano or a safe fell on him, and for a time perhaps that was true. But now he was often appalled to find himself a shell of that former self. *Thank you*, Greg mouthed to his brother. The truth was, Patrick realized, the pleasure had been all his.

At dusk, Patrick made his way to the hotel's wine bar veranda, an extension of their celebrated wine cellar. The menu boasted thirteen hundred of the finest Italian labels; Patrick had the sommelier recommend a crisp white from a smaller producer—he was in the mood for a local blend, something he had never tasted before. Now that he was alone, he indulged in a few of his love languages himself. Silence, finer things, together forever in the company of someone whose company he enjoyed (in this case, namely himself). Ordering a drink probably didn't qualify as an act of service, but perhaps keeping the vintner and sommelier employed was. In short, he was ready to exhale.

Patrick approved as the server showed him the bottle and he waited patiently as she then corked it and poured a small taste. He raised the glass by the stem, inhaled deeply, and then tossed it back in a single gulp. He'd seen many Hollywood types make a meal of this act, and he'd probably been guilty of such a spectacle in his younger days, but with no one to impress he couldn't summon the pretension. The sommelier promised hints of apricot and kaffir lime with an acidity she described in Italian as "lively." Patrick had no idea if that's what he was tasting, but it went down easily—almost *too* easily—in the warm evening air, and if it paired with anything it was with the stunning panorama. "Grazie," Patrick said, and she poured him a full glass before gently positioning the bottle in an ice bucket and stepping aside. Alone, Patrick took a proper sip and enjoyed his view of the lake.

Greg and Livia had taken the children to dinner and Patrick found himself without any responsibilities; for the first time in weeks he was not attending to anyone's needs but his own. He wasn't translating a menu, or deciding what someone else might like, or scouting the nearest bathroom. He wasn't planning the next day's activities or answering questions about the day they just had. He wasn't teaching anyone about love or why loving is an essential part of living and he blessedly wasn't being asked to stop a wedding or meddle in someone else's affairs. It was just him, a bottle of wine, and the quiet of the lake. He had truly earned this respite.

"Buonasera," a warm voice purred from behind and, although it sounded vaguely familiar, at first Patrick wasn't certain the greeting was directed at him. "Patrick?" He closed his eyes. *Why now?* The last thing he wanted was to be bothered. When he opened them, Livia stepped into view. She had changed since that afternoon and was wearing a stylish navy dress with two pockets on the front piped with white trim, hemmed short to show off her tanned legs. It looked like a designer art smock. Patrick scrambled to remember if he'd seen her in anything like this stateside, or if this was European resort wear or her attempt at looking like somebody's mom, as if the pockets might be filled with Handi Wipes and Juicy Fruit gum. "I had to come all the way to the cellar to find you."

"Turns out it's where you Italians keep the best wine." Patrick reluctantly gestured for her to join him. She pulled back the adjacent empty chair so that they both sat facing the lake and made herself comfortable on the orange-and-white-striped cushion while looking out over the water. He watched as her face relaxed—even if you were Italian, there was no taking for granted this view. "Is dinner over already?" There was still a ribbon of light in the sky.

"I didn't go. Your brother and the kids deserved some time alone." Patrick thought so, too, which is why he found this tucked-away lounge so that he wouldn't possibly intrude. But he wasn't sure if hers was an act of generosity or neglect.

His server appeared with a second glass and Patrick nodded his permission for her to pour Livia a glass. "Vino bianco?" she asked.

"Grazie," Livia replied, both to Patrick for offering and the server when shown the bottle. "A lovely vineyard. Nice family. The grapes grow on a tiny island off the west coast of Sicily. The ocean air gives them a surprising salinity."

Patrick scratched his chin, which was covered in stubble. He hadn't shaved since Austria. "Is that good?"

"If you like that sort of thing."

Patrick laughed. It was a perfectly valid observation to make, but it was also flat and laced with potential judgment—mechanical instead of warm. He knew Livia well enough to know she was less critical than people thought, but he also understood why the kids had trouble reading her. She spoke to the server again in Italian, and when the server walked away Livia explained to Patrick that they both thought the sky was threatening rain.

"Salute," she said as she raised her glass.

"Salute," he repeated, and they tossed back a good slug together. "Is Italy that small that you know everyone?"

Livia pushed her hair back from her face. "We know the important families."

"You know, when you say 'important families' . . . " He didn't need to finish the thought.

"Patrick, Patrick, Patrick. You of all people should know better than to peddle in stereotype."

Things grew awkward and they sat in silence. Patrick studied the mountains across the water, each layered with a slightly different color, haziest purples in the back, growing increasingly crisp and vibrant in the foreground. There was a small town in the foothills and its lights shimmered like fireflies.

"Greg and I wanted to thank you for taking the kids. It allowed us the time we needed to make a lot of decisions." Patrick wondered if one of those decisions was not to get married, but she was still wearing an impressive rock on her finger.

"That's some ring," Patrick said, and Livia employed her right hand to lift her left, as if it were too heavy to raise on its own. It was even more impressive than Sara's.

"Thank you. My sister, Palmina, is a jewelry designer who has a boutique on Capri. You'll meet her tomorrow."

Patrick swished a sip of wine in his mouth like Listerine, looking for the salinity Livia had mentioned. When he swallowed, he said, "It was no problem. Taking the kids I mean."

She stole a last look at her ring and then reached for her glass of wine. "You have such a way with them." This was Livia at her most complimentary.

He decided to be magnanimous in return. "*Now*," Patrick chuckled. "It wasn't always that way." He didn't mention that he was emerging on the far side of a sweet spot he'd found with both kids, and now that they were adolescents, he found it at times a struggle once again to relate.

"You sell yourself short. You three have a natural rapport." Livia took another sip from her glass before adding, "The three of *us* do not."

There was a time, not that long ago, when you could have knocked Patrick over with a feather by saying he had a way with the kids. "You'll develop your own. One unique to the three of you. It takes time." He pointed at a boat speeding by, as it struck him as quintessentially Italian, but then felt foolish and lowered his arm. "Right now I imagine they think of you as a threat."

"A threat to what?"

Patrick thought it would be obvious. "They lost their mother. I think they worry about losing their father, too."

"To me?"

To you, to anyone, to Italy.

"Is that what they said?"

Patrick clasped his hands around the stem of his glass and turned to face her. "I'm like their doctor. Or their therapist. Or their priest."

"You are none of those things."

"Like. I said *like*. In that they enjoy total confidentiality with me." He made a motion of zippering his lips. "It's the only way it works."

Livia sat with that information, either with quiet acceptance of the privilege or while looking for ways to pierce it. "How did you do it?"

"Gain their affection? Oh, I bought it. It was for sale, I had money, and I thought it would be nice to have. I bribed them over time with many things. I think it was the dog that sealed the deal."

"That hasn't worked for me."

"Yet," Patrick said. She certainly had the resources to keep trying.

"To them I'm the wicked stepmother." She smiled demurely. Patrick reached for their bottle.

"You're just going to let that sit there?" she asked. "You seem to have a smart comment for everything."

Patrick refilled Livia's drink with a heavy pour. Was that payback for her perhaps calling him a clown? "I don't swing at softballs." He returned the bottle to the ice bucket with a splash and then swept a tiny bug from his neck.

"The truth is, they don't know for years how I tried to be a mother." Livia's eyes welled and she did not make any effort to hide it. Patrick recognized a very real struggle, one she endured without shame, and in that moment he felt deeply for her. "Sorry, I don't know what softballs are," she continued. "I don't understand American sports references."

"You think I do?" Patrick placed his hand on Livia's and squeezed. He didn't want the meaning of what he had to say getting lost in a language that wasn't her first. "I'm sorry your journey has been so hard. I think the key now is not just wanting to be a mother so much as wanting to be *theirs*."

Livia wiped her eyes in stoic agreement. "You were very close to their mother?"

"I was." Patrick realized he was still holding her other hand and, uncomfortable, pulled his away. "But that doesn't mean we can't be close, too."

"Good. I would like that. The truth is, I'm grateful for her. For loving Greg and the kids as she did."

Patrick wished he could run back to his room and call Sara and share every detail of the awkwardness of this conversation. "The kids will come around, especially if you love their father. I talked to them quite a bit about love on this trip."

"I do love their father."

Patrick was relieved, even though in the moment Greg was not his primary concern.

"He is a good man."

That wasn't exactly a ringing endorsement, but to Livia perhaps that was enough. He didn't delve deeper. Patrick was more than ready to turn the page on this conversation.

"So what's this Palmina like?" Patrick asked, changing the topic. He then stifled a laugh, imagining an answer she would never give: *Like a Dutch retaining wall.*

"What's funny?" Livia asked defensively.

"Nothing. Nothing at all. I'm sorry. I'm tired."

Livia relented. "She's a lot like me, but the opposite." If she caught the ridiculous nature of her reply she didn't let on.

Their conversation faltered, and when the silence had gone on too long, Patrick said, "This feels nice." He could have been referring to anything. The wine, the hotel, the scenery, the company. What he really meant was having a moment without the kids.

"It does," Livia agreed, and he worried she meant the same.

ELEVEN

The following morning, as Livia's family descended on the Tremezzo, Patrick and Greg took the kids to the town of Bellagio across the lake. The nearest pier where they could catch the ferry was little more than a stone's throw from the hotel's entrance, and they walked single file along the narrow roadway to catch the battello. The ferry served Bellagio, Varenna, Menaggio—all the romantic villages of the central lake that were nestled into the shore. Lake Como was shaped like an inverted Y and Bellagio sat right at the promontory that divided the body of water in two.

"What did the water say to the boat?" Grant asked as they reached the pier.

Greg put his hands on his son's shoulders as they walked up to the little shack that appeared to sell tickets. "I don't know. What did the water say to the boat?"

Grant beamed. "Nothing. It just waved."

Maisie pinched her brother's arm. "There are no waves on a lake." Now that she had been reunited with her books, it was never clear exactly when she was listening and when she wasn't. Even though Patrick had taken them to a maze of a used-book store in Venice that had stairs made entirely of books and allowed them to pick out anything they liked, for today's outing she had selected a book from home: Stephen King's *Misery*. Perhaps she thought it was a subtle campaign she was waging with her reading choices on this trip, but Patrick had come to admire it for its brazenness.

Grant squirmed. "It's just a joke!"

"You're a joke," she replied, and she hit him with her book.

"DAAAAD!"

In a fluid move that couldn't have been choreographed more gracefully, Greg pulled both kids from the line. As Patrick stood at the window with his open wallet, he commended how effortlessly Greg skated right over the brewing squabble—and left Patrick to foot the bill. That was some serious talent. "Don't worry," he said to no one. "I'll get the tickets."

"Did you hear about the Bluetooth iceberg?" Greg asked, and he immediately had Grant's rapt attention.

"Any boat that goes near it will sync."

Grant squealed with delight, but Patrick turned away from them in shame. Guncle jokes were way better than dad jokes.

The battello was a two-story boat, with open-air seating in the bow. It was not even eleven and the sun already felt like it was at its full height in the sky, so Patrick ushered them to the ship's upper deck, where they could be seated under a canopy; sunburn was not a cute look for a wedding.

"Hazy today," Greg observed.

Patrick looked out from under the canopy and up at the overcast sky. "Livia mentioned something about rain."

"Is that why she didn't come?" Maisie asked. "Because I invited her."

Greg looked nervously at the cloud cover, ever the anxious groom. "Relax," Patrick instructed. "I'm sure it will pass through long before the wedding." He then leaned down to his niece and whispered, "That was nice of you to invite her. I'm proud of you."

Maisie sneered. "I was hoping she'd walk the plank."

Patrick sighed. They were raising Wednesday Addams.

Once the boat was underway, Greg took Grant to find the bathroom, leaving Maisie and Patrick alone. While Maisie read, they enjoyed the silence and the boat's smooth ride and the people watching, which was always a fun way to pass silent judgment. Maisie caught Patrick staring at her.

"What, you expect me to read *Little Women?*"

Patrick laughed and tapped the cover of her book. "Annie Wilkes is cocaine. Stephen King said as much himself." It was a daring bid to bond with her, but since her father had successfully been through rehab she was certainly old enough to understand addiction.

"Well then, he must have had a different draft, because in this copy she's a human woman."

Patrick said nothing, deciding to leave it at that. Instead he gestured toward an elderly lady whose sundress he was certain was on backward; without hesitating Maisie jutted her chin in the direction of a man who had tightened the chin strap on his hat so tightly his jowls swallowed the tie. She didn't miss a thing, even with her nose in a book. She waited until the boat reached the lake's center before asking, "Are you going to talk to him?"

"Are you?" Patrick retorted, certain he had more than upheld his end of the bargain.

Maisie said nothing and returned to reading. Patrick elbowed her to look up and gestured around them; the view was out there and the Italian Alps were not to be missed. "Livia said that on a clear day you can see Austria and Slovenia."

Maisie didn't stir. "Weren't we just *in* Austria?"

"Yeah."

"Well, then, let's not wait for a clear day." She eventually sneaked a look at the scenery, but denied Patrick satisfaction by pulling her hair down over her eyes. "Do you think Dad would let me get highlights?"

"Maybe you should ask Livia. That's the kind of thing stepmothers are for. She wouldn't dare say no."

Maisie pushed her hair back from her face and frowned, disappointed to hear him pinch-hit for traditional gender roles. "Shouldn't that be what guncles are for? Or maybe I should ask my new launt."

Patrick relented. He had yet to meet Palmina, but he wasn't about to let her have this one. "We can try some lemon juice when we get back to the hotel."

"Lemon juice?" Maisie's face was now sour as citrus itself.

"People rub lemon juice in their hair to lighten it. And then they sit in the sun. We can do that later and lie on the beach."

"People? What people?"

"I don't know. *People.*"

Maisie looked at him skeptically, but wasn't ready to put her foot down. This was the farthest she'd ever been from New England and maybe people did things differently here.

"Your mom and I, okay? We did it. Or maybe we used this ghastly product called Sun-In, but it's made with lemon juice, so we might as well go right to the source." If Patrick recalled, their hair turned an unsavory shade of orange and they went straight to the drugstore wearing ridiculous rain bonnets to procure color to dye it back. They'd laughed when they caught sight of themselves in the store window looking like frightened Mennonites. But lemon juice on its own would hopefully have a more subtle effect, especially if Patrick applied it to his niece's hair evenly, and he was pretty sure it wouldn't require an emergency run to a farmacia. "You know, I had dinner with Livia."

"When?"

"Last night."

"Traitor," Maisie mumbled, and Patrick recognized his own perfect comedic delivery; he then melted when she nuzzled against him.

"She does have a thing, doesn't she? A quality that's difficult to read. It made me wonder how your dad did it."

"Did what?"

Patrick almost said penetrate her demeanor, but what he meant was fall in love. "Get to know her, beneath the surface. It will be interesting to meet her family and see if they're the same."

"Even Palmina?" Maisie cajoled.

Patrick shuddered.

"It really bothers you, doesn't it? The idea of us having a launt."

"*Everything* bothers me," Patrick clarified as he pushed his sunglasses up the bridge of his nose. "But I'm being very brave."

"So who's coming to this wedding?" Patrick asked as they disembarked in Bellagio in front of the town's lakeshore hotels and older patrician houses; since it was the high season, the village was a beehive buzzing with life. Normally Patrick preferred to know the guest list before committing to any social event and the seemingly haphazard nature of this wedding was starting to unnerve him. "No fascists, I hope."

"No fascists," Greg confirmed. "Livia's parents, her sister, Palmina. Clara, of course, is arriving tonight."

"Oh, so *one* fascist," Patrick joked, and it was funny because their sister, Clara, while a little too serious for Patrick's tastes at times, was really anything but. And their relationship had thawed since his summer in Palm Springs with the kids, when she had tried to take custody from him in the final weeks of Greg's stint in rehab. Now she seemed more or less ashamed of the whole episode and Patrick honored her by never bringing it up.

"That's it. A few assorted friends."

"Of yours?"

"Livia's mostly."

"You know I'm actually excited to see Clara?"

"I am, too," Greg admitted. "I need someone else to stand on my side."

"Well, I'm famous, so I count as at least two."

"Actually, I was hoping you would be my best man."

Patrick was touched; Greg hadn't mentioned anything, so Patrick assumed he'd asked Grant, even though he was half a man at best. "A little last minute to be asking."

"You have other plans?"

He pretended to check his calendar. "I was maybe going to drop in on the Amal Clooneys." Greg snatched Patrick's phone and ran ahead. "Wait," Patrick called after him. "Who is Livia's maid of dishonor?"

"Her sister, Palmina." Patrick felt a jealousy weighing him down as Greg encouraged the kids to pick up their pace. How could he feel in such competition with a woman he had not yet even met? "You'll like her."

"Are Grandma and Grandpa coming?" Grant asked, too distracted by their surroundings to wait for an answer. He apparently had fewer concerns about knowing the guest list up front.

"Who?" Patrick joked once he caught up.

"*Your* parents," Grant clarified.

"I don't know what you're talking about. We were raised by wolves."

They were in fact *not* coming, but Greg mentioned they sent their regards. If there were two people even less thrilled than Maisie and Grant about these impending nuptials Patrick had to imagine it was his parents, who seemed more distrustful of foreigners as they aged. It was one thing if they took American jobs; it was quite another if they swooped in to claim American grandchildren, promising summers away in an enchanted land.

Greg pointed to what looked like a set of stairs. "Should we head up this way?" The town was cleaved in two, the grander buildings right on the lakefront, and everything that sat behind them, smaller but still charming dwellings and businesses which needed to be accessed by cobbled streets and staircases. All in all, Bellagio looked like it wouldn't take more than two hours to explore, which made it the perfect outing for the day. "We could look for gelato. It's a lot like ice cream."

"We know what gelato is," Maisie groaned. She turned to Patrick while pointing at her father as if to say, *Get a load of this boor.*

"Yeah," Grant concurred. "We had it in Venice."

"Oh," Greg said, and led them toward the stairs. "Well, if that's not of interest, we could stroll through some gardens. The grounds of Villa Melzi, I read something about. They're known to have lots of shrubs."

"No!" Grant protested. "Gelato!"

"Suit yourselves. Say, I was thinking, along the way we could shop for a little something for you to give Livia at the wedding."

"We're expected to give her a *gift?*" Maisie asked, appalled. This was getting worse by the minute. "She's getting two kids out of this marriage. Isn't that present enough?"

"You're a real gift all right," Patrick joked, and Greg elbowed him for not helping. "Let's hope you can be returned for more than store credit."

"It would be a nice gesture," Greg explained, already a few steps up Salita Serbelloni, which appeared to be the main drag.

Patrick glanced up at the sky before following; it looked more than ever like rain.

The center of town was quaint and charming and everything you'd want a stroll through a European town to be. The buildings were pale pinks and yellows and oranges, the colors of sherbet more than gelato, and the windows were framed with green shutters that hung endearingly just shy of vertical. Striped awnings hung over doors and the occasional flower box sat under windows, adding to Bellagio's delightful aesthetic. It wouldn't be hard to imagine the whole place was expertly created in a lab or at Epcot's World Showcase, except there wasn't a whiff of anything plastic or even a percentage artificial. Even locals seemed to mix in with the tourists, as if Bellagio was *the* place for luxury goods if you lived anywhere east of Milan.

"What about a scarf?" Greg asked as they entered their third shop. Como seemed to be known for its silks, and one of the shop owners had even informed them that silk production in the fifteenth century is what originally drew prominent people to the area, contributing to development around the lake. Silk scarves were plentiful and seemed to be in every shop; Patrick couldn't deny they suited Livia, as they would the Baroness.

"GUP?" Maisie asked, as if she couldn't possibly be counted on to answer such a question.

"I think it's a grand idea," Patrick said. Then, when Greg was deep in conversation with the store clerk, he added, "Perfect to strangle her with." He made a gagging sound, even though he wasn't sure why, other than to curry cheap favor with an Agatha Christie fanatic. To make up for his crass remark, he dove into a display of local designers and unearthed a Mantero scarf in blues and pinks. Instead of florals, the silk's pattern looked more like rare mushrooms. "This is the one." He held it up for Greg's approval.

"This one? Really?" He held it up to the window and then turned it around to make sure he wasn't viewing it from the wrong side. The shopkeeper "oohed" with approval, but Greg wasn't quite sold. "The pattern looks like fungus."

Maisie and Grant snickered.

"Not fungus," Patrick countered. "Mushrooms. Think, *champignons*. Like truffles, morels, and chanterelles." He said it with great confidence, even though he wasn't sure if he was listing mushrooms or sixties girl groups.

Greg squinted a last time at the scarf, reconsidering; some mushrooms *were* considered delicacies. "If you say so," he said, knowing if nothing else, gay men knew how to shop.

"I do." Patrick then turned to the kids and mouthed, *Fungus*, which made them laugh. Greg paid with his credit card and had the scarf gift wrapped as Patrick stumbled upon another display and announced to them all, "I think I'm going to get into ascots."

They reached a neighboring doorway just as the skies opened; one minute it was dry, and then sparse, splattering drops exploded on cobblestones. Then claps of thunder echoed through the streets and it was pouring buckets from the sky. Men who'd had the foresight to bring umbrellas struggled to open them, chivalrously providing cover for their anxious women. The awning was just large enough to shield the four of them, Patrick and Greg pressed shoulder to shoulder with the kids standing with their backs right up against them, which kept them dry for a time, but the wind soon picked up and rain fell sideways as much as it did from the sky.

"My book!" Maisie cried, crouching over it like she was protecting a child from the eruption of Mount Vesuvius.

Three young women ran in front of them shrieking, their hair plastered to their skulls, and their white summer dresses clinging to them like bedsheets, their flat sandals thwacking against the wet ground. People scattered like cockroaches in sudden light, and the streets quickly emptied; where people disappeared to was anyone's guess, but one had to imagine all the little shops were suddenly full.

Those who were drenched and didn't see much point in seeking refuge as the damage was already done, continued to slip and stumble across the slick cobblestone; a few threw their arms in the air like the most carefree of spirits in the mud puddles at Woodstock. A river of rain ran down the hill toward the waterfront and there was a loud clap of thunder that rattled the entire small town. Greg tucked Livia's gift-wrapped scarf under his shirt to keep it dry and Patrick did the same with his new ascots.

"Do you think the shopkeeper thought we were gay?" Greg shouted over the storm.

"We are gay," Patrick replied.

"You mean *you* are."

Patrick begged to differ. "You're marrying a marchesa. That's gayer than anything I've ever done." He watched as water streamed past them and felt grateful they were at the top of the hill and not at the bottom. "Does that make you a marquis?"

"What's a marquee?" Grant asked.

"I think in Italian it's pronounced *marchese.*"

"What's a marchese?" Grant asked again, this time tugging on Patrick's shirt with urgency while Maisie tapped away into her app.

"It's a game like Parcheesi."

"You're cheesy," Greg replied.

Patrick made a face at his brother's childish comeback. "I'm just teasing you. A marquee is a large sign over the entrance to a theater."

"Don't listen to your uncle," Greg interjected, before Patrick threw his arms in the air in protest. These kids would be so much worse off without his wisdom and bons mots.

"Don't listen to your *father.* I'm trying to give you a mnemonic device to remember. It can be a very helpful tool." Patrick then turned to his brother. "Greg, you know what a tool is, don't you?"

Greg laughed in spite of himself. "A marquis is a noble title, like princess or duke or earl. Unlike court jester or clown, which is simply a job." Greg pushed Patrick out from under the awning; the rain was surprisingly cold and he shrieked and hopped back underneath.

"Do *we* get titles?" Maisie asked. It was the most interested she'd been in this wedding to date.

"Do you want titles?" Greg seemed skeptical that they would. "They're not really something Americans have."

"Meghan Markle is the Duchess of Sussex," Patrick corrected, and then flinched when Greg glared, like he might push Patrick again. "Although, I think she's Canadian." To make up for it he told the kids, "You don't want titles. Not as Americans. It really would make you look like such tools."

◇◇◇◇◇◇◇◇

Just as the rain threatened to soak through the heavy cloth canopy above and drench them beyond all hope, it slowed to a drizzle, then stopped.

"I guess Livia was right about the rain," Greg said, extending his arm out in the open air to see if it might pick up again. Maisie shuddered, either from the sudden break in humidity brought on by the downpour or the very idea of Livia being right about anything.

The cool air became thick and muggy again. "I guess that's that," Patrick said.

"Let's hope it doesn't happen during the wedding." Greg peered up at the sky and scratched his chin the way he did when he was stressed. Maisie and Grant exchanged looks; they kind of hoped it would.

They emerged from the canopy as tourists retook the streets and the kids wandered ahead, on the lookout for gelato, undeterred by puddles, as Patrick and Greg pulled their packages from under their shirts.

"You're not wearing one of those to the wedding," Greg informed him, pointing to his brother's purchase.

"An ascot? Why not? They're my new thing!" In Palm Springs he'd had a closet full of caftans and often said Mrs. Roper was his style icon. Now he was fashioning himself after another *Three's Company* character: Don Knotts's Mr. Furley.

Greg exhaled his frustration, and they watched Maisie and Grant stomp in puddles, each trying to splash the other.

"We haven't done such a bad job with them," Patrick said, thinking for a moment, perhaps like the shopkeeper, that the kids were indeed his and Greg's. While they were certainly not a couple in the traditional sense, they had been a pretty solid team, and Patrick was feeling proud of what they'd accomplished over the past five years. He no longer just tolerated these kids, to his surprise he genuinely liked them.

"*We?*" Greg protested, as he'd done the lion's share of their raising, but it was a gentle chiding at best. It did, after all, take a village.

"Maybe they don't even need Livia," Patrick gently suggested, in case Greg was marrying her for them.

"*I* need Livia," Greg replied, and for the moment, at least, that was that, and they didn't say another word on the subject as they scoured the town for gelato.

TWELVE

The Grand Hotel Tremezzo featured three swimming pools: one built inside a floating dock in the lake designed to be memorably photographed, its azure waters in stark contrast to the lake's darker hues; an infinity pool connected to the hotel's spa, which provided the breathtaking illusion of its waters flowing outward toward the mountains; and the Flowers Pool, which was tucked in a nook behind the hotel with fragrant blossoms, mature olive trees, and Riviera palms filling the air with an intoxicating scent. The Flowers Pool deck is where they found Clara in a seafoam cocktail dress, which should have set off her tan, but instead gave her the dreadful look of unease.

"I've arrived," she announced as confidently as she could, and while she may have meant it in every sense of the word, Patrick wasn't sure she was truly selling the delivery. "Let the party begin!"

Clara's brothers exchanged glances; it was the rare social function that found its swing with their sister's entrance, but tonight they were going to go with it, as the kids were excited to see their aunt Clara—their enthusiastic hugs caught her off guard, nearly sending her into the pool. Instead of reprimanding them, she returned their embrace with equal fervor; Clara had loosened up quite a bit since her divorce was finalized, although she kept her married name, Drury, as she had muddled through enough of her life as Clara O'Hara and saw no need to return to such a metrical name. Patrick had joked she could reclaim her identity by leaning into the rhyme—divorce with no remorse, a sister with no mister, that sort of thing—but she could not be bothered with such Seussian nonsense. Not that it mattered. The single Clara Drury was much more fun than the married one and lately had been game to try new things. She had even hopped over to London on Patrick's first break from filming and they paddled down the Thames in a canoe, an activity Patrick had found skimming some magazine's list of unique things to do, before having martinis at an upscale bar called WC, which had opened in what used to be public toilets.

Greg, too, was happy to see his sister, as he was distracted with a long list of wedding chores and, if nothing else, Clara knew how to get things done.

"Patrick." Clara grabbed her brother's arms and pulled him close. "We've got to stop meeting in foreign countries like this. People will think we are spies."

"Aren't we?" Patrick asked as he scrutinized Livia's family gathered near the pool's deeper end while Clara hugged Greg and the kids. Something about the scene had raised Patrick's antennae and he could imagine himself a sort of Gay-mes Bond trying to coolly diffuse this heterosexual nightmare before it could explode.

As soon as Greg latched on to Livia and was safely out of earshot, Clara whispered in Patrick's ear, "Thank god you're here. I don't know a soul."

Patrick once again scanned the crowd. It was indeed light on people they knew. "How was your fligh—"

"You're wearing espadrilles," Clara said, interrupting his inquiry into her travels. "And is that an ascot?"

Patrick looked down at his clothes. He was indeed wearing the canvas shoes, along with a navy-blue shirt with a pineapple on it and cream-colored slacks. Not very James Bond, he supposed, although he could imagine the outfit on Daniel Craig. He fussed with his ascot. "Greg said I couldn't wear one of these to the wedding, so I'm torturing him with it now."

"Well, I never know how to pack," Clara confessed, but looking at her, Patrick thought she had done rather well. She took in the scene with a slight look of fear. "So this place is unbelievable." Even though they were on the hotel's garden side, part of the pool extended beyond the main building's edge and was open to the lake and the lush green hillsides surrounding it. "You know they gave me the room next to yours? I think the nightly rate is more than I paid for my car."

Patrick wanted to say that was more a statement about Clara's ratty old car than it was the hotel, but Greg jumped in before he had time. "Your hotel bill has been covered. We want our guests to have a good time."

"Wonderful," Clara said. "Now I'm related to two assholes with money." She was still toiling away in the nonprofit world. "Kids, why don't you go mingle?"

"What should we say?" Grant asked as he glanced around at the other faces, skeptical that any of his usual conversation starters would fly.

"A day on the moon and a year on the moon are the same thing," Patrick said. Grant's head bobbled like one of those toys.

"Is that true?"

"Who am I, Lance Bass? You're the space cadet. Go see if anyone tells you otherwise."

Greg put his hand on Maisie's shoulder. "Watch after your brother, would you?"

Maisie had other ideas. "I'd like to stay and taste my first champagne." She looked at her father with such faux-hopeful sincerity,

Patrick almost didn't recognize the bit; as soon as he did he nudged his niece in Grant's direction and the two of them scampered off around the pool.

"She's fourteen!" Greg said incredulously.

"She's teasing you. It's a line from *The Sound of Music.* We've been on a bit of a kick." Patrick cupped his hands around his mouth to call after her. "It's called prosecco in Italy!" He turned back to Greg and said, "She'll learn." But Greg wasn't certain he wanted her to.

"What is it with you and that movie?" Clara groaned.

"What?" Patrick feigned innocence.

Clara leaned closer to confide in her brother. "If seven kids start singing good night to me at this party, I'm using that time to refill my drink."

Livia approached with her parents, whom she introduced as Lorenzo and Giana Brasso. Giana was a perfect dumpling of a woman, slightly pickled, but well preserved. Lorenzo towered over her and had large moist eyes and a dry pink head, and eyebrows that met in the middle, threatening to slalom down his nose. While Giana's clothes were perfectly tailored to her round figure and flattering to her skin tone, Livia's father's were as loud as he was, over-patterned and wrinkle-prone, and Greg had forewarned them that Lorenzo's humor was his bluntest instrument of torture. Patrick and Clara offered their hands to shake, but were instead enveloped in the kind of boisterous hug that bruised ribs. "Patrizio! Chiara!"

"I'm sorry," Clara apologized. "I don't know what to call you. I mean with your titles and everything."

Greg looked at his shoes, as if his family was failing him already, but Livia's mother wagged a finger that was dripping with elegant rings. "Please. We are Lorenzo and Giana. Here we are family! We must dispense with formalities."

"How *noble* of you," Patrick said, and after an awkward beat they all laughed boisterously as the wordplay sunk in. Patrick leaned in to Clara and whispered, "Here we are family? Isn't that the slogan for the Olive Garden?" as their brother and his fiancée begged away to greet other guests.

Lorenzo placed his meaty, but likewise well-manicured, hand on Patrick's shoulder and proceeded to run down his entire family's genealogy as far back as it could be traced, before asking, "You're the comedian?"

"I'm an actor, yes."

Livia's father then launched into a very long-winded joke involving an overcured ham, circumcision, and rosary beads. Patrick returned the torture by not laughing, then caught Greg's eye from across the pool and burst into fake guffaws to keep the peace. If there was any offense taken, Patrick would never know, as Giana looked at him with sorrowful eyes.

"We had you down for a plus-one. Where is your marvelous Emily?"

Emory, Patrick thought. He tried to make eye contact with Grant, who'd made the same mistake the summer he and Emory first met.

"I'm afraid there will be an empty seat at your table." This was like a knife through the heart.

Lorenzo turned to Clara.

"And you are the sister, from where?"

"Hartford," Clara answered.

"HARTFORD!" Lorenzo bellowed, before his face was overcome with fake sorrow. "Am not familiar." Then he brightened again as he focused his attention back on Patrick. "And you. Are you any good at the acting?"

"I have a Golden Globe, if that counts for anything."

Lorenzo punched Patrick hard on the arm. "The Hollywood Foreign Press!" he cried with absolute delight. "Come! Let's away to the bar. We must drink to celebrate."

Patrick didn't know if they were celebrating upcoming nuptials or his winning a Golden Globe, but he wasn't about to say no to a drink, even if the drinks he'd been served at weddings always seemed to disappoint. "I'm always able to take nourishment in the form of a weak cocktail."

"Weak?" Lorenzo bemoaned. "We've paid for enough alcohol to fill one of these fine pools!"

"Come. You must meet our friends." Giana linked her arm with Patrick's and his mood brightened—the evening was looking up.

"Well, okay then! But you must introduce me as Golden Globe winner Patrick O'Hara."

Lorenzo howled with laughter.

"*Patrick*," Clara chided. "He's kidding."

"I am not," came Patrick's reply. "I've *earned* my titles." More riotous laughter from Livia's parents. Either they really liked him or they were already smashed.

"Please excuse Patrick," Clara said. "His favorite subject is Patrick."

"Isn't it everyone's?" Patrick asked.

They only made it halfway to the bar, when the Brassos excused themselves to intervene with some other guests, who were gesticulating wildly at a server. Clara whispered, "They don't know Hartford, but they know the Hollywood Foreign Press?"

Patrick was ready to rush to his new fan club's defense—of course they know the Hollywood Foreign Press, they were *foreign*—but she dismissed him in favor of a Bellini before he could vindicate them. Left solo, he procured himself a glass of prosecco from a passing waiter and decided to rescue the kids from their grandparents-to-be, who were now fussing and fawning and pinching cheeks like nonnas and nonnos from the old country.

Before he could move, a small commotion at the shallow end of the pool drew Patrick's eye. The crowd parted and a young woman appeared, hair slicked to one side with thick eyebrows and high cheekbones, looking very much like a young Isabella Rossellini when she modeled for *Vogue*. The woman was dressed in wide palazzo pants and a men's dress shirt that was perfectly tailored in a way that made it look both masculine and feminine. Behind her, three women undulated while wearing a similar androgynous style, and together they marched forward to join the party like they'd just stepped out of an eighties music video.

"Who is *that*?" Patrick muttered.

Grant stared all agog and Patrick had to gently slap him on the back of his head. "Her? That's Palmina," he said when he came to his senses. Patrick turned to Maisie and she was likewise entranced by the women approaching.

"*The lesbian?*"

"Yeah, why?"

Patrick stammered for something devastating to say about Palmina or her entourage, but came up short. "No reason. I just didn't know you could fit that many into a Subaru." And Livia had called *him* a clown?

Palmina torpedoed straight toward them, and as soon as she was in earshot she greeted the children.

"Maisie! Grant!" The kids hugged her tightly, and with more affection than they had ever displayed with Livia. She wore earrings that resembled brass curtain rings; were she more bullish, one of them would have been perfectly at home through her nose.

Patrick tried to mask his confusion. "You three know each other?"

"You must be GUNK," she began, with an Italian accent that bordered on Transylvanian. "We meet at last." She said it with a villainous inflection; perhaps he was more like James Bond than he thought.

"GUP." Patrick cleared his throat. "GUP is what the kids call me. Their guncle is what I am."

"GUPPY," Palmina cooed, as if that had been one of the options presented. "Like a little fish I could squish."

Maisie turned back to her uncle. "We met in New York. She came to visit Livia and we spent the day in the city."

"Where was I?" Patrick said, masking hurt feelings; a day in the city was sort of his thing. "I like the city. I *live* in the city."

"You were in London," Grant said. "Seeing a movie."

Patrick nearly choked on a sip of prosecco. "I wasn't seeing a movie, I was *filming* a movie." He looked at Palmina, who was alarmingly almost his height. "There's a big difference." He glanced down to see if she was wearing heels, but any shoes were hidden by her wide pants.

"I'm Palmina. People call me Palmina."

"Like the horse," Patrick said in retaliation for "Guppy."

"That's *palomino*," Maisie said, as if everyone knew that. "Palmina means like a palm tree."

"Like Palm Springs," Patrick said through gritted teeth. The nerve of this woman, horning in on his turf left and right. He grabbed both kids around their shoulders and pulled them in close. "These two lived with me there for a time."

"You were their guardian devil," Palmina said with a wry smirk. "These are my friends. Bruna, Carla, and Zita." Patrick pinched the bridge of his nose. He was having flashbacks of JED—John, Eduardo, and Dwayne—the gay throuple who lived behind his house in Palm Springs. "I hope to see you at dinner. We're having fagottini." With that, she motioned for her backup dancers to follow her to the bar.

"We're having WHAT?" Patrick exclaimed, but they had already woven their way into the crowd. Greg materialized by his side.

"You met Palmina!" he said with excitement. "I knew you two would hit it off."

"And the Robert Palmer girls?"

"Who are the Robert Palmer girls?" Greg asked loudly, while conspicuously waving his elbow in Livia's direction. "You and your generation!"

Patrick looked at his brother with dismay. *Was he still trying to pass as younger?* It was a performance so over-the-top it perhaps deserved its own Golden Globe, but Patrick was lost in thought studying his new rival, watching her glide through the party and everybody wanting a piece of her like the celebrity he usually was.

"I thought all gay people traveled in packs," Greg said. "Besides you."

Patrick ignored the remark. "Where did she come from?" He was as impressed as he was annoyed.

"Palmina? She's been living the past few years on Capri."

"*Capri?*" Maisie repeated with great fascination, like it was the kind of island paradise Wonder Woman hailed from; wherever Palmina lived, she imagined it had plenty to offer.

"Where is Capri?" Grant produced his notebook to take down the answer.

Patrick replied without tearing his eyes from Palmina. "It's a small island off the Amalfi Coast."

"Oh, like Rhode Island is a small island off of Connecticut," Grant said, as if it all made perfect sense; he flipped his notebook closed.

Up four steps from the pool's deck was an elegant bar with a stone pizza oven that produced some of the finest pizzas in the Como region. Tonight, the wedding party had taken over most of the outdoor space and expert pizzaioli were assembling a special menu of classic summer pizze, pasta, and insalate for the wedding guests. The tantalizing smells of tomatoes and melted cheeses overtook the pool's floral scents and everyone suddenly recognized how hungry they were.

Greg crouched to face his kids, straightening Grant's collar in the process. "Shall we get you some pizza?"

Grant thought for a moment before replying, "I could have the margherita."

"That's a pizza, not a drink," Maisie clarified.

Greg looked up at Patrick; his brother's influence never failed to delight. "Yes it is," Greg agreed. "How did you know that?"

Grant shrugged. "We're very worldly." He then headed for the nearest table, where a waiter pulled back a seat. "Grathie," he said to the server, almost as an afterthought, his old lisp creeping into his rudimentary Italian as he sat.

At dinner Patrick was seated between Maisie and an absolutely reptilian individual soaked in cologne whom the Brassos called Cousin Geppetto. If that was his Christian name or a joke, Patrick didn't know, but he still made a crack about wanting to be a real live boy, which landed with a thud. Pizzas were delivered to the table in a near-endless parade, as well as salads and pastas. Patrick even had a helping of the aforementioned fagottini, and made sure Palmina witnessed him take a bite; there was no way he was giving her the upper hand so early in the night.

"Everything smells so good," Grant observed. It always made Patrick laugh when he sounded like a little adult.

"Does it?" Palmina asked.

"Palmina," Grant continued, "what does the inside of your nose smell like?"

Palmina's friends snickered. *Oh, good,* Patrick thought. Let their new launt take a swing at fielding one of Grant's infamous questions. Patrick had years of practice answering; a newbie was sure to flail.

Palmina, however, seemed unfazed. "The inside of my nose smells like oranges, and like the lake, and magnolias, and the cool mountain air that sweeps down from the Alps, and like cypress trees because that's what is all around us."

Grant scrunched his face. "What do cypress trees smell like?"

Patrick glanced around to see who was listening to this absolute line of bullshit, but the rest of the table was engrossed in their own conversations.

Palmina took his hands. She closed her eyes and Grant did, too. "Take a deep breath. Inhale. Smell that? It's . . . How would you say? Herbaceous and woodsy, with spice."

Patrick turned to Clara and rolled his eyes, but even she seemed to be under Palmina's spell. *Does anyone not see this witchcraft for what it is?* But Grant was agreeing enthusiastically, happily lapping this bullshit up. Only Maisie seemed less than amused.

Palmina and Grant opened their eyes. "What does the inside of *your* nose smell like, Grant?"

Grant cupped his hands up under his nose and took a deep breath. "Like human flesh," he said. "And a little bit like Marlene when she's wet."

"Marlene is their dog," Clara offered.

"How wonderful that the inside of everyone's nose smells different," Palmina observed. "You must miss Marlene. That is why your nose is filled with the scent of her. That way you won't forget."

Grant bowed his head solemnly. He had never felt so very far from home. Patrick interjected; it was time to put an end to this sorcery.

"Do you have a dog, Palmina?" he asked.

Lorenzo caught wind and scoffed. "A dog? My daughter can barely care for herself."

Giana placed her hand on her husband's to quiet him. "Palmina has a bird. Named Flavia."

"Oh, come on," Patrick groused. He turned to Maisie for help. There was no way she was buying this.

"She's cool, isn't she?" Maisie said. *Another goner*, Patrick thought.

"She's something," he muttered, not ready to commit to what. Flanked by her backup dancers, the whole thing seemed like an act.

"We could call her GAP," Maisie offered. A lifeline at last?

"Like the low-rent Banana Republic? I like where your head's at, but it may need some work."

"No, like GUP. Gay Uncle Patrick, Gay Aunt Palmina."

Patrick dropped his fork and people turned to stare as it clanged on the ground. He must put a stop to this before it got out of hand.

Patrick excused himself from the table when he couldn't stomach another bite and wandered away from the crowd. The trip was becoming a real battle of the bulge and he might have to engage in some shopping, not as extravagant vacation indulgence, but as necessary waistline management—although what he really *should* be doing is hitting the hotel gym. He promised himself he would later that night, then took a seat at the bar next to the enormous pizza oven, where he watched as a few embers from the fire escaped the clay opening, burned brightly, and then blinked into nonexistence.

"Buonasera, signore," a young bartender greeted him. "Can I get you anything?"

"No, I . . ." Patrick wasn't sure exactly how to finish that sentence.

"Are you with the wedding? Are you the groom?" he asked with accelerating excitement.

"No, no. Brother of the groom. Fratello. Fratello?"

"Fratello," the bartender confirmed. "Weddings are *molto*."

"Indeed." *Weddings were a lot.* "Molto," Patrick repeated, thus exhausting his Italian.

Dusk was settling over the Tremezzo and water rippled gently over the pool lights, its blue reflections making everything dance. It was a jovial scene, people laughing, waiters ensuring no glass of wine dipped below half full, Maisie showing Palmina how to work SayHi. He inhaled deeply. *Dammit.* His nose *was* filled with the scent of the cypress trees. And the mountain air and the lake and whatever other nonsense Palmina had spouted. The scent had been there the whole time, he just hadn't relaxed enough to appreciate it.

Patrick pulled out his phone and stared at it, unsure as to why he did. That happened a lot lately. It was the interesting thing about straddling a generational divide. He'd lived more than half his life without a smartphone and everything had been fine. Now he reached for his device impulsively with an overwhelming desire to cut short the moment he was in, hoping for a different, better moment, like his entire body had been neurologically rewired. It was a sick addiction.

But since his phone was in his hand, he scrolled back for his last text from Emory, something about a package that had been delivered. Despite their breakup, he was letting Emory stay at his apartment while he was on location for the film; they'd never officially moved in together, but Emory had spent the bulk of his time at Patrick's whenever he was in New York. When Patrick needed his space, Emory had the ability to bounce around: he worked a lot, and traveled for that, and when he needed a place to crash he had no shortage of friends that took him in. It was one more thing on a long list that made him seem too young. And yet, Patrick was judging Emory for adequately dealing with a situation of Patrick's own creation, his requiring space. Which he didn't need; maybe a little in the way everyone does, but not really any more than that. He was just putting Emory through impossible tests he was destined to fail, as Patrick graded on such a steep curve. He fought the urge to text Emory now and tell him how sorry he was for being such a ridiculous creature. But Emory was a catch and Patrick had no trouble imagining he had moved on with his life.

"The most terrible poverty is loneliness." Patrick sensed the barstool next to him slide back, and by the time he snapped out of his trance, Palmina was already seated by his side.

"Oh, goody. Rock bottom has a basement," he mumbled.

Palmina tapped a box of cigarettes on the counter to pack them. "Pardon?"

"I said, 'That's rich,'" Patrick lied, doubting Palmina knew much about poverty, metaphorical or otherwise. She tilted her head quizzically, the double meaning lost in translation.

"There is a whole party happening over there. And yet you are over here."

Patrick looked beyond Palmina at the boisterous gathering; even the kids seemed to be enjoying themselves, Grant entertaining Livia's parents with a magic trick involving a napkin and his thumb, and Maisie now deep in conversation with Clara.

"I just needed a minute." Patrick held his phone up as some excuse. "I was thinking of texting my boyfriend." As soon as the word *boyfriend* left his mouth, he regretted it. Not because it was a lie so much (it was only two letters shy), but because it skirted too close to vulnerability. But what was he to say to someone who was here with three dates, when he, if you did not count the kids, had none?

"Why is he not here?"

Patrick didn't know how to answer, his face riddled with indecision. Palmina read him anyway.

"I see." She produced a cigarette from her pack and held it with the kind of effortless elegance that only Europeans could do. "You will never know what it is you want until you are certain of who you are."

Patrick bitterly swallowed that wisdom.

"I just broke up with my girlfriend," she confessed, offering Patrick a smoke. He declined with a wave of his hand.

"*Really.*"

"Sì. She was much older." Palmina lit the cigarette and took a long drag, adding as she exhaled, "Like you."

Patrick laughed. It was all he could think of to do. "She sounds beautiful. Wise."

Palmina studied him carefully, as if Patrick's English took an extra beat to compute. "She was both of those things."

"Is. Unless you killed her."

Palmina lit her cigarette, inhaled deeply and noncommittally blew smoke out the side of her mouth.

"*Did* you kill her?"

Palmina didn't answer. The relationship was dead, that's all he needed to know.

The bartender placed a small bowl of Marcona almonds soaked in olive oil between them.

"She was too old for you?" Patrick asked, feigning sympathy, hoping to extract some nugget to gain the upper hand.

"She was too possessive for me." Palmina helped herself to an almond. "Being older had nothing to do with it. Americans are too hung up on age."

Patrick could not grasp her understanding of English. He assumed it was a second—if not third—language, yet she had nailed idioms? "It has been my experience that age and treachery will win out over youth and beauty." Patrick held her gaze until she blew smoke just to one side of his face. It had a rich tobacco smell that he found strangely appealing.

"What is 'treachery'?"

Patrick reached for a definition that would make sense. "Like a betrayal of sorts."

"Did you just make that up?"

"No. Someone gave it to me on a birthday card once when I turned—" Patrick stopped cold. *Americans were too hung up on age.*

She scrutinized him further as she enjoyed a few more drags on her cigarette. "Come back and join the party, treachery," she finally said with a twisted grin. He wasn't certain, but he thought for the first time that perhaps they liked each other, or at least understood one another in a way that would make their rivalry fun. As she sauntered back toward the table, Clara approached with a curious expression.

"What are you doing over here?" his sister asked.

"Fraternizing with the enemy."

"What do you think?" Clara turned back just as Palmina resumed her seat at the table.

"Of Palmina?" Patrick took a deep breath. What *did* he think? He wasn't yet ready to say.

"Of this marriage," Clara said. "Maisie has been giving me an earful."

Patrick narrowed his eyes. "Greg's old enough to make his own mistakes." Despite whatever age he was pretending to be.

"So you think it's a mistake?"

Patrick waved his hands no. "I'm not saying that."

Applause broke out and they glanced back at the kids. After his third attempt, Grant had successfully completed his trick. He beamed.

"Greg is not the only consideration," Clara said.

That much was true.

Patrick turned to reach for some almonds and, still full, was both relieved and amused to find Palmina's cigarette stubbed out in the dish.

THIRTEEN

Patrick reclined fully on the orange cushion of his chaise to let the sun properly do its thing; the gentle breeze and the smell of sunscreen and the searing heat all made him miss Palm Springs. He was tickled by the memory of it; in the five years since he'd moved to New York, he had been back only once to clean out his house before the closing. There was no point, he thought at the time, in looking back, when so much of his life—Emory, his new show, the kids—was about moving forward. He embraced life as a New Yorker. So he was surprised now to find himself feeling oddly nostalgic. Palm Springs is where you went to do nothing; New York was a place to do *everything*. But as the sun hit his face and he felt warmth radiate through his skin, he wondered if he might not have overcorrected. There was value in doing nothing from time to time, even if it was not meant to be a way of life. And yes, he had been to the Hamptons a handful of times and twice to Fire Island, but those were like New York Lite, more than they were like Palm Springs.

He relaxed into the memory of meeting Emory for the first time in Palm Springs, their first real conversation in his own lounge chairs, much like these, except blue. But Emory quickly slipped from his thoughts as a cold shadow fell across his face. He opened one eye to find Maisie standing over him.

"Here." She held out two lemons, perfectly halved, two pieces in each hand.

"Where did you get those?" Clara asked, looking up from her book, *Women Talking* by Miriam Toews. His sister had been occupying the chair beside him so quietly he'd almost forgotten she was there. Grant was on the far side of Clara, playing a game on Maisie's phone under a towel Patrick had placed over him, as if to calm him like a macaw in a cage with a blanket.

"I nicked them from a centerpiece in the lobby." Patrick had sent Maisie to the half-moon-shaped bar under the nearby awning to have them halved.

"You *nicked* them. Who are you, Madonna? You were in England for five minutes and suddenly you're Oliver Twist?"

Patrick sat up and placed his feet on the ground, curling his bare toes in the warm sand, surprised to find it was not the warm concrete of a pool deck in Palm Springs.

"Did you see the nightly rates for these rooms?" Clara asked. "I'd argue who's robbing whom."

Patrick motioned for Maisie to sit in front of him. "Did you tell them to send over a spritz?"

"Ooh, a spritz sounds divine," Clara said, as if Aperol were a religious experience. Patrick waved until he caught the bartender's attention and held up two fingers, pointing to himself and Clara.

"Are you done being the language police?" Maisie asked, annoyed, wondering what to do next with the lemons.

Clara motioned for her to come closer and ran a lemon wedge over streaks of Maisie's hair. "Clara-all," she said, pleased.

"Are you trying to put your spin on Clairol?" Patrick's face soured as if he had just bit into one of the lemons; he wished people would leave the jokes to him. "Did you put on sunscreen?" he asked his niece as she tilted her face up toward the sun.

"Duh," she replied as Patrick took the lemon from Clara and continued as she had shown. "I don't want to end up wrinkled like you." He playfully yanked at a chunk of her hair in retaliation. "Ow." Maisie shot him a look over her shoulder.

"Sorry. Snarl." Another crack at his age; they were starting to pile up.

A deep, throaty laugh drew his attention and he watched as Palmina and her ladies-in-waiting claimed four chairs a few rows in front of them, clad in stylish one-piece sheath swimsuits that might have looked more at home on Esther Williams than this pack of *lesbutants*. "The bathing costumes," Patrick muttered, as if it were all too much.

Clara's instinct was to counter Patrick's every criticism with a compliment. "She has such an infectious laugh."

"Infectious like you could catch a disease." Patrick dropped the lemon he was holding and it landed face down in the sand. Clara shot him a look—*Serves you right*—before returning to her book.

Maisie looked down at the lemon wedge now covered in sand. "Maybe I should have Palmina do this."

Patrick yanked her hair again. "Bite your tongue." He reached for a clean piece of lemon.

"In fact, maybe I should have Palmina do everything."

"What do you mean, *everything*?"

"Stop this charade of a wedding!"

Patrick disagreed; Palmina was not right for the job. "She's Livia's sister. What's she going to do?"

Maisie looked over her shoulder judgmentally. "Well, you're not focused. Ever since we got here you've been in your own little world. Shopping for ascots. Mooning over Emory."

"I'm not mooning!"

Maisie turned back around and focused straight out at the lake. She wore a modest bikini top—a far cry from the rash-guard shirts she would wear to swim in Palm Springs—and her hair was now halfway down her back. *She's growing up too fast,* Patrick thought. But maybe she had a point. He wondered if there wasn't some underlying resentment between the Italian sisters. A bride should have attendants, not a maid of honor, and the fact that Palmina traveled with a retinue of them seemed disrespectful—like showing up to the wedding itself in a white dress. And she didn't appear at all impressed with the festivities so far, unlike her parents, who were thrilled with every lush detail. She seemed like both a member of her family and her own satellite, with a unique orbit, like his own. "Palmina can't do everything."

"She can do a lot," Maisie said admiringly.

A man in a Speedo walked by in his quest for an empty chair, chest hair glistening with sweat, and Patrick was surprised to see Clara's head turn along with his own. *Mooning over Emory.* He was doing no such thing.

"Oof," Clara said when the man was safely out of earshot. "I haven't been that attracted to a man since . . ."

"Last night?" Patrick asked before she could finish.

"WHAT?" Clara feigned innocence.

"I saw you at dinner. Flirting with everyone. You've been absolutely feral since you've arrived."

Clara swatted him with her book before relenting. "And so what if I am? I am a woman in my prime. And weddings are an excellent place to meet men."

Grant mumbled something from beneath his towel.

"Oh look, the parakeet is awake."

Clara reached over and plucked the towel off Grant. "What, sweetheart?"

"Can I get a smoothie?"

"What are you doing under there?" Patrick interjected, not entirely trusting the boy to his own devices. "You're not trying to get one off again, are you?"

Clara spun, horrified. "PATRICK."

"Moles," Patrick explained. "He picks at his moles."

"I'm playing a game."

"Does the game involve picking at your moles?"

"NO," Grant held firm.

"Say 'smoothie' like you used to."

"Stop."

"Thmoothie," Patrick imitated, to his own delight.

"You're making fun of me!" Grant protested before crawling back under his towel.

"I promise you, I'm not. You're both growing up too fast, that's all."

The bartender approached with their Aperol spritzes; the drinks perfectly matched the cushions and umbrellas in color. Patrick carefully placed the cocktails on the little table between them.

"Can we get something blended and nonalcoholic?" Patrick asked, indicating Maisie and the lump under the towel.

"Sì, signore, signorina."

Patrick made a visor with his hands and squinted as the young man returned to the bar. His white polo shirt concealed broad shoulders and his orange shorts had a five-inch inseam max—the perfect length on a man.

"And you have the nerve to call me feral," Clara said.

"You're crazy," Patrick replied, but he could not take his eyes off their bartender.

Maisie turned her head so that Patrick could streak her hair on the side. "My friend Audra Brackett said you shouldn't call people crazy. It's ableist."

"Your friend Audra Brackett is right," Clara said, and raised her eyebrows at Patrick from behind her sunglasses, challenging him to disagree.

Patrick wanted to lecture them both on the difference between hostile enemies and imperfect friends, but he knew when he was outgunned. "Tell Audra Brackett I'll try to do better."

Clara propped her chair into an upright position and layered fresh suntan lotion onto her arms. "I'd like to meet a noble person. Greg shouldn't have all the fun. A noble gentleman, in my case. I could be a, what do you call it? A maharaja."

"A marchesa," Maisie corrected.

"One of those. I'll have time to learn the lingo after we meet. But I deserve a secure retirement."

"Maybe you can Anna Nicole Smith Cousin Geppetto." Patrick ran his fingers through Maisie's hair to squeeze out any excess lemon juice. "Okay, now go lie in the sun and wait for your blended virgin beverage. But not near me because you smell like furniture polish."

"Can't you just say 'smoothie,' like a normal person?" Maisie griped.

Patrick reached for his spritz. "Calling some people normal suggests that others are abnormal and that's ableist, too." He grinned like the Cheshire cat.

Maisie pursed her lips and glared at her uncle until he gave her a little nudge and she returned to her chair on the far side of Grant.

Palmina stood, blocking his water view. She stretched, arching her back and launching her surprisingly ample breasts toward the sun. She waved at Maisie, who was fanning her damp hair across the back of her lounger. She then turned to her merry band of androids and muttered something in garbled Italian, which Patrick couldn't quite make out, save for the word madre—*mother*. Of course he gave it the worst possible translation: *It's good that after tomorrow this girl will have a mother*. And Maisie thought she was a better ally in this matter?

"Look at her," Patrick scowled. "Preening like Gina Lollobrigida."

Clara followed Patrick's gaze. "Do you know she ran for parliament?" she asked, reapplying sunscreen to her legs.

Patrick looked down over his sunglasses and mouthed, *Palmina?* in shock.

"No. Gina Lollobrigida. And she ran again for the Italian senate at the age of ninety-five."

Patrick stared blankly, unsure what that had to do with the price of cannoli.

"You say very dismissive things about women. That's all."

"I do not!" Patrick kicked at the towel underneath him, in part to straighten it, in part tantrum. It felt like everyone was coming for him today. "I just said it because it's a funny name." Patrick repeated the name to be certain. *"Gina Lollobrigida*. Come on!"

Clara stirred her drink with the straw. "Don't worry. It's not just you. There's a casual misogyny among gay men, I've discovered."

"Oh, *you've* discovered. Suddenly you're Nellie Bly?"

"There you go again!" Clara set down the drink and dropped her tube of sunscreen into her bag. "That's why you don't like Palmina. You think having female friends is beneath you."

"I have female friends!" Patrick tried his best to think of them in this moment, but his mind drew a blank.

"And don't say Sara," Clara said in a hushed tone, as not to draw the children's attention. "She doesn't count."

"Cassie!" Patrick blurted triumphantly. "I have Cassie."

"She works for you!"

"That doesn't mean we aren't friends."

Clara shook her head. "All I'm saying is I know you think you're funny, but sometimes women are more than punch lines—they're people of great substance."

Patrick rolled his eyes. "Oh-kay, Pot."

Clara adjusted her sunglasses on her face, then leaned back in her chair, exasperated. "What's that supposed to mean?"

Patrick did his best to imitate his sister's voice. "I'm going to go have brunch with my gays."

Grant popped his head out from under his towel and said, "Guncle Rule number one: Brunch is awesome."

Patrick stifled a laugh and placed his left index finger on his nose and pointed to Grant with his right. He loved a good callback, and that one went all the way back to when their relationship began.

"Is that supposed to be me?" Clara brushed the hair from her face. The colorist Patrick sent her to was doing wonders; his rates were higher than the cost of a few lemons, but to cover gray you needed more magic than a whole lemon tree could conjure.

"It's literally a direct quote. Gay people are people, not things, and they certainly aren't *yours*." Clara had a solid point—there was, at times, a casual misogyny among gay men—and Patrick could have very well thanked her for addressing it and moved on. But he and Clara had been getting on so well of late, he almost missed the times when they would spar; they'd had, after all, a lifetime of practice.

Clara stared at him for a moment and then laughed.

"What's so funny?"

"I was almost going to say that I missed this." She waved her finger between the two of them so that it was clear she was referencing their old dynamic.

"Speaking of missing. Have you seen the kids?"

Clara motioned to the two seats next to them. Maisie and Grant were right there.

"Not those kids. Darren's kids. Your kids." Clara was stepmother to two grown boys that belonged to her ex. She'd remained close with them, even as her marriage to their father fell apart.

"They're coming to stay with me for a week when we get back." She looked at Patrick, genuinely touched that he'd asked. "They're both so busy with their own lives now. College and everything. Both have internships this summer. I miss them." Clara went back to work rubbing sunscreen on her legs, which still had white streaks. "I need a man to do this for me." She looked up and down the short beach for one she could enlist, but the few men who dotted the landscape were either too young, in a "You're trying to seduce me, Mrs. Robinson" kind of way, or too occupied with women far younger than Clara. Not spying a suitable option, she glanced back toward the bar, where two smoothies were being placed on a tray. "Maybe the bartender could help me."

"Back off," Patrick hissed, forcefully enough that he surprised himself, and they laughed.

Patrick reclined again in his chair and closed his eyes. It was so much easier to attend to the kids with a partner. With Clara there he felt free to relax and trust that someone would pick up the slack. He could let his guard down if they walked toward the water or went to talk to other kids, and he suddenly had great sympathy for his brother, Greg. Yes she was beautiful and yes she was wealthy, but could this also be part of Livia's appeal? Having someone around that allowed Greg the luxury of exhaling, to not have to be on guard *all* the time? "Do you think we've done enough for Greg these past five years?" They'd done a lot for the kids, and maybe that was the same thing. But Patrick was now curious if perhaps it wasn't.

"I think we have," Clara replied. And then she wondered, "Should we have done more?"

Patrick was too focused on Palmina to answer. He watched from behind his sunglasses as she and her friends handed a stack of fashion magazines back and forth.

"Remember how you used to steal my fashion magazines?" Clara reminisced. "I'll bet you and she could be good friends."

People like Clara assumed lesbians and gay men were natural allies, and while they were, on some things—for instance, their basic human rights—they also had very little in common. Gay men were gay, but they were still men, and all men worshipped at the altar of masculinity. It's just that straight men almost always wanted to be it, whereas gay men were equally happy underneath or on top of it. Gay men and straight women shared an *attraction* to men, and in that they had a mutual interest. But lesbians weren't men, and they didn't *need* men, and thus were the rare demographic Patrick couldn't readily charm. He'd met his match in lesbians. Especially this Palmina.

"You just don't like that the kids are enchanted with her the way they used to be enchanted with you," Clara charged.

"*Used* to be," Patrick sneered. Then he dragged Grant down to the floating pool docked in the lake and they disported in the water like dolphins until the kids' smoothies arrived, just to prove that was not true.

FOURTEEN

Patrick had barely closed the door to his room when a wave of complete exhaustion overtook him. He fell face down on his bed with such force that one of his espadrilles flew into a corner. The bed linens were soft and absorbed his breath, even though his nose was squished to one side. He wondered how long he could stay like this. The kids were with their father, his next commitment wasn't for another few hours. He could lay here, face buried in bedding, drift in and out of consciousness, and still have time for a hot shower to steam some of the creases from his face. He reached for a bottle of Acqua Panna that housekeeping left for him by the bedside, thinking hydration would be smart before his snooze. He grazed the glass bottle with his fingertips and tipped it toward him until he managed a solid grip around its neck, then lifted his head the best he could and tossed the bottle back with a little too much enthusiasm. The water, which was carbonated, came exploding out of his nose. "Isn't anything here flat?" he moaned to himself as he wiped water from his face with the back of his hand. The duvet was now wet and he did his best to brush the excess water beads onto the floor. He then rolled over onto his back and hung his head off the edge of the bed, and the mountains across the lake taunted him. *No, nothing here was flat.* Italy bubbled with life.

He had just dozed into that type of afternoon sleep, the kind that was so disorienting after a day in the sun that you woke up not know-ing if it was day or night, when his cell phone rang, startling him into a panic. He fumbled for the phone, which he found underneath him; that was surprising for some reason—he was usually like the princess and the pea in that regard, needing his mattress just right. Certain it was one of the kids calling to pester him about his waning dedication to their cause, he answered, "What time is it?" as if he might have been asleep for hours.

"Ciao," a woman replied, her voice cheery and vaguely familiar. Patrick looked at the ceiling, which was adorned with molding and an ornate ceiling medallion. He rubbed his eyes, not quite able to place where he was.

"Ciao," Patrick repeated flatly. "What time is it?"

"Where you are?" the woman asked. "I'm not sure." And Patrick remembered he was in Lake Como, an unusual place for him to be.

"What time is it where you are, then?" he asked.

There was a pause as the woman checked. "It's a little after six in the morning."

Patrick sat upright in bed, wondering if he'd slept through the night. Greg would be mad, as would the kids, as he'd have one less day to stop the wedding. But the sun wasn't where it was supposed to be at six in the morning, and there was too much activity on the lake. "*Cassie?*" he asked with some hesitation.

"Yes, who did you think it was?"

Patrick didn't really know—the front desk? Livia?—someone who had a legitimate reason to say, "Ciao." "You're getting an early start," he observed, assuming this was a work call. He hoped she wasn't phoning him just to gab, as he had no gab left in him. He put the phone on speaker and rolled over onto his back.

"You're nine hours ahead." What she said next was swallowed by static.

"Time zones are overwhelming."

"The earth is hurtling through space at one hundred and sixty thousand miles per hour, but sure—time zones are what's overwhelming."

Growing bored of this call as it was currently unfolding, Patrick derailed it by asking, "Are you seeing anyone?"

"Am I . . . ?" Cassie began with a sort of stunned bemusement. She struggled to answer before observing, "We never talk about me."

It was true. The client-agent relationship was weighted in one direction. Cassie knew everything about Patrick, his taste in material, his desires, his moods, his successes . . . his *failures*. Even his income flowed through her office. Conversely, Patrick knew very little about his agent. He thought of her like a messenger on horseback, riding into his remote castle every so often with news from the outside world. All anyone in the castle wanted to know was if the kingdom seemed prosperous or in danger of collapsing, if forces were gathering that threatened them or if they could continue their way of life. No one ever cared about the messenger's journey or if they had hopes or dreams of their own—or if they even wanted to be a messenger at all. "Yes, but we're friends, right?" Patrick was still haunted by his conversation with Clara; he had to have *some* female friends.

"I just started seeing someone, in fact," Cassie announced with a burst of pride. "And Patrick, I'm so touched! I'm thrilled you think of us as fri—"

"A woman?" Patrick interrupted, bracing himself for the answer. The last thing he needed was another lesbian upending his life—he was in danger of being outnumbered. "You said some*one*."

"It's a common turn of phrase."

"I'm just wondering why you didn't say 'a guy.'"

"Is that a qualification for friendship?" Cassie asked, hoping friendship wouldn't be easily revoked. "Yes, a guy. As it so happens he's an up-and-coming director."

Patrick groaned. "Please tell me you're not dating a client."

There was a beep through the phone, as if she had pressed a button in annoyance, a sort of electronic *Bite your tongue*. "Jealous?" she asked. Cassie had grown so much in five years and of course he wanted her to be her authentic self, but selfishly he was relieved he had only one lesbian to currently contend with. "For your information, I don't represent directors," she continued. "My actor clients are needy enough. Why the sudden interest in my dating life?"

It was a good question. In the back of his mind he wondered if he shouldn't have played more of a hand in finding Greg a second wife since he'd done so well with his first. Straight men, after all, can be kind of hapless in that regard. Perhaps Cassie and Greg might be well suited. They had been introduced. They got along. And the kids seemed to adore her; at least they did that summer in Palm Springs and the few times they'd interacted since. Like with Clara, he'd assisted in finding Cassie a look that worked best with her natural features and Cassie was an absolute catch (although it had as much to do with the confidence she exuded, and despite Patrick's pride in her makeover, confidence was something that came from within). But when Patrick had introduced Greg to his best friend, his own relationship with Sara suffered. Would he want to share Cassie the way he had once had to share Sara? No was the obvious answer; Patrick didn't like to share much of anything, let alone his one female friend. But there was also very little he wouldn't do or at least try for the kids. "No reason, I was just wondering if you might like to date Greg."

This time there was no pause from her end, not even from the great communicative distance. "Greg, your *brother* Greg?!"

"What's wrong with Greg?" Patrick asked, as if she were objecting to his personality or his appearance.

"Aren't you, I don't know . . . AT HIS WEDDING?"

Patrick rolled over onto his side and came face-to-face with a wall paneled with beveled mirrors reflecting the clay-colored room and lush velvet curtains behind him. From this angle he felt like he was in a guest room at Versailles, and in that moment he wished for a tower of French macarons that he could snack on like Marie Antoinette.

"Patrick, what are you trying to tell me?" Cassie asked with obvious disappointment, and in his agent he could momentarily hear his mother. Patrick wasn't sure what he was plotting—not specifically one of those dramatic "speak now or forever hold your peace" kind of moments, but it was good to keep his options open in a situation like this.

"Tell you?" he asked, sensing it was the right time to change the subject. "You're the one who called me."

Cassie snapped back to attention. "Oh, right. I wanted to know when you were coming back to New York."

She had another offer of work. It should be every actor's dream that the phones were ringing, but her presence in his ear was adding unneeded pressure in a moment when he was already feeling overwhelmed. "Cassie."

"It's not a sequel! I swear. But where do you land on revivals?"

"I told you, I need a break."

"You're not ready to commit to film or TV or anything remotely full-time. I get it. But I thought you might be open to having some fun."

Patrick's ears pricked up at the word *fun* and he dropped his protest long enough to allow Cassie time to explain. *Grease* was the word, and she said it with groove and with meaning. The current Broadway revival was six months into its run and they were looking to goose sagging ticket sales by stunt casting the adult roles. Elizabeth Banks as Miss Lynch, Darren Criss as Teen Angel. That sort of thing. Cassie said they were negotiating a deal for Vanessa Hudgens to play Cha Cha, even though Cha Cha was not an adult and Vanessa very much was.

"Cassie, god help you if this call ends with an offer for me to play Eugene."

"Patrick, please," she replied in a way that sounded like she was smirking—either she knew better, or she thought it ridiculous that he, who was no beauty school dropout, imagined a world where he could convincingly go back to high school. "I wouldn't do that to a friend."

"Well, what is it, then?"

"They're offering you Vince Fontaine."

Patrick hung his head off the edge of the bed like a teenager and studied himself upside down in the mirror as blood ran to his head. He looked good, but not great. He had a bit of a tan from his summer travels and he flashed back to something he once told Clara: if you can't tone it, tan it—a little color masked any number of sins. Hanging upside down helped counteract gravity, and helped him look rested and fresh. But he doubted they'd let him play the role hanging from a trapeze, unless this was some sort of production from Cirque du Soleil. "Which one is Vince Fontaine?"

"He's the slick, fast-talking DJ who hosts the big high school dance."

Patrick nodded as he remembered, which was a strange gesture from this angle. "Lecherous type? Hit on Marty?" He found that amusing; only on Broadway were gay men so routinely offered straight roles. He then listened to the rustling of pages, like Cassie was flipping through the casting breakdowns to find which of the Pink Ladies Vince tried to seduce.

"I believe so, yes."

"I don't sing. Do they know that? I can't be expected to sing." Patrick said this despite having very recently performed a half-dozen numbers from *The Sound of Music*, shrieking through the streets of Austria; Austria didn't have New York critics.

"You don't have to sing. You just have to teach the kids the hand jive."

He could do that, Patrick thought. The hand jive was what, one dance? It was easier than Maria had it, trying to teach kids rudimentary singing, the fundamentals of all songs. "Can I think about it?"

"Of course. Just let me know as soon as the wedding is over. And I mean over, not off. Don't meddle where your innate Patrick-ness is not welcome."

Not welcome? He was an invited guest!

"The bride's father is a bulldog of a man with a wrinkled pocket between his eyes. I bet I could stuff a whole ravioli in the folds of his skin."

Cassie's reply was quick. "I'm begging you not to."

Patrick laughed. She was in charge of his image, so she worried about these things—an agent through and through. When he ended their call he stood up and stretched and reached for the bottle of Acqua Panna again, stubbing his toe on a period chair. He shrieked and cursed, but to his credit he held on to the bottle. Damn Livia's family for taking all the larger rooms. He imagined Palmina and her equerries luxuriating in one of the most spacious suites. He was quite certain they had plenty of room to swing cats without tripping over the chairs. He took a swig of warm Acqua Panna and his throat tickled as it went down. His kingdom for some flat water and a few cubes of ice.

Grease, Patrick thought as he sat on the edge of the bed. The idea of Broadway intrigued him and his mind started to race. His thoughts turned to Sara and their summer at the beach pretending to be Danny and Sandy. It could be fun, and a way to keep his feet wet.

Sleep was now out of the question, so Patrick entered his tiny bathroom to run the shower. At least that water was flat.

FIFTEEN

Palmina was holding hands with Maisie and Grant, a sight that made Patrick shiver as he descended the hotel's grand staircase into the lobby. He studied his rival as she stared out the windows; she looked much like any number of chic young mothers he'd see in New York waiting to usher their children across the street into a dance class. She wore coveralls like a mechanic might (albeit unbuttoned nearly to her navel), but instead of seeming like she'd put in a hard shift at the auto shop, she looked like she could throw a greasy rag over her shoulder and walk the runways of Paris. Despite being remarkably put together, Palmina also looked naked without both her entourage and enormous earrings. There was a listlessness to her demeanor, but unlike Patrick's ennui, hers was intimidating rather than pathetic. Patrick approached with caution.

"Where are the rest of the Spice Girls?" he asked. Maisie turned red when she heard her uncle's voice, like she had been caught cheating with her new launt. She quickly retracted her hand, but Grant kept his hand in Palmina's, undaunted.

When Palmina turned toward Patrick she gave him the full up and down; to his relief she seemed to approve of the ensemble he was wearing. "Who?"

"You know, Ginger and Scary and Posh."

A curious flash of recognition. "Oh, yes. Those girls. They do the spice." Patrick didn't know if Palmina was being dismissive or if something were lost in translation; either way he was suddenly very aware that there was a gay generation between them. He once took a Soul-Cycle class in New York and was on a bicycle directly behind Victoria Beckham. Watching her husband one bicycle over motivated him through the workout, specifically during sprints, when David would rise out of his seat and slowly lower himself back down again. If he ever crossed paths with the Beckhams again, Patrick would be tempted to affect his best (or worst) Italian accent to tell Victoria, *You do the spice.* "Bruna, Carla, and Zita go to the nightclub to dance." Patrick knew no self-respecting European socialite who went to a nightclub in the late afternoon; she was either lying or her friends were settling in for a long disco nap.

"You're coming to the bachelorette party, GUP?" Maisie asked, uncertain as to why he was there.

"Livia invited me," Patrick said, almost like it were a question; even he thought it was not her brightest idea.

"My sister," Palmina sighed in agreement. "She spends too much time overseas."

Modern bachelorette parties were more of an American tradition than European, and it was clear that Palmina had a distaste for the very idea. Patrick wasn't a huge fan, either; such parties had a way of invading gay spaces and wreaking havoc on homosexuals just wanting to dance, but if a male stripper was involved there might be *something* to make his attending worthwhile. Of course, that would hold zero appeal to Palmina, but since Maisie had been invited he imagined this was to be a more flaccid affair.

"Did you talk to Dad?" Maisie whispered.

He took Maisie's hand, in part to keep her from reaching for

Palmina's again. "I talked to Cassie," he offered, as if that might tickle her fancy.

Maisie's eyes brightened. "Cassie's here?"

Her reaction made Patrick wonder again about Cassie for Greg. "On the phone. She asked if I wanted to star in *Grease* on Broadway."

"Isn't *Grease* about children?" Palmina asked skeptically. In his head, *They do the spice* morphed into *They do the grease.*

"It's about teenagers," he said defensively, lest she think he was doing some tacky children's revue. But Patrick was almost impressed; if Italian lesbians could discuss American musicals, there just might be a friendship to be had.

"But you are not a teenager. Except, like all men, emotionally." She then turned to Grant and added, "Not you." The boy grinned his agreement.

Patrick didn't have it in him to defend all men. "I was offered the role of Vince Fontaine, an adult who teaches the hand jive at the big high school dance." Patrick tried to demonstrate, which, to the best of his recollection, began with slapping his knees, then clapping his hands. He fudged a few other moves before bumping his fists together and pointing his thumbs left and then right.

Palmina looked at him like he was having a stroke. "And this is the star?"

Patrick blushed. "Perhaps 'star' is too strong a word."

"My friend went to see that show," Maisie shared. "She said it was fun and she knew some of the songs."

"Of course she knew some of the . . . It's *Grease*. Never mind. It's been running for a while, so I would be a replacement."

"What happened to the Vance Coltrane they had?" Palmina asked with as little interest as she could muster.

"Vince Fontaine. He lost both his thumbs in a lawn mowing accident and can't do the— *Who cares?* Ticket sales were sluggish, so they're offering the part to a bigger name, specifically me."

Grant interrupted by tugging on Palmina's sleeve. "Palmina, what's your love language?"

"U-Haul," Patrick blurted before he could stop himself. All three of them stared at him, stumped. "What do lesbians bring on a second date? *A U-Haul.*" More stares. "Oh, come on. It's meant to be funny!" Love languages were his lessons to teach, he didn't see the need for a guest lecturer.

"What is this language you speak of?" Palmina asked Grant.

"The language you use to tell people you love them," Grant replied. "GUP's been teaching us."

Palmina locked eyes with Patrick. "What do gay men bring on a second date?"

"Yes, I know," Patrick dismissed, having heard all the old jokes. "What second date?"

Palmina crouched between both kids and pulled them in close to her side. "Thievery is my love language," she said. "I take what I love and I love what I take. And sometimes I take hearts." Patrick swallowed the lump in his throat; he hated that she was so cool.

As if to rescue him, Clara and Livia descended the staircase as a tight twosome, Clara looking particularly resplendent in a dress that definitely was not hers. Livia clocked their stares, then took Clara's hand and raised it in the air so that Clara could do a little ballerina twirl on the bottom step. Patrick thought the move was very unlike his sister, but she did it with startling conviction as the dress fanned out over her knees. "It's a loaner from Livia," she confessed. "I had nothing to wear to Milan."

"You look beautiful, Aunt Clara," Maisie stated.

"Doesn't she?" Livia agreed with great pride, as if she and Clara had been best friends for years. "It's nice to finally have a sister to share clothes." Palmina grunted and Clara turned red, not wanting to come between actual sisters.

"Please," Palmina said. "I wouldn't be caught dead in my sister's bedraggled old rags."

I'm sorry, Clara mouthed to no one in particular, but Patrick took pleasure in his rival's annoyance and he made note to exploit that later.

Livia ran her fingers through Grant's hair. "Your father is waiting for you in our room. He has a bachelor's evening planned." Grant pumped his fist and tore up the stairs with excitement. *Some bachelor party,* Patrick thought. *One sober guest, one underage.*

"Come on, girls," Clara encouraged. "Let's get drunk."

Patrick hung his head in defeat as they exited the lobby. Grant asking Palmina about love languages? Maisie thinking someone beautiful in a dress? *Clara wanting to get drunk?* This was going to be a long night, indeed.

Livia, Clara, Palmina, Maisie, and Patrick piled into the back of the hotel's stretch limousine, which Livia had commandeered for the forty-minute drive to Milan, where they had appointments with personal shoppers at Prada. Patrick had been told to make himself useful by popping the first bottle of prosecco, and he suddenly feared he was not so much a guest at this party as working it. *Was he expected to be the stripper, too?* He took several deep breaths and popped the cork while swallowing his complaints and poured each of the women a glass. Palmina glanced in Maisie's direction; Maisie looked to Patrick expectantly.

"She's underage," Patrick said firmly.

Palmina threw her head back, and then forward again in disgust until the hair piled on her head flopped elegantly over her forehead. "Once again, you Americans are uptight about age."

Patrick shoved the open bottle in an ice bucket. "I'm not uptight. It's the United States Congress, the Institute of Health, and a little something called the National Minimum Drinking Age Act of 1984 that are uptight about these things."

Palmina gestured at the Italian countryside as it whizzed by. "None of which has jurisdiction here."

Patrick turned to Clara for backup, but half her glass was already missing and she was on the verge of a giggling fit. As a guardian she was apparently useless. "Livia?" he asked, deferring to her new role as his niece's stepmother, even if that risked incurring Maisie's wrath.

Livia punted. "I think it's up to Maisie with her beautiful new highlights."

Maisie betrayed her own feelings for Livia and beamed as all three women fussed over her hair. And in the low sun that shone sideways through the limo's windows, her hair did look lighter, but the attention was all a bit too much.

"Half a glass to toast with," Patrick relented, reaching for the bottle. "But don't tell your father."

"Isn't that the point of a hen party?" Livia asked. "There will be lots of things tonight we won't tell your father." The four of them cackled, including Maisie, and Patrick was shocked to see her not only cutting Livia slack, but so completely aligning herself with this cadre of women.

Patrick poured a glass for himself last and raised it. "To Livia and Greg on the most romantic of occasions. Cheers." Maisie eyed him suspiciously; she may be allowed to enjoy herself in Livia's presence apart from her father, but Patrick was not granted permission to bless any union with her father.

"Hear hear," Clara said, and everyone enjoyed a sip. Maisie tasted her drink cautiously with good reason, the disappointed look on her face said it all; she didn't see the appeal.

"You and champagne are friends all of a sudden?" Patrick asked Clara. He had never known her to be one much to drink.

"It's prosecco, first of all. And ever since menopause I don't get migraines!"

The women cheered so loudly Patrick flinched, and they toasted his sister as if she were a soldier returning from war. Clara had faced menopause with a grim and unspoken resolve; he hoped not to be drawn into an evening of conversation about it now that it was behind her.

When their celebration died down, Palmina raised her glass a third time. "And to Patrick, who is going to Broadway."

Clara brushed the hair from her face and her eyes sparkled with genuine excitement. "Is that true, Patrick?"

Now Patrick was blushing, uncomfortable for once as the center of attention, but touched that Palmina made such an overture. "It's true. I've been asked to join the cast of *Grease*," he said sheepishly. "It's a glorified cameo, you know, for fun. And to help with ticket sales."

Palmina tapped him condescendingly on his knee. "Now is not the time for modest. He's going to give the teenagers hand jobs!"

Clara, mid-sip of prosecco, executed a classic spit take; fortunately most of the fine mist went in the direction of the open window, only some of it blowing back on Patrick. Horrified, she found a napkin to wipe down the front of her borrowed dress as she apologized profusely to Livia.

"Hand jive," Patrick clarified. *Jesus Christ.* "I'm going to give them, *teach* them, the hand *jive*. It's a dance from the nineteen fif— You know what? It's Livia's night. We can talk about this another time."

He glared at Palmina as the women broke down in laughter, making crude gestures he hoped went over Maisie's head.

"Mi scusi," Palmina said, begging his pardon. "I speak five languages, but my English? Not so good." She then held her prosecco up to the window to admire the bubbles.

"Your English is *fine*," Patrick replied sourly. Not five minutes earlier she'd said *jurisdiction*. There was nothing wrong with her ability to speak.

"I need another drink!" Clara roared.

"I need a general anesthetic," Patrick replied. He took a sip of his drink and then turned to Maisie and repeated, "Her English is fine," before refilling everyone's glass.

As they approached the city, Livia explained that Milan was the fashion capital of Italy, if not the world, and had been since the 1960s when *Vogue Italia* chose it as the location for their headquarters. The region already had a rich history of producing its own textiles, but after *Vogue* landed, brands such as Dolce & Gabbana, Armani, Moschino, Valentino, and Versace all coalesced to make Milan their home, too. The city was an amalgamation of past and present, set against the breathtaking natural backdrop of the Italian Alps. The third largest church in the world, the stunning Duomo di Milano, shared the skyline with modern skyscrapers making the whole city a contrast, and yet seamlessly, perfectly, stylishly itself. Much like fashion. Hard lines and thick textiles merged to create the most feminine beauty, while soft fabrics draped in goddess-like ways could make a woman feel like the most powerful warrior.

After entering the city, their limo headed to the Quadrilatero d'Oro, the Golden Quad, four streets that housed the highest-end boutiques, including the original Prada store, which was opened in 1913 by Mario Prada.

Clara rolled down her window and stuck her head through the opening like a dog. "Is this it? Are we here?" Patrick pulled her back inside the car before she could smack her head on a lamppost. Maisie absorbed their surroundings with nervous apprehension. Patrick understood immediately. It was one thing to enjoy being part of the girls; it would be quite another if she were expected to be *girly*—try on dresses and model them for two aunts and a stepmother, who would most certainly fuss. He took Maisie's hand and squeezed it. Everything would be okay.

"Welcome to Milano," Livia said.

"Ooh," Clara exclaimed, her head light from champagne. "Like the cookie!" Patrick slumped in his seat; tonight's experience was nothing like Pepperidge Farm. Clara straightened her dress, sat up, and announced to the group, "I would like to meet a man."

"You *what*?" Patrick asked, as if everyone hadn't heard perfectly well what she'd said. Were they talking about this openly now?

"A man," Clara repeated, drawing out *man* like it had seven *a*'s. "You know, an adult male human? Perhaps you're familiar." She turned to Livia and Palmina. "Do you know any men you could introduce me to? Men like you?"

"Like us?" Livia protested; Palmina simply snickered.

"She means rich," Patrick explained, and Clara swatted him on the knee.

"I mean *Italian*. Someone like what's-his-name."

Patrick scoffed. They *were* in Italy. "That narrows it down."

"He was in *La Dolce Vita*."

"Marcello Mastroianni," Palmina said, although she looked too bored to have been listening.

"Marcello Mastro— What *she* said."

"Marcello Mastroianni is dead," Palmina said coolly.

Clara remained undeterred. "Someone alive, then. Someone *like* Marcello." She turned to Livia and beamed hopefully.

"We'll see what we can do," Livia said accommodatingly. "But first we introduce you to Mr. Prada."

Prada was housed inside the prestigious glass-covered Galleria Vittorio Emanuele II, the whole experience was like being inside a dream. The buildings were gold, as was the inlay tile that comprised the streets; above them large glass panes arched to form incredible domes. There was a smell in the air Patrick couldn't quite place, but he wouldn't be surprised if it was money. Old money. And lots and lots of it.

Maisie clung to Patrick's side as they made their way through the arcade, looking at building facades that reminded them both of Paris. She tugged on his arm to pull him down to eye level. "I don't think we're in Kansas anymore." Patrick didn't want to break it to her, but they hadn't been in Kansas for some time.

"America has places like this," he said confidently to bolster his niece. But he couldn't think of a one that was this ostentatious.

Patrick knew rich people did this, shop after hours; Mohamed Al-Fayed gave Princess Diana the run of Harrods at night and Barbra Streisand had a shopping mall built in her basement. Patrick himself sometimes wore clothes that were sent to him through a stylist, allowing him to bypass stores altogether. But something about this experience impressed even him. The power to open the flagship Prada store in Milan after hours? Greg was *way* out of his league.

Clara, Livia, and Palmina strode toward the entrance, shoulders back, looking not unlike the women of *Sex and the City* after Samantha left and Miranda became a lesbian. The doors were flung open for them by two saleswomen, who themselves could have been models. They kissed Livia and Palmina on each cheek in a perfectly European display, even though those weren't *exactly* the cheeks they were kissing. They spoke Italian to the sisters with a lusty fluency and quick introductions were made in English to Clara, Patrick, and Maisie. Before he knew it, the store had swallowed them whole and Patrick felt like Charlie stepping into Wonka's factory.

The saleswomen explained in near-perfect English how the store had prioritized its ancient flavor, leaving things largely untouched. The custom-built mahogany shelves, for instance, were the very same commissioned by Mario Prada himself.

"Ancient? Did she say ancient?" Patrick asked. Palmina turned to him with pity.

"Yes. Are you hard with the hearing? That happens with men who are old."

"My hearing is fine." Patrick just happened to think *ancient* was a funny word choice; how can a country that included the city of Rome, which was founded well before Christ, call something a hundred years old "ancient"? He struggled to imagine what they might call him at half that age. Archaic? Antiquated? Timeworn?

Mario's little shop quickly became a favorite of the Italian aristocracy, and the more-refined members of Europe's upper crust. In fact, Prada became an official supplier to the Italian royal household and in turn it made the House of Savoy's coat of arms a featured part of its logo. Patrick and his kin kept their hands to their sides; this wasn't exactly J.Crew. But Livia and Palmina touched everything, giving enthusiastic blessings or strained dismissals, as if they were walking through a relative's house.

"Shall we have some fun?" the saleswoman asked.

"Sì. How do you say 'fun' in Italian?" Clara inquired of Livia, wanting very much to be a part of it.

"Il divertimento. Fun. Amusement. Enjoyment. *Pleasure.*"

"Sì. Sì. Sì. Sì," Clara replied to every one of her translations, as each was more enticing than the last.

Patrick jumped, startled at the popping of a cork, and was quickly relieved he was no longer the designated bartender; in the blink of an eye they were each holding fresh flutes of prosecco, except for Maisie, who waved hers away. "I had some in the car," she declined politely.

They gathered and sat in the center of the showroom and soon two racks of clothes appeared, pushed by three shorter women, who were overly tanned and clad in all black with cloth measuring tapes draped around their necks like scarves.

"Oh my god, they have Prada Loompas," Patrick gasped before Clara hit him on his arm with her borrowed clutch.

As the bride-to-be, not to mention the woman with the pull to arrange such an affair, Livia had her pick of the racks. She selected a printed minidress in green, its fabric crinkled and looking like papyrus, as well as something sleeveless and draped that flounced at the hem and a double-breasted chevron coat cut and tailored like menswear with two poofs of Muppet fur sprouting from the elbows.

"I love the shearling detail," Livia raved, and the two saleswomen made soft murmuring sounds like pigeons. Clara exchanged glances with Patrick; she clearly did not hold the shearling in the same high esteem, but wasn't about to out herself as a devotee of T.J. Maxx.

"What's shearling?" Maisie whispered.

"I thought it meant sheep," Clara whispered back.

Patrick for his part held his index finger in front of his lips and gave a consternated look like Tim Gunn about to tell a Parsons student to "edit themselves thoughtfully."

"Palmina," the saleswoman urged, once Livia had made her choices. Palmina begged Clara to go next, but Clara wouldn't hear of it, so Palmina stepped up to the rack and frowned at item after item before pulling a single selection, a quilted nylon ski suit in black. "How did that get there?" the saleswoman asked, befuddled. She looked desperately for a Prada Loompa, but none was to be found. She stepped forward to relieve Palmina of the piece, as if some grave mistake had been made, but Palmina countered by clutching it close to her chest.

"It's chic," she exclaimed, and Maisie stood up to admire its careful quilting and seams. Patrick could see a world opening for her, not all fashion had to be feminine, dresses and florals and the like; here was Palmina proudly plucking the black pantsuit off the rack, something the others would overlook as too manly or too impractical or impossible to pair with an occasion or shoe, other than a day at a chalet with Swiss boots. Patrick already resented Palmina for being such a perfect example for Maisie in a way he never could be himself and because he knew she would look so damn cool wearing this garment, like she was on her way to knock over a high-end casino in Monaco.

Clara went next and made careful study of everything on both racks, like a contestant on *Let's Make a Deal*, frightened a trapdoor might open in the floor if she picked the wrong thing. (Patrick gleefully imagined what Prada dungeon might be hiding under the glorious black-and-white checkerboard floors.) She settled on a dress in printed poplin with ties at the waist and a strap around the neck like an apron. Patrick knew she wanted to be bolder but didn't dare, fearing she'd make a fool of herself due to age or income bracket or gauche New England–ness in old Europe. Patrick grew frustrated with her timidity and pulled a second garment from the rack. Clara clearly admired it, but needed encouragement. "I don't know. Are you sure?"

"You're trying it on, not marrying it. Go!" he encouraged, and she scurried off after the sisters. Patrick had worn plenty of things in his life that elicited comments like "I wish I could wear such a thing." He never understood that reaction; you simply put your legs in a pair of pants one fabric tube at a time. Most everyone had the same ability. It wasn't until after hearing a comment like that the ninth or tenth time that he began to doubt it was a compliment.

"Signorina?" one of the saleswomen asked.

Patrick nudged Maisie. "That's you."

"I'd just like to watch," Maisie said. "For now." She hadn't quite worked up the nerve to get up close and personal with any of the clothes, but thought enough of the opportunity to leave her options open. A burst of chatter from the dressing rooms sent the saleswomen scurrying in that direction.

Patrick whispered to Maisie. "This is fun and all, but don't become like this. A fashionista. You could still do great things."

"Like what?" Maisie asked, halfway between curious and horrified.

"I don't know. Be one of those Swedish teens who solves global warming."

"I'm not Swedish," Maisie admitted as if fessing up, almost disappointed to find such a stumbling block to greatness.

"Doesn't matter. There are no limits to what you can do." Patrick raised his champagne flute, finally a sentiment worth celebrating. But even he had to admit the evening was impressive. Livia's life was much to his liking.

The women emerged to put on a show. Livia looked, well, like Livia—perfectly at home in everything she wore. But that didn't mean that she didn't love the attention, and she happily strutted and twirled with each supportive *ooh*. Clara stood an inch or two taller in her poplin dress, the difference in her demeanor remarkable; Patrick had to glance to see if she wasn't wearing different shoes. Whether it was the champagne or the garment that lowered Clara's guard, or the way the color of the fabric accentuated her skin tone, Patrick wished his sister could see how beautiful she was when she let all her tensions go. And finally, Palmina in her nylon ski suit, shirtless underneath, the straps and buckles perfectly covering the most objectionable part of her breasts (but not much else), looking every bit the ringleader of a coterie of high-fashion thieves. Maisie brightened and clapped. Even though Patrick had just told her she could do and be anything, true possibility was unlocked only once she recognized that it was possible for a woman to be that goddamn hot while wearing ridiculous ski pants.

Patrick summoned his inner Julia Roberts and addressed the saleswomen. "Remember me? Big mistake. Big. Huge."

The saleswomen glanced at each other puzzled. One of them addressed Patrick. "Of course we remember you. You have been sitting right there the entire time. What is the mistake? These women look fabulous."

The other sullenly approached Clara. "Oh, I see." She then fussed with the ties around Clara's waist and tugged on the dress until she was satisfied that it draped on her just right. Clara's relaxed face pinched back to its natural state.

"No, no," Patrick interceded. "I was doing *Pretty Woman*. It's a line from the movie. When no one would help her in Beverly Hills."

"But we are not in Beverly Hills," one of the saleswomen protested. "This is Milano."

"And we are helping you," the other said, just as Clara put her hands defensively on her hips.

"Are you saying we look like hookers?"

"No! Of course not," he reassured his sister, before catching a glimpse of Palmina. "Maybe the very high-class kind, but— NO. No, I absolutely am not."

"Then what *are* you saying?" his sister demanded. Livia and Palmina looked down their noses at Patrick, who couldn't believe the reaction he was getting.

"It's just a funny line!" Patrick couldn't recall the number of times he'd repeated it in his gay life. When he saw a bad movie with Emory. When a friend dated someone who turned out to be a mess. When someone ordered whatever Patrick deemed to be the wrong thing at brunch. *Big mistake. Big. Huge.* It was Julia Roberts at her most iconic.

"What is funny about it?" Palmina asked innocently, like she was game to laugh if only she could understand.

Patrick should have seen she was laying bait for a trap, but he was desperate to climb out of this hole and didn't yet realize he was digging it deeper. "She says it to the snooty saleswomen on Rodeo Drive who refused to help her at the top of the film. And here we are in an even *fancier* boutique. It just, seemed like the perf—"

"But these women are not snooty," Palmina interrupted. "They welcomed us into their store."

"They gave us sparkling wine," Livia added.

Patrick turned to Maisie for backup. He had shown her *Pretty Woman* just last year when they stumbled upon it on Hulu. "Not me," Maisie clarified in regards to the champagne. "But again, I had some in the car." She was still so desperate to come off as not-a-kid.

"I think something's getting lost in translation," Patrick said. "I will sit here and keep my mouth shut."

"Now there's an ideal man," Clara said to everyone's delight. "Introduce me to one like *that*."

"Perhaps I'm marrying the wrong brother," Livia crowed, and everyone laughed, and Patrick had to accept that he was going to spend the rest of this hen party as the one getting pecked. Maisie put her hand on her uncle's leg and patted it gently.

Livia extended her hand for Maisie's and Maisie accepted it with obvious trepidation. "Come. I have something special waiting for you." Maisie's knees nearly buckled as she stood, but she followed Livia toward the dressing rooms, having just enough time to look back at her uncle for help. Patrick gave her an encouraging nod, as if to say, *Play along.* He knew no good could come from his interceding, at this point it would only make things harder on her.

"Wait until you see this," Clara said once she and Patrick were out of Maisie's earshot. She peeked at the dressing rooms, pleased to be part of some grand plan. But Patrick was still stewing and refused to follow her gaze.

"You *took* me to see *Pretty Woman*. I was like fourteen. You took me to see it *three* times. We told Mom we were seeing *Driving Miss Daisy.*"

"Now *there's* a good movie," Clara said. "Drive me to the Piggly Wiggly!"

"You used to be cool," Patrick pouted.

Clara spun around, looked down at her dress, delighted anew to find herself in it, and announced, "And now I am again."

From down the hall, a gasp from Livia, to which Maisie could be heard mounting her usual protest, but she was no match for a determined stepmother-to-be. After a beat or two they both emerged from the dressing room.

Patrick saw two Maisies. One, an awkward girl, one arm over the other, her hands clasped down near her knees as if she were trying to collapse in on herself with a gravitational field so intense that no light or matter could escape, hoping to completely disappear. The other a shining young woman, intrigued by possibility and reinvention. She longed for confidence, yet stood like Bambi, unsure of how to plant her feet squarely, or take her very first steps.

"Take your hands away." Clara swatted at Maisie's arms so they could see the garment they were hiding. Slowly, Maisie released her white-knuckle grip and emerged from the cocoon she had spun with her posture.

"Satisfied?" she asked of the others, as if this were torture for her, but then she caught a glimpse of herself in a full-length mirror and

Patrick witnessed happiness creep across her face. It was beautiful to see.

Livia had selected for her a gingham-checked culotte in gray and white and a long-sleeve shirt in matching fabric with a small ruffle that snaked up the front. The shirt was buttoned tightly at her neck, and across her chest was a thin black leather strap that held a small bag by her hip. It was all age appropriate and cutting edge, soft with hard edges, feminine but not girly. In short, Livia had clearly paid attention to exactly who Maisie was, even when Maisie had gone out of her way to hide it.

"I don't know what to do with my hands," Maisie confessed under the heat of everyone's glare.

"That's what pockets are for." Livia motioned for Maisie to find the pockets in her culottes. Maisie did, and stood up even straighter. "Now take a few steps like a model."

Maisie stood her ground. "I don't want to be a model. I want to be one of those Swedish teenagers who solve global warming." She smiled at Patrick and he twinkled in spite of himself.

Palmina stepped forward. "Then do what I do." She grabbed the straps of her ski pants, making two fists. Maisie copied her by wrapping her fingers around the strap of her bag. Palmina placed her hands on Maisie's shoulders in approval. "That way you lead with two fists, ready to fight the . . ." She turned to Livia and Clara for just the right word.

"Patriarchy," Clara said.

"Patriarchy," Palmina agreed.

"But the patriarchy doesn't cause global warming, does it?"

Clara dipped her head. "*Doesn't it?* All those men and their hot air."

The women laughed again, but this time Patrick didn't hear them. He was laser-focused on Palmina, who had kneeled in front of Maisie, buttoning one of her sleeves and popping her collar just so. He saw total trust in Maisie's eyes, happy to be clay in Palmina's hands if Palmina could sculpt her into a miniature version of herself. Patrick grew hot with jealousy, and he fanned his shirt away from his chest. Maisie feared losing her dad; it was the first time Patrick feared losing Maisie.

"What's the matter?" Maisie asked when she saw her uncle fidgeting. "You don't like it?" She turned back to the mirror disappointed. She had just come to appreciate this new version of herself. "You don't like it."

It broke Patrick's heart, her thinking that he didn't. He immediately dropped his jealousy; there were more important feelings at play. "Of course I like it. *It's you.*" He crossed his arms and looked at her with great pride. He just wished her mother were alive to see her.

SIXTEEN

The limo returned Livia and her bachelorettes to the hotel's main entrance just before eleven; her lone bachelor wearily climbed out of the car, his head pounding, an early-onset hangover from both the sparkling wine and having been so unfairly maligned. The women, Maisie included, gabbed and giggled as they made their way up the stairs to the hotel's lobby. Patrick couldn't make out a thing they were saying as he trudged a dozen steps behind them like a pack mule shouldering their enormous—and heavy, he might add—shopping bags. Turns out fashion, true couture, weighed a ton. About two dozen more steps and he could drop the bags and excuse himself for the night and finally shut the world out. Never had a pillow been so insistently calling his name.

As soon as they entered the lobby, Grant leaped out from behind the circular banquette and Patrick screamed in a pitch he was not proud of and dropped two of the bags he was holding.

Greg, too, emerged from the far side of the banquette; they had been perfectly obscured by the opulent flowers positioned on top—an entirely different arrangement than the one that had greeted them when they checked in. He kissed Livia and Maisie hello.

In perfect Grant fashion, he peered through the bags one by one like he was trying to get his best peek on Christmas morning, the sound of rustling tissue like a predator making its way through tall grass.

"Which one of these is for me?" he asked before Maisie shooed him away.

"None of them," she scolded, and then pulled the bags with her items aside to guard them.

"NONE?!" Grant shouted, but his protest went unaddressed.

"Did you have fun?" Greg asked. "I can't wait to see what you bought."

Patrick almost wanted to stick around and watch Cruella de Vil don her Muppet-skin coat just to see his brother's reaction (*I'm about to marry someone who wears that?*), but all he could think about was sleep.

"I hope bringing Patrick wasn't a mistake."

Clara and Palmina looked at each other and in unison said, "Big mistake. Big. Huge." Patrick face-palmed as Greg looked wryly bemused.

"What is he still doing up?" Patrick asked, indicating Grant as he ran tight circles around the lobby like a puppy with late-night zoomies.

"I got jealous of the girls stealing you away. I thought you could join us for our bachelor's evening."

Patrick took out his phone to look at the time. Even by European standards, evening had long given way to night. "It's eleven o'clock."

"A bachelor's nightcap, then," Greg pleaded, and Patrick's heart sank. He looked up the stairs in the direction of his bed. This day was never going to end. "In the hotel bar. Just us boys." Greg's eyebrows were raised so high in concern they practically blended into his hairline; clearly something was on his mind.

"Fine. Just give me ten minutes to recharge. Ladies, it's been . . ."

There was no real way to finish that sentence, so he turned and started to walk up the steps to his room.

The last thing he heard was Greg asking Maisie, "Is your hair lighter than it was this morning?"

◇◇◇◇◇◇◇

They met inside the hotel's main lounge, an ornate room with a fireplace and elegant mahogany bar. Greg and Grant were already seated at a small table near the terrace in masculine club chairs upholstered in distressed leather; the room had an interesting palette given the walls, which were somewhere between gold and mustard. Grant's eyes were half closed like he was focused on something happening clear across the room. It wasn't until Patrick was closer that he could see it was because he was struggling to keep them open. *I know the feeling, kid.*

"Wake up, Grantelope."

"You can't call me that."

"You're asleep, I can call you whatever I want."

"I'm *not* asleep," he protested. "I'm not even tired." But then his eyes closed even further in betrayal.

"The strippers are here!" Patrick feigned excitement to see if he could startle the boy awake.

Instead Grant mumbled, "I don't believe you," then turned his neck so his face was nuzzled away from them into the chair.

"Just us?" Patrick asked. "No Cousin Geppetto?"

"It's a real name, but you're going to make a routine out of it, aren't you?"

"What do you call an old man who's into puppets?"

Greg stared at him blankly.

"A Geppettophile. Get it? I'll save that for my wedding toast."

"I'm begging you. Stop."

Patrick excused himself to the bar, where he glanced at the cocktail menu. "Buonasera, signore," the bartender said. Patrick, still longing for bed, forced a weak smile. The bartender was one of those old-school professionals who wore a waistcoat and tie and kept his arms folded behind his back until he could be of service. He seemed like he kept many secrets. "Is tonight a special occasion?"

Patrick glanced over his shoulder at their table. Greg looked out the window at the lake and Grant's jaw was now completely slack. "Just us bachelors," Patrick replied. "We're kind of a dying breed."

"Very well, sir. Perhaps I could get you bachelors a drink." He steered Patrick toward a cocktail made of mezcal, mango liqueur, lime juice, and a chili infusion. Greg, five years sober, needed an option that was nonalcoholic, so Patrick asked the bartender to improvise something off menu. Across the bar, a table burst into spontaneous laughter, drawing Patrick's eye. That's how his night should have gone; even though it was Livia's party, he had imagined himself the center of attention. Or at the very least, the evening's entertainment. He wasn't about to jump out of anyone's cake, but he could usually hold the attention of women without much effort. Alas, tonight was but one more night in a year that was not going his way. When he turned back to the bartender, he saw him mix seltzer and lemon juice, with something that may have been distilled fig, topping off the drink with frothed egg whites—a rare ingredient, Patrick imagined, as far as stag party concoctions go. But even bachelors not of the confirmed kind could enjoy a drink that was nice and frothy.

"Grazie," Patrick said once the bartender had added his final touches, and Patrick made sure to tip well for his considered efforts. He returned to their table, careful not to spill so much as a drop of the booze he would need to fortify his resolve. "Cheers," he said as he and

Greg raised their glasses, and together they knocked back a few sips. Greg carefully wiped egg whites from his stubble with the back of his hand.

"Oh my god, this is good."

"It should be," Patrick observed. "It has an omelet floating on top." He turned to Grant, who had repositioned himself yet again. "They were out of chocolate milk." But Grant, apparently down for the count, merely replied with an unintelligible mumble and a small trickle of drool.

Greg ran his fingers through his hair until it was a complete mess and exhaled something between a whisper and a groan.

"What's up?" Patrick asked. If he had any hopes of making it to his room before midnight, he had better cut right to the chase.

Greg downed half of his mocktail in a way that reminded Patrick of Grant and his Parisian hot chocolate. *That's for sipping, not gulping!* Greg then looked up at his brother with pleading eyes and asked, "Am I doing the right thing?"

Maisie had been with Patrick all evening, so it's not like she had time to say anything to her father about Livia. Would Grant have taken the lead in sowing the seeds of doubt? Patrick couldn't imagine it—the boy still had to be convinced that birthmarks didn't hurt.

If Patrick was indeed losing Maisie's favor to Palmina, was this the opening he needed to speak up and win her back? "Did the kids say something to you?"

Greg looked at his brother, confused. "Did they say something to *you?*"

Patrick feigned innocence. "So, cold feet, then." He then illuminated his phone to see the date. "The night before the rehearsal dinner. Not to borrow from Mussolini, but the trains are running right on time."

"Clever as you think you are, you can leave the fascists out of it. It's not cold feet," Greg insisted. "At least not in the way you're thinking."

Patrick motioned for Greg to fix his hair by running his hands through his own. He couldn't have a serious conversation with his brother when he resembled Cameron Diaz in *There's Something about Mary*. But his brother's hair wasn't really the problem. Greg looked . . . *defeated*. His mouth open, but his teeth tightly clenched. His arms crossed in a defensive pose, the opposite of the bartender's, to close himself off instead of willingly engage. Even his posture was stooped, like the very ground beneath his chair had a different gravitational pull.

"*Are* the kids having a hard time with this? With my getting remarried?"

Patrick scratched his head. *Here it comes.* "Have you tried asking them? There's one right here we can rouse."

Greg pinched the bridge of his nose. "Grant is picking at himself more than ever and Maisie smells like lemon Pledge for some reason and she's being downright rude to Livia." Patrick wondered if he should interject with how well Maisie did this evening, that she and Livia seemed to have a genuine moment, even if one evening did not a relationship make. "I ask what's going on, I do, but they don't give me straight answers."

"Do they give you gay ones?"

"Patrick, I'm serious. You have a way with this stuff. All this insight. The kids are always saying how you're so wise. Come on. How about you share some of it with me."

Patrick was stunned into momentary silence. "The kids think I'm *wise*?" He always thought he was, but he didn't know this virtue was recognized by others.

Greg rubbed his eyes, disappointed. That was not the takeaway from this conversation.

"I don't really tell them anything, other than give them permission to feel what they're already feeling. A courtesy I extend to you, by the way."

"I don't have time to feel what I'm feeling, I'm getting married in forty-eight hours."

Less than, Patrick thought as he reached for his drink. There was a slight breeze coming from the open doors, but the chili infusion warmed his insides, melting his demeanor just enough. "Look," he began. "You, Maisie, and Grant, you're the last survivors of a lost civilization that was your nuclear family. You had your own traditions, your own language, your own shared memories, your own, I don't know . . . You tell me. Inside jokes. You three are the keepers of your family history, your family culture. All of it." Patrick looked intently at his brother, hoping this was sinking in. "I don't want to speak for them," he continued as he glanced over at Grant to make sure he was still unconscious, "but I think, if you could get them to give you an honest answer, they would tell you that they're afraid of their civilization crumbling further under the weight of advancement. They're both furious little archaeologists trying to unearth it with those teeny brushes as fast as the present is busy burying it under more sand."

Greg didn't really know what to say, so the easiest thing was to deny it. "But I don't want to bury it. And neither does Livia. And I'm certainly not going anywhere."

"Yes you are!" Patrick lowered his voice so as not to wake Grant. "Yes you are. You're assimilating into a new civilization. One with new traditions and cultures and quite literally a whole new language."

As if to prove his point, the rowdy table erupted in cheers of "Salute!" and a woman in a wrap dress and heels sauntered past their table, met their eyes, and said, "Ciao."

As soon as the woman had safely exited the bar, Patrick gesticulated wildly. "Italy, Greg? *Lake Como?* Look at this place. What is this? Who is this for? What are you doing?"

Greg's eyes grew wet; Patrick could tell his brother didn't know what he was doing, not really, not deep down, there was no master plan guiding his every move; he was reacting more than acting. And in that moment he felt sorry for Greg. They sat in their chairs quietly, Patrick swirling a single oversized ice cube around with the last of the liquor in his glass. As much as his bed was calling, he already knew they needed another round. Eventually Greg spoke. "We did a good job with them, didn't we?"

Patrick tried not to laugh as he set his glass on the table. "Oh, *now* it's we?"

"Come on. We've been there for them, we've been understanding, we've been patient, we listen. We don't beat them."

Patrick looked at Grant sleeping so peacefully. "It's not too late to start." Grant was growing so big, and yet still had the ability to tuck in his limbs and look small. The two brothers looked at him with the urge to scoop him up.

"I love Livia," Greg confessed.

Patrick nodded. "That's good, I'm glad you do. You deserve that."

"No, really. I get a sense that you don't think I do. It's understandable. You introduced me to Sara. My first marriage owes itself to you."

Patrick held up his hands defensively; he didn't deserve that much credit.

"I've only been in love twice in my life. This isn't something I'm taking lightly. But what do the *kids* deserve? That's what I keep asking myself."

Patrick looked out the window as he wasn't really sure how to answer. They deserved their mother back. But that particular pie in the sky was of no help. They deserved a father who was happy; in that sense what Greg was undertaking was good and would ultimately benefit them all. And the kids deserved to be happy themselves. But Patrick wasn't convinced they knew what could best make them happy. Having Livia around, once they gave her more time and a bit of grace, might do just that. He even saw a glimpse of it tonight.

His thoughts were interrupted by Greg. "Can I ask you something?"

Patrick snapped back to attention. Hadn't he done nothing but ask him things since they sat down?

"What happened with you and Emory? I ask because you lost Joe. Emory seems really special. Like Livia is to me. And I'm doing everything to hold on to her and you seemed to just let Emory go."

It was the million-dollar question. "I'm going to be fifty." Patrick said it like Meg Ryan in *When Harry Met Sally*, but it wasn't followed with a plaintive *someday*.

"How old is Emory?"

"Thirty-four," Patrick said, as if Emory had chosen his age specifically to inconvenience him.

"And so what's the problem? Fifty's not as old as it used to be."

Patrick couldn't believe Greg didn't see it. "When he's my age, I'll be sixty-six. I don't want to date someone who is sixty-six. *Emory* will not want to date someone who is sixty-six."

"Has he said that?"

Patrick picked at a loose thread on his shirt and pretended not to hear.

"Patrick."

Grant mumbled something in his sleep, but it had no relevance to their conversation. Yet it forced Patrick to answer. "I extrapolated."

"I see. You wouldn't want to, so no one would want to."

"Exactly."

"You're a ridiculous person, you know that?" Greg leaned in, careful not to let Grant hear. "I hate to say that because you are my big brother and I have long looked up to you, but you are a ridiculous person. You dole out life advice and your little rules for living like candy and you don't follow any of them."

"That's not true," Patrick protested. "I always wear pants to get bottomless mimosas."

"They apply to thee and not to me, is that right?"

Patrick slumped back in shock. How was this happening again? Two events in one evening and he had somehow been cast as the villain in both? That seemed completely unfair. And yet, he never really cared what others thought of him, so why was he so rattled? He had been misunderstood at Livia's Prada party, but was the issue here in fact the opposite? Was he plainly *understood*? Of course he should have asked Emory his feelings about the future of their relationship, he knew that; he was just absolutely convinced he wouldn't like the answer. Of course he and Emory were survivors of their own little civilization, too. There was so much good that had been needlessly tossed aside. Tables at restaurants that were theirs that now sat strangers without anything approximating their chemistry or charm. Inside jokes that had no place to land, so the punch lines fizzled like fireworks whose fuses never quite fully lit. And suddenly in that moment, in a foreign bar late at night, sitting across from his brother with Grant softly snoring beside them, Patrick felt profoundly alone. He stammered, not knowing how to answer that charge; fortunately, Greg—a bundle of raw nerves—had already forgotten the question. This was observation more than accusation, but Patrick didn't exactly feel off the hook.

"What would you want in a mother?" Greg asked before motioning for the bartender. "Could we get some water?"

Patrick blinked twice. "We have a mother. You want like a list for areas of improvement?" He pushed up his sleeves as if ready to really throw down.

"I mean, if you were them. Maisie and Grant. What virtues or qualities would you want?"

"What is this, the Proust Questionnaire?"

"I'm serious."

"So am I!"

"I'll give you that Livia is not a natural in the mother department. But she has good qualities."

She's rich.

"She's kind."

She's rich.

"She's caring."

She's rich.

"And she's willing! She doesn't get enough credit for *that*. A lot of women don't want to step into a marriage like this, as it's kind of a lose-lose situation, if you know what I mean."

"Rarely do I know what you mean."

The bartender brought three glasses of water to their table. Patrick reached for his instinctually and sipped, then struggled hard to swallow. "This has no taste or redeeming value whatsoever."

"It's *water*," Greg said.

Patrick held up their now-empty glasses to the bartender and stated, "Another round, per favore." When they were alone again Patrick said, "I don't think the point of marriage is to enter into it with just *any* woman who says yes."

"You say that, but any woman I meet will never live up to memories of Sara. Not in the kids' minds at least. They've practically deified her, no thanks to you."

"What did I do?" Patrick asked, employing the most innocent tone he could muster. Had he filled the kids' heads with stories that lionized their mom? Sure. But never before this moment was he accused of doing them—or Greg—a disservice. Had some of these stories taken on a life of their own? It was hard to say what space they occupied in their little minds, but in his own he had to confess that maybe they did. That was the thing about grief; each memory had a way of amplifying in importance, lest they, too, be lost forever.

"Most women would be happy to come in second. But we're not talking a reasonable second, getting touched out at the finish after a valiant effort. We're talking a *distant* second, which in this case, since there are no other entrants, also happens to be last." Greg reached for his second drink, snatching it directly from the waiter's tray, forcing him to expertly shift his balance to rescue Patrick's cocktail from spilling. He then took a sip too quickly and choked, coughing egg white foam across Patrick's lap. "WHAT IS WRONG WITH THIS DRINK?!"

Patrick reached for a napkin and dabbed his pants, taking back his earlier thought. Straight men were not ready for frothy drinks. "What is wrong with *you?*"

Greg snapped his fingers like Patrick had not been paying attention.

"What?! I'm not following."

"Exactly," Greg said, scooping some of the egg white away with his finger like he was giving his mocktail a close shave. "Just like any woman wouldn't be able to follow Sara. But Livia . . . Livia doesn't feel in competition with—well, *anyone*—let alone Sara. Do you know how rare that is to find?"

Patrick didn't exactly, but decided to agree. "Rare."

"*Extremely* rare." Patrick handed Greg his napkin so he could wipe the foam from his finger. "I know what I'm doing, Patrick. You may not think so, Clara may not think so, the kids may not think so. But I would like a little credit here, a little support. From you." And then, as if he felt guilty for demanding anything, Greg reached over and tied Grant's shoe as he slept quietly in the chair. Patrick watched his face soften in the knowledge that at least in the moment his son felt at peace with everything happening. "Sara would be proud of us, right?"

Patrick took in their surroundings. "We brought a kid to a bar."

It was obvious that to Greg it did not matter. If he had become adept at anything in the last five years it was learning not to sweat the trivial.

Patrick thought of Emory, very much aware now that he had torpedoed their relationship for a reason that perhaps didn't exist. How Sara had orchestrated that summer Patrick had with the kids in Palm Springs and how she imagined it would be a season of healing for him, too. He'd had a second stab at happiness and blew it. Would he get a third?

"Well?" Greg asked again, very aware that his question was still floating in the air unanswered.

Patrick pushed the last of his second cocktail away from him, ready to end the night. He then looked at his brother and said honestly, "She would be proud of you."

SEVENTEEN

The rehearsal dinner was on the lawn of the Villa del Balbianello, a breathtaking estate once home to Franciscan friars that was left by its most recent owner, the Italian explorer Count Guido Monzino, to the Fondo Ambiente Italiano, the National Trust of Italy, upon his death. The house sat on the very tip of the peninsula of Dosso d'Avedo, and was famous for both its terraced gardens and stunning views of the lake. It had also been a filming location for the Bond film *Casino Royale* (it stood in for a hospital, where Daniel Craig convalesced just before the film's climax) as well as for *Star Wars: Attack of the Clones*, largely regarded as one of the worst entries in the series, which meant that it was Grant's favorite.

"The Clone Wars happened here?" Grant asked breathlessly as they stepped off the private water taxi that had shuttled them from the hotel.

"Not really, mind you," Patrick said, stifling a yawn, as if there had been actual skirmishes with clones. Over the last few weeks they had seen a lot of historical landmarks and Patrick didn't want the boy confusing fiction with fact. *Star Wars* may have taken place a long time ago, but in this moment it was only Patrick wishing he could transport himself to a galaxy far, far away. "But, according to Livia, they filmed the movie here." Livia had given them a rundown on the property that morning at breakfast, but Patrick was still exhausted after his night and had only been half listening while popping espressos like pills.

"Not even the Clone Wars part," Maisie informed her brother. "The romantic scenes. The parts you usually skip." Patrick perked up; if Maisie had been listening to Livia that morning and was now passing along her observations as unassailable fact, it might mark a thawing in their relationship. She was even wearing the Prada outfit that Livia had selected.

"Oh," Grant said, disappointed. That was obviously much less interesting.

"Is that one of the movies with Natalie Portman or Carrie Fisher?" Patrick asked as another yawn escaped.

"Why are you so tired?" Maisie asked with a slight air of disgust. Now was not the time to drift off.

"I'm not tired, I'm relaxed." Patrick had spent the afternoon at the hotel spa getting a treatment called the Sleep Ritual, which he'd hoped would afford him a nap before the evening's festivities. The Ritual was described on the spa menu as a total body experience that calms the mind as well as soothes the body by incorporating the plants that grow naturally on the shores of Lake Como. Exfoliation with everlasting flower, soft packs of lavender, sage, and mint—that sort of thing. Patrick was promised the sensation of pure wellness. What he received instead was sudden-onset narcolepsy; he felt in danger of falling dead asleep on his feet.

"Are you going to get through this?"

Patrick steeled his posture. "You know me. As long as I get near-constant attention I'll be fine."

Maisie gave her uncle a push and Patrick realized he'd been blocking the steps. He trudged ahead, following members of Livia's family, who had mostly ascended the steep embankment on their way to the lawn, where dinner would be.

The wedding party was given tours of the property in shifts as everyone waited with bated breath for the bride and the groom to arrive. Since the property had once been a monastery, two towers stood near the villa marking what remained of the original church. The estate passed hands a number of times before Count Monzino, who had led the first Italian expedition to Mount Everest, acquired it. He was buried along the shores of the lake, and there was even a little museum on the property of the count's many things, including dogsleds from his 1971 expedition to the North Pole.

"That's pretty cool," Patrick said of the sleds, trying his best to get Grant to reengage.

"Meh," was the kid's reply, not finding any of this notebook-worthy. None of them had been to the North Pole, but sleds and toboggans were a dime a dozen in Connecticut and Grant himself had been the owner of several. He didn't perk up until their tour guide showed them several secret passages that were added to the estate after the assassination of Prime Minister Aldo Moro in 1978. Patrick leaned on Monzino's desk in an attempt to keep himself upright. The tour guide scolded him immediately when he emerged from a second hidden door.

"Sir!"

Patrick snapped awake and removed his hands from the desk. Touching in museums was a no-no.

"Why did he need secret passages?" Grant asked his uncle.

Patrick whispered in case he was wrong. "Because he was worried about pirates."

Grant's eyes widened and he produced his notebook at last. "The ARGH kind?"

Patrick meant the terrorist kind who might storm the properties of the rich from the water, but it was no skin off his back if Grant wanted to imagine the Jack Sparrow variety. It might even elevate his report from a B to an A. "Sure."

The kid spun in a complete circle with a look that could best be described as "Dinner is looking up."

The water taxi made several additional trips and more and more guests arrived. Patrick resisted champagne offered to him from a caterer with a tray, announcing proudly he was not drinking tonight, but ordered the kids two Shirley Temples. "Seven maraschino cherries each," Patrick instructed, as some things never change. They walked across the plush green lawn, which was made for croquet; it was flat and level, free of weeds and divots. It was so comically perfect it reminded Patrick of the queen's garden in *Alice in Wonderland*, where they played croquet with hedgehogs for balls and flamingos for mallets.

"You have to talk to Dad tonight," Maisie implored. There was new urgency in her voice. "We're running out of time."

"Off with their heads!" Patrick cried, still lost in his *Wonderland* dream.

"Now we're talking!" Maisie replied. "Although, maybe just Livia's." She was willing to extend a pardon to her dad.

"We're not decapitating anyone. Did you read *Alice in Wonderland*?" Patrick asked, and Maisie looked at him doubtfully.

"Did *you*?" Maisie challenged. Since she was the bookworm, he thought it best not to press; Patrick was pretty certain the Queen of Hearts only threatened to behead the losing players save for Alice, but maybe he wasn't remembering the scene correctly. He wasn't even sure why it popped into his head at all, beyond his drowsy state, although perhaps there was some metaphor there. He was the nearest queen in a seat of power, and Maisie was pressing upon him to act. But the rules in this land were maddening and didn't make much sense, just like they hadn't for Alice. Patrick led them over to a stone wall overlooking the lake, where the waiter found them and gave the kids their drinks.

Patrick fussed with the collar on Maisie's blouse until it was just perfect. "You really want to stop this wedding? I'm not joking anymore. After all we did and saw, after all our talks about love, after the nice evening you had with her in Milan?" Just the previous night Greg had asked for his brother's support and he wanted very much to honor the request. But Patrick was being pulled in too many directions to keep up. "You can't envision happiness with Livia at all?"

Maisie stood silently, crossing her arms in defiance at the foot of a large stone statue depicting a friar wearing a hood, lifting his robes just enough to expose sandaled feet. His beard was impressively detailed, but his hand didn't have any fingers—whether they were never chiseled or worn down by time, Patrick didn't know. He stepped into its long, thin shadow, hoping to disappear. But there was no slipping into the shadows with Maisie; she was holding her ground.

"What if she wasn't your stepmother. What if she was just your father's wife. You couldn't imagine a way to make peace with her? Over time. Even for the sake of your dad?"

"Dad's not going to be happy with two miserable kids."

"Grant?"

Grant was conspicuously silent.

Patrick had no choice but to concede the point. Greg would never be happy if Maisie and Grant were not. This would hurt, but maybe in the long term it was what was best. There would be drama, there would be raised voices, there would be humiliation (frankly, under slightly different circumstances, all things gay men thrived on), but then it would be over, and they could all start rebuilding their lives. *Again.*

"Okay, you're right. I have been distracted by Palmina. And I kept thinking you'd come around. I mean, you're kids. Kids don't know what they don't know. I thought you would listen to me. Except, you two have experienced things. You've been forced to grow up faster than most. I didn't take into account that you might listen to me and still disagree."

Maisie tapped her foot impatiently. What was Patrick trying to say? Even Patrick wasn't quite sure.

"Okay."

"Okay, what?"

Patrick yawned again, then closed his eyes in defeat. "I'll talk to your father."

"Now?"

"Is he here?" Patrick forced his eyes open and scanned the lush lawn, where a long banquet table was being set. He hated to ruin a beautiful dinner. Last night he had come around to his brother's way of thinking, but perhaps Maisie was right all along. Livia was like a rejected organ transplant—they could apply bandages and try medication and monitor the situation closely, but in the end she just wasn't going to take. Their engagement was on life support. "Tonight."

"Good." A wave of relief washed over the girl's face, and getting what she wanted, she excused herself to explore the grounds.

Patrick took Grant by the shoulders and placed the boy between him and the awkwardness to come.

"GUP?" Grant's voice was reedy and thin. He had to ask for his uncle again before Patrick replied.

"I'm sorry. What?"

Grant hesitated as he took everything in. A soft pink dyed the late afternoon sky and a gentle breeze tickled the tall olive trees that grew and twisted like stately guards across the vast property. "I like it here," he confessed. "This trip has been the best time. I don't want it to end." He threw his arms around Patrick's waist, hugging his uncle tightly.

For the first time Patrick recognized daylight between Maisie and Grant. Their whole lives they'd been one unit in his mind, where one went the other was not far behind. But they were growing up, growing into different people, it should not have been a surprise that they'd have different needs. Grant was so young when Sara died. Maybe he secretly wanted another shot at a mom. "Grant—" Patrick began, ready to dig into this further. Tonight would be that much harder if he needed to carefully thread a needle.

"Oh, look, there's SAC!" Grant exclaimed as another water taxi approached shore.

Patrick gripped his temples. "Who on earth is 'sack'?"

"Straight Aunt Clara," Grant giggled. "I just made it up." It had been right under their noses this whole time.

Indeed, Clara was standing in the back of the water taxi, the wind on the lake sweeping her hair like she was on the cover of an eighties romance novel. "Wait, *is* that Aunt Clara?"

Patrick did a double take, then cupped his hands around his eyes to be sure. Clara was wearing her new Prada dress with sunglasses that were either new or he hadn't seen. But it wasn't the dress or the sunglasses so much as an even more startling accessory that transformed his sister's demeanor—a man in a seersucker suit and mirrored aviators had his hand pressed against the small of her back, protectively, in that intimate way that suggested they were—Patrick almost couldn't complete the thought—*together.* How long had he been in the spa?

"Who's that with Aunt Clara?" Grant asked. But Patrick could only yawn a nonresponse.

"Let's go see!" Grant said, and he tore off across the lawn like a roadrunner.

"No running!" Patrick called after him, but it was too little, too late, and he wasn't even sure why he'd said it, as an open lawn over-looking a lake was the perfect place for a kid to run free.

"SAAAAAAAAAAAC!" the boy screamed, and his voice echoed off the retaining wall.

Overwhelmed, Patrick looked up at the friar and said, "You lucky bastard." The friar, made of stone, did not respond, so Patrick took off in Grant's direction.

The mystery man held Clara's hand as they disembarked the boat and was just as attentive as they ascended the stairs. "Grant!" Clara cried as she spotted her nephew. "Where's Maisie? I want you to meet someone special. This is Gustavo."

"Gustavo?" Patrick asked as he arrived, out of breath. He braced his hands on his knees while he waited for confirmation that he had heard his sister correctly. He angled one eye up at the man, who ap-peared to be sixty, with thick graying hair that looked like a tamed Brillo pad and a dark pair of caterpillars over his eyes to match. His skin was red, and Patrick couldn't tell if it was from the sun, or from skipping his blood pressure medication that day or, god forbid, pop-ping Viagra. The newcomer was not unattractive as older men go, but hardly seemed like his sister's type.

"Sì," Gustavo said, and he shook Patrick's hand vigorously.

"Isn't he great? He owns a chain of supermarkets."

"Gustavo," Patrick repeated.

"Sì, Gustavo," Gustavo said again, and shook Patrick's hand like he hadn't just done that seconds before.

Clara's eyes grew wide. "It means staff of the gods." She then nudged Patrick and whispered, "He doesn't speak a lick of English."

"Then how do you know his name means . . ." Patrick struggled to remember what she had just said.

"'Staff of the gods.' I googled it." Clara sparkled with pride, as if she were the first person on earth to think of googling a paramour. She leaned in even farther, gripped Patrick by his lapels, and said, "And here's hoping," before breaking out in a Cheshire grin and making like she was Groucho Marx with a cigar.

Patrick groaned as his face folded in on itself in disgust. "This family needs an HR department."

Clara laughed. "He was at the valet when I was coming back from the beach."

"Parking cars?" How desperate had his sister become?

"No! Checking in. I told you he owns supermarkets. Or owned supermarkets. The verb tense is tricky. At least I think he was checking in. He's very difficult to understand. Where's Maisie?" She scanned the lawn for her niece. "I could use her app, to be honest. What was it called again?"

"SayHi."

"Hi. But what was the app called?"

Patrick looked up at the sky, trapped in this "Who's on First?" nightmare from hell. "No, the app is called SayHi."

"And where is she?"

"Where is who?"

"MAISIE."

"Oh, sorry. Auditory recency bias."

Clara ignored her brother's antics, unable to peel her eyes from Gustavo's wide face and bold features. "Not understanding him will eventually be an impediment. Then again, *you're* impossible to understand and people seem to like you." She drank in Gustavo another moment before deciding they needed a cocktail, stat.

Patrick placed a hand on her arm. "Actually, could we talk for a—"

But Clara already had a tight grip on Grant's hand. "Come on," she said, pointing them straight toward the action. "Let's go find your sister."

Patrick glanced politely at Gustavo, who announced, "Villa del Balbianello!" as if he were offering brand-new information.

Annoyed, Patrick, Clara, and Grant all muttered, "*We know.*"

Patrick was startled awake by applause. He felt along the bench beneath him with his hands, confused; he must have nodded off. Damn that massage. The ovation was for Greg and Livia, who arrived on the last water taxi—together they made a grand entrance onto the lawn looking absolutely resplendent, and everyone began snapping photographs of the bride and groom like they were movie stars walking the Croisette at Cannes. If he hadn't been so absolutely exhausted Patrick might have been jealous, not just of the attention they were receiving as the evening's stars, but also because they looked so damn *happy*. He scanned the lawn, hoping the kids would see and recognize at last that this was a union to be built up and not torn down. Alas, Grant was arm wrestling with Gustavo and Maisie stood with her arms crossed, looking at Patrick like Drew Barrymore in *Firestarter*. Disturbed, Patrick watched as Clara pulled Greg aside to point out Gustavo and then the table, where an additional setting would have to be arranged for her spontaneous plus-one. Gustavo stepped forward and said his name as introduction to a stunned Greg, who looked around either for help or to see if he was being pranked. When his eyes landed on Patrick, Patrick shot back his best *Don't look at me*. For once, he was the sibling better behaved.

It was then that someone whispered in his ear. "I do the toast." It was Palmina, clad in another of a seemingly endless parade of jumpsuits, this one a color somewhere between mango and squash, a shade Patrick didn't consider very wedding-y, although it might come in handy masking stains if the menu offered some sort of gazpacho. The way she made her pronouncement was so seductive and secretive

Patrick momentarily thought she was confessing having just had sex with a dry piece of bread.

"You do the *what?*" And then he understood. He looked around for backup, but Greg was talking to Grant and Livia was deep in conversation with her mother. Even though he had just admitted to Maisie that Palmina had been a distraction of his own making, he couldn't help but be sucked back into the rivalry. "No, I do the toast," he corrected. "I'm the best man." He hadn't prepared exact words, but that wouldn't stop him; he wouldn't cede the spotlight to someone who looked like they were dressed for hang gliding. Actors, after all, were good on their feet.

"I'm the best *woman,*" Palmina countered.

"I'm Greg's brother."

"I am Livia's sister." The way she glared made it clear she thought this was some sort of patriarchal spitting contest.

How could Patrick best explain? The difference was not that he was a man, but that he was famous. People wanted, no—*expected* to hear from him. He was always what made the price of admission worth it. Of course, that might not really serve his cause when the bulk of the evening's guests were related to her and his fame didn't necessarily translate overseas, but that didn't matter, as Patrick also had another motive in mind: he was best suited to deliver remarks that could work on multiple levels, not just for Greg and Livia, should he decide to throw them a lifeline, but for Maisie and Grant as well. Palmina didn't even understand this to be a requirement of the gig. Since their back-and-forth could easily go on through the appetizer course, Patrick relented and said, "Fine. We both give the toast. Final offer."

Palmina heaved a heavy, disappointed sigh. "The trouble with men is they think everyone wants to hear what they have to say."

Patrick didn't disagree. He looked over his shoulder and flinched, surprised to find Maisie scowling behind him. "Jesus. We should put a bell on you."

"I need to speak with you," Maisie said, eyeing Palmina in a way that pleased Patrick: suspiciously. He was winning her back over to his side. "When's dinner?"

"We rehearse first," Palmina explained. "Then dinner."

"Why do we have to rehearse having dinner?"

Patrick jumped in. "Because apparently you aren't doing it right."

Palmina fished in her clutch for a cigarette.

"Then I need to talk to you now." Maisie motioned with her head to one side. "*Alone.*"

"Later. Let's not be rude to your launt."

Palmina's interest was piqued. "What is this 'launt'?" Her cigarette bobbled up and down in her mouth as she lit it.

"Lesbian. Aunt." Patrick mashed his hands together to demonstrate. "Launt."

"Like a portmanteau." Palmina blew smoke out the side of her mouth and offered Patrick her pack. He declined, despite the intoxicating scent of her tobacco. He had smoked in college, but he had never looked that cool, like the cigarette was a natural extension of his hand. Holding a cigarette, Patrick always looked pained.

"You speak French?"

"I speak five languages," she reminded him.

"How many do you speak, GUP?" Maisie asked.

"Just two," Patrick admitted. "English and Connecticut tween." He allowed Maisie to pull him away by the arm. Palmina locked eyes with her trio of friends standing in the shade of an olive tree and excused herself to join them.

As soon as they were alone Maisie held up her phone. "I've got Livia cold." She barely tried to suppress a wicked grin. "This wedding is over. She's so dead."

Patrick blanched at her word choice. This was all becoming a bit too cutthroat.

"She thought she could sneak one past me in Italian? SayHi, Livia!"

Patrick reached for Maisie's phone to see what she thought she had heard, but she snatched it away just in time.

"Let me see what she said."

"Oh, you'll see."

"Come on. She at least deserves a chance to defend herself."

Maisie challenged him with her eyes. "Fine. She can do that at dinner."

Patrick grabbed a glass of champagne from a passing waiter.

"I thought you weren't drinking today."

"Yeah, well, you've driven me to it." Patrick took a large gulp, hoping the bubbles would settle a rapidly growing anxiety. If he was going to insert himself in what was about to go down he would need a little *Nerve* Clicquot.

At dinner, Patrick was seated next to Groot, which is what he and Grant had taken to calling Gustavo, since all he ever said was his name, and across from Clara, as Livia felt couples—even last-minute additions—should be split to encourage conversation. *Some conversation*, Patrick thought as Gustavo grinned at him with baseball-sized teeth. On Patrick's right was Grant, and across from him Maisie and Palmina. Only Greg and Livia were seated together at the center of the table, with Livia's parents, Lorenzo and Giana, on the far side with Cousin Geppetto and Palmina's friends. When they were seated at the table there was only water in goblets to drink, so Patrick, still ill at ease, emptied his on the lawn and reached for a carafe of white wine to refill it. He didn't wait for a toast to start drinking.

Clara, perhaps needing to galvanize herself for further conversation with Gustavo, reached for the carafe after Patrick. "How is the wine?"

"Thick," Patrick gagged.

"Thick?" Clara asked.

Patrick petted his throat in the way one might when trying to get a dog to swallow a pill. "It's olive oil," he managed, struggling to speak.

"We press our own!" Lorenzo bellowed proudly as Patrick tried his best not to retch into a napkin.

"Great. *Lorenzo's oil*," Patrick muttered; no one appreciated this as a dig against Susan Sarandon, who somehow wrangled an Oscar nomination for a forgettable film of the same name. He grabbed for bread from a basket to soak up the last of the slick remnants in his mouth.

"I don't think I've seen you eat carbs," Greg confessed.

"Italy rules," Patrick said with his mouth full.

"YEAH, ITALY RULES!" Greg said, misunderstanding, oblivious of his kids' mood and the Mack truck that was about to hit him.

Patrick stopped a passing waiter and asked, "Could I get like a vase of actual wine?"

Dinner was catered by one of the lake's five-star cooking schools and they were served bream baked in a salt crust. This was apparently a Sicilian tradition, salt lagoons being abundant on the island, and provided a showy presentation that failed to impress Grant, who, while at first intrigued, was slowly horrified when an entire fish—head and all—was excavated from the mountain of salt. He and Maisie both winced as the fish was filleted, and they stared at their servings when plated in front of them.

"What's the matter, you don't like fish?" Livia asked.

Grant did his best to explain that it wasn't the fish that was the problem so much as the scales and the head.

"They are used to it in the form of sticks," Greg explained with a wink. As always with new things, he liked his children to have a taste, but they wouldn't be forced to eat the whole thing.

"Is there any salt?" Patrick joked, doing his level best to diffuse a tense situation (and for once using his powers of stealing focus for good). But the joke was on him when he took a bite and found the bream to be incredibly flavorful while not the least bit briny. He leaned into the table to catch Clara's attention. "Will you ask Groot to pass the lemon?"

Greg nearly choked on his bream.

"Why do you call him that?" Clara groused. "His name is Gustavo."

"GUSTAVO!" Gustavo said, leaning in to acknowledge everyone, as if they hadn't already been introduced a half-dozen times.

Patrick stood up and reached for the lemon himself. "That's why."

Greg held his hand tightly, clutching his fork in front of his mouth to hide his laughter. He cleared his throat and changed the subject.

Growing weary of polite conversation, Patrick studied Palmina, who seemed equally glum, and his spirits momentarily lifted. Perhaps it was only because she, too, was seated separately from her friends, but, with a glimmer of hope, he suddenly wondered if Livia hadn't likewise come to her, asking if *she* was making a mistake. Livia didn't have her own children to consider, but certainly there was a world of eligible men available to her that were better suited—men who had less baggage and made more geographical sense. What might Palmina have counseled? She seemed to be a fan of both Maisie and Grant, as evidenced by how tenderly she stood by them, and lesbians as a whole seemed pro-marriage. They were so pro-marriage, in fact, some lesbians Patrick knew had been married two or three times. But in truth, Palmina was impossible to read. Was she in favor of this union? Or did she need to invite the Robert Palmer girls to fortify her spirits just to see this week through? Perhaps Palmina even had her own doubts, and the very reason she wanted to "do the toast" was so that she could put a stop to this wedding herself. Could Patrick be that lucky? Could he be off the proverbial hook? But if Palmina stole this task from his to-do list, would that make her the hero in Maisie's eyes? She would no longer be her launt by marriage, but would she be elevated to some new role—savior—that would eclipse his own in her esteem? His head was swimming with obsession.

"Patrick," Greg interrupted. "It's Italy, you can't possibly be so dyspeptic."

"Sorry," Patrick apologized while shifting uncomfortably in his seat. "I think I had some bad wine."

"Nonsense!" Lorenzo said before leaning across the happy couple to squabble with his wife in Italian.

"Have you traveled much with your brother?" Livia asked, attempting to engage Clara in the conversation. In truth the three of them hadn't traveled together much since they were kids.

"Have you?" Patrick shot back at Livia, thinking perhaps there was a fuse he could light that would lead them to self-destruct. Wasn't that his best hope, after all? Absolving himself without boosting Palmina? "Greg is an awful travel companion."

"Hey now," Greg protested.

"His face is in a guidebook the whole time."

"Guidebook?" Livia repeated with a judgmental air. Citizens of the world didn't need guidebooks. Patrick hoped it made his brother seem small.

"Nonsense," Greg protested.

"Remember Maui?" Patrick asked. They had taken the kids for Christmas one year, trying to reinvent the holiday without Sara.

Greg turned to Patrick, betrayed. "Are you going to bring up the triplets?"

Livia turned to Greg and cocked an eyebrow.

"The triplets were three sister waterfalls," he reassured her. "Three waterfalls we found because of my guidebook."

"And what happened at the three sisters?" Patrick asked.

"I fell in."

"And why did you fall in?"

Greg was cornered. "Because my face was in a guidebook."

Palmina tapped her wineglass with her spoon with such force Patrick was shocked it didn't shatter. She continued until she had everyone's attention. The table grew quiet in hushed anticipation and even Gustavo fell silent, his eyes sparkling at Clara. Palmina stood with her glass and Patrick's heart began to race. "Amici, amiche. Old friends, new friends."

"Gustavo," Gustavo said, introducing himself to Palmina and the last few at the far end of the table he had not met.

"There was some discussion as to who should do the toast, and unable to come to a peaceful conclusion I have agreed to share this duty with Patrick."

Patrick's face grew hot as eyes turned to him.

"But we have not decided who shall do the first."

Patrick realized people were looking to him to respond. "Oh," he said, stalling. Now that the time was here, he desperately wanted Palmina to take the lead. "Ladies first," he said, challenging her to dive in.

Palmina held his gaze unfazed. "So, it is decided, then." Patrick exhaled, relieved. "Patrick?" His heart sank. She gestured to him as she took her seat, winking across the table at her family.

Patrick closed his eyes and swallowed, even though his mouth was dry. Was this stage fright? He'd always felt a rush of adrenaline before entering the spotlight, but this was something new entirely and he needed a moment to diagnose it. But all eyes were upon him, most searingly Maisie's. So he picked up his glass and stood.

"First of all. I want to thank the Brasso family for their incredible hospitality. Livia. Lorenzo and Giana, especially now that my glass is filled with wine and not olive oil." Patrick sniffed his glass to be sure.

"Vino, vino!" Giana declared to the tune of "Hear, hear!"

Patrick gritted his teeth as he turned to his new nemesis. "Even Palmina, for allowing me to say a few words first, the dig at my manliness notwithstanding. This is a lovely evening and a beautiful estate. In fact, it reminds me a bit of a mosquito-ridden summer cottage we vacationed in as kids back home." Greg and Clara laughed, but the others not so much. "I'm the comedian," he explained for those who needed context.

"Hollywood Foreign Press!" Lorenzo shouted, and everyone raised their glass as if that were the toast.

"No, no! I'm not finished." Patrick then focused on the bride and groom. "Greg, Livia." He took a deep breath and tried not to melt under the heat of the kids' searing gaze. "I've done my best these last few weeks to teach Maisie and Grant about love and the different love languages we can employ to express it. But there's one we didn't discuss. And that's protection."

The color drained from Greg's face and he whispered hoarsely, "Patrick, we *use* protection."

Patrick, doing his best to ignore that, gripped his wineglass so firmly he was again surprised it didn't shatter. "Love is something special to be protected. Because if you don't protect it, if you don't honor it as something rare and precious, it's easy to walk away from. I did that, and I regret it." Patrick's voice cracked as he thought about Emory, before his thoughts turned to Sara and Joe. He did his best to carry on. "My brother and I both know loss. Too well. And we also know not everybody gets a second chance at love. But Greg and Livia do." Patrick turned to face them. "Let's just say the beating of my heart is a drum that is lost, and it's looking for a rhythm like you."

Maisie kicked her uncle under the table. This was not going in the direction they had discussed. Clara, meanwhile, leaned across Maisie to address Greg. "Is he quoting Air Supply?"

"Yes. Yes I am quoting Air Supply. Because these two are making love out of nothing at all." Patrick bowed his head, to avoid Maisie's stone-cold glare. "And so tonight, I choose to protect the bond you have created. Celebrate it. Even if it means disappointing someone else I love, too."

Greg, at a loss, looked to Livia, who was equally confused. "Disappoint who?"

"Whom," Grant said to everyone's surprise.

"You promised," Maisie whispered.

"Well, I shouldn't have. That's on me." He could sense Greg glaring at him and easily read his brother's thoughts: *Whatever's going on here—shouldn't you have mentioned it last night?* "I tried to teach you about love. Perhaps I'm a bad teacher. Perhaps there are certain things you are still too young to understand."

"I'm not too young!"

"Fine. Too angsty, or hormonal or, just, you know—fill in the blank with whatever word you choose."

"Hormonal?" Maisie stood up, enraged.

Concerned, Greg whispered, "Maisie, are you having your period?" He started counting weeks on his fingers.

Maisie grabbed clumps of her hair in her hands and tugged in frustration. "Everyone stop talking about my body. I don't have a body! Okay? From now on I am a head. ONLY A HEAD!"

"Okay, calm down," Patrick urged. He then turned to the others at his end of the table. "This is a very heady performance."

Palmina stood in Maisie's defense and slammed her fist on the table. "Never tell a woman to calm down."

"Palmina," Patrick begged. "This doesn't concern you." Palmina was right, of course—it was perhaps the most annoying thing about her. But the situation called for de-escalation.

"Don't talk to her that way," Clara barked, jumping in to fortify Palmina's position.

"Great," Patrick said. "It's the Sisterhood of the Traveling Aunts."

Palmina brushed Clara aside. "I don't need anyone to defend me."

"Right," Patrick said, sucked back into a rivalry he had vowed to let go. "Because as we *all* know, you're the greatest thing since Sappho herself."

Palmina groaned her displeasure. "Who died and put you in charge?"

Patrick went from annoyed to enraged, and before he could stop himself he said, "Their mother, for one." The table gasped.

"PATRICK." This time it was Greg who was enraged. "If anyone's in charge here, it's me. Now sit down."

Palmina extended an arm, indignant. "Of course. Another man!"

Livia squirmed uncomfortably in her seat, torn between her sister and her fiancé, uncertain whether to jump in.

Patrick ignored Palmina's protest and kept his focus on Greg. "If you were so in charge of the situation, why did you ask me to take the kids?"

"WHAT IS GOING ON?" Livia finally demanded.

"Fine." Maisie produced her phone from her little bag, her eyes locked on Patrick the whole time. "I'll do this myself."

"Do what?" Greg asked, thoroughly stumped.

"I overheard Livia talking."

Livia moved her napkin from her lap to the table. Clearly the meal portion of the evening was done. "Overheard me talking when? What is it you think I said?"

Maisie swallowed a large gulp of air. "That you didn't want to be a mother!"

Livia grew very quiet. She looked to her own mother, not certain what to say. Giana sat perfectly still.

Greg looked from Maisie to Livia to Maisie and back again. "Livia, is that true?"

Livia looked like she'd been caught with her hand in the cookie jar. "Maisie. That's simply not true. I would never say such a thing. I have wanted for years to be a mother. I tried very hard."

It was Greg's instinct to jump to his daughter's defense. "Are you saying my daughter is lying?"

"I—I was speaking in Italian. How did you know?"

Greg's head drooped in grave disappointment.

Maisie held her phone aloft. "Say hello to SayHi!"

"What is SayHi?" Giana asked her husband, still playing catch-up.

But Clara knew. "It's Maisie's translation app."

Livia stammered. "I was only saying what Patrick and I had discussed."

All eyes turned to Patrick. Even Maisie's; she had now been betrayed by her uncle twice in one night.

"Patrick?" Greg asked. People were entering the chat faster than Greg could keep up. "You knew about this?"

"Maisie. It was a mistranslation," Livia promised.

Greg took Maisie's hand. "Perhaps we should give Livia a chance to explain."

Maisie pulled her hand out of her father's. "You hate me. You all hate me." Tears welled in her eyes. "EVERYBODY HATES ME!"

Grant started to cry, out of fear, in his sister's defense, out of sheer confusion.

"Everyone hates *you*?!" Patrick protested. "Try having a movie open at nineteen percent on Rotten Tomatoes! *Nineteen percent!*"

"Patrick!" Greg hollered, urging him once again to be calm.

"Oh! I see," Patrick complained. "No one thinks twice about telling a gay man to calm down. Well, they should!"

"Patrick. I mean it."

"GREG. Let me handle this. Please."

"Let my sister explain," Palmina demanded.

"Livia?" Lorenzo inquired. He, too, was ready for this to end. They had paid for a perfectly fine meal that was now ruined.

"Palmina," Giana said, encouraging her daughter to sit back down.

"Maisie," Patrick began, hoping the right words would come.

"GUSTAVO!" Gustavo bellowed.

The whole table shouted, "NOT NOW!"

"All of you be quiet!" Patrick yelled.

"No, Patrick." Livia had had just about enough of this. "There is a time for uncles and there is a time for parents." Livia got out from behind her chair and kneeled before Maisie, taking her hand in her own. Maisie tried to yank free, but Livia refused to let go.

"Maisie. It's true. I did say I didn't want to be a mother. Or rather, just anyone's mother. What I was trying to convey is that I want to be *your* mother. And Grant's." She wiped tears from Maisie's eyes with her thumbs. And Maisie, momentarily, let her. Until, overwhelmed, she found the strength to pull away.

"But you're not my mother. *You're not!* And you never will be!" She began pleading with Greg. "You can't marry her, Dad. You can't. I *hate* it here. I want to go home. I want my friends. I want MOM."

"MAISIE, STOP!" Grant climbed on top of his chair. He was the first of them to get the table to fall quiet. "I want a mom. You got to have one for nine years and I only got six. I like it here. I like Livia!" Livia looked up at Grant, her eyes melting. "I want a mom for birthdays and summer vacations and to wake up with on Christmas and to buy us Santa presents and regular presents and stocking presents."

Patrick put one arm around Grant and hugged him tight. "Let's not get ahead of ourselves, Tiny Tim." To explain, he added, "Grant's love language is gifts."

"Maisie," Greg managed, while looking at Grant. He didn't know which of his kids to address first; the bottom of his whole world was falling out.

Maisie stepped back from the table, equal parts horrified and enraged.

"Where are you going?" Livia asked.

"Connecticut."

"Maisie."

Maisie's face twisted in overwrought teenage agony. "I don't care if I have to swim!"

"Oh my god," Livia said, then discreetly reached across Greg for her napkin. Maisie looked down mortified to discover a trickle of blood running from her culottes down her leg.

Completely overwhelmed, she turned to Patrick and screamed, "*This is all your fault!*" She then buried her head in Livia's shoulder and sobbed as Livia lovingly attended to her needs.

EIGHTEEN

It was late. Patrick found his way by moonlight to the Villa Emilia—a second building on the hotel's property, which housed some of the more exclusive guest suites—and he paced with his sister, Clara, in the hallway in front of Palmina's door. What a mess. Greg and Livia had retreated back to their room with Grant in tow and were most likely in for the night; no doubt they had some hard thinking to do. Maisie rode back to the hotel in a separate water taxi with him, Clara, and Palmina. Clara and Palmina tended to her feminine needs, and then, in the privacy of Patrick's room, he held her while she cried until there were no tears left and, drained, she fell asleep in his bed.

"Are we doing this?" Clara asked impatiently. "I have someone waiting for me in the hotel bar."

"Yes, we all know. Groot."

"His name is Gustavo. Why do you keep calling him Groot?"

Patrick ran both hands through his hair, uncharacteristically mussing it. "Hasn't Grant forced you to watch *Guardians of the Galaxy*? Groot is a big dumb tree who can only say his name. He hangs out with a raccoon."

Clara considered this new information. "Not *that* dumb if he can say his name."

"What?"

"I know that you mean it as some clever insult, but how many talking trees do you know?" Clara fanned herself with her hand, her frustration making her temperature rise. "Does the raccoon also talk?"

"*Does the raccoon also*— Can we *focus*, please?"

Patrick pressed his ear against Palmina's door, wondering if they would find her alone. Despite their squabble at dinner they had made fragile peace on the boat, and Patrick felt an emergency summit of the siblings was in order—something that would be much more difficult to convene with her backup singers hovering.

"What are you doing?" Clara whispered hoarsely, checking the delicate watch on her wrist. She looked back wistfully in the direction of the main lobby.

"Listening."

"For what?"

Patrick wasn't sure. "Movement, scissoring, women's lacrosse. I don't know—I'll know it when I hear it."

"That's it, I'm out." Clara turned and headed back for the elevator.

"Clara, *wa*—"

Palmina whipped open her door, causing Patrick to tumble forward, his head landing squarely on her breasts.

"What is all this bickering in the hall?" Palmina seemed more bothered by the unwelcome noise than she was about Patrick's presence against her chest, as if everyone eventually ended up in her bosom. Patrick scrambled upright, trying to look equally nonchalant. Palmina had removed her makeup and changed from her jumpsuit into sweats and her hair had flopped to one side; she looked more reasonable with her guard down. The sleeves and waist on her sweatshirt had been cropped, and it was emblazoned with a pitched trident, which may or may not have been the logo for Maserati. Or maybe she'd paid an outrageous amount and it came that way. It didn't matter. This was a Palmina that Patrick could do business with.

"Are you alone?" Patrick asked, peering beyond her into her room. "We were hoping to find you alone."

"I'm flattered, but I'm not into threesomes."

Clara gasped, then giggled, but Palmina just glared, then retreated into her room. Was that an invitation for them to follow? Patrick ushered Clara inside before Palmina could change her mind and quietly closed the door behind them.

The room was wedge-shaped, the widest end where they stood now, and as they passed a marble bathroom, Clara pointed to a tub that was so long and thin a very small person could almost swim laps. The bed was in the room's center and was still immaculately made. Feeling frustrated with their hosts, he whispered to Clara, "I knew they booked the best rooms for themselves."

Palmina moved undaunted to a sitting area at the room's far end, which had two modest couches, a small table with chairs, and an antique desk that held her laptop and a stack of books with Italian titles including an Elena Ferrante. Outside her open floor-to-ceiling windows, the long track of the moon rippled across the lake's choppy waters as a surprising wind made dance partners of the drapes.

"There's champagne," Palmina informed them, indicating a bucket on the coffee table next to an enormous conch shell, which Patrick hoped was not dredged from the lake.

"Not prosecco?" Patrick asked carefully, in as dry a tone as (hopefully) the champagne. He knew better than to rock the boat (it was already a small miracle she had let them in), but he couldn't help himself.

Palmina waved her hand dismissively. "Sometimes the French do things better." It was a rare concession on her part. She leaned out the open window and piled the hair back on top of her head before the wind caught it and swept it back down. "I'll kill you if you tell anyone I say that. And they will never find your body."

Patrick imagined the Robert Palmer girls weighing his corpse down with enormous shells like the one on the table, and pushing him off a boat into the lake under the cover of darkness. They'd then undulate back toward the boat's wheel and grab it in unison, speeding off into the night, hair gelled so slickly to their scalps, nary a strand would be out of place when they were questioned about his disappearance later.

"We've probably consumed enough for one night," Clara said. They both had observed Palmina's face as they left the rehearsal dinner. There was not even a hint of pleasure at the evening's unraveling; quite the opposite, in fact—her forehead remained furrowed in concern. "Besides," she continued, "Gustavo's waiting."

Patrick, ignoring her, released the bottle's cork with a satisfying pop and a spiritous fog escaped from the bottle's neck.

Clara relented. "Well, maybe just one glass."

Patrick poured three, waiting patiently for the bubbles to fizzle and fade, then slowly filled each flute with more. He handed one to his sister and one to Palmina as she closed the drapes over both open windows so they blew dramatically into the room, then sat on the floor like she was Demi Moore at the end of *St. Elmo's Fire*. "I want to start by apologizing for my behavior tonight," he began. "I was less than my best self."

It didn't feel like Palmina needed an apology. In fact, she seemed not to desire one at all. "I would hate to see more." She grabbed a bottle of pills from the desk and tossed them to Patrick, who—with surprising athletic grace—caught them. The bottle rattled like a tambourine.

"I don't need pills," he announced. Alcohol, for him, was enough.

"They're for Maisie. She could be in for rough days."

"See, this is where guncles are better than launts, as even I know not to give a child Valium."

Clara, understanding Palmina perfectly, rolled her eyes.

"They're for her period, you bastardo," Palmina croaked.

Patrick's face grew hot as he scrutinized the bottle's label. "Oh," he said, and tucked the pills in his pocket. A change of subject was in order. *Moving on.* "Just so you know, I've always liked Livia." He thought it important Palmina knew where he stood.

"As have I," Clara added, wanting to do her part to make peace.

"And I have always liked Greg." Patrick wasn't looking for reciprocation, but he appreciated Palmina's words nonetheless. She gestured for her guests to take a seat on the couch.

"We can fix this. Can't we?"

"*We?*" Palmina challenged, but she said it with a wry leer.

Clara tried not to overdo it, wanting to stay alert for Gustavo, but the champagne was better than any she'd ever tasted. "Why have we not been drinking this all weekend?"

Palmina stretched on the floor like a cat. "My parents don't like the French."

Patrick stared into his glass, transfixed by the bubbles rising to the surface. *Come quickly, I am drinking the stars.* Those were words supposedly spoken by Dom Pierre Pérignon the first time he discovered bubbles in one of his bottles, at least according to a book on sparkling wines Patrick had read. The line, pure poetry—as romantic as champagne itself. The truth of course was less intoxicating, the bubbles were CO_2 gas; there was enough in the average bottle to create twenty million of them. *The magic is in the bubbles,* he thought, even knowing it was not magic at all. Anyone who had tasted flat champagne would know what he meant. The same was true of relationships—you introduce too much air and the bond between any two people could fizzle. In this case, kids were a lot of ether.

"So what do we do?" Clara asked.

Clara usually thrived in a crisis. Patrick stared at her, wondering who'd kidnapped that version of his sister. Sadly, he knew—he was sitting patiently at the hotel bar introducing himself to everyone and everything down to the potted plants.

Palmina held her champagne flute by its base, as coolly as she held cigarettes. "Why do we need to do anything? Time, I think, fixes most things."

"Yes, but we don't have a lot of it," Patrick pointed out.

"We have the night, that is plenty. Then I will talk to my sister."

"And I'll talk to Greg," Clara offered.

"Okay," Patrick agreed. "That leaves me to talk to the kids." He and Palmina once again held an intense eye contact that made Patrick uncomfortable, and he thought it best in the moment to agree. "A good night's sleep might help cooler, may I say prettier, heads prevail."

"Grazie," Palmina said, in unison with Clara's "Thank you."

"I was talking about me," Patrick protested. He stood and began to pace. "Grant will be fine. He's made his desires clear. It's Maisie I'm worried about. I know you both look at me and see someone who has it all together . . ."

"My father is right. You are the comedian."

". . . but the truth of the matter is I'm a little out of my league."

Palmina clutched nonexistent pearls. "Patrick. Are you asking for my help?"

Patrick gripped his temples at the absurdity of it all. They were now the unlikely partners thrown together by a job-weary chief in every cop movie ever made. "Misery acquaints a man with strange bedfellows."

Clara set her champagne down on the coffee table. "Speaking of bedfellows, I should probably . . ." She pointed with both thumbs at the door.

"It's an expression," Patrick said, plopping back down on the couch. "Shakespeare. *The Tempest*, if I recall."

Palmina agreed. "Prospero was the Duke of Milan."

Patrick tucked his chin to his chest and looked down at her on the floor. "Yes, I'm sure next you will tell me you were related."

Clara was exasperated with her brother's antics. "Patrick, she's only saying that because we were just *in* Milan."

"Right." They had been in the city not two nights prior. Europe was extraordinary that way, so different from the States, Patrick thought, which felt far from the center of everything. Patrick settled on the couch and kicked off his shoes. Clara glared at him, annoyed he was making himself comfortable instead of starting their good nights. "You know, there was a time I thought Maisie was like you."

"Beguiling?" Palmina purred.

"Gay," Patrick corrected.

Clara glanced at her watch again.

"And now?" Palmina asked, with genuine curiosity.

Patrick adjusted the conch shell with his bare foot so that the opening was not facing him, suddenly afraid of something crawling out of it. "I don't think about it. Now she's just Maisie. She's a young woman, something I don't have any experience being."

"This is where Maisie could benefit from someone like Livia," Clara observed. "If she would just stop pushing back against everything all the time."

Palmina dissented. "Pushing back is the job of a young woman. It is, what is the word—*imperative*." She laid flat on her back and studied the ceiling, before rolling her head in the direction of the windows. "Some people believe there is a monster in the lake."

"A *monster*?" Clara recoiled.

"Lariosauro. Over the years there have been many sightings."

Clara laughed nervously. "Have you told this to Grant? He would love you forever."

Patrick glared. *Traitor.* If he was losing Maisie's favored status to Palmina, he didn't want to lose Grant, too.

"Do you believe there is such a monster?" Clara asked, blocking her brother's annoyed gaze with her hand like one might blot out the sun.

"Italian folklore," Palmina dismissed, returning her attention to the ceiling. "There are many stories of witches and demons and ghosts. That's just Italy. The Christianization of our myths."

Patrick understood. Religion seeped its way into everything. But monsters living under the water seemed to take things to a new and chilling depth.

"But folklore has its place," she continued. "Because that is what it is like to be a young woman. To have a monster inside you. Raging." Patrick turned to Clara; while she looked a little uncomfortable with Palmina's phrasing, she was clearly in agreement. "And there are sightings. Occasionally. People see it from time to time, despite your best efforts to keep it hidden."

"Like at rehearsal dinners?"

Palmina winked, glad to be understood.

"But isn't that true for all adolescents?" Patrick pressed. "Young men, too?"

"Young men can become their monster and not be judged for it. They are allowed to show anger, be violent and growl. Young women are different. They know they have to contain the monster to get what they want. And it's frustrating to be young and to first see how the world works and to learn how much of yourself you have to hide. The unfairness of there being two sexes. And how lonely it can be to see your future mapped out and to know that part of your light will be dimmed."

Patrick hated the idea of Maisie being lonely or dulled. Is that why she spent so much time with her nose in a book, where the world might still seem vibrant? "Greg doesn't want that. *I* don't want that. We go out of our way to make sure that she is encouraged and cele-brated for exactly who she is." He turned to Clara for back-up.

Palmina glanced down at her sweatshirt as if contemplating cut-ting it shorter. "At home."

"Yes."

With her foot, Palmina knocked her cigarettes from the desk chair where they sat next to a book of matches. "But she won't be celebrated that way in the world. Not by everyone. That's not how the world works." She propped herself on an elbow to reach for the matchbook, too. When she lit her cigarette, she held the match upside down so that the flame crawled toward her fingers; it was the way Patrick and Clara's grandfather had long ago lit a pipe and he found it both mas-culine and strangely sexy. She inhaled deeply and it was a long time before she exhaled. "Your sister is right. The irony is she could use a strong woman like Livia to help it all make sense."

Irony was a bit strong of a word for Patrick's liking, and he didn't like the suggestion that he wasn't enough to light Maisie's way. "All this monster talk is wonderful feminist theory, but we have a very real-world problem facing us. So unless you can tell me how to tame this monster . . ."

"Oh, you never tame it."

"Train it, then."

Palmina shook her head. *Wrong again.* "You encourage it."

Feeling like he was the only one dealing with the matter at hand, Patrick punched a sequined pillow in frustration, then blew on his knuckles when they burned.

"See?" Palmina said to Clara, who looked ashamed on her broth-er's behalf.

"I'm not a monster!" Patrick insisted.

Palmina exhaled several smoke rings. *If you say so.*

Clara polished off her champagne. "You know, you two are not as different as you think."

Patrick and Palmina aligned their gaze.

"You're not! Here." Clara checked her watch a third time, hoping she could make this quick. "I play this game with Maisie and Grant when they're fighting."

"We don't have time for games," Patrick protested. "We have a wedding to get back on track."

Clara pushed ahead. "What's your favorite color?"

"CLARA," Patrick objected, burying his face in his hands.

"Humor me," she insisted. "What's your favorite color?"

"Blue," Patrick answered, without looking up.

"Black," Palmina countered at the same time.

Clara snapped her fingers to get them to focus. "Great, together you're a bruise." This was already not going how it did with the kids.

Patrick turned to Palmina. "Black is not a color."

"Yes it is."

"Black is the absence of light. It's the very nonexistence of color!"

"FORGET COLORS," Clara exclaimed, losing her patience. "Favorite shapes."

"Parallelogram."

"Circle."

"*Parallelogram*, Patrick?! Honestly. How about a shape that people have heard of."

Patrick threw up his arms. "Fine. Square." They were wasting time. "Which I might point out *is* a parallelogram."

Palmina scoffed. "Talk about *square*."

Clara was losing her patience. "Musical instrument, then." She was grasping for straws.

"Clavichord," Palmina said.

Which overlapped with Patrick saying, "Triangle."

Clara stood up and brushed the wrinkles from her dress. "If you're not going to take this seriously, I have better things to do."

"WAIT," Patrick said before his sister could go. "I may have been stuck on shapes."

"I have kept Groot waiting long enough. *Gustavo.*" Clara clapped her hands over her mouth, horrified. Patrick laughed, which angered Clara further. "You know, you may not think he's the smartest tool in the shed, but he could probably *build* me a shed. And frankly that's all I need for tonight."

"A shed?" Palmina asked, as if needing the word translated.

"That's what she shed," Patrick said by way of explanation and they both laughed, causing him to wonder if they ran reruns of *The Office* in Italy.

"Honestly, you two deserve each other." This time Clara skipped checking her watch and headed straight for the door. "If you figure out this mess you can call me. But don't be surprised if my phone's on do not disturb." Patrick and Palmina waited until they heard the door close and latch before they burst out in riotous laughter. Then it grew awkward again, so Patrick reached for the champagne and topped off their glasses.

It was the first time the two of them had been alone.

"It feels good to laugh," Palmina admitted. For once on this trip Patrick took pride in being the comedian; it was no longer a diss.

Patrick reclined on the sofa and covered his face with his hands. "I hope Maisie's asleep," he said.

"She is," Palmina assured him, as if she knew firsthand that emotional outbursts were exhausting.

"I just want to *fix it* for her, you know?"

"Americans try to fix everything. Maybe it fixes itself. Or maybe it doesn't. And we make peace with some things that are broken."

As much as it wasn't the answer Patrick hoped for, she did have a point. Perhaps their predicament wasn't that dire; maybe everyone was not as far apart as they seemed. "It's beautiful here. Lake Como. I'm sorry it became such a mess."

Palmina hesitated before saying, "Don't be."

Patrick turned to her, surprised.

"This entire . . . *production*? Prada. Milan. The Grand Hotel Tremezzo. It's not me. I had to bring my friends just to endure it. I'm not so sure it's Livia, either, but she is better at pretending." She became transfixed by her cigarette as it burned perilously close to the filter.

"It's definitely *me*," Patrick blurted. He couldn't help himself. He might have tried to mask his enthusiasm before, but this wedding was his dream affair. He even wondered if he could replicate it one day; all he had to do was find a willing groom.

"Of course it is," Palmina said, disappointed, and they laughed.

"Oh, hell. Give me a drag of that thing before it goes out." Patrick reached for her cigarette and Palmina relinquished it to him. He inhaled deeply, letting the smoke hit his lungs, holding it there momentarily before doubling over in a coughing fit when it was time to exhale. She laughed again, this time at his very predictable predicament. "Oh, shit!" he exclaimed as he dropped the butt; Palmina swooped in and extinguished it between two moistened fingers before it could burn a hole in the rug. Once again, unflappably cool.

"Should I light another?"

Patrick waved her away as he caught his breath, reclining further on the couch. They were like two teenagers staying up all night at a slumber party. Patrick even wondered if he could crash right here, leaving Maisie undisturbed in his bed. But he also knew his niece would be frightened if she woke up in a strange room alone. His eyes followed the room's ornate molding to a corner, where it joined seamlessly with the door frame. Two different things, blending against the odds, just like him and Palmina.

"I start every day by crying for nine minutes," she divulged.

Patrick propped himself up on his elbows. Nine minutes was very specific. "Are you that miserable?"

"No. I'm that happy. They are tears of joy. I was just thinking you should try it sometime."

"Yoga might be more productive. Or even taking up smoking for real." And then he thought about it. "You cry. For *nine* minutes."

"Yes, but with joy."

Patrick didn't feel like he had that much to be joyful for lately, but maybe this would help find things for which to be happy. "I'll think about it."

"Think soon," she said, as if he were the victim of one of the Italian folk tales she mentioned, cursed by a witch while sands in an hourglass were running out. She couldn't have let it just be a nice moment between them.

Patrick took a few deep breaths. "Just so you know. These are limited circumstances in which we are aligned."

"Very limited." Palmina agreed. Then added, "You worry too much, trying to control everything."

"Controlling things is what gay people in my country do best."

"There will be a wedding," Palmina assured him with an airy conviction.

"I wish I had your confidence."

Palmina tossed the extinguished cigarette butt in the dregs of her champagne and made herself comfortable again on the floor. "You can just feel it in the air."

NOW

NINETEEN

A knock on the door. Either Maisie had forgotten her phone (which seemed unlikely since it was practically an appendage of hers), or there were no seats for brunch in the shade and Clara was returning the kids to his care. Or possibly it was Grant's grape juice arriving too little, too late. (He had to stop giving that kid carte blanche to order room service.) Patrick tightened his robe and placed the cold compress he had made for himself tightly against his head, then opened the door and instinctively stepped aside to allow either Maisie or the room attendant to enter. Except it wasn't room service standing in front of him with an unwanted pitcher of juice nor was it his niece or nephew, but rather someone else—someone who took his breath away.

"It's you."

"Is that an accusation or surprise?" Emory asked with a wry smirk. His hair was longer—longer than Patrick had ever seen it—and flopped perfectly over one eye; Patrick couldn't tell if it grew out of his head that way or was the result of a three-hundred-dollar cut.

"How?"

"You may have heard there's a new invention called the airplane? New York to Milan, then I rented a car. I got here as fast as I could." No one had ever looked so handsome after a long red-eye flight.

"Why?"

"Are we going to do this one word at a time?" Emory looked beyond Patrick and into the room, perhaps checking for Maisie and Grant, perhaps to make sure Patrick wasn't with anyone else. "The kids said you needed me. And given that you have a compress stuck to your head, I'd say they were right."

"When?" Patrick asked, wondering how much Emory had heard about the rehearsal dinner the night before.

"Honestly, the monosyllabic routine is getting old." Emory's smile betrayed his annoyance. "They called me yesterday morning. What can I say? I was on the next flight."

Patrick didn't have the energy to decipher if yesterday morning in New York, or wherever Emory had been, came before or after the calamitous events of last night. But none of that mattered. Without a thought, he gripped Emory and held him as tight as he could recall ever doing. After a moment that was perhaps a beat too long for Patrick's liking, he felt Emory's long arms embrace him back.

"Are you going to invite me in?" Patrick glanced down, noticing two bags at Emory's feet.

He answered unintelligibly, his words muffled by his ex's shoulder. After realizing his words probably were not clear he crouched down and grabbed Emory's bags, his robe slipping open again. He caught Emory staring.

Feeling sheepish, Patrick set Emory's bags next to the bed, as there was limited floor space, and fumbled with his robe's tie. "We had a trainer on set. I guess I've become a bit of a gym rat." Emory helped Patrick secure his robe, cinching it playfully tight. Still nervous and out of sorts with Emory now standing so close, Patrick added, "That means I go to the gym after midnight and eat their garbage."

Emory laughed, much to Patrick's delight—it was a much needed icebreaker.

"Would you look at this," Emory said, turning his attention to the room. Out of his ex's sightline, Patrick allowed his knees to buckle.

"It's small," Patrick said apologetically, regaining his footing. When Palmina had stopped by his room earlier to check on Maisie he was haunted by her upturned nose. She said his room was *piccola*.

"*Small*," Emory repeated, rolling his eyes. "You can never just appreciate what you have." It was a pointed observation and not the least bit about the room. His eyes passed the side of the bed where Maisie had slept; two pillows side by side, and they had both been used.

"Maisie," Patrick explained. "Maisie spent the night." Patrick hoped it registered with Emory that Patrick *did* appreciate what he once had—that there was no one else in his life, at least not romantically—but if it did, Emory made no mention.

"So where are they now?"

Patrick looked around, as if unsure.

"The kids, I mean."

"Oh. Clara and Palmina took them down to brunch."

"Palmina?"

"Livia's sister. She's their launt." Patrick looked up at the ceiling. "Or, was going to be."

"Launt . . . *Lesbian aunt*?" Emory's lips fluttered. "There's no such thing."

"That's what I said!" Patrick exclaimed, relieved to finally have backup. "And yet this hotel is crawling with them. Lesbians, not launts, since that's not a thing. The whole fourth floor is like a road company of *The Vagina Monologues*. You should see them all with their snide looks and remarks." Patrick grunted his frustration. "They get my testosterone roiling."

Emory's face soured. "Well, try not to get any on people."

"*Emory.*"

"Oh, like you've never made snide remarks."

Patrick flopped on the bed, guilty. Emory knew him too well to believe him a victim.

He leaned over Patrick and straightened the compress on his forehead. "My perfect invalid."

Patrick smiled, because he called Patrick his. "You shouldn't call people invalids. It's ableist."

"Says who?"

"Someone named Audrey Buckets, I think? I wasn't really listening."

"Big surprise." Emory continued his tour out onto the balcony. His silhouette against the bright water and distant mountains made for a perfect, romantic tableau.

After they were quiet for a moment, Patrick inquired, "They just called you *yesterday*?" which overlapped Emory asking, "*Was* going to be?"

Emory turned and the two stared at each other, drinking in every detail, and this time Emory spoke first. "Yesterday. I told you. Early."

"And that gave you enough time . . . ?"

"It's six hours earlier in New York."

"Right." With Patrick having been in Europe as long as he had, Emory could have told him it was both yesterday *and* tomorrow in the States and Patrick would have believed him.

"Is the wedding off, Patrick?"

"Huh?"

"You said Palmina *was* going to be their launt."

"Oh." Patrick scanned the lake for signs of Greg and Livia's boat; he imagined they would return with crucial, up-to-the-minute information he was currently missing. He turned back to look at Emory, whose eyes were as blue as the lake. In his head, Patrick had carved this image of Emory as boyish, but the person before him was very much a man. Not just his deep-set eyes, or the cut of his jaw, although they both played a part. It wasn't the few days' growth on his chin or the very first hints of graying at his temples. But instead because he was someone who cared deeply, someone with obligations who would drop everything to help a loved one in need. Maisie, yes. Grant, obviously. But maybe—*just maybe*—Patrick, too.

"What?" Emory asked, uncomfortable but not withering from Patrick's stare.

"You look older than I remember."

"I just took the red-eye, asshole. And navigated a car rental agency in a language I don't speak to race straight to be by your side. I'm sorry I'm not *refreshed*."

This was coming out all wrong. "No, I mean older than when we first met."

Emory chuckled. "Time isn't standing still, Patrick, not for any of us." He sat on the edge of the bed and rested his hand against Patrick's cheek and the warmth of his palm caused tears to well in Patrick's eyes. "And yet somehow you figured out how to get better with age."

Patrick had never in his life felt more foolish. So convinced was he that Emory would lose interest with the years, it had never occurred to him that his love for Patrick might grow.

"What?" Emory asked, not understanding Patrick's sudden emotion.

Patrick wasn't yet able to form coherent thoughts. "You stayed in touch with the kids," he finally said, expressing his disbelief.

Emory play-slapped his cheek. "I wasn't just in a relationship with you, you dolt. I had a relationship with your whole family. That means Greg and Clara, too."

Patrick braced himself, thinking Emory might tell him that he and Clara met twice a week for coed pickleball, but he could only cross one bridge at a time. "That's very sweet, but they're growing up, you know. They're not all young and cuddly like they once were."

"Greg and Clara?" Emory joked.

"Maisie is a young woman now, and Grant—Grant takes long showers. God knows what he's doing in there."

Emory was unfazed. "*You* take long showers."

"No, I mean *looooong* showers."

Emory shot him a look.

"I have to exfoliate! I'm not a caveperson."

"You shouldn't use the word 'caveperson.' It's ableist."

"How is it ableist?"

"*You're* able to live outside of caves."

"Isn't that classist?" Patrick sunk his head deeper into the pillow, hoping he could disappear. "You know what? This isn't about me, and it's certainly not about cavepeople or Audrey Buckets."

"No one is named Audrey Buckets."

"This is about the kids not being kids so much anymore." It was like having a small dog. When a dachshund wanted to go the wrong way you could just pick the thing up and redirect it. Now it was like Patrick was herding two Saint Bernards.

Emory rolled over Patrick to flop on the bed beside him. "Isn't it great?"

Patrick furrowed his brow. *Is it?*

"They're growing up and getting really interesting. Maisie always wants to talk about books she's reading. Her head is filled with ideas and it's so fun to see her reconcile them with her worldview. And Grant, he's no longer Maisie's tagalong, you know? He's his own little man with his own desires and needs. My favorite is when they disagree."

"I haven't noticed that so much."

"Really? They remind me of you and Clara and Greg."

There was a time not long ago when Patrick would not have thought this a good thing. But he and his siblings had become close over the past couple of years. Part out of necessity, but part because they were—at the core—his oldest friends.

Emory continued. "This is a time to know them better, not pull away. All the hard work that went into raising them? It's paying off in great dividends."

It was the second time Emory expressed aging as a virtue.

"They're less charmed by me than they used to be."

Emory laughed, but avoided saying *Aren't we all*. He fluffed Maisie's pillow with a few well-placed thwacks and together they leaned back to stare out the open doors at the water.

"Some lake, huh?" Patrick asked. And then he said the name in Italian. "Lago di Como."

"Remember Vegas?"

Patrick said that he did, as he was just recounting that trip to Grant. "Maisie got annoyed with me just now when I inadvertently suggested Greg getting remarried was the end of her grief over losing her mom."

"That doesn't sound like you." Indeed the observation was clumsy.

"I meant the end of the beginning." Patrick groaned, wishing he could have the conversation over again, but she was resilient. She would forgive him. "I was so young when I lost Joe. Not Maisie young, but still young."

Emory rolled his head to look at Patrick and he gently took his hand. It had been a long time since they had talked about Joe's accident.

"Trauma like that stays such a part of you. It changes your DNA. And yet I survived it. In part because I *was* young. So I know Maisie will be okay."

"Then who are you so worried about?"

Patrick remained very still. It sounded almost selfish to admit. "*Me.* The pendulum has swung, and I'm terrified of loss when I'm old. That because of our age difference, you will eventually lose interest and walk away." Patrick looked first down at his hand in Emory's, then he rolled his head, too, so that their noses were almost touching. His heart began beating faster. "And I'm not sure I would survive that."

"Have I given you any indication that I was going anywhere?"

Patrick tried his best to hide his face, his nose mushing into the pillow.

"Have I done anything other than fall more in love with you with each passing year? As ridiculous as you are?"

Patrick whispered, "No."

"Then what are we going to do about that?"

"I have work to do. On myself."

"Clearly." It was a little stab to Patrick's heart. Then Emory mussed his hair. "But. Don't we all."

Patrick took the deepest breath he could muster, like oxygen might bring him clarity. "Are you saying you would consider getting back together?" It was an honest question; in the moment Patrick felt so unworthy.

Half of Emory's face was lost in a pillow, his good side, Emory would say. But this other side was pretty perfect, too. "I hate to break it to you. But I don't think we were ever *really* apart."

Patrick grinned broadly, Emory had been staying in his apartment. But then his expression just as quickly flattened. "I was with someone named Pip," he blurted. It was best to have these things in the open.

"Pip?" Emory stared at him for a moment in a way that was hard to read. Patrick could hear a boat's motor cutting through the lake. "Is that short for something?"

Patrick bit the inside of his cheek. *Pippin? Pip pip hooray?* Emory wasn't the type to get jealous over the occasional Pip. It was emotional fidelity that had always been more of his thing. But Patrick wanted to start this new chapter as cleanly and honestly as possible. "But I don't think we were ever really apart, either."

Emory nuzzled into Patrick's chest.

"You don't think this is a terrible idea? Us getting back together, I mean."

"I do," Emory said, and Patrick's stomach dropped. But then he rolled on top of Patrick, grabbed the collar of his robe and smiled that winsome Emory smile. "But aren't terrible ideas always the best?"

They kissed deeply, and slowly Patrick pushed Emory off him, and they wrestled playfully until Patrick's wet compress fell on Emory's face with a perfect *plop* that made them both laugh. Emory brushed it aside and they continued their passionate embrace, Emory undoing Patrick's robe with one hand while unzipping his own pants with the other. Just as they were about to hit a point of no return, they were interrupted by a knock at the door. Emory froze. Was Patrick expecting anyone else?

"That would be a pitcher of grape juice." Patrick then laughed, picturing the Kool-Aid Man giving a polite knock before bursting through the door.

Emory laughed, too, but for a different reason. "I see you spared no expense welcoming me back."

TWENTY

When Greg and Livia returned from their meditation on the lake they summoned the family to their impressive suite. Their panoramic windows slid into the wall, making the living room and terrace one great open-air room in which they could hold a summit. Livia had ordered bites to eat, which were inside on the coffee table and out of the sun, and pitchers of lemonade (and a bottle of limoncello) were set out to drink. Livia ushered everyone in like a proper hostess and in her Marimekko dress looked not sad but properly bronzed, as if the reflection of the sun's rays off the water had restored her back to health after the calamitous wedding rehearsal dinner that would have sent a lesser woman running to a sanitarium to convalesce. Patrick and the kids were already peeling from sunburn and were in need of their own regeneration, but not Livia; it was like she slept in a hyperbaric chamber.

Clara arrived first, dragging Palmina behind her. Livia's parents appeared next, and then Patrick, followed by the kids, who clung tightly to his side, perhaps afraid they were about to be grounded for weeks. Emory snuck in last and pulled the door softly closed behind him.

"Emory?" Greg asked once he spotted this new arrival through the crowd, surprised to find that their party had grown by one in the brief time he was on the lake. Emory waved sheepishly, as though he were intruding. "In the flesh." He winked at Patrick, who'd just experienced every inch of it.

"Does this mean?" Greg pointed to him and then Patrick, and then back to Emory again. Clara's head turned with the same question.

"We're doing a soft *re*launch," Patrick said. "Let's not everyone make a big deal. We don't need to draft a press release, or alert the Passages page in *People*."

"But it *is* a big deal," Greg said, and Patrick was moved by the genuine happiness his brother mustered in a moment when other things were potentially falling apart. Greg then hugged Emory and enthusiastically introduced him to Livia and her family. Grant high-fived his uncle, and then immediately crossed to investigate the "snappetizers," borrowing an old word of Patrick's. Even Clara gripped Patrick and Emory tightly.

"Well done," she whispered to Patrick as he peeled her off him so she wouldn't smear his shirt with her wedding makeup. "I shouldn't be the only one having great sex in this magnificent hotel."

"I beg you, stop talking."

"Great, animalistic sex. Come on, I'm *dying* to tell someone."

"Buy a diary," Patrick pleaded as he squeezed between the kids and a wall to get away.

"So you are the mysterious Emily!" Lorenzo trumpeted when they had finally made the rounds. Emory looked back at Patrick, who scrunched his nose; it was easier just to go with it. Emory greeted the Brassos warmly, before his gaze fell on Palmina. She, too, had her face done for the wedding, and her enormous earrings were back. Her hair was swept up in a faux-hawk that made her look more in vogue than ever, irritating Patrick to no end.

"And you are Palmina. I've heard so much about you."

"All bad, I hope," Palmina murmured as her mother whacked her in the arm. Emory laughed.

"I can already tell I like you."

Patrick stepped in to curtail this budding enthrallment. "Okay, that's enough introductions."

Grant pushed himself into the center of the room. "Where Palmina lives there's a sea cave where the water inside is blue."

"All water is blue," Patrick insisted. *Honestly.* They didn't need to be impressed with *all* things Palmina.

"No, but like *really* blue. What's it called?"

"The Grotta Azzurra," Palmina replied.

"Grotta Azzhoo—" Grant attempted before giving up. "All there is where GUP lives is Central Park."

Palmina looked at the boy with great pity. "Central Park is so plebeian."

Patrick turned to Emory to say, *See what I'm dealing with?* But Emory had already turned his attention to Livia.

"I don't mean to intrude on your family meeting. I just wanted to say a quick hello and I'll leave you all to it. Patrick, meet me downstairs when you're done?"

Livia turned to Patrick for explanation.

"The kids called him," he said, holding his hands up to proclaim innocence. "I had nothing to do with it." Maisie shot daggers his way, thinking he could only get her in more trouble where Livia was concerned, but Grant was pleased to get credit.

But Livia was nothing if not gracious. "If the kids called you and they want you here, then you are part of the family and I want you here, too."

"Let's get you some antipasto," Giana offered, and led Emory to the bountiful spread. "You've had a long flight. You must eat." It was clear from the look on his face Emory was enjoying the Brassos; how much of his enjoyment stemmed from it annoying Patrick was as yet undetermined.

That morning they had followed their plan. Clara cornered Greg early and had given him a good talking to, and Palmina likewise had taken Livia aside. They did their best to reassure them that the kids were just that—kids—and while they were an important consideration, they perhaps shouldn't be the *only* consideration when they had proven to be so resilient. Both Greg and Livia listened to their respective siblings politely before stating firmly that they, and they alone, would make any final decision. Meanwhile Patrick had done his best to make headway with Maisie, but her general discomfort led to her standing her ground, lest she expose even more vulnerability by allowing a public change of heart. As lifeguards in this situation, Palmina, Clara, and Patrick had jumped into the riptide with both feet and were now in danger themselves of being swept out to sea.

"Greg," Patrick tried, making one last-ditch effort. But Greg held a finger in front of his lips to shush him.

"Why don't you all sit down." Livia gestured at the tufted sofa and chair. Palmina took an awkward seat on the sofa's arm next to her parents, and Patrick for the first time saw the vulnerable girl underneath her queer swagger. Giana fussed with the food, arranging everything to look presentable as Lorenzo swatted a buzzing fly. Emory procured two chairs from the terrace's dining table for him and Patrick, and Grant hopped on Emory's lap, looking more like a ventriloquist's dummy than ever. Maisie receded into the far corner next to a potted plant, not wanting anything to do with this torture. Greg took Livia's hand in his and they stood facing the gathering. Emory, realizing he was the only one holding food, discreetly handed his plate to Patrick, who slid it under his chair.

Greg began. "First of all, I want to thank Lorenzo and Giana for their incredible hospitality this week, not to mention the generosity and the kindness they have shown my children. That I won't ever forget. And Patrick, Clara, Maisie, and Grant—"

"And Emory!" Grant excitedly exclaimed.

"And Emory," Greg agreed. "I thank you for putting your own lives on hold and traveling all this way to celebrate with us. All of it means so much. But we have come to a . . ." His voice cracking, he turned to Livia for strength.

Livia pursed her lips stoically. "We have decided that now is not the time to get married."

The room sat quietly with this news. Even Lorenzo, who never met a passing thought he couldn't express boisterously, could only mutter to himself softly. Patrick glanced at Maisie; instead of relief, he saw genuine anguish. As much as she thought she wanted this, victory, now that it was at hand, apparently was not so sweet. He then turned back to Greg and read bona fide heartbreak on his brother's face. And so he broke the silence. "Bullshit."

Everyone turned to Patrick, appalled.

"No, I'm sorry. That's bullshit."

"Patrick," Greg cautioned. "Let's not get into a repeat of last night. The decision has already been made."

"And it's wrong! Once again I am right, and the rest of you are behaving like morons."

"GUP," Maisie protested. But Patrick was having none of it.

"No, Maisie, that's not ableist. Being an idiot is not a medical condition. I'm talking garden variety, actors who don't know not to read the stage directions out loud type of imbeciles here. Get serious."

Emory swallowed uncomfortably, then tried to cut some of the tension. "No, no. Back off, everyone. I saw him first."

Palmina laughed her throaty laugh. She liked this Emory character, too.

"Maisie, I know this is what you wanted, but I need you to open your eyes and your heart and remember the love languages I taught you. 'Silent All These Years.' Livia has been nothing but silent since you first met as she endured your chilly embrace. 'The Finer Things'? Oh my god, have you seen this hotel? It's nothing but the finest! Even my room, which yes, I know—piccola. But still, wow. And she wants to share them all with you. A tour of the Villa del Balbianello? A once-in-a-lifetime shopping trip to the Prada flagship store, where she shared a few of her favorite things? And she picked up the bill? 'Don't need no credit card to ride this train.' Hello!"

Emory whispered to Grant. "The Prada flagship store? Is that true?" Grant, however, merely shrugged. Greg, meanwhile, looked thoroughly baffled. What were these lessons Patrick had been teaching the kids?

"And 'Making love out of nothing at all.' Putting off her own wedding at the last minute to build a relationship with you. Maybe you haven't spent enough time with Livia to see it yet, and yes—seeing is believing. Even I was slow to come around. But she wants to take a vow to join your family in front of god and everyone until death do you part." The god stuff was perhaps a little over the top, but Lorenzo, finding his mojo, gave him a spirited thumbs-up. Maisie looked down at her shoes.

"Patrick," Greg said again. "These lessons seem well intended—"

"Because they are! But the one thing I didn't get to say about love is how rare it can be. And what a miracle it is to find it once. But to find it *twice?*" Patrick held out his hand for Emory, who happily offered his in return. "Maisie, Grant. We all loved your mom. I dare say even Livia loves your mom because of the love she had for your dad and because she brought you into this world."

"It's true," Livia said quietly, leaning into Greg.

"Just as your mom and I loved Joe. But now they are both gone. And they both want us to be happy. I know this in my bones." Patrick scanned the room to see if this was sinking in. "Do you remember Guncle Rule sweet sixteen?" He hoped that was the right one—it had been such a long time. "I want you to really *live*. And change is the biggest part of living."

Grant slipped off Emory's lap and crossed to his sister, pinning her arms to her side with a tight hug. "It's okay, Maisie. You're just scared because we're the last survivors of a lost civilization that was you, me, Mom, and Dad. We know all the traditions and the jokes."

Everyone's jaws dropped in amazement, except for Greg's, who instead caught Patrick's eye. *I thought he was asleep*, he mouthed.

I know, Patrick mouthed back.

"But we can teach Livia about our ways. About birthdays and Christmas."

"Ease up on the presents," Patrick cautioned before his nephew could ruin the moment by opening a registry.

"We can rebuild our civilization. And make booby traps with spears and poison darts, and a giant boulder that can roll down from the attic if anyone tries to attack—"

There it was. Patrick stepped forward and covered Grant's mouth with his hand. "Nailed it, kiddo. Right up until that Indiana Jones bit."

Grant wriggled free of Patrick and pumped his fist. "I'll bet you thought I was sleeping, huh?"

Patrick was too stunned to answer, his mind already racing to think of what else he and Greg might have absentmindedly discussed in front of the boy.

"Magic! I'm training myself to sleep with my eyes open and be awake with my eyes closed." Patrick tried to imagine the résumé that listed those as special skills.

"What an excellent use of your time."

Livia stepped forward. "It's true, Maisie. I really would like to learn. I know you're the keeper of your family's memories. So I am going to need your help. Your father and I still very much want to get married. But we've agreed we need to do a better job of including you in the planning. And that maybe it should all happen closer to home."

"My home?" Maisie asked tentatively. She might be better able to wrap her head around a wedding in Connecticut.

"*Our* home," Livia said as Greg embraced her.

Maisie took a conciliatory step away from the wall and toward the group. "I would like that," she said. She still looked like she hoped the floor would swallow her, and it was only a small step. But it was one giant leap for Maisiekind.

"Are you sure, sweetheart?" Giana asked of her daughter, hoping perhaps that this was enough in the way of reconciliation to put things back on track. "We are here all together. In this stunning hotel. Surrounded by the most breathtaking view."

"We have all this food!" Lorenzo added. "And the wine. Oh, so much wine."

"Someone should get married today," Giana pleaded.

Maisie's thin voice broke through everyone murmuring their regret. "It should be GUP."

Grant, however, was on another track entirely. "Can we get an Italian greyhound?" he asked Livia. "A dog like that might help you feel more at home."

Only Greg registered what Maisie said. He turned to Livia for confirmation, but she was focused solely on Grant as he continued pleading his case. "Maisie," Greg interrupted, covering Grant's mouth with his hand. "What did you just say?"

The color drained from Patrick's face when her words finally sunk in. "Maisie didn't say anything."

"Yes she did," Clara said, coming around.

"I only heard something about Italian hounds."

"That's because you have auditory recency bias," Maisie charged.

Livia turned to Patrick, concerned. "Is it serious?"

"Is it fatal?" Palmina asked, her eyes gleaming with excitement. Lorenzo and Giana exchanged glances.

Emory jumped in to put them all at ease. "Sadly, made-up diseases rarely are."

Patrick turned to the kids. "It is not made up . . . Kids, are you just going to let that hang there?"

Maisie stepped forward. "We think launts are better than guncles." She extended her hand to Patrick. "Could you hand me a plate?"

Without thinking Patrick reached for a plate from the table, but he snatched it back before Maisie could take it. "For the last time, there is no such thing as launts!"

Maisie threw her arms in the air. "OH MY GOD, HE'S CURED!" Patrick spun in a tight circle as a dog might as everyone laughed at his expense. "You heard exactly what I said. All the things you said about Livia, they're true about Emory, too. He keeps silent when you are at your most ridiculous."

"Like right now, for instance," Emory teased, uncertain where this was going.

"And when Grant and I stay with you, you and Emory make the bed with eight-hundred-thread-count sheets. Even though we have no idea what that means. *Finer things.*"

Patrick turned to Emory for backup. "It's a guest room, not a barn."

"You do everything together, as you have the same favorite things. And he dropped everything to fly over an ocean to be here for us when we needed him most. You love spending time together, and you mope around when you're apart."

"I do not *mope* . . ." Patrick protested, covering his eyes. This wasn't happening. Now it was him hoping the room's floor would suddenly open.

"So, what are you going to do about it?" Maisie challenged with newly gained confidence.

This was such obvious payback, Patrick should have seen it coming; he'd walked himself right into this trap. All eyes were on him, including Emory's. "No, I said a soft relaunch. *Soft.*"

"What if we made it hard?" Emory smirked. It caused Patrick to do a double take. Patrick scanned the room looking for someone—*anyone*—to rescue him from this tight corner, or at the very least point the way out.

"Patrizio," Palmina began. "Giving the teenagers hand jobs is fine for a while, but is it really a life?"

Emory's head spun like an owl's. "I'm sorry, giving teenagers WHAT?"

"Hand JIVE. Jive. And not giving, *teaching.*" Beads of sweat gathered on Patrick's forehead. "I need to lie down."

Palmina stood, and then one by one so did the others until only Emory remained seated. Patrick closed his eyes and breathed deeply, reminding himself how sad he'd been the past few months. Palmina's words from their very first encounter rang through his head. *You'll never know what you want until you know for certain who you are.* It was the one thing this moment had going for it: Patrick had never felt more like himself.

Fuck it, he thought as he opened his eyes. "Carpe diem," he muttered. And then since Maisie's SayHi app was set to Italian, he said, "That's Latin for seize the day." He dropped to one knee and groaned when his kneecap hit the floor.

"Did you just groan?" Emory asked.

"Give me a break. My knees are old."

"They're not old," Palmina opined. "They're *wise.*" She then dropped her bravado and tugged on her earring, exposing the hidden soft spot she had underneath. She gestured encouragement for him to follow through; he had already confessed that this was his dream wedding, it was up to him now to make that dream come true.

"Emory." Patrick inhaled and the scent of cypress trees brought great calm. "I have all these rules for others and my life is best when I apply them to myself, too. I want to truly live, and that means living my life with you. I don't always deserve you, but I do always love you. And I would be honored if you saw fit to live your life with me." Patrick took one last deep breath, the weight of all eyes on him. "Will you marry me?"

In this fairy-tale world of old European castles and wicked step-mothers (who turned out to be empathetic and kind), could this really be it? Patrick had always been more fairy godmother than Cinderella, but as he waited for Emory's answer he knew he was now ready for his happily ever after.

TWENTY-ONE

The Belle Epoque was a period of European prosperity that began in the late eighteen hundreds and ended with the outbreak of the First World War. It was a time of opulence and affluence that celebrated life and style and European cultural influence before the hardships of the early twentieth century took hold. And in hosting special events like weddings, the Grand Hotel Tremezzo did everything in its power to mimic the exuberance and frivolity of the period and to bring everyone together in celebration back to that singular time.

Patrick was calming his pre-wedding jitters with an Italian spritz on the hotel's main terrazza, flanked by Maisie and Grant. The early-evening air was warm, but the sun was flirting with the mountaintops and would soon say its own buonasera, the occasional breeze providing just enough relief across the back of his neck. There were a few mosquitoes, but not many; the crawling sensation on Patrick's skin was mostly nervous anticipation, and the slight peeling from sunburn. On the lawn below, caterers scurried about putting the finishing touches on a grand banquet table for the post-ceremony meal, lobster mostly, and caviar. Centerpieces were being finalized, orchids for drama mixed with peonies. Wine was unloaded from the boat dock in crates. Everyone was working with great haste to pull off a spectacular affair; in fact, it seemed for the first time in his stay the hotel had more employees than guests.

"Is there anything to eat besides lobster?" Grant asked, looking skeptically at the buffet.

Patrick strained to remember. Lorenzo and Giana had given them a full rundown of the menu they had planned for their daughter, but in the moment it was all a blur. "Ravioli. Tagliatelle. Don't worry. We'll find you something." In this moment, Patrick was more concerned for himself. They were on a lake, for god's sake. *Do lobsters live in lakes?* What had Livia's parents wrought?

"Lobsters spend their whole lives in the water, but they are poorly designed for swimming. Did you know that?" Grant asked.

Patrick knelt down and tugged at the hem of his nephew's dinner jacket. "Is that so?"

"They mostly just walk on the bottom. I'm not really sure they're designed for us eating them, either. They're like the insects of the sea."

Patrick smirked. "In some cultures insects are delicacies."

Grant frowned. "Is this one of them?" If it were, he would have to reassess his opinion of Italy. "What are you doing?" he asked when he felt a sharp tug on his jacket.

"Giving you crisp shoulder lines. Might as well show off those seven push-ups you can do."

"I did ten this morning!"

"Three of them were on your knees," his sister reminded him.

Patrick glanced at Maisie, who was dressed in another outfit Livia had arranged for her, pants with a short linen trench coat and stylish belt. "You look absolutely perfect," Patrick said, standing up.

Maisie replied, "I know." No book in sight, her hands were confidently in her pockets. She surveyed the grounds and offered a higher opinion than Grant's. "Everything does."

"Are you happy?" Patrick asked. After all they'd endured, he should have sought their blessing earlier.

The kids looked at each other, then at their uncle with wide jack-o'-lantern grins.

"Okay, good. But dial it back a notch, you're creeping me out." But even Patrick couldn't contain his delight. Then suddenly the world went dark as his eyes were covered from behind. It could only be one person. "It's bad luck to see the bride before the wedding."

"Then it's a good thing this wedding has two grooms."

His fiancé removed his hands and Patrick spun around. Emory was wearing a suit that matched his own—the Prada shawl collar tuxedo in light blue. He wasn't sure how she did it, but Livia and her Prada Loompas had worked real magic, right down to the silver onyx button studs and black grosgrain loafers in exactly their size. Patrick adjusted Emory's bow tie. "Are you sure?" he asked.

Emory replied with a quizzical look. "Shouldn't you save that question for the ceremony?"

Patrick gestured at everything. It may have aligned perfectly with his tastes, but it was someone else's venue, someone else's banquet, someone else's guest list, someone else's cake, someone else's vision. "Are you sure this is our wedding?"

Emory scanned the property, slowly absorbing each detail. The bar set up with aperitifs to hand to each guest as they arrived. The Edison lights strung over the lawn. The speedboat that waited to take just the two of them on a brief spin after they said their I dos. "Will you be there?" he asked when his eyes landed back on Patrick.

Patrick said he would indeed.

Emory bit his lip to keep from grinning. "Then it's my wedding."

"I'll be there, too," Grant hollered. Emory scooped him up and threw him over his shoulder.

"Me too," Maisie said, beaming. She looked like a kid again despite her very adult clothes, and Patrick realized she had been this whole time. She had just been carrying too much weight on her shoulders.

"Okay, well, both of you don't wrinkle your jackets," Patrick said, wresting Grant from Emory to set back on the ground.

"I can do ten push-ups," Grant said to Emory as he began to slip out of his jacket. "Wanna see?"

Patrick pinched the bridge of his nose.

"What's your deal?" Maisie asked.

Patrick held up his half-empty glass. "This drink needs fortifying, and frankly so do I."

They were married on the terrazza at sunset, the light glinting off the far windows of Bellagio on the distant side of the lake under a cloud-dappled sky. Eschewing tradition, Patrick and Emory walked themselves down the aisle. Greg stood just behind Patrick, wearing a suit Patrick hoped hadn't likewise been demoted when his brother went from groom to best man. Palmina joined them on Emory's side, wearing yet another jumpsuit and a silk scarf printed with tigers that made Patrick long for his ascot. It wasn't Patrick's first choice to include his rival in their wedding party, but since he was old and the venue was borrowed and the suits were blue he let his great love have his something new. Grant stood with Patrick next to his dad, Maisie behind Palmina and Emory. It was the kids' first time being part of a wedding, and they were giddy that it was one they approved of so much. And good practice for a future wedding back home. Livia sat in the front row of a small gathering of chairs next to her parents; Lorenzo and Giana both seemed genuinely pleased their planning and hard work were not going to waste. They had been more gracious than ever in gifting the venue to Patrick and Emory. Only Cousin Geppetto seemed unsure as to what was about to transpire, distracted as he was by an enthusiastic Gustavo doing his best to remind everyone who he was and how he was connected to the affair. Clara stood between the couple to officiate. She wasn't ordained, but that didn't matter. As marriage equality was not yet the law in Italy, they would have to do it all again in New York to make it official.

Clara and Emory hadn't started on the right foot when they met five summers before, but she had been wrong about him, and over the years she admitted as much, and Emory was not one to hold a grudge. Today as she opened the ceremony, Clara sang his praises, and expressed gratitude for the joy he had brought into their lives—*all* of their lives. Patrick glanced over his shoulder at Greg, happy to be absolved once again for any perceived misdoings he might have been blamed for that first summer in Palm Springs. But Greg's attention was focused squarely on Livia. Patrick forgave this slight; even though in a just world the betrothed couple should rightly be everyone's focus, he was the center of enough attention and was happy in the knowledge that one way or another Greg and Livia would work things out.

Patrick and Emory recited their own written vows, though *written* was too strong a word. With little time to prepare, there was no room for writing and they were forced to speak off-the-cuff. Patrick recognized in Emory what he was feeling himself—an unusual case of stage fright.

"Don't worry," Patrick whispered. "Most of our guests don't speak English."

Emory's face glowed in the last of the day's northern Italian sun, and the anxiety that had spread through both their bodies suddenly lifted, shed as easily as their suit jackets would be when later it was time to dance.

"Patrick. Where to even begin. When we met you were like the best home on a bad block. People would advise one against buying it. There was a gloomy sadness in your neighborhood, but all it needed was someone to restore it to glory. I wasn't always certain I was up for the challenge, building an entire world back up around you, no matter how much I was sure you were worth it. But of this much I was always sure: there are times when one's heart dictates and it's best to simply stop arguing and obey."

It was the one use of the word *obey* in wedding vows that Patrick could readily embrace. Still, he had no choice but to chuckle. Arguing was what he did best.

Clara turned to her brother. "Patrick?"

Patrick shifted his weight from one foot to the other, then steadied himself before speaking. It would take his full self to get through this. "It's true that when we met I had stopped living, so completely crushed was I by the loss of young love. The truth is, there are a thousand ways that love ends, but there is only one way it begins and that's by opening your heart to another. It's something I didn't think I dared do again until two rotten kids stepped into my life and reminded me of everything love could be." Maisie and Grant snickered at being called rotten. "And you. You linked your pinkie in mine as we stood around my piano singing Christmas songs in the sweltering heat of July. And you made room in your life for mine, as messy and imperfect as it was. For these kids. For my family. For the memories of Sara and Joe. And I finally moved, not on, but *forward*." Out of the corner of his eye, Patrick saw Clara rest her hand on Greg's shoulder, happy.

Emory held out his left hand until it found Patrick's, and he gripped his husband-to-be tight as they made additional vows to be patient, forgiving, and kind, and Clara asked if they freely took each other to be their lawfully wedded spouse.

"If only we'd had time to get rings," Emory said forlornly.

Rings! Even Greg pat down the front of his suit, as if he was supposed to be carrying them. It was a best man's job, after all. Palmina stepped forward, mildly annoyed like she had to do everything, and

Patrick feared she would offer her earrings, which were more like bracelets than rings. But instead she untied the silk scarf from her neck, stepping forward to lash it around the grooms' wrists until they were bound tightly together, the tigers of the scarf's pattern running circles around their arms. Patrick winced slightly as she tied her knot a little too tightly; she seemed to find enjoyment in administering pain.

"Kinky," Emory whispered, sharing in Palmina's delight.

Clara grasped their arms where they were joined and said, "By the power vested in me . . ."

Patrick cleared his throat. "You have no power," he reminded her.

"Fine." Patrick read the annoyance on his sister's face; he couldn't just leave her be. "As someone who loves you both, then. Does that work? I recognize you as united. You may now kiss your husband."

Patrick and Emory did just that, sharing a deep soulful kiss that went on perhaps just a moment too long.

"I guess they're over their stage fright," Greg remarked.

Maisie and Grant reached into their pockets and pulled out fist-fuls of golden confetti and tossed it in the air. It rained down on Patrick and Emory and pulled them out of their kiss. They looked up in wonder, as if they'd awoken from a dream not knowing where they were. Confetti, strangers clapping, rolling green hills sloping down into the most magnificent lake. Twilight. The warmth of summer air, the cool of an evening breeze. The Edison bulbs blinking to life above a banquet table on the lawn below.

The distribution of loss is inequitable, and Patrick and his family had endured more than their fair share. But he was done being sad.

It was time now to celebrate.

TWENTY-TWO

Night fell. The wedding party feasted around the long table that had been placed on the lawn, its white linens hanging like a bride's veil perfectly masking their stuffed bellies. Patrick and Emory sat together at the table's center with the best view of the lake; they gorged on lobster and pasta, and Livia lovingly helped find Maisie and Grant dishes that were acceptable to their more limited palates, and they let her do so without showing derision or scorn. Patrick looked around at the gathering of both family and strangers and was filled with admiration for the Italians for their ability to shift the direction of their hospitality so effortlessly. It didn't matter who they were gathered to celebrate, so much as *that* they were gathered to celebrate. There was a real lesson in that. They raised glasses, they popped corks, they shouted boisterously in both English and Italian, and they laughed generously; at times it felt like the whole table shook.

The sky was black when they moved back up to the terrazza, which had been cleared of chairs, for dancing. A few boats were scattered across the lake in the soft mist of darkness, lit just enough to form new and unfamiliar constellations in the water that was their sky. Above the terrace, a cream-colored awning rippled like low soft clouds; Patrick stood on his heels and poked it.

"Are you wearing lifts?" Clara asked.

To which Patrick replied, "Bite your tongue."

He saw Emory at the railing looking across the lake. Patrick tip-toed up from behind until he could wrap his arms around him. "Come quickly, I am drinking the stars." Emory leaned back into Patrick's embrace. "Husband," he then whispered in Emory's ear.

"Say it in Italian."

Patrick had reached the limits of his vocabulary and took a wild stab. "Husbandito."

"Close," Emory replied. "Marito."

Patrick pulled back far enough for Emory to see the puzzled look on his face. "Did SayHi teach you that?"

"No, Palmina told me to call you that." Emory's enthusiasm dimmed. "But knowing you two, perhaps it's a slur." Emory pulled the scarf she had tied around their wrists from his pocket. "I borrowed this. I thought we could put it to use later."

"Wonderful," Patrick said, but he wasn't sure he wanted any part of Palmina invading their bedroom. He glanced over and saw Greg standing alone and asked Emory to excuse him.

Patrick walked over to his brother and hugged him. "Were you thinking about how all this should have been yours?"

Greg looked wistfully at the reception. "Yes and no. I was actually just thinking about Sara."

Patrick was taken aback.

"Don't look so surprised. I think about her every day." Greg then pretended to study his cuticles before fidgeting with his empty ring finger. "I'm looking forward to having a ring on this finger again. We're not dishonoring them by loving again, are we?"

Patrick swallowed the lump in his throat. "I think quite the opposite, in fact."

◇◇◇◇◇◇◇◇

Soon it was midnight and the band played one last song before packing their instruments to leave. Without music, things fell eerily quiet, the silence pierced only by the chatter of small conversations clustered around them. Patrick watched as the last of the table settings were struck and cleared before the Edison bulbs were turned off for the night, blanketing the lawn in darkness. Only the floating pool lights remained glowing, the pool water a beckoning aqua blue against the surrounding gloom of the lake. Emory was charming Livia's family; they were perhaps more taken with Emory than they had been with him. But that was okay. That was the thing about love. Somehow people adoring your partner reflected well on you. He walked over to the kids, who were fighting to stay awake.

Patrick knelt beside them. Grant leaned against his bent leg and Maisie rested her head on his shoulder. "I was thinking back to our summer in Palm Springs," he said.

"Oh yeah?"

"Remember the pool floats? There was a slow leak in one. The pineapple, perhaps."

"Or Pegasus!" Grant offered. *Pegathuth.*

"Maybe. You were so upset that it kept deflating."

"I was?" Grant seemed skeptical.

"You both were. And me a little bit, too. The thing of it is, so much air had escaped from our lives. Your mother kept us all afloat. But I look around me tonight, and I think we did a good job patching the leak." There was suddenly a lump in Patrick's throat.

Maisie gripped his shirt tightly and he didn't admonish her for wrinkling it.

"Your mom is missing so much. It's really not fair. She's missing your accomplishments. She's missing your crying. She's missing your dancing. All of it." He could feel Maisie's head bobbing in agreement against his collar. "I wish she could be at my wedding. I think she would love Emory. Don't you?" Grant played with the button studs on Patrick's chest. "And my god, she would love you. The incredible people you are becoming. All the things you are going to be. She'd be so thrilled. And she'll love you forever. I've only ever wanted you to be secure in that knowledge. And to be happy. I just want to squeeze you right now and demand you be happy." He shook them both until they cracked and giggled. "But I can't do that. I can't snap my fingers and order you to be anything. I can *ask* you to choose happiness when you can. I can ask you to try. I can show you what happens when you let new people into your life." He looked across at Emory and did his best to contain himself. Greg sauntered over to listen, but stayed far enough back not to encroach on their moment.

"I'm sorry you're sad about missing Mom," Grant said.

Patrick undid a button on his shirt. "That's just the thing. It doesn't feel like sadness. It feels like love."

Patrick jostled them again until they cracked.

"How does it feel for you?" Patrick leaned from Maisie to Grant and back again, as if they might whisper the answer in his ear. "Are you happy?"

Maisie hesitated. "For Emory and you?"

"*About* Emory and me."

"YES!" Grant screamed as he pumped his fist in the air.

Patrick held both palms up waiting for two high fives, which came in perfect unison. He then stood and looked his brother, Greg, in the eye. "And that's—"

"Don't say it," Greg pleaded. Emory, who was just joining them, likewise encouraged him to quit while ahead.

But there was no stopping Patrick from employing his character's catchphrase from his first TV sitcom. "—how you do it."

Maisie looked like she was going to be sick.

"Oh come on," Patrick protested. "It was meant to be funny!"

They had the terrazza reserved for another hour. Soon it would be hosed down, and tables would be set for breakfast service, which began at six. But Patrick wasn't willing to cede the night to those who rose with the sun. Not his night. Not *their* night. The wedding would soon be over and a new life would begin. He would head home, say goodbye to the kids, and figure out everything to come next.

"Someone must have speakers or something. We need more dancing!"

Palmina offered the Bluetooth speakers in her room, which was closest to the terrazza. When she returned with them, Patrick snatched the speakers from her grip before she could plug them in.

"Why don't you like Palmina?" Maisie asked, having observed this interaction go down.

"Who says I don't like Palmina?" Patrick protested. But as he waited for his phone to pair with the speakers, he earnestly replied, "I like Palmina very much."

Palmina closed her eyes in disgust. There was no need to get mushy now.

"Lesbians, then," Maisie pressed, as if she wasn't buying his response.

"Let me tell you something," he said, looking up at Palmina. "Lesbians are heroes. They were at the forefront of earning women the right to vote. They helped pave the way for marriage equality and were on the front lines to normalize the idea of gay people raising kids. They held our hands when we were dying of AIDS. Sally Ride was the first woman in space! Also, they went to the prom with us when we were scared queer boys and allowed us to hold our heads high. And, if that weren't enough, they lend you their speakers when you want to dance."

"Then why do you bicker so much?"

Patrick thought this was obvious. "Why do you bicker with Grant? Gay men and lesbians are brothers and sisters. And sometimes you tease your family because you love them the most." Maisie seemed to find this acceptable just as the speakers blipped their connection. "But you can't dance to anyone who played Lilith Fair, so we're going to play music from *my* phone." He winked at Palmina, who found Patrick's references as outdated and square as the kids did.

Patrick pulled up an old standby playlist that never failed to get people on their feet.

"We didn't get you anything," Grant said panicked, looking at the few gifts that had been hastily procured and placed in a sad little lump in the corner. Presents again his love language.

Patrick placed his hands on their shoulders and turned them out-ward to face their spectacular setting—the lake, the moon, the stars that punctured the sky. Emory wandered into their sight line and waved. "Correction," Patrick whispered so only they could hear. "You got me *everything*." He then pressed play on his phone and the open-ing synth-pop beats of Starship's "Nothing's Gonna Stop Us Now" unspooled from the speakers.

Emory groaned. "Not oldies."

But Clara squealed with recognition, as did several others, and Patrick amped up the volume and had just enough time to spin Emory onto the makeshift checkered tile dance floor and say, "*Oldies*. Don't make me marry and divorce you in the same night." He then lip-synched the opening lyrics. *Lookin' in your eyes, I see a paradise . . .*

Emory relented and whispered the next lyrics back. Indeed the world that they found seemed too good to be true.

Clara and Gustavo, Greg and Livia, even Palmina and the Robert Palmer girls all took the dance floor, unable to resist a power ballad. "*Oldies*," Patrick scoffed over the music. "CLASSICS!" Even Maisie and Grant couldn't hold themselves back from dancing. Grant had long lost his little suit jacket and he'd rolled up his sleeves to get down. As always, he was a natural, and over the years Patrick had encouraged his interest in dancing by introducing him to all kinds of music that kept the kid on his feet. Maisie was just a half step off the beat, much as she was in life. Awkward, but also beautiful, like a baby giraffe first standing tall. But they were at the heart of it all; Patrick, Emory, Palmina, Livia, Clara, and even Groot couldn't help but break in to have a turn dancing with each kid.

Patrick eyed Emory from across the dance floor. If the world ran out of lovers, they'd still have each other. There were challenges ahead, and a new life to get used to, but indeed—nothing could stop them now.

Except for the event staff at the Grand Hotel Tremezzo, who eventually *did* stop them just after one in the morning. Drenched in sweat, a slight chill descended over Patrick and the kids once they stopped dancing, and Grant asked if he and Maisie could have hot chocolate. Livia agreed the nightcap was a fine idea and offered to join them.

"We've had the best in the world," Grant warned, looking back at his uncle, as if this would be a make-or-break test for Livia. *Finer things.*

"In Paris?" she asked, looking to Patrick for confirmation. Livia didn't seem too concerned. "Well, let me tell you, there is a difference in French and Italian hot chocolates. We both use heavy cream, but Italians add cornstarch to thicken the drink into something special."

"Cornstarch?" Maisie frowned, unsure. It didn't seem like an ingredient that screamed rich dessert.

"How about we go to the kitchen and I will have them whip some up, and you can tell me who has the best in the world."

"DEAL," Grant said, and he spit in his hand before offering it to shake.

Livia stared at Patrick, trying her best to mask horror.

"He didn't learn that from me!" Patrick protested, who was more likely to spit bons mots than saliva.

On Livia's other side, Palmina did her best to look innocent. Sadly, innocent was not her default setting and it was clear to everyone who encouraged this. She cleared her throat to get Livia's attention, a little familial encouragement. Livia hesitated only a second before spitting in her own hand and grabbing Grant's to seal their agreement. "Deal."

Patrick applauded and tossed her a nearby napkin. *Well done*, he said with his eyes as Livia turned to lead the children inside.

He looked around at the motley assortment of lingering guests, the ones that were somehow still standing. Part of the joy in not growing up imagining one's wedding was the security in knowing it could never be a disappointment. Emory and Patrick were an unlikely pair that worked *because* they each let the other be exactly who they were. *Let 'em say we're crazy*, Patrick thought silently to himself, not wanting to incur Maisie's friend Audra Brackett's wrath. He then put his hand in Emory's and neither of them looked back.

TWENTY-THREE

Their flight departed Milan Malpensa in the late afternoon arching them over the Atlantic Ocean on their way west to New York's JFK, where new chapters would begin for them all. Maisie would start high school in the fall and Grant middle school. Patrick and Emory would ease into the fresh challenges of married life. Greg and Livia would plan another wedding, this time including the kids. Even Clara saw a future for herself dating, although she left Gustavo behind. They flew first across France, enjoying a glass of French wine in their first-class seats, and nosed over the ocean just before sunset. Patrick watched the sky turn orange and then pink, reflecting across the vast, flat waters, until they were in near darkness with only thin ribbons of color kissing the horizon. The flight would be nine hours in total, six of which they would gain back.

"You okay?" Emory asked as he took Patrick's hand. Patrick had been looking out the window in uncharacteristic silence for quite some time. "You've hardly touched your wine."

"What? Huh? Oh," Patrick muttered as he snapped back to attention. He glanced up toward the front of the cabin and saw Greg and Livia. In the window seats on the far side of the cabin, across from a center row of passengers, sat Maisie and Grant. Clara had her own seat two rows back. "It's just . . . Flying over the ocean is unnatural. The ocean is unnatural."

"The ocean is not unnatural. It's like seventy percent of the planet."

"Whales can grow to be the size of a bus."

"So can your ego."

Patrick ignored him. "A blue whale's heartbeat can be heard from two miles away." Patrick took a sip of his Sancerre to cover his smirk; it was a nugget he was once told by Grant.

"And yet I have to press my head against your chest just to hear yours." Emory placed a hand over Patrick's heart, and Patrick clasped his own on top of it to hold it there. "You just don't trust anything saltier than you are."

Patrick laughed. No wine could mask that.

"Were you having second thoughts?"

"About us?"

Emory nodded.

"No, not at all," Patrick replied firmly. "A prenup, maybe." Patrick elbowed his husband jokingly, and Emory pulled his hand away. But he wasn't offended.

"I'll sign a prenup," Emory offered sincerely.

"It's a little late for that, hence the *pre*. There's no bargaining chips for a postnup."

Emory didn't see the issue. "We still have to make it legal back in the States." A flight attendant appeared at the front of the cabin with a meal cart.

Patrick scrutinized his husband. "What do you know that I don't?"

"You want like a list? There's only seven hours until we land." Emory grinned, amused.

"Have you booked something?" Patrick asked, suddenly worried he was prenupping himself out of a windfall.

"The role of your husband. It runs for the rest of my life."

"I'm serious!"

Emory remained noncommittal. "I've had offers."

"So have I." Patrick wondered if he shouldn't use this time to tackle the new batch of scripts Cassie had emailed, but his attention was focused squarely on the meal cart as Livia and Greg were handed their dinners. "Look at us. We're like the Doublemint twins."

Emory whistled while making a gesture of the reference sailing right over his head.

"It had to do with Wrigley chewing gum. Double the flavor, double the something."

"Double the obscurity." Emory hummed a few bars of Icona Pop's "I Love It." *You're from the seventies, but I'm a nineties bitch.* His face then hardened into an inscrutable expression. "We can make this work, right? I mean, we're good for one another."

Patrick turned to Emory. "Is this a pep talk for you or for me?"

Emory chuckled while Patrick watched the meal cart nudge closer.

"I think I'll get the chicken." Patrick loosened his seat belt. He'd be dancing on Broadway in a matter of weeks; the time for pasta was over. "Of course we can make this work. We're so silly. Overthinking everything. Trying to make the right mark on the world. And yet one day, not that long from now, someone will think of us for the very last time and we will be forgotten from the universe entirely."

Emory tucked his chin into his neck. *That was maudlin.*

"Not if you eat the *Mona Lisa.*" Patrick turned to see that Grant had materialized next to him in the aisle.

"WHAT?!"

"You said one day you will be forgotten. But not if you eat the *Mona Lisa.*" Grant stood confidently as if he had done some quick math in his head and the figures turned out right. "People wouldn't ever forget that."

"So much for the chicken," Patrick muttered.

"The kid has a solid point." Emory didn't see a reason to argue.

"What do you want, Grant?" Patrick asked. "They're about to serve the meal."

"Is there going to be ice cream?" The proverbial midnight must be approaching. Gelato was turning back into ice cream.

"Is that really what you came to ask?"

Grant snapped his fingers, recalling his actual reason. "Maisie wants to talk to you."

Patrick looked across the plane to Grant's empty seat and Maisie sitting quietly in hers. He expected her to have her nose in a book, but instead she fidgeted awkwardly, unsure where to focus her gaze. "Keep Emory company?" Patrick asked Grant, and before he had even stood to his full height in the aisle, the kid had already buckled himself in his uncle's place.

"Want to see a magic trick?" Grant asked his new guncle as Patrick crossed the center row of seats to find Maisie.

"Excited to be going home?" Patrick sat himself in Grant's empty seat, flinched, then produced the kid's game console out from under him. Maisie didn't respond, so he added, "We're both going to high school when we get back." It was true enough, even if he would only be a guest at Rydell High.

"Funny," Maisie said, but not in a way that suggested it actually was. "These seats are a waste of space."

"You'd prefer to stand? This isn't the subway."

"No, first-class seats. You could fit so many more people up here and it would reduce everyone's carbon footprint."

Then it wouldn't be first class, Patrick thought, but he knew better than to say so out loud, as he'd risk Maisie's friends canceling him. "I already do plenty for the environment."

"Like what?" Maisie asked, but it was more accusation than genuine question.

"I recycle a lot of my jokes." Patrick waited for a laugh that never came. "You know, when I said you could be one of those teenagers who did anything, I didn't mean for you to start this week." Patrick noticed she was clutching an envelope in her hands. "What you got there?"

Maisie was the master of the dramatic pause. "It's a letter," she said. "From Mom."

Patrick's heart raced. "Did you say from your mom?"

She pulled her mouth to one side as if reluctant to confirm, but eventually she did.

"Where did it come from?" The postal service got a lot of fair knocks, but if they could deliver a letter from heaven to a moving airplane, then they were a lot better than people thought.

"Dad."

Oh. That made much more sense. "Did Grant get one, too?" Patrick looked over his shoulder. He'd made no mention of such a thing.

"It's not to me, it's to Livia."

"*Livia?*" Patrick exclaimed. How could Sara possibly have written a letter to Livia?

Maisie studied the envelope, turning it from front to back. "Not Livia, exactly. But to the woman who marries Dad. He was supposed to give it to her on their wedding day, but he gave it to me to read instead."

Patrick's eyes welled with tears. *Dammit.* Sometimes he missed the days when his heart was made of stone. "What does it say?"

Maisie handed him the letter without tearing her eyes from the window. Patrick subtly ran the envelope under his nose, wondering if it might still smell of Sara, but of course it didn't, living years in Greg's sock drawer or some other tucked-away place. He carefully opened the envelope, and then the letter, which was folded in thirds.

It was written on hospital stationary.

The first thing Patrick noticed was Sara's loopy handwriting. Whereas he wrote everything in block letters, she much preferred script. He instantly flashed back to the series of birthday and holiday cards that came like clockwork, even during his darkest years when he couldn't be bothered to send cards in return.

"Well?" Maisie asked.

Patrick realized he'd been staring without yet reading a word. "Sorry," he said. "Hold on." And slowly, he began to read.

To the woman who marries my Gregory,

Please know I like you already, as my husband has excellent taste in women. I imagine you're different than me, but not in the important ways. I imagine you're kind. I imagine you have a big heart. You'd have to, to get Greg to fall in love. I'm in no position to ask you a favor, but ask you a favor I must. Please use part of that big heart to be patient with Maisie and Grant. Maisie especially, as she's so loyal and brave. But if her dad loves you, she will one day, too. And I promise it will very much be worth the wait.

I spent my life loving those three, and what an incredible life it was. Just as I know it will be for you. You'll see. I'm envious. Because if I could have one wish, I would live this life over, just so I could love them all again.

With love and gratitude, Sara

Patrick wiped the tear on his cheek with his sleeve while handing Maisie the letter back. "That's your mom," he said with great pride, putting his arm around his niece and letting her nuzzle into his chest the way she would when she was smaller.

Maisie's voice was very frail. "I should have spent more time with her, at the very end."

"With your mom?"

"I was just so scared."

Patrick couldn't think of anything meaningful to say, so he just squeezed her tighter. "You were only nine." He closed his eyes and wondered for the first time if it wasn't some strange blessing that Joe's family kept him from Joe's side at the end.

"I was just so scared all the time."

"And yet you read what your mother said. You put on such a brave face for your brother." He stroked Maisie's hair, which no longer smelled of lemons, and they sat there quietly for a moment until the meal cart came to them and Patrick quietly asked the flight attendant if she could give them a moment and come back.

"A brave face is not the same thing as being brave."

Patrick watched his niece's head move with the rise and fall of his chest. He sat with his own regret, wishing he had spent more time with the kids when they were young, had been more a part of their family. "Oh, I very much think it is."

"Anyway," Maisie whispered. "I wish I could go back and change that."

"I don't know," he finally said when they had been quiet long enough. "I think anyone who wants to time travel is unhinged. But you could try spending some time with Livia."

Maisie groaned and buried her face deeper in his chest. "What would that do?"

"I don't know, exactly." And that much was true. Maybe he was high as a kite in a postnuptial bliss, but Patrick desperately wanted something happy to come from something sad. He wanted for Maisie to see that was possible. "You can't change the past. But some people come into our lives to give us a second chance and set some wrong things right." Patrick glanced back at Emory, who had done just that for him. Grant was in the midst of performing his magic trick.

Magic. Isn't that what life was?

Maisie emerged from her uncle's embrace and fidgeted with her seat until she reclined as far as she could and crossed her hands on her chest like she was on a therapist's couch. "What, *now?*"

Patrick shrugged so subtly it would be easy for one to think that he hadn't.

Maisie knew when she was defeated. "Fine. Send her over."

Patrick looked at her amiss. "What, are you holding office hours from here?"

"Just do it," Maisie croaked. Patrick had cut the kids plenty of slack on this trip, and was desperately hoping for a return to normal when they got back stateside. But for now he obeyed, standing to stretch his quads in the aisle. He then walked around to Greg and Livia's row. They were happily ensconced in their meal and, reluctant to intrude on this happy tableau, Patrick cleared his throat gently to announce his presence. "Maisie would like a word."

Greg glanced over at his daughter and moved to unbuckle his seat belt before Patrick placed a hand on his shoulder to keep his brother from rising.

"With Livia."

Livia's eyes brightened and she and Greg exchanged glances. She pushed her meal tray to the side, unbuckled her seat belt, and squeezed past Greg to join Patrick in the aisle.

"Thank you, Patrick," she said, resting her hand on his arm. Patrick then told her he had asked the flight attendant to circle back and that Maisie might need help choosing something to eat. Livia was grateful for the motherly task. Patrick then assumed her seat next to Greg.

"Is she walking into a trap?" Greg asked.

"She's not, but you could have warned me about Sara's letter."

Greg placed his silverware down on his meal tray. "For real, though. They'll be okay?"

Before they boarded the plane, Maisie deleted SayHi from her phone and Patrick had helped her replace it with Duolingo. The best way to avoid future misunderstandings was to learn the language for herself. "More than okay. How are you holding up?" Patrick asked gently. Greg had imagined himself returning from Italy married.

"I'm good," Greg assured him. "*Truly.* I am. We did the right thing."

"That doesn't mean it didn't come at a cost." Patrick absentmindedly buttered Livia's dinner roll and lifted it to his mouth.

"What are you doing?" Greg pointed to the roll.

"Oh, right. I'm supposed to be off carbs." He set the roll down, as if that had been Greg's concern. "But one day I will be best man at your wedding. And I can't wait."

Greg crossed his fingers hopefully.

"Kids. The gift that keeps on taking."

It was a funny line, but Patrick had it all wrong. "You get so much more in return," Greg insisted. He looked first at Maisie, deep in conversation with Livia, and then back at Grant still trying to dazzle Emory with magic. "Should we rescue your husband?"

Husband. It took some getting used to. "Soon," Patrick said. If they waited much longer and Emory continued to pretend to be impressed with Grant's magic it would be Emory's dignity in danger of disappearing.

"Vis-à-vis our bachelor party conversation."

"*Party,*" Patrick repeated, making air quotes. A full third of the guest list had been snoozing. Or so he'd thought.

"I want you to know Sara would be proud of you, too."

Patrick placed his hand over his heart, grateful for Greg saying so. He hoped very much that was true. He studied Greg, waiting for him to produce another letter—one this time for him, but alas none came. Then Clara's shadow fell over her brothers, interrupting the moment. "Go ahead. Get it out of the way."

"Get what out of the way?" Greg asked innocently.

"The two of you sitting together? Snickering? I know you have some smart remark to say about my vacation romance. Let's have it."

Patrick looked at Greg. "For never was a story of more woe, than this of Juliet and her Gustaveo." They both giggled like idiots.

It had been Clara's curse, to live a life with two brothers. "Juliet was Maisie's age, you know."

Greg's laughter dried up instantly and he looked to Patrick for correction. "That can't be true, can it?"

Patrick ignored him and tried to engage earnestly with his sister. "Was it hard to say goodbye?"

Clara bowed her head. "Ultimately? No. It was fun and all, the idea of fantasizing about his money. Italy, the fancy hotel, trying to keep pace with you morons. But I fear we didn't have much in common."

"You'll meet someone. Someone better. Someone just right for you," Patrick assured her.

"I know I will."

"You were married a long time. Who knows? Dating could be fun."

Clara considered that possibility, thinking back on her week. "Oh, it was definitely fun."

Patrick grimaced, thinking of their shared wall. "We don't need the gory details." He grabbed Livia's wine and raised it to his mouth to drink.

Greg stopped him. "Patrick. Honestly." Patrick looked down, surprised. He didn't know why he was so determined to consume Livia's meal.

"With that, I'm going to pop an Ambien and see you two fools in New York. I hope I don't talk in my sleep." Clara winked at her brothers, who were both appalled.

Greg turned to his brother, still aghast, and asked, "Was Juliet really fourteen?"

"Just shy of, I think. Good luck with that," Patrick said, patting his brother on the shoulder and stepping over his legs to get back to the aisle.

"Where are you going?"

Patrick pointed to the food cart, which had just reached his own seat. "Dinner is served."

As soon as the cart had cleared the aisle, Patrick grabbed Grant by the neck of his shirt and gently lifted the boy out of his seat. "Your father wants you. He said he hasn't seen that trick yet."

Grant's eyes lit up. "Oh, cool." He scrambled up the aisle and Patrick finally had his assigned seat back to himself.

"Making the rounds?" Emory asked.

"It's like I'm running for mayor." He would need a campaign manager other than Maisie, as "Squeeze in More Seats" was likely a losing slogan in first class. Patrick eyed the food that was placed on the tray in front of him. "I said I would have the chicken."

"I know, but I got you the pasta. One last supper won't kill you." Patrick frowned. That's usually what last suppers did. "Do you have a pen?"

Patrick produced one from his personal bag and handed it to Emory. "I stole this from the hotel." The room was probably three grand a night, so they owed him at least a pen.

Emory began scribbling on a napkin.

"What are you writing?" Patrick wasn't sure he could take any more correspondence.

Emory kept writing and quickly filled the napkin on one side. He promptly turned it over to continue. "I'm drafting a prenup."

"A prenup," Patrick said skeptically.

Emory placed the pen down when he finished and began reading what he drafted. "I, Emory Reed, of sound mind—"

"You're not of sound mind."

"I'm not?"

"You married me!" Patrick thought that was as clear a definition of insanity as anything. He reached for the napkin and dunked it in the last of the Sancerre in his glass.

"Hey!" Emory protested. "That was a legal document."

"Sure it was."

Emory turned to look at his husband directly. "Patrick, I don't want your money. I never did. All I ever wanted was you."

Patrick wondered how it was possible that someone he'd known for five years could still take his breath away. "And you have me." What a joy it was to belong. Not just to Emory. But to a family.

"I will take this pen, though." Emory gripped it by both ends like an ear of corn.

Patrick was happy to let it go. He raised his hand to get the flight attendant's attention. He was in need of a fresh glass of Sancerre.

TWENTY-FOUR

Patrick sat in his dressing room backstage at the Belasco Theatre and took a good long look at himself. He remembered doing high school theater, a production of *The Diary of Anne Frank*. The director, their English teacher, taught him and his castmates the art of old-age makeup. A sallow-toned foundation was applied with a sponge and a stippling technique, topped with age lines, which they drew on themselves with eyeliner pencils. A dark line blended with a lighter one underneath made the appearance of age lines under the hot stage lights. Young Patrick would raise his eyebrows to wrinkle his forehead and then draw a flat line in each crease, before moving on to crow's-feet. No such techniques were required now; he was more or less the same age as the character he was playing. A young person in old-age makeup looks just like that—a child playing dress-up. He and his school castmates used to laugh in horror at how they might one day look given the ravages of time, but they had no way of knowing how that horror might one day be pride. For Patrick, now with a little stage makeup, looked devilishly good. He was almost remiss to remove it.

A knock on his dressing room door interrupted his thoughts. It was Adam Rucker, who played Putzie. "Did you see David? Heather says she saw him last night disappear into a mirror."

"Heather drinks."

"No she doesn't."

"She vapes, then. Or takes pills."

Just then Heather, a world-weary woman from wardrobe, snatched Patrick's costume, which was hanging on the back of his door. "Heather does none of those things," she muttered in her own defense. She was responsible for cleaning the costumes between shows, and since there was a matinee the next day she didn't have time for such gossip.

"Good night, Heather!" Patrick called after her.

"No, seriously," Adam stressed when she was out of earshot. "She saw David walk into the big mirror out in the hall and—*poof*—disappear."

David was the long-deceased Broadway pioneer David Belasco, who was known in some circles as the Bishop of Broadway for his penchant for wearing cassocks and clerical collars. Not that his identity much mattered. Almost every theater had its rumored ghost, every opera house its phantom. These spirits would moan at night after the shows were done, turn on lights or drop sandbags from the rafters. Belasco was no different in that regard. It was part of the lore of doing theater.

"Heather huffs glue."

"I think you *sniff* glue," Adam corrected. And then he stood there looking both awkward and up to no good. "You huff bath salts."

"What?"

Adam looked just beyond the door's frame and whispered, "*Not you*," presumably to Heather, just as Patrick registered the opening notes of the mournful dirge we all know as "Happy Birthday." If looks could kill, Adam would be a goner.

One by one the cast crowded around his dressing room door, a decked-out Cassie among them holding a cupcake. *Et tu, Brute?* Patrick mouthed disappointed, but in truth it was good to see her. And at least the cupcake, red velvet if he was right, only had one candle, its flame reflected in Cassie's sequined top.

The song finished on a high note, quite literally as his castmates jumped an octave and harmonized, reminding him of his time with the kids on the *Sound of Music* tour alongside Jam and Bread. The thing is, the cast seemed absolutely thrilled to celebrate him, there wasn't a hint of pity humoring the old man. He may have come in as an elder statesman, but the entire production team had been so kind and immediately embraced him as one of their own. They looked up to him and were entertained by his stories—more than that, they listened until *he* was worn out, no small feat, as Patrick, like most actors, enjoyed talking about himself. This cast of young artists was raised watching a golden age of sitcoms, including *The People Upstairs*—the show that made him a star. Patrick had worked the jobs they themselves dreamed of booking, even if the sitcom itself was dying.

"Thank you," he said, doing his best to mask his discomfort. Cassie thrust the cupcake forward, and Patrick made his birthday wish. He wet his thumb and forefinger and pinched out the flame, just as he remembered Palmina doing to put out her lit cigarette; he hoped it looked half as cool.

Someone in the back began the second verse—*How old are you?*—but was mercifully shushed by Adam.

The musical's director, Juliane Ford, stepped forward from the bunch and flipped through notes on her clipboard. "Once again during the hand jive you crossed downstage and walked in front of every single dancer, blocking them."

Assorted giggles from the cast.

Patrick winced; it was a note he'd been given before. "I'm sorry. I don't even realize I'm doing it."

"*Keep* doing it," Juliane said. "We only have you for six weeks, we might as well get the most bang for our buck. Besides . . ." She flipped her pages of notes flat against her clipboard. ". . . It's exactly what the character would do. Good job."

Adam followed her out with the others all shouting various birthday wishes, before remembering why he had stopped by his dressing room in the first place; it had nothing to do with ghosts. "Hey, are you coming out with us after? The usual place."

Patrick smiled in the mirror so Adam could see. "Will Heather be there? I hear she has all the good drugs."

"You're incorrigible," Adam laughed.

"I heard that." Heather stuck her head back in the dressing room one final time and handed Patrick a manila envelope. "Andy wanted me to give you this. It was delivered to you at the box office."

Patrick took the envelope and thanked her. He turned to Adam and said, "I'll meet you there."

Adam tapped the wall twice, *Goodbye for now,* and disappeared into the hall. Only Cassie remained, and he thanked her. Not only did she show up time and again for him, but she did so with advice that was right. This was exactly the break that he needed, which is to say not much of a break at all.

"Happy birthday, Patrick," she said, kissing him on the cheek, leaving a print of her lipstick like Marilyn Monroe. "I'm here all week, if you'd like to grab dinner."

"I eat dinner at five o'clock," he said. "And sometimes again at eleven." It was the life of an actor on Broadway.

"Five is fine," she agreed. "It's two in LA, so I'll think of it as lunch."

"Or lupper," he said.

Cassie laughed. "Yes, yes. I know. All your meals are portmanteaus."

She left and things fell quiet again, and a light bulb outside his dressing room flickered and dimmed. Not that it spooked him. To Patrick, all ghosts were friendly, and he liked knowing that they were nearby. He took his time wiping off his makeup. He enjoyed being one of the last to leave the theater, when the crowds outside had thinned and the younger kids had had their fill of glory. He was here as a guest after all, it wasn't his show. He then reached for the photos on his dressing room table. He and Sara splashing in the waves the summer they spent at the beach acting like John Travolta and Olivia Newton-John. Patrick and the kids in Paris. Patrick and Emory, dancing on the terrace at the Grand Hotel Tremezzo the night of their wedding. He took a moment to cherish each one, then grabbed his bag and slung it over his shoulder as he bounded down the stairs to the alley.

There was loud cheering when he came out the door, which startled Patrick, catching him off guard. It was Greg and Livia, Clara, Maisie and Grant jumping up and down, making fools of themselves. Patrick almost didn't recognize them, bundled as they were for the unseasonable cold. Patrick was not ready for winter; since their return from Italy he once again craved warm weather. "I never took you for stage-door Johnnies," he grumbled. "What are you doing here?" He signed programs for the few people waiting that weren't related to him by marriage or blood.

"We thought we could use a night in the city," Livia explained.

"But it's a school night."

Maisie and Grant exchanged looks and giggled. They might as well be getting away with murder. He prayed they, too, were not about to burst out in song.

"Seriously, am I the only responsible one here?"

Livia and Greg parted as someone thrust a last program between them for him to sign. He scribbled his name without looking up, and when he heard the familiar voice, his Sharpie skidded off the program's edge. "What good is a launt if she can't get her niece and nephew excused from a day of school?"

Patrick grimaced. Mischief like that used to be squarely the purview of a guncle.

"HAPPY BIRTHDAY!" they exclaimed, except for Palmina, who said, "Buon compleanno."

"Palmina, what are you doing here?"

"Palmina's in town for a jewelry expo," Maisie explained.

Patrick cocked an eyebrow. "Who's taking care of your bird?" he asked, trying to sound as dismissive as he possibly could. He leaned in to pose for a selfie with a fan who added his own *Happy birthday*, and then at last it was just him and his family.

"We took Palmina to see your show!" Grant exclaimed. He then looked up at Livia's sister. "Who *is* taking care of your bird?"

Palmina took Grant's hand. "Bruna and Carla and Zita."

The Robert Palmer girls.

"Flavia is in good hands."

"You were really good, GUP," Maisie exclaimed.

"Yes," Palmina purred. "You were very good at giving the . . . hand jive." She winked at Patrick playfully; she'd been messing with him all along.

"Thank you. It's all in the wrist." He winked back and she laughed.

"Did you always want to be an actor, GUP?" Grant asked. "Maybe I should be one, too."

"When I was your age I thought I would be a weatherman. The weatherman was always the most handsome man on TV."

"I've already been in a movie," Grant continued. "Not a lot of kids can say that."

"You've been in a what?" Greg asked, always a step behind.

"Oh, did we not tell you?" Patrick asked. He mouthed, *Whoops* to Maisie and Grant.

"Kids, you may be missing school, but you still have a bedtime. You can tell us about it as we head back to the Plaza."

"Can we walk?" Maisie asked. "Despite the cold, it's such a nice night."

"Certainly," Livia said, and she took Maisie's hand. "But first say good night to your guncle."

The kids threw their arms around Patrick, hugging him tight. His phone vibrated. *Emory.* "It's my husband calling," he announced. "I should probably . . ."

Greg motioned for him to go.

"My last show is the third week of November," Patrick called after them. "You'd better set two extra seats at Thanksgiving." He waved as he jogged backward a few steps down Forty-Fourth Street, watching them get smaller as they walked in the other direction.

He answered just as he heard Palmina ask, "Is that the one with turkey?" She then instructed her sister to set a place for her, too. Patrick groaned into the phone.

"That's a fine greeting," Emory said.

"Sorry, that wasn't for you. How's LA?" Emory was there for a few weeks on a job.

"Great. I love the director, she has such a vision. How was the show? Did you get my envelope?"

"Envelope?" Patrick asked. That's right, he'd been delivered an envelope and had shoved it right in his bag. "Hold on." He fished in his messenger bag. The envelope was lumpy and had an odd heft.

"I hate not being there for your birthday."

To Patrick it wasn't such a big deal. This year had already given him so much. He found the envelope in his bag's outside pocket.

"Listen, I did something," Emory explained. "Don't be mad." If it was possible to hear a smile through the phone, Patrick could.

"Is that what marriage is? Us doing things and telling the other not to be mad?" He ripped open the envelope and a set of house keys spilled into his hand. "Keys?" he asked, confused. Patrick took a right on Sixth toward Bryant Park just as an ambulance went by. "Emory?" he asked when the siren had died, and then checked his phone to make sure they hadn't been disconnected.

"Okay, but you have to promise not to be mad."

"I promise," Patrick said, he was even pretty sure it wasn't a lie. He pinned his phone between his ear and his shoulder and blew on his hands to warm them. How was it this cold in October?

"Okay," Emory said. "Here goes. I couldn't think what to get you for your birthday. So I bought us a house in Palm Springs."

Patrick froze in the middle of a crosswalk and laughed. It dawned on him a final Guncle Love Language gift-wrapped in the words of Rosemary Clooney: *Come on-a my house*. Grant could have presents. Patrick would take real estate. A place for his whole family to gather.

"Patrick?" Emory asked, making sure his husband was still there.

"Maybe you should have had *me* sign a prenup," Patrick said, and they both laughed, although Emory too hard for his liking.

The walk sign started blinking an angry red hand and Patrick skipped to the far side of Sixth. So much for dreading winter; there was about to be a great thaw.

Acknowledgments

The Guncle was published in May of 2021, at a time when we were emerging after a very dark year. I didn't get to tour with that book as all events were still virtual. Because of that, I don't think I fully grasped the extent to which the original resonated with readers until I was able to do in-person events again. I'm grateful for every one of you who read *The Guncle*, followed me, messaged me, came to see me, bought the book, reviewed the book, recommended the book, read it with your book club, borrowed it from the library, or otherwise let Patrick, Maisie, and Grant into your hearts. It's not a stretch to say *The Guncle Abroad* would not exist without you.

Thank you to every writer who has ever written a sequel or series. I read many second chapters in plotting this new adventure. All of you who have undertaken this challenge inspire me.

I couldn't do what I do without my incredible team. Rob Weisbach, my agent, my confidant, my right-hand man. Your unwavering belief in me means the world. This career we've built together feels like a perfect dream. Sally Kim, my editor, my Auntie Mame, my friend. I trust you implicitly. I'm so grateful you agreed to this journey abroad with me. I can't believe we get to do this again and again. G. P. Putnam's Sons is staffed with rock stars, and I'm so lucky to have them beside me. Ivan Held, Alexis Welby, Katie McKee, Ashley McClay, Molly Pieper, Samantha Bryant, Jazmin Miller, and Tarini Sipahimalani. I'm grateful for everything you do on my behalf and there's no one I love celebrating with more. And once again Tal Goretsky delivered the perfect cover.

To my friends at Thurber House, I'm still humbled you chose to honor *The Guncle*. Thank you for acknowledging that humor can be both riotously funny and incredibly kind. To anyone who thinks it's impossible to be funny in politically correct times I say you were most likely mistaking cruelty for humor in the first place. Likewise to Jenna Bush Hager and my Read with Jenna family. Your continued enthusiasm for my work means the world.

Thank you to Whoopi Goldberg for loving these characters as much as I do. And to Kristin Burr, Jessica Friedman, Jason Moore, James Meyers, Scott O'Brien, and the wonderful team at Lionsgate for their work in bringing *The Guncle* to the big screen. My gratitude also goes to my wonderful film agent Matthew Snyder and the mighty team at CAA.

Bookstagram. Wow. I am grateful to this community for many things—its camaraderie, its creativity, its diversity—but at the top of that list has to be the priceless friendships Bookstagram has brought into my life.

As a gay man, I've been fortunate to live in a time when we have gained incredible rights in a historically short period of time. When that happens, there is an inevitable period of backslide. There are cowardly politicians hell-bent on taking hard-fought and -won rights from minority communities while banning our stories in an attempt to deny our basic humanity. We cannot allow that to happen. Thank you to the brave teachers and librarians, parents and readers who have stood on the front lines fighting book bans. Every hateful comment I receive about *The Guncle* is validation I'm doing something right.

ACKNOWLEDGMENTS

My own niblings, Evie, Emmett, Harper, Eli, and Graham, continue to inspire me. I love you. I love seeing the dynamic people you are becoming.

To the incredible LGBTQ+ people raising families, I see you and you are beautiful. And to my own family, Byron and Raindrop and Shirley—I love you, I need you and yes, we can go for a walk. I just need to write five hundred more words.